Sonia J⬛⬛⬛⬛⬛⬛⬛⬛⬛⬛⬛⬛⬛⬛d two young
children.⬛⬛⬛⬛⬛⬛⬛⬛⬛⬛⬛⬛⬛⬛on officer,
and has ⬛

Three Mothers

Sonia Lambert

PIATKUS

f151 341
£19.18

Acknowledgements

Many thanks to Anya and Nina, whose stories I've so distorted. Thanks to everyone who helped look after my children: Debbie Baker, Sinead Belcher and the hard-working teachers at St John of Jerusalem Primary School in E9. Thanks to the other friends who get me through the week and to my sister, Judy. Thanks to Jai Durai, Simon Trewin and Emma Callagher. Most of all, thank you, Ben.

For my family

The Adversary

Mothers are hardest to forgive.
Life is the fruit they long to hand you,
Ripe on a plate. And while you live,
Relentlessly they understand you.

Phyllis McGinley
1959

Chapter One

Susie

Until she got ill, I thought I knew everything about my mother.

Three months or so after her death, we started clearing the house. My aunt Lottie persuaded us to do it. She was trying to help, of course, but even so, she annoyed me.

'Already?' I said, listening to my voice wobble, like a tightrope walker, down the telephone line.

She paused. 'You must take anything you want. Anything at all.'

'Really? How generous.'

'Of course you must,' she didn't seem to notice my knee-jerk sarcasm, although she must have registered my reluctance. 'But for Steve and Gus, you know, we ought to try and sort things out a bit.'

'I know, I know, we can't expect them to live in a shrine,' I said, although that's exactly what I'd have liked them to do. In fact, my brother Gus had moved in with some friends ('it's too freaky to be there,' he said), and Steve, my stepfather, was sleeping at his shop, but Lottie didn't know this, and I didn't tell her. She was bound to have an opinion of some sort, and anyway, it only strengthened her case.

So we set to work, one autumn weekend, Steve, Lottie and I, picking through the layers like forensic scientists, with black plastic bin liners, as the leaves fell from the cherry tree in the wind-swept garden. It was hard work, in every sense. There was so much stuff: pots and pans in the kitchen, blackened with use, the books (hundreds of faded orange Penguins, or cream-coloured *Livres de Poche*), the pictures on the wall, the clothes in the cupboards – the things that defined my mother. They seemed to be waiting for her, rebelling against the facts. They had to be brought into line, I could see that; they had to be made to understand. It was difficult to do, though, wiping her from the world, almost like watching her die a second time.

I had some tapes already, my precious salvage. They were tiny little cassettes, which I'd recorded using a Dictaphone from work, during Mum's illness. I'd marked them 'Vera' or 'Helene' instead of 'Mum' and 'Granny,' perhaps pretending to myself that by using their names, I'd make it more of a dispassionate exercise, and I'd numbered them in sequence. For a long time I just left them in a box. I was superstitious about hearing Mum's voice, and besides, I needed time to absorb their contents. Her illness – and her death, which we'd known was coming – had forced me to try and see her as a person, but she wasn't quite the person I'd expected. I felt as if I'd found her and lost her, found and lost myself, all in one go.

I kept most of the photographs. Many of them were of us, me and Gus, and when Mum appeared she was often in the background, or out of focus, but there were a few nice ones, from over the decades. There was one of Mum getting married the first time, in very pointy shoes and a Jackie Kennedy hair-do, and getting married the second time, in a white trouser suit with shoulder pads. There was Mum as a toddler, with a floppy hat in a tropical garden, or as a young woman, sitting on a tartan rug at Devil's Dyke, smiling up at the camera, her pale legs curled awkwardly beneath her. There were a lifetime's worth of holiday snaps – pregnant, in the South of France, standing on bridges in any number of European cities, or with Steve, in Montreal, in a reindeer patterned jumper, with big, layered hair. There was a white-bordered snap of Mum outside hospital gates, clutching a tiny bundle to her chest, with a defiant smile, and stunned, car-crash eyes.

I didn't want the other stuff. It would have been too difficult to pick a few objects over the rest – I could see myself with crate-loads, it was just the kind of trick she might play from beyond the grave, to make me hobble through life, laden with her things. I left it to Steve, who dealt with such situations for a living, and could despatch furniture and kitchenware to the four winds with professional detachment, and Lottie, whose ostentatious efficiency felt like a flimsy defence against despair. I thought I was being restrained, but you don't get away that lightly.

Up until that spring, I thought I knew who I was and where I came from. I had my story, and I was sticking to it: I'd grown up, and moved on. That May, however, I began to feel that the past wasn't over, it was flowing in my veins. I realised that the people nearest to me were too close to see – they were the prism through which I viewed the world, and a puzzle I'd come back to for the rest of my life. I thought I'd escaped, but I was wrong.

So here it is – the story of my mother, and her mother, and the things they didn't tell me, until it was almost too late. Now I can see that it's also the story of me.

Helene

I sat on a bench in King's Cross, still amid the cross-currents of purposeful passengers, the shouts of the porters, and the panic-making whirr of the announcement boards. It was raining outside, and the station floor was slippery with mud. The crowd wore damp woollen uniforms, glistening oilskins, and soggy tweed, and from time to time someone flapped an umbrella open, or closed. I watched the slow progress of the large station clock, and was anxious in case I had been forgotten. Another young woman sat a few feet away from me on the same bench, apparently engrossed in a paperback novel, and I glanced over at her curiously from time to time, wondering if she was waiting for the same reason I was.

I had been there nearly an hour. I thought of my baby daughter, and wondered if she'd settled easily for her nap. I remembered the last, illicit breastfeed I'd given her that morning – she was supposed to be fully weaned, in the few days before my departure, but still half-asleep, I'd allowed this secret consolation for us both, as we lay beneath my candlewick bedspread, the grey dawn seeping in around the blackout blinds. She'd clawed at me with such greedy absorption, her arm making a clumsy, flailing caress, and my tears, as they so often seemed to, had come with the milk.

By breakfast, the redness around my eyes was gone, and the baby was slurping a precious mixture of egg yolk and sugar enthu-siastically from a spoon for my mother. Sitting together, opposite me, they had looked rather alike – their lively eyes peering out from within the folds of their chubby faces, my mother's hair drawn back in a tight bun, Lottie's few short wisps still thin and

3

patchy. As usual, the similarity made me feel both reassured and a little excluded. Baby Lottie held a spoon, which she banged against the table delightedly: my mother and I leaned forwards simultaneously, to move a tea cup out of her reach.

'Remember, cover your head in the sun. And ask for tea,' my mother said. 'The water will make you sick.' She was intent on practising her English, which added a theatricality, I felt, to our exchange – and she was a theatrical woman to start with, always playing to an invisible audience. 'Anything precious, keep it close. Inside the brassière is good,' she mouthed conspiratorially, although there was no one else to hear. How can she irritate me so, I wondered, even while I'm already missing her? She was a popular woman, mother-figure to many of the other tenants in our building, but the little quirks which others found endearing, I found tedious and affected.

I reached over, and took the baby from her. It was like a non-verbal language we'd developed, passing this plump parcel between us, attending to the small practical details of her care, communicating anger, annoyance, or affection, and most of all, perhaps, sharing the chance to be useful, in those months when powerlessness ate away at us like a wasting disease.

The baby searched my face for a joke, and I kissed her too hard. I knew her body better than my own: the rolls of fat around her limbs, the squidgy little hands, the exact degree of support she needed to sit, and to stand. I wore a new suit for my journey, with shoulder pads and a vaguely military cut, and I was worried that Lottie might mark it. 'Does she know?' I wondered again, 'can she sense something?' I reminded myself that of course she couldn't, but somehow the fact of her not knowing made it feel all the worse, as if I had to know for both of us.

Until a week before, I had been expecting that we would all travel together. Folded next to my ticket and papers, in my fawn leather handbag, was a hand-written letter, and the paragraph I knew by heart, picking apart the sentences as though they contained coded information, until I could probably have recited them backwards. 'Dearest,' my husband had written, 'the climate here is not healthy for a child, and the political and military situation is still unstable. I really think it best you leave her, for the time being at least, with your mother in England. However' (he always wrote and spoke as if he had access to the highest, most

4

privileged sources, and for a long time, I trusted that he did) 'the news in general is good, and I am confident the waiting will soon be over, and we will be able to begin our life together as a family.'

He had never seen our baby, and so, perhaps, it was easier for him to imagine she would wait – like a dry seed, patient in the dark earth, unfurling at some mysterious starting signal, as the first irregular droplets of his attention came seeping through the topsoil. I, on the other hand, had been a closer witness – although no less passive, I often felt – to her slow-motion explosion from my ovaries, the rapid doubling in weight, the inbuilt compulsion to smile, to grasp, to sit, to crawl.

Leaving the flat, alongside the sick sense of disbelief that lay in my stomach, there was also a fluttering excitement. Train times were not divulged, and the secrecy around the journey added a certain glamour, and made me feel a part of the war. I was young, and found it hard to 'also serve' by wiping up dribbles and keeping vigil by the radio. Stepping out into the street alone, I pretended to myself I was on some secret mission of national importance.

I sat on the bench, and watched the clock, and listened to the rain rattle on the station roof. After some time, a uniformed private appeared, and asked me politely to follow him. Although I had been waiting for so long, I still felt startled and unready. I gathered up my things, and hurried off to find my train.

Susie

The year after I graduated, I spent a weekend in Paris with my mother. Mum had been attending a conference at the Sorbonne, and I had been visiting my boyfriend Toby, whose family had a house in the Loire. We arranged to meet at the last minute, realising we'd be in the city at the same time, and stayed together in a cheap hotel for two nights. '*Maman et fille,*' the proprietor kept remarking, with a smile, as if there were something wonderful in this fact, although perhaps he was just bored with, or offended by, all the romantic weekenders, or just trying to be friendly.

As time passed, the weekend acquired a glow in my memory, partly because of the beautiful spring weather. It had been a long time since we'd been on holiday together, and it felt strange to spend time alone with Mum. She was recovering from a bad cold

5

– her hoarse voice and general fragility alarmed me. Later, this concern became linked in my mind with her subsequent illness, although in fact, they were a couple of years apart.

Mum had a life-long love affair with France ('weird, considering she's a kraut really,' Toby said, in the jokey, ironic tone he used as a sort of habitual disclaimer, to indicate he knew this was stretching it a bit). It was something to do with a wish to identify herself as a continental, anyway, or perhaps just her age and class, since a lot of my friends' parents are the same, going on about their second homes – and it made her a great, if sometimes rather gushy travelling companion.

There were the usual irritations, of course. She had an annoying habit of peppering her conversation with sarcastic asides in French ('*tant pis*,' or '*ça se voit*'), and a memsahib manner in the Moroccan restaurant on the first night (she tended to reminisce self-importantly about her colonial childhood to waiters, and I was never sure quite how this would go down). She wounded my pride by smiling at my attempts to speak French, and was characteristically vague, forgetting the hotel keys in her room, and leaving either her bag or her glasses behind almost every time we sat down. There were so many old resentments and flashpoints to be navigated carefully around for the trip to be a success, and these cast shadows over even the more mundane topics. The new context, however, helped me to transcend these frustrations, and to see her with a bit of distance. I enjoyed sitting opposite her in restaurants, listening to her translate the menu with such enthusiasm. For moments, we managed to relate to each other simply as two grown women together, and I think it was a novelty we both enjoyed.

While we were crossing a bridge from the Ile de la Cité to the Left Bank, the sun came out. We squinted in the unaccustomed brightness – almost the same pucker on almost the same brow – our faces pale as mushrooms, after months of overcast weather. The light danced on the water, and behind us, Notre Dame crouched like an insect, heavy with scribbled detail. 'Do you remember that awful joke Gus used to tell, about Quasimodo?' I said, and Mum shook her head, and smiled, the very mention of his name drawing us closer, making us a family. I related it badly ('his face rings a bell') and she pulled a face, and laughed, and the warmth was bliss on my skin, and all my senses strained to absorb

6

the softness of the sunshine.

'I sometimes wish I had a video camera inside me,' I said, 'which could record sensations and smells as well as sights.'

'You do, darling,' Mum said. 'It's called your memory.'

'Yes, I suppose so,' I said. 'I should remember to switch it on more often.' A pleasure boat passed beneath us, under the bridge, the passengers pointing, and shading their eyes. 'Do you ever do that thing, of deciding to remember a particular moment?'

'Oh yes,' she said.

'I'm always doing that. And then a better moment always comes along just after, so I try to remember that instead.'

'I remember the very first time I did that – or the first time it worked, anyway. It was outside the white house we had in Dhaka, so I must have been really quite little. There had been a heavy rain, and there were puddles in the yard, and one of them had that oily, rainbowy effect you sometimes get, and I said right, I'm going to remember that *forever*. And, evidently, I did.'

We made a small detour, to avoid some tourists taking a photograph on the pavement. 'Bit of a banal thing to pick, when you think about it,' Mum finished up.

That day stuck in my memory, though – Mum's childlike delight in finding the restaurant in St Germain still open, the fish soup, the view over crisp tablecloths on to the busy street. It was surprisingly warm, and the white wine made me woozy. I was missing Toby already, which was perhaps why my conversation was fuller than usual of his views and ambitions, veiled beneath the first person plural – we think this, we hope that.

I could feel a distance in my mother which usually signalled disapproval – something she deliberately wasn't saying – and it irritated me intensely. Perhaps because of the wine, I decided to confront her about this. 'You don't really like Toby, do you?'

'What makes you think that?' Mum asked, carefully.

'Oh, I can tell. It's pretty obvious. The way you talk about him. The way you don't talk about him. It's OK, I don't mind.'

'Actually, I think he's very sweet, most of the time. One does have to be a little cautious, though, with these college relationships.' She paused, fished in her handbag, and lit up a Benson & Hedges, with a long, hungry drag.

'When are you going to give up?' I said. As a little girl, I used to hide her cigarettes. I knew, at an early age, that cigarettes could kill you, but she seemed so invulnerable to me that this was a rather abstract concern. I think it was more that I liked the rare sense of power it gave me, and the feeling of being in the right.

'God, sweetheart, I don't know.'

'Anyway, you met Dad at university.'

'Precisely. Actually, I met your father before we started, but I suppose the real *coup de foudre* came then, yes. Heady stuff, of course, but it can be rather, I don't know, a thing of its time. You're still changing so fast at that age.'

'People grow up faster these days,' I said, resentfully. 'And Toby's not like you think – he's quite insecure, actually – although I suppose he can seem a bit full of himself sometimes,' I conceded.

'Can't they all, babe,' Mum laughed her big, throaty laugh. 'Can't they all.'

The weekend was quite enough: we were beginning to get on each other's nerves, embarrassed by the infantilising effect we seemed to have on each other, and keen to beat a retreat into the blissful independence of adulthood. We wanted to control each other. We each took the other's deficiencies far too personally, or perhaps we were frustrated by the possibilities we saw in each other, which only an infuriating stubbornness prevented from being fully realised. After a while, the effort would become too much for one of us – the slow, ominous rise in atmospheric pressure would lead inevitably to headaches, tetchiness, and then an explosion, usually over something quite trivial. I was keen to go before the pattern ran its course.

Even so, on leaving her at the Gare du Nord, I had a moment of panic. It seemed an unnatural place to say good-bye – one wants to leave one's parents at home, waiting on the doorstep for one's return. It was partly something about seeing her at a distance, in that great cavernous space, a stout, middle-aged woman in a dark green raincoat and violet scarf, her short, dark hair streaked with grey. She looked so small, from far away, and so like all the other people in the crowd.

For a moment, I had a sense that there was something important I'd forgotten to ask her, or to tell her, or to give her. I wanted to call out to her, to find some reason to go back. Instead, I waved to her on the concourse. I could still feel the imprint of her forceful kiss, on my cheek, as I made my way through the crowds.

8

I'd had maternal feelings for as long as I could remember – even as a child, perhaps. I dreamed about small things – alive, and in danger of being squashed or accidentally eaten – that I had to look after. Tiny, talking tangerines needed my protection; I gave birth repeatedly, painlessly, to a half eaten corn on the cob, or to a kitten ('they're all little animals to start with,' the midwife said). Sometimes there were actual babies, with spooky, see-through bodies, the size of a finger. Invariably, they met some horrible end.

We had no money for a child, though, and there was plenty going on; I disentangled the dreams from my waking thoughts each morning, as I brushed my hair. I supported Gregor through his doctorate with a variety of translation jobs. I paid the rent on our cluttered little flat in Camden Town, with its gas meter, dusty cheese plant, Indian cotton bedspread – picking up socks, newspapers, ashtrays and leaflets off the floor, and drawing the curtains, daily, to let the light in. We got a cat, called Leon, after Trotsky.

We spent a lot of time with a tall Canadian called Steve – a friend of Gregor's with a Frank Zappa moustache which seemed a little ridiculous, even at the time. Steve flirted with me, supplied Gregor with the occasional joint, and brought his new women round for approval and spaghetti bolognaise. Many of the people we'd known at college were in London – there were pubs and parties to go to, and benefits and talks and demos. In the summers we travelled, hitch-hiking around the Mediterranean, sleeping on beaches, living on bread and tomatoes.

Back home, however, my stomach gave a little lurch when I saw babies on buses, and I tried not to stare. I became interested in the children of friends, and a little too anxious to coax smiles from them. Their warmth and weight called to me – I wanted an excuse to touch, to smell, to bury my head. These embarrassing, sometimes quite frightening urges felt strangely like a perversion, and I learned to hide them. On visits, I played the role of everyone's favourite young auntie, letting the children pull on my beads and my hair, chasing them round the kitchen, until some over-indulgence, some imbalance of power they could feel but not name, made them uneasy, or over-excited, like hounds that scent blood. Their mothers looked at me with sympathy, but took back the fractious infants with an easy, tired familiarity that, in itself, stung me. I tried to curb my growing interest in buying presents for friends with new babies. Fingering a rack of baby-gros, I felt a tightness in my chest, and had to make an effort to breathe and speak normally. 'It's as if you're high in here,' Gregor said.

Then, as the decade drew to a close, Gregor was offered a lectureship at the new university in Sussex. He'd always found financial dependency difficult, so this role reversal was a relief to us both. We put down a deposit on a narrow, cream-painted house in Brighton – bubbling and flaking on the outside, as though suffering some dreadful skin disease – with peeling wallpaper inside, and a long, sloping garden. Steve, who had a van, helped us move down, but his relentless references to suburbia, or 'plastic people', and his clowning around – lampshades on the head, gurning at the other drivers on the motorway, endless renditions of 'Oh I Do Like to Be Beside the Seaside', with a Canadian accent – suddenly irritated us more than before.

While Gregor was still unloading his books, Steve and I sat under the cherry tree at the bottom of the garden, smoking. 'Don't do this,' Steve said suddenly. 'It won't suit you.' I looked up in surprise, from behind my hair, but saw only his spindly, denim-clad legs, as he rose to his feet and strode back towards the kitchen door. I wanted to ask him what he meant, but I suppose I must have had some idea that there were things there I didn't want to unearth. I didn't get a chance, anyway, because after that he said his goodbyes, and walked out of my life for over ten years.

The house used to be a bed and breakfast, and we kept the old sign that said 'Vacancies/No Vacancies'. hanging over the fireplace, as a memento. We stripped off the worst of the flowery, mildewy wallpaper, and had gas fires installed. We put some of our posters back up, this time in clip frames (a Cezanne print, a bull-fight poster, and a poster from the Paris demonstrations, of a sinister-looking gas-mask behind a microphone, 'La Police Vous Parle, Tous les Soirs à 20h'). We bought a sofa from Habitat, and some big glass jars to keep pasta, rice and pulses in. We had a kind of tacit agreement not to mention the number of bedrooms – Gregor colonised one of them, at the top of the house, for his books, papers and typewriter. When I forced open the rickety, sash windows, I could smell the sea.

I found a job teaching French at a local sixth form, where I was

10

regarded with some suspicion, with my long hair, my scruffy clothes, and my radical views (the other teachers were mostly older, brisk and neat). I stopped taking the Pill – Gregor was actually the one who suggested it, and I agreed, with a mixture of fear and relief. I knew he wasn't entirely ready, but I wasn't sure he would ever be. Besides, I felt I was in danger of becoming a stalker.

At that point, the strange dreams stopped. Ironically, I had never felt less broody. Brighton seemed full of women with rainproof head scarves and string bags, or tired-looking girls with pushchairs. There was a seediness to the city, particularly out of season, that made me think of the darker side to the dirty weekend stereotype – young mothers in bedsits, back-street abortions, or the suicides that, I was told, sometimes washed up on the shingle. Our new life made me feel as if the pair of us were acting the part of adults, pretending to be grown-ups in some kitchen sink drama, or perhaps on *Mr and Mrs*, that grotesque TV show in which a married couple answered questions to show how well they really knew each other, to win a holiday, or some desirable consumer durable.

I went to see our new doctor, without telling Greg. I'd had my suspicions for a while: the butter was rancid, I couldn't bear the smell of rubber in the car – it was either a baby or a stomach bug. I didn't want a big song and dance about it every month, though – I wanted to be sure – and moreover, part of me didn't believe it was possible. I sat in the waiting room, surrounded by battered copies of *Reader's Digest* and *Women's Realm*. The doors and windows had that blobby, grid-effect glass in them, and I could just see the muted colours and blurred shapes of the people moving outside. Inside the consulting room, there was a high, leather examining couch, and the smell of surgical spirit. The doctor sent me off to pee into a small plastic pot, and told me with a beneficent smile, almost as if he'd inseminated me himself.

I stood in the kitchen, while the cat wound himself ingratiatingly around my ankles. It was dark outside and the windows were cloudy with condensation, from the potatoes boiling on the stove. I heard the yank of a handbrake in the street outside, an engine hum into silence, and the slam of a car door.

Suddenly, I felt scared. Telling people these things is what makes them feel real. Part of me felt remote, watching from the outside with a kind of detached interest, and thinking 'am I react-ing normally?' This is the kind of moment, I thought, that you rehearse for in your head, and I wished I had the courage to do it with flair, in a way that would make a good story, later on ('. . . and Gregor nearly fell off his chair,' I imagined myself saying, to general hilarity).

Then footsteps, the key in the lock, and Gregor was standing in the hall, unbelting his leather jacket, raking one hand through his hair, humming beneath his breath. I thought of you inside me – a tangerine, corn-on-the-cob, kitten creature – the size of a microbe, perhaps, of an unformed idea, doing a leisurely backstroke, through the mysterious depths of my amniotic fluid.

Susie

That night, I dreamed about Mum. I was massaging her forehead, the way I used to as a little girl, when she had a headache. Mum had always made great claims for the success of this treatment – it made me feel clever and powerful, with my 'magic fingers'. It was more of an atmosphere, really, than a story. I woke and saw the light streaming into the bedroom; mounds of clothes lay all around, and Toby sprawled beside me beneath the duvet. I remembered that the results of Mum's tests were due.

I hadn't seen her for some time, although I received reports on the telephone – later, with that irrationally self-absorbed guilt such things provoke, it seemed almost as if the world had been waiting until my back was turned. Apparently, Mum had been feeling ill for several weeks. She'd lost weight, and her skin had developed a yellowish tinge.

Hepatitis, the GP said, and they needed to find out what kind (after a little anxious research, I could only ascertain that A sounded the best and D sounded the worst). It made sense, because she'd made a trip to Asia and North Africa a few months earlier, a big-deal nostalgia-tour, revisiting some of the places where she'd lived as a child. I couldn't at first understand why she'd sounded so relieved about this diagnosis. 'To be honest, darling, I was scared it might be, you know . . .' she tailed off, on the other end of the line, suddenly uncharacteristically coy.

'What?' I said.

12

'You *know*. The Big C.'

I was living in a shared house in Camberwell. My boyfriend Toby and I had the largest bedroom. Toby was going to be a formidable human rights lawyer, but for the moment, he was doing a law conversion course, working in a bar, and growing a goatee beard that seemed rather silly, even at the time. We lived with my best friend from college, Zoe, a pretty Texan with a stud in her nose. Zoe wanted to work in the media, and was making coffee and doing the photocopying for a TV production company. The fourth tenant was a large German postgraduate student, called Christina. I had signed the lease – I was the one who knew what day the bins were emptied, and the one who most often went shopping (although we all stole Christina's crisp bread, when the cupboards got really empty). Our hall was full of other people's post, a big batik wall hanging (a present from Mum's trip) and boxes of stuff waiting to be recycled.

I climbed out of bed, and searched the bedroom for something clean and uncrumpled enough to wear to work. It was the 90s, and we were young – full of easy self-righteousness about the Criminal Justice Act, the cones hotline, and 'back to basics'. I had just started what I thought of as my first *proper* job, although I'd done plenty of crap jobs – waitressing, temping and so on – and it was turning out to be less different than I'd expected. I dressed quietly, so as not to wake Toby. Then I found a patch of exposed cheekbone to kiss, between the rumpled duvet and the rumpled blonde hair – the pull of his warm, sleeping body hard to resist – before gently closing the door, on my way out.

I worked in a cramped office, full of overflowing box files, overlooking a square in Bloomsbury. Midway through the morning, I telephoned home – which is how I still thought of the house in which I'd grown up – to ask about Mum, but after eight rings, the answerphone clicked in, and I decided not to leave a message. When I got back after lunch, there was a post-it note on my desk: 'Gus rang.' This alarmed me. Gus was my younger brother. He almost never called me, and wouldn't have rung just to chat.

I called back again, and it was Gus who answered. 'Oh, hi Suze,' he said.

'I got your message. What's wrong?' Out of the window I could see pigeons and plane trees, and office workers eating their sandwiches on benches.

13

'It's Mum,' he said. He sounded gruff and peculiar. 'She's here. I think she wants to talk to you. Suze ...?' for some reason, I could feel my heart thumping, and taste the coffee I'd drunk earlier rising in my throat. 'It isn't good.'

'Hello, Susanna,' Mum said. Just hearing her voice reassured me. 'We just got back from the hospital.' She paused. 'I'm afraid that they say it is cancer, after all.' She managed to sound both apologetic and melodramatic at once. Because she was on the end of the line, talking to me, I couldn't really take it in. My first thought was, 'Well, it can't be all that bad.'

I asked questions – what kind, what next. She didn't seem to know very much, but mentioned an operation. 'They've not been particularly reassuring about it so far,' she said, dryly.

'I'll come right down,' I said.

'Only if you want,' Mum said. 'I don't want this to be too ... disruptive.' Her 'courage in adversity' voice made me feel bizarrely irritated with her.

'I want.'

'That would be nice,' she said, as if conceding a small defeat. 'You've nearly missed the blossom for this year.'

I told my colleagues – surprisingly calmly, it seemed to me, but when I wrote down my home phone number for them, I noticed that my hand was shaking. I rang Toby. 'I've got some bad news,' I told him; he thought I meant I'd have to work late.

A sympathetic colleague gave me a lift back to South London. Watching the ornate roofs of the big Bloomsbury hotels go by, I had the feeling that perhaps I ought to be crying. I tried to talk through the news with her, hoping to clarify things for myself. 'I hope you don't think I'm cold,' I said.

'God, no,' she said. 'It's not a competition.'

Back at the house, Toby was in, with the TV on, and a large book on 'The Law of Tort' lying open on the coffee table. He followed me upstairs, and I began throwing clothes into a shoulder bag. 'I'm here for you,' he kept saying, and he kept trying to hug me. It hadn't occurred to me that he wouldn't be there for me, and seemed to be missing the point, somehow. I hugged him back, briefly, and worried about catching my train.

In the back of a minicab, weaving through the traffic to London Bridge, I remembered my dream, and wondered for a moment if I still had magic fingers. Then I started to cry – big, dry, gulping

14

sobs, almost, I was distantly aware, like a bad actor. Losing my composure so completely in front of a stranger was frightening: I panicked for a moment that I might not be able to get it together again.

'Are you OK?' the driver asked, with precise, African articulation, 'do you want me to stop?' I wondered where he was from – Mum would have known, probably, and might even have been there. Unable to speak, I waved at him helplessly, to drive on.

Helene

The train gathered speed as we left King's Cross. London was laid waste around us. The rows of houses reminded me of rotten teeth, with blackened gaps, some crumbling away, the few, here and there, that still seemed good, like a joke really, a reminder of the others' deficiencies. Doors opened onto nothing, bedroom wallpaper was exposed, lavatory bowls hung over thin air. It seemed so brutally invasive one almost felt embarrassed, but compelled to look.

The logic of our lives had disintegrated, and those things we thought of as permanent had been exposed as matchstick and dust, precious possessions reduced to rubbish and filth. Some places looked like a stage set, a flimsy façade, so jarringly, recently rearranged; the older sites, already overgrown with brambles and buddleia, made me think of the ruins of some ancient civilisation. It made me feel hopeless, as we thundered through the suburbs – it left me suspecting a futility in all of our attempts to construct order and meaning. People sometimes think that it was just the East End and the docks that were destroyed, but all I can say is, you should have seen the rest of it. The whole city was an immense field of ruins, from end to end. There was something deeply depressing about the mess.

The countryside looked more normal, as we made our way north, although the station names had been painted out, at the start of the war, to confuse the potential invaders. All the way, I had the idea that I might change my mind: at the last minute, I could just say no, and turn around, and the thought made me panicky. I ate the cheese sandwich which my mother had given me, in the tin box which I used to take to work. Dusk fell, and then the thick, blanketing, pre-industrial dark roared by the windows. We drew down the blinds and I tried to sleep.

In the night, I woke suddenly, as if someone had spoken my name. For a moment I couldn't remember where I was, and felt for the baby next to me – since her birth, I'd been subconsciously aware of her proximity, in the way one is aware of one's own limbs, even when asleep. The rhythmic rattle soon reminded me I was on a train, and I could feel the strangers sleeping around me. I had to remind myself that she hadn't fallen down a crack, or onto the floor: she wasn't there. My breasts were hot and hard, still in tune with her hunger, uncomfortably full with her bedtime feed. I tried to conjure for myself, over the miles, the fast, shallow breathing that usually calmed me back to sleep, and the extraordinary way she radiated peace.

The next day, I changed trains in Glasgow. By now, there were almost a hundred of us, other wives, with square-shouldered coats and jaunty hats, carefully set hair, chunky heels, and nervous, scarlet smiles. They had suitcases and trunks; some of them had their children with them, and seeing them was uncomfortable for me. We exchanged details about our husbands, as a sort of short-hand for ourselves, and I told a few of them about Lottie.

I felt worse by then. I was agitated and dizzy, hot and frantic. My poor breasts burned and prickled, and it felt as if the ducts within them had solidified into seams of iron ore. We got off the train and took a bus, to a field on what felt to me like the very edge of the world. By then, the chirpy enthusiasm of the rest of the group was also fading, and we gradually became less like a schoolgirls' outing, and more like the groups of refugees on news-reels, our carefully set hair-dos ruined by the wind, our chunky heels sliding in the mud. We waited in a row of Nissen huts, crowded with our luggage and some rudimentary metal furniture.

Tearfully, I confessed my discomfort to some of the other women. 'Milk fever,' one of them said, knowledgably. 'We ought to find you a doctor.'

The naval doctor I saw seemed bemused and rather embarrassed. He dosed me up with vast quantities of Epsom salts. I had to pump the wretched stuff out myself, bending over a basin like an animal. I spent three days tossing and turning in the rough blankets, making the trip back and forth to the nearest privy. The other women were kind and sympathetic, but I was miserable and humiliated, and it was extremely painful.

Gradually, my wretched, ridiculous bosoms went down, and my temperature subsided. I had felt essential, full of love, and milk, and now I just had soft little rags, squeezed dry. There was no longer any question in my mind about turning round and going back. We had been warned not to communicate our location to anyone, and I hadn't been able to telephone home. It seemed to me I had been travelling for a week, and I felt as if I should be in another continent already. It was almost as if I'd had something amputated, the shape of which I could still feel in the air. I was left feeling empty and drained, but also strangely light and free.

Then, finally, word came to get ready, and we hurriedly snatched up our stuff. I wrapped myself up against the wind, and trod carefully, and watched the choppy grey water, and it wasn't until the vast cliff face of the ship was almost upon us that I really looked up. The enormous, dizzying bulk of a great ocean liner loomed above me. One huge funnel belched smoke into the sky. There were rows and rows of faces, peering over at us. At that moment, even from the depths of my misery, I thought to myself, well, this might not be quite so bad after all. There were thousands of men, all in uniform, lining the decks, and gazing down at us: just *staring*.

Vera

We carried on going to work and doing the house up, but the new information added a surreal undercurrent to life. Gregor was daunted by the news ('bloody hell, that was quick'), and, at first, alarmingly quiet. Then, for a day or so, he was triumphant, and wanted to announce to the world that we had 'a bun in the oven', or that I was 'up the duff'. I didn't want to tell anyone yet, and made him promise, on the verge of tears, suddenly so adamant that he agreed to hold back. After a couple of days, he didn't seem to want to talk about it any more, either. 'You're right,' he said. 'Let's keep it quiet for a bit.'

I wanted a chance to get used to the idea myself, first. It still felt as private, and as tenuous, as a missed period, and I didn't feel ready for excitement and congratulations. I felt as if the announcement would turn me, and my insides, into public property. I had a

17

dream in which my womb had been placed in a glass case as a science exhibit. I worried about my new job – perhaps they'd feel that I'd tricked them, or let them down. The stories about 'fallen women' and 'the wages of sin' that I'd heard all my life were so powerful that I had to keep reminding myself that I was married, and grown-up, and it was actually OK for me to be pregnant, and not a dark, shameful tragedy. There was also the secret fear that, after years of quiet yearning, I suddenly, perversely, might not be able to seem as unequivocally happy as perhaps I ought. I even worried, for God's sake, about the cat, and how he would adapt.

Not telling people was also peculiar, however, and made me feel a little mad. 'Oh, we're fine, pretty much the same,' I said to friends on the telephone, and enthused defensively about life outside the capital; 'yes, thanks, settling in well,' I replied to my colleagues, and gushed about the sea air.

I spoke to Sheila, my oldest friend and co-conspirator from school, with whom I'd set the world to rights so many nights – over barley wine and Woodbines, or cider and mentholated cigarettes, and lately over red wine and the Gauloises that Gregor and I bought in bulk on holiday, in soft, blue-paper packets. Sheila was feeling jaded – she was just coming out of a relationship with a beautiful young Australian, who'd done industrial quantities of LSD, developed a paranoid fear of electricity, and lost all interest in sex. I did my best to console her, but after I put the receiver down, I felt lonely and strangely guilty, as if I'd been secretly plotting to change teams.

We went to dinner with some of Gregor's new colleagues, in a big house in Lewes, with a hallway full of the debris – blotchy paintings and teeny tiny wellington boots – of the sleeping children upstairs. Over the *coq au vin*, I searched the faces of the parents around the table for clues, and read too much into every little sign of contentment or complaint. The thing that was different was so much in my head, so much in my daydreams – it actually felt very like my old, illicit fantasies about what it would be like to have a baby, and it was sometimes hard to believe that anything real had changed.

Yet inside, my whole mental landscape was shifting; my whole internal world was turning on its axis. Alone with Gregor, sitting in the bath or over the washing up, I initiated a few conversations along the lines of 'can you believe we're going to be parents?' in

18

which I'd go a little further down the path each time, tentatively verbalising my thoughts, until I reached the point at which it felt uncomfortable, hearing something so intimate, so risky, and so fantastical, spoken out loud.

Gregor didn't seem to understand, 'What's there to talk about?' he said. 'Isn't it a bit late for that?' While handling fruit at the greengrocers, while cycling into work, with the wind in my face, or driving across the downs in our rattly little Triumph Herald, I felt pangs of betrayal towards my girlhood, and all those imagined futures I might once have had; sudden moments of mourning for my free, simple, empty self, and for a state of solitude that I felt I'd never quite have again.

I felt slightly sick all the time, as if life had suddenly become a never-ending car journey, and I was overcome, at intervals, by a debilitating tiredness. Ironically, I was introducing the upper sixth to 'La Nausée', and I would discuss the text with the class, fixing my eyes steadily on the clock at the back of the room, and breathing deeply in an attempt to overcome my own queasiness. Sometimes it was too much for me, and I had to make a dash for the white tiled toilet across the hall, retching into the ceramic bowl whilst holding my hair back with one hand, and then dabbing ineffectually at my mouth with the hard, green-paper hand towels, before returning to my bewildered students, and the next agonisingly slow paragraph.

During free periods, the exhaustion would overcome me – a powerful undertow, dragging me down in great, enticing waves – and I would sometimes lose consciousness, as suddenly and completely as if I'd been drugged, slumped forwards on my marking. I would wake to find dribble in the margins, and fragments of a seventeen-year-old's scrawl imprinted across my forehead. At lunchtimes, if I had the staff-room to myself, I would lie on my back on the floor, and stare up at the sunlight filtering through the orange woollen curtains, and the dust particles dancing round the brown checked easy chairs and ring-marked coffee table. It was hard to keep up the pretence of normality.

My breasts were growing. The feeling reminded me of adolescence – they were hot, and sore, and heavy, swelling up like one of the bawdy cartoons on the postcards they sold at the sea front. It was strange, this feeling that my body, which for many years now had simply delivered the expected degree of pleasure or pain

19

at the appropriate moments, suddenly had an agenda of its own. Even my T-shirt hurt, and my bras were suddenly too small. I'd always had a fairly average bosom, certainly in comparison with the film star icons of my teenage years, and although I didn't waste my time with some of my class-mates' methods ('I must, I must, I must increase my bust') and later grew to appreciate the infantile nature of society's fixation with the breast – well, there was a part of me that was also secretly rather impressed with my magnificently curvaceous new cleavage.

On Saturday, I consulted books about pregnancy in the municipal library, checking neurotically for any of my students who might be around as I did so. The books available were either briskly medical, with intricate line drawings of the foetus in utero, or filled with matronly advice for new mothers, with diagrams on the different ways to fold a nappy, and sections entitled 'He's Apt to Change His Eating Habits'. They were compelling, but scary – I felt rather as I had as a teenager, reading 'Lady Chatterley's Lover' under the bedcovers, trying to work out what exactly was going on, with the added intrigue of wondering what the nuns would make of it all. It was rather like a language, I told myself, practising the words under my breath – episiotomy, post partum, layette – and there was nothing like knowing a bit of the vocabulary to make me feel better about things.

That night, though, in bed, hot tears welled up and slid down my cheeks. 'I'm going to lose my figure,' I sobbed on to Gregor's shoulder, and then, amending the thought, 'I'm not sure I'm really cut out to be a mother. It's a bit much, to have to go through all this for someone you don't even know yet.'

'But you're like a goddess,' Gregor whispered, tracing my flank with one hand. 'A fertility goddess, swollen with fecundity.' We had been together a long time – he knew the sing-songy tone of voice which would soothe me, but I felt he was going through the motions, lacking in real empathy.

'A puking goddess, you mean.' One of the library books that afternoon had insisted that pregnancy wasn't an illness, but a completely natural, healthy state. It felt like an illness to me, though – and besides, I reasoned, feeling unwell was presumably just as 'natural' as feeling great. I sometimes consoled myself, when I had flu, with the thought of epic battles being fought out in my mucus and my bloodstream, and there was a similar sense of something big going on in my body in which I – as a person – was only incidentally involved.

'Ten per cent extra for free,' Gregor drew me closer. 'Two for the price of one.' The wooden wind chimes at the window murmured to themselves, and the silver light from the street lamp outside spilled through the curtains. 'Your body's working miracles, behind your back. It's bound to take it out of you.'

He started to press himself against me. My skin felt too tender to be touched, even by the sheets. The aching exhaustion reminded me of a feeling from childhood, which my mother had briskly dismissed as 'growing pains' – I wanted unconsciousness to swallow me up, and could already feel the downward spiralling towards sleep when I kept my head still. 'Please, don't,' I moaned, rolling away, and burying my face in the pillow.

Susie

Out of the window, I watched the countryside spool past: green and gold pastures, stately old trees, pillar-box red station furniture. People slept in their seats, a look of drained suffering on their faces.

My brother, Gus, met me in the station forecourt, waiting behind the wheel of Mum's big old Volvo. He got out as I approached. He had the same boyish face as before, but transplanted on to a taller body, with broader shoulders. He looked bewildered, lost, as if he had been expecting someone else.

I kissed him on the cheek. 'Are you OK?'

'It's so fucked up,' he said, as he lobbed my bag into the boot. We got in, and he slammed the door. 'She's been talking about dying.'

I released a deep, shaky breath. 'Typical,' I said.

'Yep,' Gus echoed. 'Drama queen.'

There it all was, the same tatty old town – the greasy cafés and wrought-iron balconies, the chimney pots and gulls, the peeling cream house-fronts and steep elegant streets, sloping down to the sea, which still surprised me with its scale. There was something strange about the way time passed there. On my intermittent visits back, I felt as if I saw it as a time-lapse film, all sped up – the accelerated blossoming and withering of districts, a flash of colour as bars and shops opened, changed their name, then closed, the swarming growth of new glass, fresh brickwork, or scaffolding. I recognised street names with surprise, as we passed. The information belonged to a part of my brain, a part of myself, no longer in use, buried in the substrata of my personality.

It was also strange to see Gus driving, changing gear unthinkingly with his large, man's hands. He was talking about Mum's eyes. 'She looks like an alien,' he was saying. 'She frightens little kids.'

Gus was on a 'year off' that threatened to become longer, retaking an A level, working at Oddbins, and partying hard. Usually he irritated me, because things seemed to come so easily to him. He had that inconsistent maturity that the kids of divorcees often acquire, and was a master of manipulation, it seemed to me. Gus took after Dad, with his mass of unruly ginger curls. I have straight brown hair, and pale blue eyes; 'you've got your mother's eyes', people sometimes said. Usually, I was indignant, cynical, a little jealous, but now, I felt a surge of protectiveness towards him.

Mum met us in the hallway. Seeing her hit me as no telephone conversation could. She looked shrunken, frail, and suddenly, much older. It was as if she'd been freeze dried. Small folds of flesh, around her neck, her cheeks, her arms, had gone, as if they'd been sand-blasted away, taking a certain softness from her face and leaving new angles beneath. Her normally pale skin had a vivid, mustard tinge, and the whites of her eyes were a stunning lemon yellow. I thought of the plastic we'd stuck on to the car headlights for long-ago holidays in France, when I was a child, to change their colour. I felt sick, and scared.

'Well, this is a bit of a bore, isn't it?' Mum said, and kissed me. I started crying again.

We went into the kitchen, where crying seemed to be the new conversation.

Steve, my stepfather – a big, well-meaning bear of a man – heated up tomato soup and made a salad. An old friend of Mum's, Cathy, was also there: she was almost like an aunt to me, a small, birdlike Liverpudlian with blonde hair and a maternal way about her. Mum was itching so badly she couldn't sit still. She said that her tears stung her. 'I suppose they must have bile in them,' she said.

Steve, who was Canadian, was trying to be positive, 'we're

gonna fight this, hey?' he kept saying, 'we're gonna beat this', and 'it's not such a bad time of year to get sick'.

'It's OK, we're allowed to cry,' Mum said. 'We've been so brave all day. I always thought I was one of those excitable continental types, but I surprise myself. It seems I do have a stiff upper lip, after all.'

I looked around the table. The faces, in a pool of light from the low hanging lamp, were distorted with shock, and shining with tears. It was like a bad dream in which everything was familiar but altered. The kitchen looked the same as it always had – the cork board with postcards, lists and timetables pinned to it, two spindly avocado plants, grown from stones, on the window sill, and the faded Provençal cotton curtains which hung from the work surfaces, concealing saucepans, colanders and earthenware oven-dishes.

'It's funny. These are the kind of things you rehearse for, in your head,' Mum was saying. 'Yet when it comes to the point, one's thoughts are really quite banal.'

The meal was punctuated with telephone conversations, close friends and family ringing to ask about the tests. I didn't want Mum to tell anyone about the cancer – childishly, I felt that if she didn't tell them, it might go away – but she was almost brutally direct. It seemed as if through telling people, she was forcing the news into herself. I could hear her voice, from the hall, in crisis mode, and could all too easily imagine the other side of the conversation: shocked, practical, sympathetic. It was my way of reacting too – very female, very British, adamantly coping, spinning a swift web of solidarity against the unknown – 'yes, of course, I'll keep you posted.' Hearing it from a distance, however, something in it also revolted me. I hated listening to this new reality becoming established, and taking root, as well as the speed and efficiency of the process, the jostling to be at the centre of things, and a barely-concealed hunger for drama.

Mum came back in, aware of our eyes on her, and sat back down. We talked about the hospital. She told us about lying in a tube, inside a scanner that clunked and vibrated as it looked through her flesh in slices, like a loaf of bread. Despite the shock, I could hear her beginning to make it into a story. 'I couldn't believe that sign on the shelf,' she said. She sounded perplexed. 'In the room where they told us. Did you see it? It said HAVE A

23

NICE DAY. Someone should take that down.'

'That's terrible. You ought to mention it to them,' Cathy said.

'You're an old hand at all this,' Mum said. 'I suppose.' Cathy's husband had died of cancer, six years earlier.

'This is very different,' Cathy said. 'Cancer is such a catch-all term. This isn't what Mike had.'

'And who wants to be a cancer veteran, anyway?'

Cathy began to blink rapidly, and then to cry. 'I'm sorry,' she said. 'It just seems so . . .'

'I'm sorry, I didn't mean to . . .'

'Do you want a tissue?'

I tried to change the subject. 'How's Will?' I asked. Cathy's son was the same age as I was, and we'd been to the same school. He was abroad, teaching English.

Cathy pulled herself together. 'He's OK, I think. Still in Bratislava, but he says he's coming back in the summer. I was beginning to worry he'd be over there for good.'

It grew late, and Cathy said her goodbyes. Gus had vanished into his room, and Steve went to his study, ostensibly to work, but really to finish his beer and play patience on the computer. I wanted to help Mum clear up, and she wouldn't let me, an edge of irritation in her voice that nearly started me crying again. She said that she wouldn't be able to sleep because of the itching, so she might as well have something to do. I sat in the kitchen chair, watching her. We talked about my new job.

'It's OK, I mean, there's nothing actually wrong. It's just not like I expected.' I didn't know how to communicate the disappointment I felt with the world, and my intimate relationship with the office photocopier and fax machine – what scared me most was that she might be disappointed on my behalf, so I focused on the bigger picture. 'It's as if you learn this secret language, all these catch-phrases, social exclusion, capacity building, gender empowerment, blah, blah, and then people will give you money. It all seems so cynical, somehow. It's almost as if they're spending money to keep things pretty much as they are.'

'It sounds incredibly interesting, though, darling. We're so proud of you, doing something so worthwhile. I'm sure, when you've been there a while, you can change the way they do things, shake things up a bit, cut down on all the red tape and so on.' She sounded exhausted.

'Huh. I doubt it.'

'Oh, I'm sure you can. Just what the world needs, a few more sparky young women in charge. Show those men in suits a thing or two.' I could hear her feeling for a familiar interpretation – left versus right, wimmin versus patriarchy, idealism versus pessimism. As usual, it frustrated me: I felt she wasn't really listening to what I was saying.

I couldn't bring myself to say goodnight. I had that same feeling again, that there was something important that I'd forgotten to ask, or to say. I was like a child, afraid of the dark, and just being near her seemed to help. I was scared that once I left her, the news would begin to sink in. After a while, though, she must have got the feeling I was waiting for something. She enfolded my hands in hers. 'I'm sorry,' she said. 'I don't have anything very profound to say. I didn't want to put you two through this.' She ran a hand over my hair. 'Why don't you go to bed? You look terribly tired.'

I slept in my old bedroom. Orange light, from the street lamp outside, leaked in through the curtains, making familiar shapes on the walls. The shelves were filled with books from different parts of my life – *Letts Revision Guides*, battered paperback copies of *Ballet Shoes* and *The Little House on the Prairie*. Dear God, I thought, this is all wrong, there must be some mistake. I will wake up and everything will be back to normal.

I slept badly, my brain troubled with formless thoughts, and an enormous problem I had to work out, in diagrammatic form. In the middle of the night, though, I woke with a powerful sense, almost like the continuation of a dream, that everything was going to be OK.

Chapter Two

Helene

I lay in my bunk in the dark, listening to the deep, consoling rumble of the engine, rocked by the gentle pitch of the ship.

I was used to fielding polite questions about my background, still startled by the compulsion of the English to place me – so swiftly and subtly – within their mental scheme, pinning me down, wriggling, like an insect in a display case. London was full of refugees, and there I had been nothing special – rather reassuring, even, as proof of civilised British values, in contrast to the unsporting behaviour of the enemy. These army wives were different, however, with their own notions of status, enmeshed in complex hierarchies I only half understood. I gave different versions, all true, featuring my husband heavily, but slanted one way or another, depending on my mood.

I grew up, as you know, in Vienna. My family were Jewish, but had converted to the Lutheran Church; my father and grandfather were both doctors. My childhood memories are set in comfortable apartments, crammed with a multitude of clocks, and fringed silk lampshades, with everything polished to a shine. My grandparents were respectable, conservative, and at first quite taken with National Socialism, if it weren't for the distasteful anti-Semitism with which it was associated. I remember them arguing with my father, whose views were more radical. Perhaps it was just a 'childhood disease,' I remember my grandfather saying indulgently, a temporary phase.

In March 1938 I'd been a gawky teenager, unused to my suddenly longer limbs, and prone to knocking things over. I had

26

several days off school for the referendum. My mother and I went for a walk in the Vienna woods. It was early spring, and the buds on the trees were just about to open, so that the whole wood gave off a pinkish glow.

We met a police officer who was also out walking, and he started to talk to my mother. He was desperately worried, he confessed. He feared the Nazis wouldn't wait for the referendum to take place, they'd seize power, and he was afraid of what the police would be called upon to do. This complete stranger, who spoke to us so openly and frankly, brought home the seriousness of the situation to my mother. For the first time, I think, she became really concerned.

The next day, my mother and I went to the Opera with some friends, to see *Eugene Onegin*, by Tchaikovsky. It was a long opera – it certainly seemed so to me – and when we came out, our ears still ringing with the music, everything had changed. My father appeared in the foyer to meet us with a white face. On the Ring Strasse, there were thousands of people milling around, perching in the trees, up on the lampposts, all very excited. The posters about the referendum had been torn down, and there were swastikas absolutely everywhere, crawling over everything, like a swarm of cubist spiders. My father walked us home swiftly, with our eyes on the pavement. The German army had crossed into Austria, and the Chancellor was under arrest.

After that, there was hushed talk of suicides, people jumping out of top-floor windows. My family became very tense and would snap at me for the slightest thing. The older of my two brothers, Michael, had joined some patriotic organisation a few days before, and had put on a uniform, just to have to take it off again very quickly. I tried to keep out of the way, and nobody paid me much attention.

At the weekend, Hitler and Goebbels addressed the crowd from the Rathaus, to announce the Anschluss – Austria had become part of the Reich. I went along to listen. I got myself a little swastika to pin on to my lapel, so that I would blend in, and I pushed my way right to the front of the crowd. Everything was in rhythm, 'ein Volk, ein Reich, ein Führer! Ein Volk, ein Reich, ein Führer!' I was part of a great sea of people, completely hysterical, their arms going up like a wave, with a huge rush of air, roaring with energy and excitement. Before Hitler spoke, hundreds of homing pigeons were released, back to Germany, blacking out the sky, to carry the news that Austria was part of the motherland. It was incredibly dramatic; I didn't feel afraid at all. Afterwards, when they discovered where I'd been, my family were frantic – how could you? Why didn't you tell us where you were going? My God, what's that on your coat?

I went back to school. The father of one of the girls in my class had been arrested, which gave her a sort of solemn glamour to the rest of us – she was sick with worry. There were other very unpleasant things. They made old Jewish gentlemen scrub the pavements, or do knee bends in the street, people like my grandfather. Ordinary Austrians put on brown uniforms, and they just became bullies.

Opposite my grandparents' apartment, there was a small grocer's shop. If she ran out of something, my grandmother sent me there, or her maid. When she went in herself, they were very subservient and smarmy – 'Ja bitte sehr, ja danke schön', 'Küss die Hand gnädige Frau'. After the Anschluss, my grandmother and I went in to this shop to buy a bit of semolina, and as she always did, my grandmother went straight up to the counter.

'Go to the back of the queue, you Jewish sow,' the shopkeeper said. 'Saujüdin dreckige.'

My grandmother seemed to shrink inside her mink collar. She simply couldn't understand what he was saying – she'd never heard such words. I felt deeply embarrassed for her, and then angry. It seemed so hypocritical: after all those years of Frau Doktor this, Frau Doktor that.

An Englishwoman, a friend of my mother's, telegraphed to say that my parents could send me to England, and that she would be responsible for me. I went to the English Consulate to queue for papers. There were queues going round the block several times.

I travelled out to England by myself, with just what I could carry. The train went to Linz and then through Germany, and then over the border from Aachen into Holland. People sat bolt upright in the compartment, and nobody slept. Everyone wore a little swastika on their lapel. They checked our papers constantly: the SS, the SA, up and down the train, slamming the doors. They asked each of us questions, and we explained how we were going on holiday, or to visit relatives, or to improve our English. We held our breath each time; they could be very arbitrary.

28

Then we crossed into Holland, and suddenly we began to make eye contact, and talk. One person opened the window, and then we all took off our little swastikas, and threw them out, into the ditch, in a rain of metal pins. The sense of relief was enormous. 'I'm not going back there,' people said. Some of them started crying.

I stayed with the British family for nearly a year. I had a good ear for languages, and picked up English quite easily, although I think they thought I was rather funny. The more progressive English schools offered some free places to refugee children, and I got one of these. After Krystallnacht, the family with whom I was staying decided to get my mother over as well. My father and my two older brothers stayed in Vienna.

My mother found work keeping house for an elderly city gent, and after that we lived in a series of rented rooms in and just outside London. We were united in our dislike of English food – the horrors of custard, and junket – and would reminisce lovingly about Mohn Palatschinken and Sachertorte. My mother was good at making things feel like an adventure. In the public shelters, she'd get out a small bottle of cooking sherry, and a tablespoon, and share it around, like medicine. When the Blitz started we were staying in Hampstead. Looking downhill towards the city was incredible. Truly, the night sky was red and orange.

I was courted by a sweet German Jewish boy called Franz, with whom I developed an intense friendship. He was called up into the Pioneer Corps, which we jokingly called the Schpioneer Corps – the spying corps – since Germans weren't allowed to join the proper army. If he did well, he explained to me, he'd have the chance to get British nationality, and maybe change his name – he made it sound a bit like an offer. We were both young, however, and the world was changing fast, and perhaps somewhere in the back of my mind I was aware that there was another way for me to change my life, and my surname.

I passed my Higher School Certificate, and I could have gone on to University, but I was keen to find work. I earned some money teaching German to officers of the Intelligence Corps. They were supposed to know languages, but some of them didn't very well, so I gave them extra tuition, to learn to speak like ordinary people, not just the way that Goethe or Schiller wrote.

Charles was one of my more diligent students. He was twelve years older than I was, a tall, blonde man, with conventional, film star good looks, a small, wispy moustache, and a rather pinkish complexion. We began to hold our lessons over dinner. At the time, good food was in short supply, and he knew the better restaurants, ordering the waiters around and refilling my glass with the easy confidence of his class. He seemed to consider women an alien and very delicate species, and his clumsy gestures in my direction – speaking as if from a script in his head – amused me. He seemed reassured by my brisk, teacherly attitude (several times he remarked, with surprise, how much easier I was to talk to than most of the young ladies he knew) as well as impressed, and perhaps a little shocked, by my appetite. He wooed me with further gifts of steak and tinned tomatoes. After several months, he invited me to see a Bing Crosby film, the road to somewhere or other, and afterwards, he blurted out a kind of declaration: 'You will think this awfully sudden.' It was all I could do not to laugh – only an Englishman would think it sudden, and I had been expecting it for weeks.

His kiss was hard and bony, like a collision of faces. He made strange, mechanical movements with his mouth, but the sensation was not unpleasant. I closed my eyes, and tried to lose myself (I had read novels about this, and seen it at the cinema) but as I drew away, I noticed that his eyes were still open, watching me as we kissed, and the effect was disconcerting. He was very serious about everything.

My mother liked the fact that he was older, and an officer, and thought that he might provide me with security and stability. We hadn't heard from my father or brother for many months – she had plenty to worry about, and seemed hopeful that I, at least, might be safely taken care of. Perhaps she also felt, in the darkness of the night, that life might be easier for me as a Perkins than as a Rosenbaum.

Before our marriage, Charles and I took a train down to meet his parents. Charles seemed more nervous than I was, and was very concerned about my comfort on the journey, jumping up and down to open and close the carriage window, or to fetch and then stow my handbag. We got off at a little station in the New Forest, where his father was waiting to meet us in his motor car. He drove us back to a large, mock-Tudor house, separated from the road by a thick rhododendron hedge, and surrounded by steep banks of fern and heather.

30

Charles's mother was waiting at home, and it quickly became clear to me that she was the real power in the family. She set her husband to work, with an array of bottles and a cut-glass decanter, positioned us around the room, and guided the conversation smoothly along preordained lines.

Charles's father used to build canals out in the Punjab before his retirement, and had been an enthusiastic photographer. I asked a few questions, out of politeness, and immediately, the family album came out. There were many, muddy-brown pictures: people in jodhpurs and frock coats, at durbars and gymkhanas, ranked in rows or seated straight-backed on horses. They were shown standing on concrete structures, or at home, surrounded by servants in improbable headgear, and once with a dead tiger. I quickly became confused by all the different names, but grasped that Charles had an uncle (who had been knighted, it was pointed out to me, several times) who was the Governor of a whole Province.

'We miss it terribly,' his mother said to me, 'although of course nothing's the same with this dreadful war.'

I could sense a polite distaste behind their exaggerated good manners towards me. There was something else, however, in the barking and backslapping towards Charles, and in his mother's high-pitched laughter. It came to me over dinner, when I thought of my own mother – relief, of course, they're pleased he's found someone at last! I bristled with a protective resentment on his behalf – why on earth they should worry, when he was so good looking, I couldn't imagine – but he was in his thirties, and I suppose they must have been concerned that he'd never settle down.

His mother spoke a language of convoluted connections and name-dropping, but was strangely silent on the subject of my own family, as if frightened of the horrors which probing might reveal. When discussing my care of Charles, however, and his particularities over food and dress, she was suddenly warmer. I was such a strange fish to them, such a nobody, that they seemed to think I'd be malleable at least, and hard-working, eager to earn the unexpected honour which had been conferred upon me. His father went further. 'I think you could be the making of him, my dear,' he growled, after his second glass of wine.

I watched all this with a detached, almost anthropological interest. 'So this will be my new world,' I thought. I believed that when

31

you married, you took on your husband's identity and attributes, and shed your old self like a dead skin. This was quite appealing to me. My mother had always been a strong influence, and our abrupt displacement had thrown us even closer together. I was beginning to find this claustrophobic. She was not particularly well educated, but enormously strong-willed. Increasingly, I found her an embarrassment, with her irrational pronouncements, her over-powering sentimentality, and her effusive, broken English. Through Charles, I felt I could assert my difference from her, and remake myself, as a member of the British ruling class. I truly believed that a ring on my finger would bring about this magic transformation, or at least camouflage my differences. Charles and his family knew more about camouflage, however, than I realised.

I took instruction into the Catholic faith. Some of it struck me as rather silly – the concept of Limbo, for instance, for unbaptised babies. Surely if anyone deserved to go to heaven it was children, I argued, with a passion which surprised even me. The nuns had to call in a priest to talk me round, and in the end I gave way, and accepted it, although I never really warmed to the religion. We were married in church: I had a beautiful dress, and Charles looked very dashing in his uniform.

Sex was an awkward, embarrassing affair, but after a few drinks each we managed it, and almost immediately, I became pregnant. At the same time, Charles was posted to India, where there had been some land fighting with the Japanese in Burma, right on the frontier. I saw him off at the station, and came home, and had a haemorrhage, and I thought I'd lost the baby. My mother arranged for an excellent Austrian gynaecologist to visit, and he told me to lie flat for a month. After that, baby Lottie came out perfectly all right.

My mother looked after me during the confinement, and after the birth she looked after us both. I named the baby Charlotte, after her absent father. Charles's mother came up to see us, once, after Lottie was born, and pronounced her 'very healthy looking', although I was struck by the fact that she didn't take off her gloves. My time with Charles came to seem like a brief, peculiar interlude – we'd never set up home, and barely even lived together.

Now, in the belly of the huge ship, I had his photograph in my luggage, and spoke of him to the other women, but with a strange sense of fraudulence, as if to conjure for myself a context. I didn't know his moods: his highs and lows, his hopes and fears. In my mind's eye, I placed him in a picture I'd seen of his father, with a topee on his head, and a rifle pointing down at a dead tiger. It seemed implausible, already, but it was all I had to go on.

Susie

It was agreed that I would tell my father. I went up to the University to do it in person – it seemed like a good way to catch him alone, and I didn't want him to be subjected to one of my mother's hit-and-run phone-calls. Once I arrived, however, I lost my nerve, and wondered if I was doing the right thing.

He was giving a lecture. I crept into the back of the hall and sat down. He noticed me, and I saw a flicker of concern cross his face, but he carried on speaking.

The stuffy lecture theatre brought it all back – it was only a few years since I'd sat in one myself, but I'd forgotten already. The students around me were sprawled on orange chairs in attitudes of frozen torment, like victims of some terrible disaster – heads in hands, legs akimbo, twitching remnants of life in a doodling wrist, a foot pulsing to some inaudible beat. He held them paralysed with his voice, the focus of the room, and their attention seemed to somehow magnify him. It was like listening to someone else speak – someone I didn't know at all.

Dad still had the same curls as Gus, but his were no longer ginger but greying, and receding. He was talking about the battle of Cable Street – he'd written a book about it, along with several about dock workers – and although it was an old story, one he'd told many times, with the certainties of good and evil rumbling reassuringly beneath the surface, it was stirring to hear, with the slight break in his voice, his eyes shining, from behind his glasses, 'No pasaran!' One of the strip lights in the room was faulty, and flickered fitfully. The female students at the front leaned forward a little, still touched by his enthusiasm, although there was a murmuring at the back, and then a burst of coughing that could have covered a laugh.

I felt an almost unbearable pity for him, for his innocence. To start with I'd felt a responsibility to protect them both, trotting between the two of them at parents' evenings, amending myself

33

and the facts, with a child's natural deviousness, as far as possible – further, sometimes – in an attempt to make things better. Later, as a teenager, I'd held Mum to blame – as she became my adversary, it was easy for me to understand how she could be his. As usual, I couldn't imagine them ever having been together. I sometimes noticed faint similarities of language and attitude, the geological clues that they had once, before the rift, been part of the same landmass – my little island – but these were buried very deep. I couldn't imagine them not being angry, exasperated and disdainful towards each other.

I listened to the soothing rise and fall of his voice, with its faint, rather beautiful Scottish inflection. He was summing up, now, turning things inside out, looking at them back to front, and even though I wasn't really paying attention to what he was saying, I could feel a satisfying shape beneath his words. He listed three short-term results, and three longer-term results: the pens around me all began to scratch, and I thought how nice it would be if the world around me were always that clear. He wound up his lecture, bang on time, his wristwatch lying face-up on the lectern, and I made my way over, as he was gathering up his notes.

'What's wrong?' he said, immediately, and I felt a wave of panic, of unreadiness – should I tell him straight away, or somewhere more private? Should I launch right in, or was there a gentler way to do it? He removed his glasses, and rubbed his eyes, which made him look terribly vulnerable. When did my parents both start wearing glasses, I wondered? I didn't notice it happen – they didn't, in the photographs, and then suddenly, they did. It was hateful, this new position of power, and I wanted to be shot of it as soon as possible. 'I thought I must have forgotten your birthday or something,' he said.

I laughed, relief mixed with reproach. 'Dad! My birthday's not for three months!'

'I know. That's what I thought next.'

I couldn't hold out on him. 'No, it's Mum,' I said. 'She's not very well.'

'What *really* not very well?'

'Yes, really not very well.'

I remember the look on his face as he sank into a chair. The students were leaving around us – the room, held in frozen tension for an hour, fragmenting into its constituent chaos, a churning sea of bags and papers and coats. I told him the details quickly, and briefly. He'd always had a horror of illness. 'Oh God,' he said. 'Good God.'

I didn't bear him a grudge. Mum did, of course – she had based her whole personality, it sometimes seemed, around this – and Gus did too, partly out of loyalty, and partly for reasons of his own. Poor Dad made a great scapegoat, but I'd always felt it wasn't really his fault – he was foolish, perhaps, or emotionally incapable, or maybe just male, but I was his ally, and still felt like his clever, bonnie, grown-up girl. He stood again, and put his arms around me, and I surprised myself by bursting into tears, and felt better that he knew, because he was part of it, after all, even if, by then, we didn't see that much of each other.

He drove me back to his house in Hove, in the Espace he'd got after the twins were born. 'What an extraordinarily beautiful evening,' he said, as the countryside rolled by the tinted windows. And then, 'Such a large part of one's life . . .'

Carole, my stepmother, was in when we arrived, with their two three-year-old children. Carole was younger, and temperamentally more cheerful than Mum, but not, as Dad was discovering since the birth of the twins, any less demanding when backed into a corner. They lived in a large, 1930s-built semi, newly furnished and painted in pastel colours. Despite the fact that Carole bought his clothes – something Mum would never have considered – Dad sometimes looked a little out of place, a little crumpled and faded, in this setting. At the school gate, people mistook him for the twins' grandfather. ('Ha!' Mum had said triumphantly, when she'd heard about the scan, with its two pulsing heartbeats – 'so there is a God! He'll be wiping their bottoms well into his fifties'). Carole was stretched by the demands of their offspring – the late and longed-for result of years of fertility treatment – and had limited energy for anything beyond the immediate domestic battlefield. When she noticed me at all, on my visits, I sometimes caught her looking vaguely puzzled, as if she couldn't quite work out what I was still doing there.

I played with the twins for a while, reading them stories and letting them chase me round the first floor, while Dad explained the situation to Carole, downstairs. Low murmurs of shock and concern floated up the stairwell, hushed mutterings that I was glad, for once, not to be a part of. I rested my chin on top of Billy's soft head, turning the pages, and Megan nestled into my side, and I breathed in their smell. The bright, well-equipped room, and their cute, trendy clothes, made theirs seem a safe, appealing, idealised world.

The two of them always intrigued me – the bane of twins, I suppose – with the kaleidoscope of resemblances and differences I glimpsed as they changed and grew. They had Dad's eyes but Carole's determined chin: it must have been her genes, too, that touched their hair with gold. They were not particularly alike: Megan was larger, more athletic and physically competent, Billy more thoughtful and frail, but there was some distinct similarity, perhaps just their colouring and gestures, that made you see instantly that they were from the same mould.

They were tired. There was a disagreement over which book to read next, and Megan started to wail, 'I want Elmeeeeeer . . .', and trivial as it was, something about her desperate fury made the tears well up in my eyes as well. They knew nothing of illness or death, yet it struck me that their own disappointments seemed just as intense, their pain just as real. Small things wounded me dispro-portionately. I couldn't bear to see my feelings mirrored back by the world, in any form.

When they saw the tears running silently down my face, the twins stopped shouting abruptly. 'Why are you feeling a little bit sad?' Billy inquired, brightly.

'My Mummy isn't very well,' I explained, blotting my eyes with my sleeve.

'Do you still have a Mummy?' Megan sounded intrigued.

'Of course.' I struggled to hit the bright, reassuring, grown-up note, but it made me feel a bit better. 'I've got a Mummy and a Daddy, just like you.'

'Silly. Her Daddy is Gus,' Billy admonished.

'No, my Daddy is your Daddy.'

They looked at me suspiciously, and just as quickly, seemed to lose interest. 'Don't worry, the doctor will make them all better,' Megan said, 'and then they can have Smarties.'

Dad drove me home. The streets were full of people, spilling out of pubs and restaurants, overflowing pavements, stumbling into the road. 'This place is really changing,' I said.

'I suppose so. We don't get out much,' he gave me an anxious glance. 'Is Gus OK? I do wish he'd come and see us more.' When we were younger, Dad went through a phase of trying to be firm with Gus, 'setting a few boundaries', as he'd put it – I suspect on Carole's insistence. It was deeply unconvincing, and Gus had at first laughed it off, and then just taken himself out of the equation. He didn't make the same effort I did; he was less pathetically eager, I suppose, to paper over the cracks.

'We're all a bit shaken.'

'Yes, of course,' he paused. 'Should I go and see her? Do you think?'

This irritated me. 'I don't know,' I said. 'It's up to you.'

Perhaps he noticed my resentment: we drove in silence for a while, in our large, air-freshener-scented bubble. 'You know, if there's one thing in my life I regret,' he said, after a bit, 'it's how much I hurt your mother.'

He stopped the car outside the house, and felt in his pockets. Carole had made him give up smoking, and instead, he had taken – somewhat incongruously – to chewing gum. 'I won't come in,' he said. I was relieved; I found it difficult to be with both my parents at once. It was as if I knew who I was with each of them separately, but was unable to fuse the two roles.

We kissed cheeks. 'Send my regards,' he said, as I got out.

Vera

At the weekend, we drove out of town. I had quickly grown fond of the landscape, with its storybook simplicity – the downs tumbling into the town, and the town tumbling into the sea; the whole lot seeming to slide, like the scrapings off a giant plate. We stopped at Devil's Dyke and looked out over the Weald. Between us, we had rather a lot of hair at that stage, mine thick and straight, Gregor's wild and curly, with sideburns that seemed to accentuate the length of his face – and it whipped around our heads in the wind, like seaweed underwater. On Gregor's lapel, he wore a tiny CND badge.

The end of the world had always loomed large in our relationship. We'd met nearly a decade before, in the early 60s, on the Aldermaston peace march. Sheila and I were still at school, at the time, and Gregor was working as a wages clerk in his father's business, before starting university. In fact, Sheila was the one he got chatting to first. 'He's Scottish,' she hissed to me, as we stood in the rain, amid the embroidered banners and home-made placards, 'and rather dishy, don't you think?'

I accepted a proffered cigarette. Gregor was handsome, dressed in a black roll-necked sweater and duffel coat, with his curly ginger hair, and prominent cheekbones and Adam's apple. My clothes were solidly respectable – a rayon jersey skirt and matronly shoes, my only concession to bohemia an oversized jumper. I suppose that Sheila was the adventurous one, the one who usually interested the boys (in fact, by then she was already making the acquaintance of a couple of art students marching to the other side of us), and I was her swotty side-kick. My studied lack of interest in fripperies was intended to mark me out as more cerebral, superior to other girls, with their giggles and their bouffant hair. 'Can't you hear the H bomb's thunder, echo like the crack of doom?' we sang, shoulder to shoulder.

Gregor was very fired up about the march. It was his second one, and he pointed out the different contingents to me helpfully – the Quakers behind us, joining in the singing with a thin, reedy warble, the trade unionists, in their overcoats and trilbies, and the Communists in front, with more robust voices and the advantage of a guitar.

'They don't look in the least bit sly or sinister, do they?' I remarked. 'Rather wholesome and jolly, actually.' I was a little disappointed to find that the seditious elements against which I had been warned had all the rosy cheeks and high spirits of an Ovaltine advertisement.

'No horns and tails, then?' Gregor said, teasingly. 'You should judge people on what they say, not on what's said about them. Have you ever read any Marx?'

'Oh I agree, he makes a lot of sense,' I added, hurriedly, although as a matter of fact, I hadn't. 'If I didn't believe in God, I might even be tempted by Communism myself.' I had the feeling – irritating but not entirely unpleasant – that he was laughing at me.

Gregor had travelled down from Edinburgh to 'stand up and be counted'. It was exciting to see so many people who felt the same way, to feel we had a common cause with each other and with all these complete strangers – 'they'll have to listen to us now,' he said. He told me elatedly about the people he'd met on the train

38

who had told him how much they admired 'you Ban the Bomb crowd'. I was relieved to hear that he had no intention of getting arrested. 'The Civil Disobedience Campaign is surely misguided,' he said, as if I'd disagreed with him. 'The best hope for CND has to be in proving itself a mature and respectable political movement.' I found myself admiring the lilt in his voice, to the extent that it was hard to concentrate on his words.

We had plenty of time to talk, as we shuffled slowly through Reading. We cautiously name-checked our heroes (Simone de Beauvoir and Edith Piaf in my case, Jack Kerouac and Charlie Parker in his) and criticised our parents. He was having a rather dull time working. 'I've seen enough of small industry to know I never want to see it again,' he said emphatically, as the rain cleared, and we shared his fish-paste sandwiches.

'What would you like to be, in that case?' I asked.

'Oh, an intellectual, I suppose!' he said, with a disarming grin. 'Or failing that, perhaps a high-class debauchee.'

We exchanged addresses, and then, later on, long, increasingly intimate letters, in which we questioned our faiths (although I confessed that I seemed to get pimples whenever I stopped believing in God), and developed our views. He mentioned authors, and I raced off to read them – Salinger (we agreed that the world was full of phonies) and Camus (we began to describe ourselves as 'existentialists', although I'm not sure how much we understood by the term). We railed against the small-minded consumerism of Macmillan's Britain. Later on, when I had to care for a family myself, it made me blush to recall how we despised washing machines.

I liked the fact that Gregor was Scottish – the sexy accent, and his impatience with the South, added, in my mind, to his angry young man credentials. He liked the fact that I was half Jewish, which he saw as cosmopolitan and chic (and often bracketed in his mind with 'intellectual'), and the unlikely coupling with the fact that I was a (rapidly lapsing) Catholic, which would satisfy a lustful curiosity about 'convent girls'. When we discovered we were both going up to Oxford at the same time, it gave our attraction the kind of cosmic nudge on which long-term relationships are based.

The women's college in which I found myself was far more like school than I had expected, a stifling environment of curfews, 'cocoa parties' and intense female peer pressure. It took its 'in loco' responsibilities rather more seriously than my own mother, and as a result, it took us a long time to get round to sex – we were also hindered by a few remaining religious scruples, and our general inexperience. We stumbled around the streets of Oxford, drunken with desire, feeling out of step with the world, in our own private time-zone, sharing fish and chips and cider on park benches, and kissing passionately in back-streets and hallways.

'It feels rather childish, doesn't it, all this sneaking around?' I said, adjusting my hair in a car window.

'If only we had a place to ourselves—' he pulled me back towards himself, and his voice had a serious intent that made my stomach do back-flips of desire '—we might suddenly find ourselves feeling very grown-up indeed.'

We kissed again, and then came up for air. 'Anyway, I'm told Catholics get very good at heavy petting,' I said, with what I hoped was sophisticated insouciance.

'You lot think you invented everything,' he said, letting me free this time, with a resigned pat on the bum.

The imminence of nuclear war continued to feature. When our opportunity finally arose, in the form of a friend's rented room, empty for the afternoon, Gregor used a rather clumsy line about what we would do during the four-minute warning. I didn't need much persuading, and had wriggled out of my blouse almost before he'd finished his speech about 'Time's winged chariot hurrying near'.

We kissed again, as waves of giddiness swept over me, undermining the strength in my knees, and igniting a hot, melting sensation between my legs. Lying down beside one another on an actual bed felt novel, and incredibly grown up. 'Are you sure about this?' he asked, perhaps unnerved by his success, or just a little guilty about using the prospect of universal annihilation to get his wicked way with me.

I wasn't sure what to say, and besides, was finding it increasingly difficult to speak. His groin was pressed firmly against my thigh, as if trying to influence my answer. 'The point of no return,' I said, breathlessly, playing for time.

He laughed, and then looked down at my bosom, encased in a sturdy white brassiere, with a mixture of awe and apprehension, like a man about to scale a mountain. 'And that must be the crack of doom,' he said.

40

Afterwards, I was shocked by how little changed I seemed to be. We lay in his friend's bed, and giggled at the photographs of his parents, and listened to his 'Beyond the Fringe' record, and made ourselves a cup of tea on his single hob, and then, reassured by the absence of thunder claps and police sirens, decided to try it again.

I visited the Marie Stopes clinic to have myself fitted with a cap, and a few years later, I went on the Pill. We had many boozy discussions on the flaws in the domino theory, the labour theory of value, and the relative merits of 'sit-downs' versus direct action as a means of protest. During the Cuban Missile Crisis, we discovered that the world did not degenerate into a frenzied love-in, but just continued, with a kind of weird hyper-normality. We sat together by Gregor's grey plastic radio, sipping tea with a sick feeling in our stomachs, rather as we did before an exam.

We stayed together, despite the efforts of a pretty, posh blonde who introduced Gregor to the writings of Kropotkin on anarchism, and a job-offer that took me to Paris (which I resigned after two months, missing Gregor so badly I couldn't eat or sleep). Perhaps the fact that we were both quite distant from our families – physically and emotionally – strengthened our bond. As the years passed, and our friends fell, like dominoes themselves, to their own versions of domesticity and parenthood, Gregor argued nervously that it would be immoral to bring a child into the world just in time for the nuclear holocaust, the bloody death throes of capitalism, or some kind of (as yet fairly unspecific) environmental disaster.

The Cold War felt futuristic and frightening, almost like a grotesque exaggeration of one of the sci-fi movies of our youth. Although the nuclear threat was real, it also had the force of a parable: the white heat of technology turned against us, the forbidden fruit of the tree of knowledge. After thirteen years under a Conservative government, we were excited by Labour's victory, but quickly disillusioned with their modernising, technocratic style, their betrayal (as we saw it) of socialist principles, and their support for the Americans in a brutal and misguided war. Like many of our friends, we grew more frustrated, and radical, as the decade wore on. We marched on Grosvenor Square, chanting 'Ho, Ho, Ho Chi Minh' – I saw, in the fear and hatred on the face of a young police constable in the crowd, how easy it was to become the enemy. Watching running battles on the streets of Paris on our

41

grainy black and white television, we exchanged bewildered, exhilarated glances, wondering if this was really the beginning, really the revolution: it was thrilling to see the whole edifice of power start to wobble, but there was also a surreal sense of self-fulfilling prophecy to it, and I couldn't believe that it was quite so much like we'd expected. We'd seen the internal contradictions, the writing on the wall, and it was only a matter of time, we feared but also hoped, before the whole thing went off with the most almighty bang. In the event, however, the end of my world came much later, in 1977, and the apocalypse was of a more personal nature than I'd envisaged.

And before this, but several thousand cigarettes on from our first, Gregor cupped his hands against the wind to spark up a light, and we stood on Devil's Dyke, and the wind roared in our ears, and our cheeks ached from the cold. 'Feeling any better?' Gregor asked.

I nodded, although I wasn't, and the nausea seemed to blur with the fear inside my stomach. 'I think I'm scared,' I admitted. We could see for miles, over the patchwork of fields, and the clusters of farm buildings and brown, 1930s semis, into the misty distance. Faint chalk tracks scored the curve of the hill, like stretch marks.

'Of course. You're bound to be,' he said.

'Not so much of the birth, although I dare say I will be. Of how it will change me. Of not having any control, or any power. It's as if I'm jumping off, and you're the only one at the bottom to catch me,' I said, taking the cigarette from him, leaning back against him, inhaling the smoke.

Gregor worked his icy fingers under my layers, and, finding the warm flesh beneath my jeans, cupped my belly with his large hands, and kissed my neck. 'But did she fall, or was she pushed?' I went on. 'Is she trapped, or was she tripped?' For someone so passionate about his work, Gregor had remarkably little sense of poetry. As so often, I think he just thought I was being melodramatic.

'I'll catch you,' he muttered into my ear. 'I'll catch you both.' We turned and walked back towards the car park, with its lonely Wall's ice-cream van.

Bright sun bounced off the many square windows; cars and ambulances crawled in and out of the gates. The incinerator chimney stood, blatant against the bright blue sky. Something about it troubled me, in the corner of my eye, as it followed the curve of the Volvo in the car park – perhaps its conspicuous insistence on suppressed hospital realities, on clinical waste.

Steve carried Mum's bag ('stop fussing, will you?') and Cathy and I walked behind, like bodyguards. The automatic doors slid open and shut with a hiss, making their autocratic distinction between the worlds of the sick and the well, spewing the bandaged and the bewildered out into the roaring, dazzling daytime. In the foyer, you could buy Cornish pasties, bumper crossword books, and multi-coloured teddy bears. There was a Thorntons, next to a large advertisement for a legal firm ('Had an Accident?' it demanded, mockingly). In the last few years, public spaces had begun their mutation into shopping arcades – the whole Socks Shop thing was happening in the stations – and Mum made some comment about how comforting it was that sickness need not diminish one's relevance as a consumer.

We asked our way at the reception desk. Inside, the building made me think of a giant body, signs indicating the different organs – cardiac care, maternity wing, mental health unit – a constant flow of dazed patients, or deferential visitors, pumping through its veins. In the huge metal lift, a disembodied voice intoned the levels. The floors shone like liquid, beneath a thick, plastic skin. The harsh strip lights made it feel as if it were always about three o'clock in the morning.

We found our way to a ward high in the building, and were shown to a side alcove with four beds. There was an old lady in the bed opposite. 'Morning,' Mum said to her.

'Is it?' said the old lady, weakly.

Mum walked over to the blinds that covered the large window, and parted two of them with her fingers to look out. Then she found a blobby plastic string and raised them about halfway, to reveal rabbit-box houses and tiny trees, far below. 'It is out there,' she said.

On the wall there was a poster, outlining the ward's 'Philosophy of Care' on a hazy pastel background (Each patient to have a named nurse. Promotion of independence. A high standard of individualised care. Privacy and dignity. Relevant information and good communications while safeguarding privacy. Unconditional positive regard/respect). The white bedside cabinets were crowded with scratched plastic water jugs, 'get well' cards, and wilting flowers. It was very warm.

Mum placed her overnight bag on a vinyl-covered chair. The iron bed seemed to take up almost all of her allotted space, like a threat.

'It's a nice view, isn't it?' Mum said, scratching her forearm distractedly. In the distance, we could see the sea. 'Don't feel you have to hang around.' Cathy, who used to be a nurse, was staying with her. 'She speaks the lingo,' Mum said. 'I need her to converse with the natives.' Her brisk jokiness made me flinch – some of the nurses were black or Asian, and I was worried they might overhear and misinterpret her.

'Go on,' she said again. 'Off you go.' We hesitated. It felt like a betrayal to leave her there: like giving in to something, delivering her to a world of disease.

'I'll call you to let you know what happens,' Cathy said, more gently. It was often her role to soften my mother's corners. I remembered the number of times that she'd found me a tissue, as a child, or a sticking plaster, or a boiled sweet, in the bottom of her bag. Mum had never been a tissue-carrying type.

'See you later,' I said, and Mum waved us off.

Vera

A while after we became 'an item', Gregor took me up to Scotland to meet his parents.

We drove up in his Morris Minor convertible, the first car he had, before we got the Triumph Herald. It had been raining for days, and the car leaked in several places, so we had newspaper on the floor to absorb the puddles. On the way back, I enjoyed the privacy of the front seat, behind the misty windows, as the windscreen wipers parted the drops like a bead curtain. We both felt relieved to have got the meeting over with, and closer, because of it.

His parents had tried hard with me. His genteel, soft-spoken

44

mother, and gruff, impatient father were clearly bewildered by their son, and his peculiar new girlfriend. His mother served us cakes on paper doilies in the drawing room of their large, grey Edinburgh house, and they had done their best to welcome me. His father made small-talk about our studies, recalling the set-texts of his own youth with a frown of effort, and his mother was concerned about our diets, but careful not to enquire too closely into the exact nature of our living arrangements. Gregor sprawled over the damask furniture in his boots and donkey jacket, and slurped his tea, and tried, through his sarcasm and body language, to exhibit his contempt for their petty-bourgeois values. I'd felt a little embarrassed by his obvious disdain.

'Well, I thought they were lovely,' I said.

'Oh, aye,' he said distractedly, over the loud ticking of the indicator. 'They're nice enough, if you can see past the blimpish, neo-fascist prejudice, suburban ideals, and political apathy.' We were both intrigued by the idea of each other's families, as you are when first in love, and his curiosity was stoked by the fact that he hadn't met mine. 'I imagine we'll not be taking tea with your mama, then?' he said.

'No,' I said. 'A stiff drink might be more her style.'

'Sounds like a woman after my own heart.'

I was silent. We were overtaking a lorry, which sent great arcs of water from its wheels, splattering our windows.

'Isn't it time you told me a bit more about her?' he said.

Gregor knew quite a lot, by then, about my parents. He knew my mother was Jewish, from Austria, and had arrived in London as a refugee, where she met my father (older, English and a Catholic), during the war. Lottie and I were both born in England, but spent our early years overseas, where our father worked in various colonial administrations, first in India and then in Africa. When we were deemed old enough, we were packed off to a convent school near Bath.

After the bright colours and fierce sunshine of my early childhood, the grey skies, over-enthusiastic nuns and atmosphere of zealous piety came as something of a shock. While Lottie sought solace in food, I tried to regain my parents' attention by being good (embracing Catholicism), and then bad (taking up smoking with Sheila, hacking off my hair with scissors, reading the few vaguely subversive publications I could get my hands on). I passed all my exams, and was offered a place at Oxford. None of it had the desired effect. The summer my results came through, my father was suffering renal failure at a mission hospital in Accra, and my mother was busy meeting her second husband, an American business man.

'What would you like to know?' I said, as brightly as I could.

'Tell me about the Big Row,' Gregor said. 'Tell me why you don't speak to your mother.'

'She's in another country, for a start.'

'Oh I know, but it's not as if you even write. And there's that sour-puss, prissy-miss face you pull, every time I talk about her.'

I blinked back tears. Gregor was lighting a cigarette, one hand on the wheel. I really wanted to tell him the truth. He'd be sure to have some theory about it – bourgeois decadence, or the corrupt, hypocritical moral standards of the ruling classes. I could even imagine him laughing about it. Part of me longed to hear him reduce it to this, distancing my past and removing the sting. At the front of that flimsy little car together, side-by-side, watching the road, we had our own special window on to the world, protected from the rain.

I really wanted to, but I found that I couldn't. The windscreen wipers followed each other back and forth insistently, like an argument that is just tilting over into physical violence, and each time I thought now, now, now, but I didn't know where to start. The years of silence had become something stronger than mere habit in me: they had hardened to concrete in my bones. A Catholic education is not easily overthrown, and guilt and secrecy had become second nature. I suppose a part of me was scared that he might stop loving me if he knew.

'So ...?' Gregor prompted gently. 'What kind of schism are we talking about, exactly? Sworn enemies, or just, I don't know, different taste in shoes? Or do you deny there's even a rift?' He smoked as he drove, taking drags between gear changes.

'You're right,' I said, since that was something Gregor always liked to hear, 'I suppose we aren't particularly close.'

That was clearly the moment, but I didn't tell him. At the age of fourteen – the age, in any case, at which most of us start to notice the bad in the world, and to react with a child's uncompromised indignation – my mother had confided in me, and had shaken my faith in human nature. I clearly wasn't strong enough to hear him joke about it, after all.

'She's a strange woman,' I said, instead. 'Hard and secretive. You can't tell what she's thinking. I've always worried that I might be like that with my own children.'

'My poor honey. You're warning me that you might eat your own young?'

'Something like that.'

There was a pause, which alarmed me a little, despite his obvious amusement, but he was just chewing over his reply. 'I'm a great believer, as you know, in the sanctity of the sexual act for the purposes of procreation. But if you insist, baby, we can just have gratuitous sex. Let's waste my seed wantonly.'

I looked out of the window, at the outskirts of Carlisle. 'How romantic.'

He laughed. 'No kiddies, then,' he said. He sounded rather pleased. 'You unnatural woman. Oh well. We can always get a cat.'

Chapter Three

Susie

Back at the house, a lot of people came and went. I hadn't realised that my mother having cancer would be so much like holding a party. My aunt Lottie arrived, and sat in the kitchen sipping herbal tea. 'She's never really taken proper care of herself, has she?' she said. 'These high-octane people. I did try to tell her.' A neighbour dropped in to say how dreadful, she couldn't believe it, and to ask if we needed anything from the supermarket. Gus emerged from his bedroom, and padded round the house in a Nirvana T-shirt and boxer shorts, his hair standing on end. I offered people drinks, and sat by the telephone, waiting for Cathy to call.

I felt as if the past kept welling up around me. It was in the objects and the furnishings, barely visible, they were so familiar – the green plastic telephone, with its old-fashioned round dial, the wicker fruit bowl, the hall mirror. It was in the smell of the rooms, the slant of the light through the curtains, the books and papers piled everywhere, the dust on the ledges, or the creak of the boards. Away from home, I carried my own stuff carefully with me, and unpacked posters and books and clothes, as ballast in the whirling chaos of London. Here, though, the accumulation of debris, over the years, felt stifling: it scared and unbalanced me. It seemed to threaten my adult sense of self, making it feel fragile and recently constructed. I could close my eyes, or take a small step back, and it was all still there, more real than the present, a fundamental reality, a basis time, in which the truths about the world were established.

She was still sedated, as I stood at the foot of her bed. Her face was completely relaxed, and her look of abandon made me feel protective, and strangely maternal towards her myself.

She opened her eyes, and lifted her heavy arm, and blew us a kiss with her forefinger. She beckoned us closer. 'What happened?' she whispered to me. She was bitterly disappointed, and frustrated, that the procedure – to ease her jaundice – hadn't been a success.

'Hello, you,' she said to Lottie.

Lottie's chin started to wobble. 'Hello, you.'

'Come here and kiss me,' she said, and we filed by obediently, and kissed her one by one. 'I'm so lucky,' she said, sleepily, like a docile child, and it was a strange thing to say, under the circumstances, but I knew that she meant lucky to have us.

Mum talked to Aunt Lottie for a while. Lottie's latest enthusiasm was for alternative medicine. She'd brought her sister a 'healing stone', and a little bottle of Arnica, 'for stress', which she clutched like a talisman.

'You have to be careful not to touch them before you swallow them,' she said, clearing a space for them on the bedside cabinet. She was two years older than Mum, but she suddenly looked like the younger of the two. They had always been different, physically – Lottie had always been more like my grandmother, with olive skin and dark brown eyes, while my mother had been blue-eyed and paler. The fact that Mum was suddenly so shrunken, in her hospital gown, added to the contrast between them, so that Lottie seemed vast beside her, her flowered Monsoon dress stretched over her bosom, her upper-arms like sides of meat. It was uncomfortably warm on the ward, as usual. Lottie shifted in the vinyl-covered chair, which made a squeaking, farting noise.

'How do you get them into your mouth, then?' Gus asked. He was standing, a dark shape, by the window. The floor was so highly polished that he cast a reflection.

'Sounds like witchcraft to me,' Mum muttered, from her pillow.

'Have you spoken to Mummy?' Lottie asked, choosing not to respond. It always seemed bizarre to me that they still referred to my grandmother in this childlike way.

'Not yet,' Mum said, and then, 'I know, don't worry, I will.'

She was very tired. After a while, the others went to the cafeteria, and I sat with Mum, while she dozed. I watched the other people on the ward – the old lady opposite in a knitted bed-jacket,

49

doing a bumper crossword, an orderly wiping a sink clean.

Watching Mum's sleeping face, I remembered the last time I'd seen her, before she was diagnosed, in London. She'd been so different: large, vital, and irritating. I hadn't enjoyed her visit. Her voice had seemed unnaturally loud, and jarringly middle-class, on the bus – 'you are lucky, darling, to be living somewhere so wonderfully multi-cultural'. A couple of kids were riding a moped through the estate where we got off, whooping as they went. I stepped aside and ignored them, so used to avoiding trouble that it had become second nature. 'Do you think they're high?' my mother asked.

'God, Mum, I don't know,' I'd said, in exasperation.

At my house, Mum had been a big hit. She bought us all an Indian takeaway – from a grotty-looking place that I'd been avoid-ing, for fear of food poisoning – and plenty of beer, from the corner shop, where she made friends with the proprietor. She'd quizzed Toby on his world music, and asked Zoe all about working in the media, and filled the living room with clouds of smoke, and even Christina didn't have the nerve to object. 'These tight little tops you wear these days look rather good on you,' she said to me, as I was rationalising the remains of the meal into a couple of foil dishes, to go into the fridge, 'I must say, they show off your little titties beautifully.'

'Mum!' I groaned, looking down, becoming awkward and self-conscious as a teenager.

On our way back to the station, she'd asked intrusive questions of the Nigerian minicab driver ('which tribe are you from? Ah yes, the Igbo have a reputation for being rather intelligent'), drooling over his tales of persecution and discrimination, although he seemed quite happy to find a sympathetic ear, unaware of the patronising, stereotyping nuances which so embarrassed me.

I'd been relieved when she'd gone. 'Your Mum's great,' Zoe had said.

'Yes,' I'd said, wearily, 'I know.'

A consultant arrived, on his rounds. Mum opened her eyes, demanded her glasses, and raised herself weakly to a sitting posi-tion. 'The really important ones are called Mister instead of Doctor,' she hissed, in a stage whisper, perhaps to make me take notice, but also intended to show the rest of the ward she wasn't intimidated. He drew the threadbare curtains round the bed, and spoke to us both.

50

'It's not looking good, is it?' said Mum, first of all – a pre-emptive strike. I could tell from her voice that she needed the consultant to take her seriously – to realise that she was educated, and intelligent.

'No, it's not,' the consultant agreed. He wore a name badge that announced him as Mr Thompson. He had glasses and a big chin, and he spoke formally and slowly, seeming to choose his words carefully. Under the circumstances, he said, although they had limited information from the scans, he was inclined to recommend an operation. Mum asked about what that would mean. Mr Thompson said that it would take some time to recover, and that she would have to take enzyme capsules afterwards.

There was a pause. It almost seemed as if the conversation might be over. Afterwards, it made me angry that we'd had to work so hard to draw the crucial information out of him – he didn't make it easy to get to the heart of the thing. I felt that there was so much I wanted to know, but I wasn't sure how to ask, and was scared to formulate the questions. Perhaps he was waiting to see how much we really wanted to be told. Perhaps, if Mum had overdone her display of being well informed, he was assuming that we already knew.

'Can I ask something?' I said. They both nodded, of course. 'When they talk about whether it's malignant or benign, I mean, what are the implications of that?'

'It's very likely indeed to be malignant. Almost certain,' he said.

'And what does that mean?'

He said that he would recommend a course of chemotherapy and radiotherapy after the operation. I watched the various defences on my mother's face – the mask of receptive interest she used for car mechanics and parents' evenings – start to fall away, leaving a look of bewildered hurt beneath. It was like a new language. He said that at some point, decisions about quantity versus quality of life would have to be made. He started, for some reason, talking about time. 'Time scales can vary tremendously. It depends on the extent, and on other factors which will be revealed by a histological investigation. I have to say that what we've seen on the scan indicates that things are relatively advanced.'

Suddenly, with an awful clarity, we knew what he was talking about. He talked about percentage survival rates after two years. 'After five years, survival rates are very low indeed,' he said.

51

'How low?' Mum asked, fiercely.

'Almost non existent,' he said.

'So you're saying that I'm dying?'

The consultant looked at his notes, and hesitated. 'Arguably, we're all dying.'

'You know what I mean. Are you saying this will kill me?'

'Well, yes, if you choose to put it like that, I'm afraid I am. Except in the unlikely event that something else gets there first.' He hesitated, seeming to sense that something else was required. 'I'm sorry,' he concluded.

There it was. I had the confused impression that I had somehow known it, without knowing it, all the time. Perhaps it was something to do with shock, a sort of sub-conscious petulance, my mind defensive with surprise on gulping down a large lump of information all in one go. Suddenly it made sense, just from the things that hadn't been said, the consolations that hadn't been offered.

Mum's face was unbearable, like a caricature of grief. With her overfilled eyes and her down-turned mouth, she looked like a small child who's had a terrible disappointment, or one of those Greek masks signifying tragedy.

The consultant left. 'Well, that's that, then,' Mum said. I hugged her. I had always imagined that at a moment like that, one would lose all self-consciousness, but the small details of life – the uncomfortable metal bed-frame, on which I was balanced, the sound of dinner being served, from behind the curtain, the question of how to be from one moment to the next – were, I was surprised to find, still an issue. After a few seconds, Mum extricated herself from the hug. 'I'm glad Gus wasn't here to hear that,' she said.

We sat in silence. There was nothing I could think of to say. I found myself utterly unable to absorb the news properly – it was as if I had to fall back on my acting skills in an attempt to convey an appropriate response. 'Well, I suppose it's an enforced holiday, at least,' Mum said, after a bit.

Steve was the first to join us. I was afraid when I saw him. I must have been afraid for him – afraid of what I knew and he didn't – but it felt as if I were afraid of him, and of how he would react. Men are different in such situations, less bound, I suppose, by social constraints, and less predictable. 'Could you leave us alone for a bit?' Mum asked me.

52

'What is it?' Steve demanded. 'Tell me, Susie, tell me!'

He sounded angry, and his face had a dreadful suspicious look, as if he were beginning to doubt reality. I felt torn. I wanted to respect Mum's request, but empathised with his position – it could so easily have been me who'd been outside at the time – and felt it would be a kind of torture to leave him hanging, especially after such a direct appeal. I hesitated, and Mum intervened. 'It isn't good, sweetheart. He said that an operation might give me a bit longer, but they think . . . .they think it's going to get me in the end.'

'Who said that?'

'The consultant.'

'That's crazy. Jesus. They can't write you off, that's not their job. Your chances go up, if it doesn't come back. That's what they always say.'

'Maybe we got it wrong,' I said, hopefully.

'No,' Mum said. 'We didn't.'

Steve sat down. I had been scared he might make a scene – start yelling, or smashing things up – but now I almost wanted him to. He looked crumpled, as if someone were slowly letting the air out of his large frame.

The others arrived back from the cafeteria. 'What's happened?' Gus said, immediately.

'The consultant came by,' I said. There was a dreadful pause. Telling people was actually worse than hearing it yourself.

Mum got into some clothes, and we walked along the shining corridors, down in the large metal lift, through the automatic doors, and outside. She still felt weak, and leaned on Steve's arm. We passed other people walking through the hospital: families with new babies, people in wheelchairs or with limbs in casts, and I wondered about their dramas and tragedies. The evening was beautiful – the sky so blue, the sun so golden, even the cars basking in the forecourt looked luminous, gleaming beneath a thin film of dust. The astonishing weather gave everything a sense of unreality. I felt as if we were in another country; one in which nothing was familiar.

We found a wooden bench not far from the main entrance, next to a small patch of grass and a raised flower bed filled with wood chip. Mum lit up a cigarette, and blew out the smoke with a long sigh. 'What a week,' she said.

'Couldn't we just leave, get on a plane somewhere?' Steve said. He buried his head in his hands. There were cigarette ends all over the tarmac, around his feet.

Helene

The ship was a P&O Liner called the *Orion*, which had been converted into a troopship. German U-boats were still active in the Atlantic, so we had to travel in convoy as far as Gibraltar.

As if I hadn't been miserable enough already, at the start of the voyage, I was dreadfully seasick. On the first morning, I awoke to the vast grey sea, slopping beneath a small round window. The stateroom I was in had been built for four, and there were ten of us crammed in there, so there were overflowing suitcases, and stockings draped everywhere, and every surface was cluttered with the feminine debris of hairbrushes and compacts, and it was difficult to move. We were travelling 'Officer Class' because we were officers' wives. I felt queasy, so I dressed quickly, and escaped the close, chatty atmosphere, in the hope I'd feel better outside.

The rest of the ship was just as crowded. I made my wobbly way to breakfast, stepping over bodies and being waved gallantly through doors. There were so many men in uniform: standing, smoking, sprawled in deckchairs, embarking on epic card tournaments which would last the whole voyage, all over the grand Art Deco chrome and bakelite interiors of the ship, the galleries and the lounges, the elegant curved stairway, the polished wooden floors. The sight of a woman was clearly of great interest. I was overwhelmed by this vast, unsteady city, in which all the usual fixed points – walls, floors, furniture – were susceptible to sudden swings and lurches, and I was finding it harder and harder to control my nausea. I just wanted to sink into a chair and put my head down, but was having enough difficulty fending off enthusiastic offers of help and concern, and was afraid of being submerged by chivalry if I did.

At last, I found my way to the first-class dining-room, where breakfast was just being served. Murmuring a vague apology, I found myself a seat, amid the crisp table linen and atmosphere of suppressed, hungry enthusiasm. Stewards moved between the tables with steaming coffee pots. There was a sign on the wall that

54

said 'Fear God, Honour the King'.

A large, silver tureen was placed in front of me and the lid removed. 'Mmm, kedgeree!' came an approving snort from beside me (a young fellow who seemed already to have embraced the mannerisms of the middle-aged was tucking a napkin into his collar). A great wave of fish-loaded steam hit me, and the floor lurched again, making the cutlery rattle, and another wave of nausea broke over my head. I knew I was going to be sick, and stumbled from the table with a napkin clutched to my mouth, just making it through the door before vomiting violently onto the floor in the corridor outside. A kindly steward helped me quickly away, and organised someone else to clean up, but I imagined the disgust of the whole room, burning into my bent head and heaving shoulders.

On deck, I held the rail, and watched the waves, far below. My cheeks burned, and my eyes were watery with humiliation and self-pity: the wind blew into my face, carrying the smell of oil and the call of the gulls.

I could feel someone hovering behind me. I wanted to be alone, but had the growing suspicion that on this ship, solitude would be an impossible luxury. His indecision was obvious, and irritating – I tried to look as absorbed and unwelcoming as I could. Undeterred, he edged closer, another shift of the vessel removing the attempted nonchalance from his move.

'I say, are you all right?' he asked.

'Yes,' I said.

He held out a handkerchief. 'Only ...'

I waved it away. 'Please don't,' I said. I couldn't help myself.

'Don't what?'

'I'm sorry,' I said, aware of my rudeness. 'Don't tell me your remedy for seasickness. I promise you I've heard it already.'

He laughed, awkwardly. 'I wouldn't dream of it. I know exactly what you mean. You see, I suffer from insomnia. It's dreadfully boring. I try not to tell people any more. Warm milk, hot baths, and the funny thing is that they all think it'll come as a complete surprise.'

'If it were that simple, we'd be real idiots to put up with it, wouldn't we?' I said.

'Too right.'

He wore RAF uniform. His skin, I noticed, was very pale,

55

almost translucent, and – as you might expect – he had dark smudges under his pale blue eyes. His hair was short, and dark, and oiled flat. 'I tell you what,' he went on, 'you try counting sheep, and I'll have the little tot of rum. Might make a nice change.'

In spite of myself I smiled, and realised it felt peculiar to do so. 'Anyway, by the Bay of Biscay, we'll all be green about the gills,' he said.

'Ah. Something to look forward to, then,' I said. I noticed his white hands, grasping the rail.

'I hope you feel better, anyway,' he said.

I spent most of the day in my bunk, and by the evening, I did, a little. A glass of wine over dinner helped, and suddenly he was there again, at my elbow, offering me a cigarette. I didn't smoke much as a rule, but I had the feeling that on this voyage I probably would.

'You again?' I said.

'Me again.' We smiled, like old friends.

'Tell me, what do you do with all the extra hours?' I asked, as he lit my cigarette, and then his own.

He looked confused.

'When you can't sleep. You said you were an insomniac. I've always been a bit jealous. You must have so much more time than the rest of us for saving the world, or at very least leading a double life.' I was feeling rather light-headed.

He looked embarrassed, and I wondered if that was the faintest hint of colour I could see on his porcelain-pale cheekbone? I regretted asking, and wanted to tell him it didn't matter, I hadn't been serious. 'Oh, I do less than you'd think,' he said, coyly. 'It can be quite useful, sometimes, when I'm flying. And the rest of the time, well, the truth is, I have a rather time-consuming hobby.'

'Really?'

'Flight Lieutenant Robert Miller by the way,' he said, reaching over. I swapped my cigarette into my left hand and we shook, solemnly. 'My friends call me Bobby.'

'Helene Perkins.' The surname still sounded odd.

'Helene,' he repeated carefully, rolling the word around his mouth like someone tasting wine. Charles had always called me 'Helena', with a resolutely English pronunciation, just like the teachers at my English school. 'I write verse. Absolute tosh,

56

mostly, but it fills the hours.'

'So you're going to be the great poet of this war?'

'Does it mean I have to get killed?'

'Of course not,' I said, quickly. ('Not even in joke', my mother would have said). 'In fact, I expect it would help considerably if you don't.'

'Then maybe,' he said, smiling. 'If I can find my muse.'

We smoked our cigarettes, and he suggested a walk out on deck. On the stairway, we passed one of his friends, and I could see from his smirk that assumptions were being made. Outside, it was a cold night, and we could hear faint music coming from below, over the steady chug of the engine.

'I suppose you can't say where you're going?' I said.

'Burma, I imagine. "Get me knees brown," as the men say.' He laughed. It was hard to imagine him with brown knees.

Something unspoken hung between us. 'I see you're married,' he said, after a moment, looking down at my ring.

'Yes.' I looked down too, at the black, churning sea. In its wake, the ship ploughed a great wide furrow in the dark water, fringed with white foam.

'Happily?'

I was startled by his cheek. The truthful answer was that I didn't yet know, but I certainly couldn't tell him that. 'Very,' I said.

'Jolly good. And I suppose you're joining your husband?'

'He was sent out by the army, but he's been seconded to the Indian Civil Service. He's a Magistrate, apparently.' I imagined Charles sitting under a tree, dispensing justice, like Solomon.

'Lucky chap.'

I thought he was referring to the cushy posting. Knowing of Charles's important uncle, I assumed that a string or two had been pulled on his behalf. 'He's quite well connected, I suppose,' I said, by way of explanation.

'That's not what I meant,' Bobby said, meaningfully.

After that, the days resolved into a sort of lazy, dream-like rhythm, centred largely around meals. There was an effortless sense of achievement to be had simply from covering the miles. Surrounded by a new set of people, in a completely new environment, I felt like a different person myself, untethered by past or future.

The first shock was how little, after all, I seemed marked by

57

motherhood. After so long in which I'd felt subsumed by it – in which I'd reluctantly accepted that things would never be the same again – I felt it should be written on my face, somehow, as it had been on my body. Yet here I was: slim, light, and flat-chested, drinking and smoking, the old curiosities and appetites, which I'd thought dead forever, tingling to the surface as I shed my skin. Suddenly it was as if I'd never had a child.

I didn't admit it to myself, but increasingly, I searched the crowd for Bobby, and I found myself secretly disappointed during the odd mealtime in which he didn't appear. We talked for hours, wandering the ship, watching the endlessly changing waves: I told him different versions of my life, he told me different versions of his. He read me Yeats, and gave me meaningful looks, which I tried to laugh off, or pretend I hadn't noticed, but which nonetheless made my stomach turn somersaults. The other women in my cabin started to refer to him as my 'admirer', and I had to struggle to suppress an unseemly grin.

The Mediterranean had already been cleared, so after Gibraltar, progress was a lot faster. Bobby grew bolder, and confessed he'd written me a poem, which he then consented to recite. 'Under this troubled sky/ your heavy eyes/ drawing me with promises then withdrawn/ dragged by currents to our uncertain destinations . . .' I was flattered – although his flat delivery made me want to giggle. I'd never been written a poem, and he gave me a copy to keep. There was a straightforward confidence to his unspoken demand: I want you, therefore you should be mine. He made it seem almost a patriotic duty to flirt with him. It was childlike, and irrational, and uniquely male, but for all those reasons, it was also curiously powerful.

The ship became our world, and waiting a way of life, and it seemed it would go on forever. We females mixed only with the officers, and I don't think I even spoke to an Other Rank, although at night we could hear the sounds of singing from below, and each morning, the sound of the men doing their physical training on deck. At Port Said, vendors came alongside to try and sell us things, which could be winched up in a basket, and boys on the quayside tried to attract our attention and dived for pennies. It grew hotter, and people changed into tropical dress, the men wearing a different, lighter uniform.

We drifted slowly through the Suez Canal, and everyone else

took refuge from the stark, blazing sun below decks, where nerves got frayed and there was a good deal of bickering. Bobby and I stayed out, finding what shade we could beneath the lifeboats, and enjoying the eerie quiet, as we floated past the large, brown banks of Egypt, so close they seemed within touching distance. The heat made us dizzy and drained, and we spoke in short, truncated phrases.

'We should go in,' I said.

'The thing is, we don't want to.' He was turned a little away from me, towards the sea, so that all I could see was his thin white wrist, dangling listlessly from the arm of his deckchair. 'We don't want to do what we should.'

I couldn't answer. I knew something was coming.

'Helene?' he said. 'Do you *know*?'

'Let's not,' I said, but stayed put, powerless to move.

We made a last stop for supplies at Aden, after dark, where coolies carried provisions in buckets on their heads, up planks from the shore. Then we were launched once more into the dazzling blue, with no land in sight for days on end.

I had a little portable typewriter, and wrote letters to my mother, which I hoped I would be able to post when we reached land. The females on board were still the subject of a good deal of attention – once there was a competition to find the woman with the best legs. I didn't go in for it, but a chap came round anyway, and scrutinised my legs as I typed a letter on deck.

Light music was played over the loudspeaker system, and the ship's radio officer announced important news as he received it. The Allies were advancing in Europe. Amsterdam was liberated; the Americans were in Austria; then came the report that Hitler was dead. Can you imagine how we felt on hearing this? The war in Europe was drawing to a close, and here we were amid the sharks and flying fish.

A stirring of activity on board, and an imperceptible change in the air – a smell, perhaps, or a change in the light – suggested land. I felt a sudden and quite disproportionate pang at the thought of leaving Bobby – after all, I barely even knew him – but the intensity of that time together, and the momentous international events taking place, made it feel as if he'd always been there, a reassuringly attentive presence at my side. Almost without realising it, and certainly without admitting it, I had grown to depend

59

on his friendship, and the strong, silent tug of his attraction towards me, which cheered and fortified me on a daily basis.

'Perhaps you'll come and visit us?' I said, a note of desperation in my bravado. 'Surely you'll have some leave?'

He smiled, acknowledging that we both knew that this was missing the point. 'Anything might happen. I might arrive on an elephant and bring you the Kohinoor diamond. We've still got the Japs to see to – I might get killed. We just don't know.'

'Don't be ridiculous.' I felt his melodrama was a little manipulative.

'Sorry,' he said. 'I know, I'm a silly ass. Only it strikes me sometimes that perhaps we have to make our own happiness in this life. Not just drift along in darkness.'

'Like ships that pass in the night?' I said, regretting my reflex irony as soon as it left my mouth.

'Exactly.'

I hesitated. 'So what are you saying?'

He sighed, and paused, and seemed to consider, and then reject, a number of possible replies. Then he took my hand. We had barely touched, except by accident, on the whole voyage, and I felt my heart beating harder, in the base of my throat. 'Sweet Helene, the face that launched a thousand ships that pass in the night. Only that I wish you all the luck, and love, and happiness in the world,' he said, and kissed my fingers.

That afternoon there was an announcement that the ship's radio officer had received a message for me. Charles could not get away from his work to meet me, and I was to make the rest of the journey by rail. The following morning, we sailed into port. It was VE day.

Vera

Different shades of sickness coloured the whole of my life. I became familiar with toilet bowls all over town. Sometimes, I was sick in the street, retching into the gutter like a dog, at bus stops or in the park. Losing control in public was humiliating. People turned away, with disapproval or revulsion – I imagined they thought I was drunk. Old ladies would put a hesitant hand on my arm, 'are you all right, dear?' My insides were like the changing sea, which was also suddenly a backdrop to our world – thick and grey, some mornings, sloshing and tilting, wild and inky in the evenings, churning and dragging, with brief moments of deceptive calm.

I felt as if I'd been poisoned – as if I were allergic to the foreign body that had taken up residence inside me. I had dreams in which I was forced to eat paper clips and treasury tags, or in which I was shovelling in mouthfuls of rotten food. I developed an intense, uncanny sense of smell, and thought I could identify all the ingredients in any dish, and the type of oil it had been cooked in – walking past restaurants or pubs, great waves of fish, cabbage or beer-loaded air would ambush me on the pavement, and I could smell what had been on each plate, as I did the washing up. One morning, I went downstairs and threw out the entire contents of the curvaceous, cream-coloured refrigerator, convinced that it had all gone off.

At first I lost weight. I worried for the baby, and kept trying to eat – dry toast and sips of milk or Bovril – hoping I'd find something I could keep down. This developed into the vague sense that there was something out there that would make me feel better, and an increasingly urgent need to find it. Between bouts of vomiting, I would stuff food into my mouth desperately, refilling my strained, fragile stomach. And bizarrely, when food was good, it was amazing, better than sex – certain tastes made every cell in my body scream with hysterical approval, like a crowd of teenaged girls at a concert. Suddenly, after years of moaning about English cooking, and priding myself on my sophisticated palate, I found that bland foods were best. I visited the baker's across the road from the school several times a day for iced buns, custard tarts, or white rolls filled with sweaty cheese and wilting, pale-green lettuce, and then the chip shop near the house – where the Chinese is now – for a saveloy snack before supper. Whole packets of bourbon creams or Ritz crackers disappeared, and my coat pockets were always bulging with empty paper bags and food wrappers. It was like having an eating disorder. A weird mixture of gluttony and nausea seemed to have overtaken my whole being.

My stomach began to swell. Increasingly, I had to leave the top button of my jeans undone. It felt different to flesh – harder, full of fluid, and I didn't like pressure on it. Luckily the mini-dresses I was wearing that year were fairly accommodating, but I thought

61

they'd look ridiculous with a proper bump, as would the very long skirts that were also around: the fashion was for pale, ethereal sylphs, and clearly not dreamed up with reproduction in mind. I remembered the women I'd seen as a girl, in Africa – the servants' wives and stallholders who'd seemed to always have a new baby on their backs – and realised, for the first time, why they wore wraparound skirts, or dresses that fell from the shoulder.

Gradually, I began telling people about the baby. I practised on less important people first – the secretary at my school, a couple of kindly colleagues, sworn to secrecy. The first time, I felt as if I might be lying, but every time I spoke the fact, it seemed to become a tiny bit truer. People with children themselves were the most loudly enthusiastic, as if welcoming me to some enormous but clandestine club, with rules I did not as yet quite understand. Their excitement made me a little nervous, because I suspected there was a tinge of *schadenfreude* to it – great, finally you'll be under all the same constraints as us, sustained through the tiredness and hard slog by all the same irrational instincts, finally you'll understand. People without children seemed to be waving me off from the shore – depending on their own circumstances, with sadness, curiosity or there-but-for-the-grace-of-God relief.

Occasionally, I stumbled onto some terrible secret sadness, and could feel my confidence causing pain as well as pleasure – I felt the worse for it, given the swirling mess of emotion I had felt about the subject myself. Mostly, though, I was just stunned, and humbled by the goodwill that radiated from the most surprising sources. My head teacher, whom I'd expected to be irritated by the news at the least, embraced me warmly and sent straight out for tea and digestive biscuits. Usually, 'we've got some news' did the trick; sometimes I'd hear myself say 'we're expecting a baby', and think about how odd it sounded – as if we were awaiting a parcel, which might contain something else entirely. It was as if the pregnancy, which I had thought of as a rather embarrassing private indulgence, meant something altogether different to the rest of the world.

'Good for you,' said Lottie, my sister, by then a straight-laced vet's wife, living in Yorkshire. 'You should tell Mummy, you know.'

My mother was living in California with her second husband, a wealthy businessman. Although we didn't speak to each other any more, she was still in my head: at any significant point in my life, the whole thing had a tendency to come back at me. Whatever else, she had carried me, as I was carrying you, and the experience made me feel closer to her.

I could hear her talking to the operator, before we were connected. 'Hello Mummy,' I said. 'It's me, Vera.'

She had been expecting my sister, and there was a strange silence as she absorbed this fact, while the whole of the Atlantic seemed to roar in the background. 'Vera!' she said, at last, and I could hear surprise, eagerness, and nervousness in her voice.

'I've got some news.'

'Oh God,' she said, 'what's happened?'

'Good news,' I said, 'I hope. I'm pregnant.'

'Preggers?' she breathed down the echoey telephone line, reverting to pre-war slang in her excitement. 'Oh, dahling! How wonderful!'

I could tell there were lots more things she wanted to ask, and to say, but I didn't want to lose the initiative. 'Yes, well,' I said briskly, as she drew breath, 'I just wanted you to know.' I replaced the receiver quickly. My heart was thumping. I sat alone in our house, the black plastic telephone suddenly silent, with its expressionless round dial.

Gregor was taken aback when I told him. 'I thought we agreed not to tell anyone,' he said.

'Just for a bit. We can hardly keep it quiet forever.'

'No, I suppose not,' he said, but he didn't sound happy.

Mostly, the never-ending queasiness, and my apparently limitless capacity for sleep, depressed me. I spent almost all my spare time in bed, just to get through the days at work. For the brief moments when I was all right, I felt as if I'd been let out of prison. I could feel my life shrinking, to the invalid's limited world of crumpled sheets and eiderdown, bedside table and permanently half-drawn curtains.

Gregor was not a natural nurse. He began to spend more time at the university, and had given up trying to touch me. He woke, most mornings, to the sound of vomiting, in the toilet down the hall.

'I had no idea it would be this bad,' I said, one Sunday, climbing back into bed, taking a sip of water from the glass beside me. 'I don't think I can stand much more.'

63

'What can I do?' he asked wearily, reaching out an arm for his cigarettes.

'Nothing. I'm just telling you.'

'I know. You've told me already,' he drew deeply on the cigarette, and then coughed. 'Several times.'

I started to cry, quietly, and he softened his tone, propping himself up on one elbow. 'I'm just a bit bored with it, sweetheart. It's all we ever talk about, already, and we've got six months of this to go.' He was naked in bed, and his slender, curly-haired torso was beautiful, although I couldn't stand the musty, sweaty smell of the sleep-filled room. 'There's nothing I can say. I do want to be, you know, sympathetic, and enlightened about this, but the whole situation makes me the villain, whatever I do. It's not fair.'

'Oh boo hoo, well, *tant pis*. You think I'm not bored with it?' my voice wobbled. 'You think I'm not sick to death – quite literally, actually – of being like this?'

This time, Gregor didn't bother with the soothing tone. 'I'm going to do some work,' he said, scratching his chin, and then reaching for his dressing gown with a shiver. 'Go back to sleep.'

I turned onto my side, and drew the paisley eiderdown over my shoulders, and closed my eyes in an attempt to quell another wave of nausea. I felt very sorry for myself. Gregor and I had been pretty equal in our relationship, passing back and forth the paperbacks, forming our views of the world together, over a succession of kitchen tables – in fact, I reminded myself, I had been the one who kept the money coming in. We had put our faith in communication and imagination – as a linguist and a historian, we were confident these could overcome any barrier of culture or time. Yet here was an experience, and hardly an unusual one, that divided us instantly, irrevocably, with the finality of biology. When I tried to convey my feelings about it, or to get a little distance from my bewildering new status, the words seemed to shrivel as they left my mouth, their meaning revolting against me, mutating into whinging complaint or banality. My God, I thought, why did I believe we would be different? Suddenly, like it or not, I was the weaker sex.

It was getting colder, and wilder, outside. The noise of the wind in the pipes sounded to me like a baby crying.

I spoke to Toby on the telephone. He offered to come down ('I'm there for you,' he said, again), but he had so much reading to do to stay on top of his law course, and to be honest, I wanted to be alone with my family. Although I didn't articulate this to him, or even to myself, I wasn't sure he had the sensitivity to handle the situation.

Toby was my first real boyfriend. We'd met at university, in 1989. The first time I saw him, he was busking in front of Boots, on a bleak, windswept Saturday afternoon. He wore a long, dark-green Army Surplus greatcoat, which looked like something out of the First World War. He had angelic, curly-blonde, shoulder length hair.

He only knew three chords, at the time, and was singing one of his own compositions, most of which were faux-naive little ballads about the issues of the day ('Tiananmen Square, Act like it's not there, Keep on doing your hair, Yeah'). There was an up-turned beret on the pavement in front of him. So far he'd accumulated 9p, a piece of Wrigley's Juicy Fruit, and a lot of good-natured abuse from the passers-by – who considered 'student' an insult to start with, and embellished this with a range of choice adjectives. (People are dying, While your burgers are frying, Their mothers are crying, You just don't fucking care . . .') I scuttled along, head down, in my DMs and my long floaty skirt, avoiding everyone's eyes. Normally, I wore the kind of expression which made strangers tell me to 'cheer up, it might never happen'. There was something about his ludicrous defiance of both the weather and his audience, however, as well as the lyrics, which made me smile to myself.

I was very self-conscious, and desperately homesick. The students I'd met so far, of both sexes, were keen on drinking games, and on wearing stockings and suspenders and satin ball-gowns at the slightest pretext. I'd bonded a bit with Zoe, who'd come to the UK expecting Morrisey and John Lennon and police-men in silly hats, and got instead a bunch of wannabe Yanks setting off fire extinguishers at three in the morning. Mostly, though, I was miserable, and to make matters worse, I was deep into my first essay crisis. I thought I recognised a kindred spirit in Toby, and put 10p in his hat, thereby doubling his takings. ('The tanks they are rolling, Down the high street you're strolling ...')

He broke off, and smiled at me. 'Thanks!' he said, with a heart-felt gratitude that took me aback. 'Aren't you a friend of Zoe's?'

We spent his earnings on two cups of coffee – McDonald's was out of the question, he explained, but there was a teashop round the corner. Normally I would have been too shy to accept, but I thought of the essay question waiting on my desk, and had spoken to no one all day. He talked such a lot, and had such strong opinions, that I found my awkwardness evaporating. He had a kind of puppy-dog excitability, which made a satisfying counterpoint to my own studied efforts at cynicism, whilst infecting me with some much-needed enthusiasm, in spite of myself.

It surprised and intrigued me to learn that Toby – despite his carefully toned-down accent, and his clothes from Oxfam – had been to a very posh public school in Cheltenham, and that his father was a High Court Judge. In the sixth form, he had joined Young Socialist Worker and grown his hair, and although he'd got fed up with selling papers and defected pretty swiftly, he'd retained something of the zeal of a recent convert. One thing led to another, and we quickly became an item. He couldn't believe that I'd been born into the left-wing orthodoxy he worked so hard at emulating. I think this confused him – he was never sure if it was unbelievably cool or just cheating. It certainly confused me, since I'd always regarded my ageing hippie parents as tragic and embarrassing, and was startled by his eagerness to borrow old copies of the *New Left Review*, or yellowing tomes on Trotsky, from Dad.

In our second and third years, Zoe and I shared a flat over a bookie's, living on takeaway curry and breakfast cereal, and Toby and I spent a lot of time in each other's beds. We went down to London on demos ('Whadda we want? Grants not loans! When do we want them? Now!'). At parties, we sat on the floor, and someone would turn the music off, and Toby played his guitar, his blonde hair falling over his face, and people clapped and laughed in the right places, and I felt proud to be his girlfriend.

The world around us was changing with bewildering speed. On TV, we watched our contemporaries clambering the Berlin wall, swaying with candles in town squares, and running between bullet-pocked buildings. The day after Nelson Mandela was released from prison, Toby wore his 'Free Nelson Mandela' badge, just so that when people pointed out that it was a bit out of date, with an elated grin, he could fix them with his earnest eyes, and say 'Think about it, man. Think about it.'

Toby continued to write his ballads – some political, some just surreal, 'Can't Pay, Won't Pay', 'The Brown Telephone' trilogy, and the immortal 'Bastard Cheese'. He tried very hard to be tormented. While we were revising for our finals, he had a kind of mini-breakdown, and had to go back to his parents for a few weeks. He wrote to me every day – I kept all his letters – and you'd have thought he was Siegfried Sassoon, on leave from the trenches. 'This morning, I sat in the garden with my mother,' he wrote. 'The sun was out, and Mum was reading the newspaper, while I worked on a new song. "I'm home now, Mum, aren't I?" I asked. "Yes, Toby," she replied. "You are."'

He recovered, however, in time to take his exams, and we graduated, and all three of us moved down to London, to be in place for the great life opportunities, when they started coming along. The economy was in recession. Toby was a little crestfallen when he discovered that no one was particularly interested in his great works, and it gradually dawned on me that none of the NGOs I approached particularly wanted to pay me to end world poverty or rescue street children. Zoe had dramatic on-off relationships with older men, Toby embarked on another extended life crisis, performing his songs from time to time at a pub near the Oval, and I worked as a temp. We spent some time travelling, and a while longer stuffing envelopes for good causes – in the run-up to the 1992 election, we canvassed some extremely scary corners of the North Peckham Estate. After a few years, Toby applied to his Law Conversion Course. His father was relieved, and agreed to fund him, on condition that he cut his hair.

By then, we had become more like a family than a couple – me playing mother, Toby as a troubled father, and Zoe as our feckless teenaged daughter. Only we weren't really a family; I should have remembered that. Relationships have their defining moments, and Mum's illness was ours.

'It's OK,' I said, on the telephone. 'You don't need to come down. I'll see you in a couple of days.'

'Are you sure?' he said. I could hear the anxiety in his voice, mingled with relief.

'I'm sure,' I said.

The hospital seemed to me to have a logic of its own, and an authority that exerted its power beyond the Victorian, red brick building with its tangle of newer extensions, reaching invisibly across town, and into the rest of my life. Leaving my bicycle in the forecourt, I had a superstitious sense that the place itself would create my condition – that the pregnancy might disappear unless validated by medical professionals. 'But I'm perfectly OK,' I thought, pushing against the heavy doors for the first time.

Gregor wasn't with me. He was spending a lot of time at work, in a panic, perhaps, at the thought of the looming deadline, and the implication of his own mortality. He seemed to blow hot and cold about the pregnancy, sometimes being very considerate and affectionate, making ardent, unprovoked declarations of love and elaborate plans for the future, and at others, seeming withdrawn and even angry. 'If you don't mind too much, I'd rather get on,' he said. 'You know I don't like hospitals.'

Waiting with my paperback to be called, I could feel the building working around me – the squeak of the nurses' rubber shoes on the polished vinyl floor, the whirr of the lifts, the smell of disinfectant and cabbage, the clank of metal trays as lunch was distributed. I felt the suck of the place was very powerful – watching the staff go about their work breezily, noticing the personalities, the orders, the little rituals, I could tell how easily it could become my world. The temptation to submit struggled against an urge to rebel. An instinct to disrupt, question and criticise in my clear, well-educated voice tugged against a fear of slipping up, a nervous need to belong. It was as if all the many establishments in my life had been a kind of training for this one; I could feel myself becoming institutionalised with every tick of the large, round clock. Next to the reception desk, there was a sign for the delivery room. I had my first premonition of pain, and felt afraid.

Brisk women weighed me, on heavy metal scales, took blood samples, measured my bump with a tape, or felt it with strong, expert fingers, and asked questions about my dates and gynaecological history. There were never results. It was an endless examination with no marks. After a while, I stopped waiting for a conversation in which things became clear. I just had to trust in the system, to assume that no news was good news. I was shocked by the scale of this vast parallel universe, the world of the sick, the entrance and exit point for so many, and by how easily it assimilated me. After a while I relaxed, and learned to be a good patient; seeking their approval was second nature. I submitted myself to their care like a child.

I lay on another high bench, my small bump – taut skin over hard, quivering fluid – exposed. The young doctor listened with a metal cone, something like an ear trumpet – the cold made me flinch as he moved it. 'Very good,' he said, and I raised myself to a sitting position, adjusting my clothes with a strange sense of embarrassment. I saw him write something on my notes.

I hesitated for a moment, my curiosity struggling with my deference. 'What's that?' I asked.

The doctor looked surprised, as if he'd forgotten I might be able to talk, and I pointed. 'What are you writing?'

'Oh, that,' he said. 'Nothing to worry about. Little chap's doing fine. I was just listening to his heart beating.'

Susie

I introduced Toby to my family in my second year at college. Mum plied him with Campari sodas in the garden, and hectored us about the ambulance strike ('so why aren't you out there doing something about it? Honestly, talk about Thatcher's children! You lot are pathetic'). Toby wasn't used to being on the receiving end; he seemed to rather like it. 'Your mum's cool,' he mumbled, later, collapsing into my bed upstairs.

'No she isn't,' I tried to explain, the following day. We had been wandering the streets of Brighton for a while, and had ended up in a vegetarian café in town. There was a menu chalked on a blackboard, and a cool-cabinet full of baps stuffed with grated carrot and bean sprouts. The place was almost empty, and rather dark due to all the dove and rainbow stickers and plants in the window, but I checked behind me anyway, since it was just the sort of place where someone might know her.

'There's a lot to be said for boring parents,' I said. 'Kids need stability. We had a lot of freedom, and she treated us almost as equals, but in the end, I don't think that makes for a secure upbringing.'

'She brought you up on her own, more or less, didn't she? That can't have been easy.' Toby took his own dramas rather seriously, but could be more even-handed about mine. I was drinking fennel tea, and he had a cup of fair trade coffee.

'Dad always did his bit,' I replied, indignantly. 'I mean, maybe he has his faults, but she isn't a patient woman. She was on her voyage of self-fulfilment, or whatever, and we were obstacles to her liberation, as she never tired of letting us know.'

I had faint memories of the chaos of those early years, and the fall-out from my parents' separation. Along with the headaches, I remembered seeing Mum cry a fair amount, and other details I'd discounted at the time – the urgent, angry conversations with female friends, lighting one cigarette after another with shaking hands, and the evenings, when Gus and I were supposed to be in bed, and she got drunk and melancholy to Van Morrison with Cathy, or drunk and combative to Joan Armatrading with Sheila. I made strange concoctions for supper (which I relished forcing baby Gus to eat) and helped with the housework from a very young age. Life lurched along in its way, but the world seemed precarious, and arbitrary, and a bit crazy, rather like her. I blamed her passionately for all of it.

There was a procession of boyfriends. Their things appeared in the house, when we arrived back from weekends with Dad; some-times they were in Mum's bed when we came tumbling in, in the mornings. The first was a Chilean exile – I remember the dark allusions my mother made to his terrible 'wounds' (although, thinking back, I'm not sure if these were physical or mental) and his occasional but alarming explosions in Spanish. He was followed by a Sikh bus driver (I remember his long, blue-black hair on the pillow, his unfolded turban stretching the whole length of the hall, as we helped him fold it, and his evident disapproval of our unruly behaviour). Then there was a leather-jacketed social worker – I remember him best, because unlike the others, he'd got on with Gus and me extremely well, playing Monopoly with us for three hours solidly, while Mum's carefully prepared lasagne turned to concrete. Gus and I waited out each upheaval, confident that our universe would revert to its rightful configuration sooner or later, and sooner or later, were left feeling relieved (and perhaps just a little guilty), when it did.

When I was a teenager, Mum got a new job, lecturing in French

70

at the polytechnic, and suddenly, we weren't so broke all the time. She left us for a week-long conference in Montreal, and after that, letters started arriving from Canada. After a while, we had one of the new fax machines installed and watched incredulously, as it traced Steve's quirky doodles out of the thin air. Mum, who up until then had apparently regarded the far side of the Atlantic as the preserve of that Great Satan Uncle Sam, 'the do Ron Ron with the neutron bomb' (as one of her protest songs had it), now went on glamorous North American holidays without us (a fact which outraged us both, since at the time, Gus harboured futile yearnings towards Disneyland, and I had a crush on Michael J Fox).

Then Steve came over for Christmas, and Mum behaved like a lovesick teenager herself, repeatedly checking her reflection nervously in the mirror – her spreading hips in stonewashed jeans or brightly patterned trousers, topped with little waistcoats and long, dangly earrings. The adults disappeared upstairs 'for a nap' in the afternoons, giggling on the stairs. Gus looked on in horror, and I worked on a new line in supercilious disdain: we both agreed that it was 'totally embarrassing'. Then, just as things should, according to the rules of the game so far, have been about to get back to normal, Steve announced that he'd been to look at a shop which was to let in the Lanes. This information was received with blank looks. 'He's coming to live here, with us,' Mum elaborated, her face alight with pleasure.

There were a few rocky months. Mum was called in to speak to Gus's teacher, and my irony tipped over into open hostility, with as many nights as I could arrange over at my friend Karen's. After a while, though, we settled for a kind of peaceful coexistence, held together by Mum's diplomatic efforts, Gus's underlying certainty that he was really top dog, and Steve's dread of appearing 'heavy'.

There was still a sense of freedom in the house – we and our friends could come and go as we liked, borrow Steve's LPs (Bob Dylan, Pink Floyd, and so on, which were suddenly regarded as cool, rather than comical, by some of my classmates), and we could drink and even smoke openly (although, perhaps because there was precious little potential for annoying my mother in this respect, I remained puritanically abstemious). Our increasing prosperity cheered everyone up, and, once the shop began to turn a healthy profit, and as Mum climbed the career ladder, the adults embarked on little projects – an attic conversion, a small place in the South of France – from which we benefited, without having to drop our studied cynicism. We were one of the first of our friends to have a real computer (an Amstrad, with nine-inch floppy disks) in the house.

The first time I tried marijuana, it was Steve's (in a cheese dip – 'just one cracker, then,' Mum said, uncomfortably). When Gus started to nick Steve's stash, they just said it would be nice if he'd ask next time, and when he complained about his teachers, or got into trouble, they laughed along with him, and sympathised with his anti-authoritarian stance. Often, as a teenager, I envied my friends the kind of parents who imposed curfews and stopped you wearing make-up – who would make disparaging comments about pop music instead of asking interested questions. It was a relief, sometimes, to visit homes in which the only way to get drunk was by raiding a teak-effect drinks cabinet when the adults were out.

I tried to explain something of this to Toby. 'It doesn't sound that dreadful,' he said.

'She's strange, messed up in ways I don't get. I can understand my grandmother being a bit weird – with the war, and everything – and it doesn't really bother me the way it does with Mum. I don't think she really trusts people, for all her hippie ideals. She's always acting. I don't know who she's going to be from one moment to the next – I don't think she knows herself.'

'I think you're probably more alike than you realise,' Toby said.

'Thanks a lot. I have no intention of screwing things up like she has. I'm going to do it completely differently.'

'Plenty of people dislike their families, and try to see them as little as possible. What makes me suspicious is the fact that you always seem to be getting a train down here.' I frowned. 'You look a bit like she did, anyway,' he said, mischievously, entwining his fingers with mine over the sticky oil-cloth on the table. 'That photo in the hall, that could be you.'

I glanced at my reflection, in the glass of the door which led back into the toilets. I was wearing a stretchy black top that looked a bit like a leotard, under an open baggy shirt, and my hair was fixed back with a plastic tortoiseshell comb. I'd often been told I looked like Mum – same pale blue eyes, straight brown hair, very pale skin, completely impossible to tan. The superficial stuff, I noticed with relief, looked OK – my eyeliner hadn't run, and my hair wasn't too ruined by the wind – but of course I was too famil-

72

iar with my own reflection to see myself with any objectivity.

'God,' I said, with a theatrical groan, taking his chin between my thumb and forefinger, 'you must be kidding. Shoot me now,' but he kissed me instead.

Helene

We disembarked in the morning, but the sky was already a fierce, relentless blue, and without the gentle breeze – which we'd barely noticed on the ship – the heat seemed to give the air a new, pulsing density. Walking down the gangplank was like opening the door of an enormous oven, and the solid ground, beneath my feet, felt as unsteady and treacherous as the shifting deck had once seemed.

I felt sad to leave the *Orion* there – our home, our rock, empty and desolate amid the debris of the docks. The quay was stacked with mountain ranges of luggage, huge trunks and leather suit-cases, whole cliffs of stacked tea chests, great pools of rope, coiled like snakes, and mounds of chain. Tall cranes bent their dutiful necks, and bare-chested Indians, gleaming with sweat, called out in strange languages, or stared at us with an unnerving directness.

The road was a dusty chaos of trucks and bicycles, rickshaws, troop lorries and mangy donkeys, choked with the vast movements of war and commerce. The smell – the stink, really – on the hot air, struck me very strongly: a mixture of rotting vegetables, sweat, petrol and spices, which I found quite disgusting. I had an impression of palm trees, and cliffs, and the great, teeming, filthy mass of the city. Then the dim station, crammed with life: goats and chickens, small children, and beggars with stumps for fingers. It was like a strange dream.

I watched my fellow travellers with a new admiration. The English seemed to glide through all this with calm authority and easy self-assurance, like pale swans on a stream, dispensing baksheesh and instructions, the crowds parting before them, bearers staggering in their wake. I had to struggle hard to keep my wits and my luggage about me.

Luckily, one of the women I knew from the ship was taking the same train, and we found a compartment together. It was a large monster of a locomotive, parts of which, I could tell from the engraved lettering, had been built in Birmingham. Our carriage

73

seemed rather empty, even with our luggage in it, since it was expected that you'd travel with your own bedroll and basic equipment, none of which we had. We were frightened of the huge spiders which lurked in the corners.

While the train waited at the platform I felt hot and claustrophobic. I had to resist the temptation to stare at every group of men in uniform, in the hope of catching a last glimpse of Bobby, and the clamour of people outside, doing business or bidding elaborate farewells, was exhausting. 'Phew,' said my companion, fanning herself with her ticket. 'Welcome to India. Are you feeling all right? You do look a bit dicky.'

'I'll be fine once we get moving,' I said, not really believing it.

In a few moments, we were off, with a great creaking and squeaking and an uncertain lurch. With the air on my face, and the blinding sunshine, I closed my eyes, and tilted my head back against the seat, leaving the station behind. The sense I had of Bobby stayed with me, however. 'Oh dear,' I thought to myself, 'I've got this worse than I realised.'

He seemed the more powerful for being purely inside my head. He was a mood, and a sensation, which both distanced and intensified the rest of the world. He was a sickness churning in my gut, hard to distinguish from the upset stomach which coincided with my first step on Indian soil – accompanied by hot and cold flushes, and the dread that things might, at any moment, slide out of control. He was in the dazzling sky, the foreign smells, the sudden sense I had of potential, of my life as a story in a book. He was a caress, like the warm air, whispering over my skin.

Chapter Four

Vera

I was growing. My belly seemed almost to wax and wane. Sometimes, particularly in the evenings, I looked in the bedroom mirror and it seemed enormous. I felt distorted and ungainly, with spindly legs and bulbous protrusions, like a Biafran child. On other mornings I woke up and it seemed laughably small again. It was like looking into a fairground mirror every time, unsure of what I'd see. I realised why pregnant women touch their bumps so much – it felt bizarre, and uncomfortable, to be changing shape so fast.

The sickness had mostly gone, and I felt that after that, I could face anything. Bewildering surges of emotion, however, left me exhausted and drained. I cried inconsolably at the television news, and could barely bring myself to look at the newspaper – I felt a terrible new empathy with the Vietnamese mothers, and the big eyes of their children slid into me like a knife. Certain adverts, particularly those for good causes in the back of the *Listener* or the *Guardian*, made me choke up with feeling. At work, I had to skip passages of text in class that I felt might undo me.

I still spent a lot of time imagining the future. Walking in the windy park, it was as if I had a kind of double vision, superimposing myself and Gregor, and our phantom offspring, onto everyone I saw. I day-dreamed about gurgling babies in prams, apple-cheeked toddlers running across the grass, little children riding tricycles or feeding the ducks. Every corner of the house and garden became infested with these tiny ghosts.

My old school friend Sheila arrived to visit us for the weekend, wearing a theatrical, wide-brimmed hat. It was wonderful to have

75

someone to talk to: I hadn't realised how isolated the sickness had made me. I felt sorry for her, on her own again, but she seemed to be on fine form, and was full of new ideas. She'd been going to a Women's Group in North London, she told us, and she had taken to posting stickers in the tube: 'This Advertisement Exploits Women'.

I was careful with her, worried that the pregnancy might be a difficult issue – perhaps she'd be jealous, or feel our friendship was threatened by it – but in fact, her straightforward curiosity was a relief. She was fascinated by the physical side of things in a way that Gregor never could be, and her interest gave him a welcome break. 'Do you love it yet?' she asked me. We were painting a bedroom – smothering the yellowing rosebud wallpaper in white snow.

I had to think for a moment to answer her question. It wasn't like loving a person, someone I knew, but I was certainly growing very attached – perhaps dangerously attached – to the idea of it. 'It's hard to say. I'd feel very bad if something happened to it,' I said.

'And Gregor?' she said. 'How's he been about it all?'

'I don't think it's a reality for him in the same way,' I said, quickly. 'He just thinks about it in terms of how it will change our lives. He doesn't experience it like I can.' I bent to dip my brush into the paint pot. My face felt hot, and I was annoyed to find my sight blurred by tears.

Sheila turned to face me. 'My darling, are you all right?' she said.

I put down my brush, and wiped my face with the backs of my hands, carefully so as not to get paint in my hair, and took a deep breath. I felt I should be happy. I was the lucky one, with the new house, the man and a baby on the way. 'Of course I'm happy,' I said. 'I'm sorry, I just get a bit emotional.'

'Well, it's hard. Don't get me wrong, I think Gregor's super, and if you ever . . .' She must have noticed my expression, or some stiffening in my demeanour, because she swiftly abandoned whatever joke she'd been about to make. 'But he can be rather thick-skinned, can't he?'

'What do you mean?' I said, warily.

'Well, for example, his career comes first. You don't question your role. It's just assumed that you'll give up your friends, and

76

move, and change your job, and have babies, and not even think twice about it all, but it wouldn't be surprising if you found it a bit difficult. You shouldn't have to give up your whole life to be a good wife.'

'I wanted this baby more than Greg,' I said. 'And he's been great about it all.' She is jealous, after all, I thought, and angry that I've moved away.

'I'm sure he has, sweetie,' she said.

'Gregor says that inequality is an inescapable by-product of capitalism, and it's only in a socialist society that everyone, both men and women, will be able to achieve true emancipation,' I said.

She hesitated. 'Just make sure you don't let him have it all his own way.'

The pity in her eyes was what got to me. 'Look, I'm not oppressed, OK?' I snapped. 'I want this. I don't need rescuing, or saving.'

That afternoon, Sheila caught a train back to London. Gregor was out. I was tired by the decorating, and worried by our conversation, so I went to bed early.

I woke in darkness, and found that Gregor's side of the bed, next to me, was still empty, the sheet cool. It was midnight. The headlights of a passing car swept the ceiling of our bedroom like a searchlight. As I lay there, I felt it again, and this time I was sure of it – a very faint sensation, like bubbles, percolating in my abdomen.

Susie

It came in waves. Fear and sadness seemed to overtake my body like a physical sensation, at unexpected moments, without apparently connecting with my mind. I took a train back to London, and went back to work. I couldn't settle to anything, but switched tasks with a restless, absent-minded energy, pacing the floor, tidying up, and rehearsing new angles in my head. The fact of my mother's illness attached itself to my surroundings – my desk, the stairwell, my journey into work. A sickening daily dread followed me, and something ugly seemed to crouch around every corner. It was like a lens, through which I saw the world, re-tinted.

I'd always had problems getting to sleep, and these became

much worse. Bed became a scary place, my pillow full of the bad thoughts from the night before. I watched telly on the sofa, instead, until I finally lost consciousness. Every time I woke, there was a gut-churning moment when I remembered. Sleep generally seemed to help, though: afterwards, I felt calmer, and told myself how much better I felt.

I became very superstitious, half-believing in a complex personal mysticism, offering up secret sacrifices to the Gods of the wardrobe, the traffic lights, or the kitchen appliances. If I give to this beggar, I found myself thinking, if I can just finish washing up these cups before the kettle has boiled, then maybe she'll be OK. Perhaps it's because I got my new job, I even thought, insanely. Perhaps this is the price.

Toby and Zoe tried to hug me a lot, and asked if I wanted 'to talk', but most of the time it only annoyed me. One evening, however, I had a kind of a crying fit – sobs that were more like screams overtook my whole body, and I stared at the wall as if something terrible were coming towards me. Zoe held onto me and called me 'honey' and tried to calm me down. The feeling of crying aloud like that reminded me of being a very small child, and my hands tingled from lack of oxygen. I scared them. 'I'm glad Zoe was there,' Toby said, afterwards, 'I don't think I'd have known what to do.'

Some of my colleagues also seemed afraid of me. 'How's your mother doing?' people asked, and I didn't know what to tell them. People offered up their own experiences of illness: suddenly the world was full of suffering. As we queued for coffees in an Italian café opposite our office, one of my colleagues told me how his mother had recovered from breast cancer.

'My mother's cancer is quite advanced, they say, and, well, it doesn't look good at all,' I said. Sometimes I felt I should have prepared a press release – a carefully crafted list of acceptable euphemisms. Sometimes the information I gave surprised me. Hearing myself tell them, it shocked me afresh, or I told them things that I wasn't aware that I knew.

'Oh,' he said, and flushed. 'I'm sorry. Do you want to talk about something else?'

'I'm OK,' I said – in fact I almost preferred to talk about it, since it was in my head all the time, anyway. Then I realised that it was a plea, rather than a question. I divided the world into people who understood, who'd been through something equivalent themselves, and people who didn't, with two healthy parents, whom I could barely tolerate. I spent a lot of time looking out of the window at the people on the grass below, hating them.

'People live with cancer for years and years,' Toby said. 'I can't help feeling you shouldn't give in to it like this.' He lay on the sofa, in our living room, cradling his unplugged electric guitar. As usual, the throw we draped over the brown velour upholstery was falling off. Every so often he would play a few quiet, tinny chords, humming beneath his breath, as if he could hear the music in his head. 'With these kind of things, they say your attitude can make a big difference.'

I wanted to believe him. 'I suppose were all going to die at some point,' I said, tapping into the stream of thought that was a constant undercurrent to my waking mind. 'So it's hard to get a handle on it. Perhaps the main difference is just that we know, in her case, what it's most likely to be of.'

'And it wouldn't be, like, a total wonder of medical science if she survived, would it? Your mum's a toughie. I'm sure she'll put up one hell of a fight.'

That evening, Zoe had suggested a 'house outing': a bonding exercise she insisted on once in a while, with Polly Anna-ish brightness, and the confidence of a pretty girl who is seldom refused. There was a comedian she wanted to see, performing in a pub in Balham. We were used to following her around London on complex nocturnal manoeuvres – often to bump into, or even avoid, some new love interest – and we all went along, dutifully. It had worked well in the past, combating domestic bickering and inertia, and Toby suggested it might be good to break my cycle of work and worry.

The pub was grand and old-fashioned, with smoked-glass doors, and gleaming tables and mirrors. It was crammed with young professionals, with ruddy faces and denim shirts, guzzling their Alcopops like over-grown children. I couldn't concentrate on the comedian, there was no space for his words in my head, but I watched the crowd, roaring at intervals, each time his voice reached a crescendo. I realised, almost immediately, that I shouldn't have come, but it would have seemed melodramatic to leave, and I felt I had no option but to sit it out. Mum was so much in my head that she might almost have been at the table with me:

I felt as if I saw things through her eyes, and was filled with distaste. 'Laugh,' I thought, 'but you're all going to die, and the sooner the better, for most of you.'

Afterwards, the conversation slid over me, and I felt alone amid the clinking and chatter. Toby was teasing Zoe, as he always did – making disparaging remarks about 'Yanks', and convoluted, rather personal political attacks. We were on our fourth round of drinks, and there was an elation in the air. Zoe was giggling uncontrollably, and even Christina was smiling.

Toby looked good, I thought, distantly. His sharp, impish face was alive with laughter – he seemed, in his very expression, to be urging you to get the joke. He wore a leather waistcoat and jeans, and his shorter hair suited him, although I wasn't so sure about the goatee. He'd always changed so fast, especially at college, hearing new ideas one day, and then trying them on for size the next. He'd been an environmental bore one term (the rainforests had been a big concern, at the time), a communist the next, and for a while even a Lib Dem, with an interest in the finer points of proportional representation. We'd kept up, as best we could, but it was a risky business, and he'd make us the butt of humorous, Ben Elton style rants, or put us in one of his songs, for using aerosols, or eating dolphin-unfriendly tuna – 'it's like living through the Cultural Revolution, round here,' Zoe once said.

He'd obliterated the influence of his family so completely that it was uncanny when something seeped through. We were out shopping once, for instance, and in the middle of a loud digression on sweat-shop conditions and child labour, he'd added, 'And if you want real wool, of course, you've got to pay for it.' He came back from his parents' with his grotty old clothes – the granddad shirts, and second-hand suit jackets from Oxfam (which he wore rolled up at the sleeves), the long khaki greatcoat – smelling of 'spring breeze' fabric conditioner, or the disintegrating Greenpeace T-shirts carefully pressed and folded by their housekeeper, and there was something in his attitude to money that implied he knew he'd never be really short for long. I think it was his very restlessness that attracted me to him – it made him far more interesting than the flat, complacent posh kids around us, who'd inherited a world, and lived in it unquestioningly. There was something a little ruthless, however, about the way he dropped people when he moved on. I'd lost count, for instance, of the various student societies and later, the local pressure groups, which had flourished through his attentions, and then collapsed shortly after he lost interest, leaving some bewildered Japanese student, or little old lady, with a flat full of un-posted newsletters. His capacity for reinvention had been so suited to the artificial, transitory environment of university that he'd found leaving particularly hard, and was now flourishing, once again, at law school.

The song on the juke box finished playing, and I noticed a lapse in the conversation, as if someone had put a foot wrong, or said more than they intended.

'Why don't you two just shag, and give us all a break?' Christina said. Zoe looked anxiously at me, but I laughed, to show what a good sport I was, and cover the fact that I hadn't really been listening. Zoe said 'no thanks, hon, not my cuppa tea,' and then snorted with laughter, because she was slightly drunk, and even after seven years in England, she still thought this expression was hilarious.

The bright night bus brought us lurching to our stop, with its strange cargo of ranting drunks and muttering schizophrenics, and we wobbled our way home down orange-lit pavements. Music throbbed from the flats and cars we passed, and someone was screaming a few streets away. There was a madness and a self-absorbed brutality to the city at play: I wondered why I'd never noticed it before.

Christina went ahead and unlocked the door. Toby and Zoe were wrestling on the kerb. I stood under a street lamp. 'How can you?' I turned on Toby. I had hardly spoken all night, and talking made me realise that I was also rather drunk.

Zoe seemed to sober abruptly. 'Um, I'll go warm up the couch?' she said.

'What?' Toby said. He sounded surprisingly guilty.

'How can you carry on as if everything is the same?'

His silence, I thought, spoke volumes. For him, everything *was*. Compassion fatigue, I suppose you could call it. My mum's illness had become like the conflict in the Balkans, or the unspeakable things being uncovered in Rwanda – something you feel bad about, but would rather not think about on your night off. The scaffolding I'd created for myself was an illusion, I thought. I was alone in this. No one else could feel my pain.

He sighed, and folded his arms around me. His hands on my hair, and on my neck, calmed me, and made me feel real again.

'Come here, you,' he said. 'I'm sorry. It's OK to feel like that. You're bound to. It's all OK.'

No it's not, I thought, it isn't all OK. But I didn't say it – I just wanted to be quiet, and in his arms, and to stop thinking. I just wanted to feel young and carefree again.

The front door was open. From inside our house, I could hear that someone had turned the TV on. It had always seemed so convenient, and cosy, until now, with my best friend and boyfriend both on tap. We all got on so well, I'd always thought – all the hugging and kissing and teasing proof that we were beyond those boring adult hang-ups. They'd been my insulation against the world, only now they just made me feel more isolated.

'Do you think we might look into finding a place of our own?' I said. 'Perhaps we could afford something, now that I've got a proper job. Just the two of us?'

'Let's see, shall we,' he said. I knew he liked the sociability of our house, and I think the idea of being just us maybe rather scared him. 'It's probably not a good time for you to be taking big decisions.'

I leaned against him, my nose at the base of his neck, too tired and comfortable to move, drawing strength from his self-confidence. 'Can't I just live here?' I asked.

'It's far too expensive,' he said. It was a joke we had.

'Really?' I whispered.

'I expect I could do you some kind of a deal.'

On his skin, I could smell our curry, and the pub, and underlying this, the unmistakable smell of him, and it was like a summary of my day, and a foretaste of my night. Physical contact felt like a simpler, safer language. I felt a relief that wasn't put into words, but was something like, thank God, he's my home now.

Helene

The train journey came to seem like a prolonged hallucination. Exhaustingly vivid panoramas rolled past the window, day and night. It was like sitting in the front row at the cinema – I slipped into that utterly passive state which travelling can induce, and spent much of my time dozing.

We rumbled slowly right through a bazaar, the people gathering

82

up their wares and scrambling to clear the tracks before us, just in time: voices called out to us, and hands reached into our compartment, as we shrank back into our seats. As we left the city, I had the impression of travelling not in miles, but in centuries, glimpsing medieval tableaux of peasant life, as we sped by. At night, I awoke as we crossed a wide river, gleaming in the moonlight. The next morning, we were on a steep embankment, the jungle canopy, below us, hung with enormous creepers, and tiny villages were dotted over the hills.

As our journey progressed, gradually the countryside grew more pastoral. At one station, there was a man with a bear: 'Look, look!' my companion squealed excitedly. After being prodded viciously by its owner, the beast ambled over obediently and shook its chains in a slow, swaying movement. The man spoke to us in English: 'Look, look, dancing cha cha!' I searched my purse reluctantly for a coin, but closer up, my companion's initial delight had turned to horror – 'poor creature, it's disgusting, we shouldn't give money to that,' she announced. The man was angry at being called over for nothing – although we couldn't understand his words, his displeasure was clear enough – and it was a relief when the guard blew his whistle and we were off again.

The other girl from the boat reached her station before me, but finally I arrived, smelly and crumpled, stiff and disorientated. Charles met me on the platform. It was very odd to see him again somewhere so strange – he seemed utterly incompatible with the 'husband' I had referred to so often, and tried to sustain in my mind. His hair was fairer, from the sun, and his skin pinker, and he seemed a different size, somehow – although whether smaller or larger, I wasn't sure.

He seemed rather nervous, too, and anxious to impress me with his control of the situation, and his authority in this new environment. He had a tonga waiting outside, with a silent driver and an elderly, fly-bothered mare. Charles helped me up, my suitcase was safely stowed, and with a jingle and a gentle rocking motion, we were off towards the hotel.

We started along a wide, tree-lined boulevard. Two men in baggy white trousers pruned roses on a central island. Everything looked bright in the sunshine, and I thought of Alice in Wonderland. Charles pointed out Government House to me, as proudly as if he'd built the place himself. 'Look, darling. That's very typical,

83

very Indian,' he kept saying. A stray cow wandered sedately over the road. There was a policeman in an elaborate blue turban (which Charles explained was called a puggaree). We passed the compound walls of fine British bungalows, overgrown with scarlet bougainvillea, glimpsing the vivid green of well-watered lawns behind.

We turned a corner, and suddenly there was more traffic – bicycles, more army lorries. We passed the Post Office, and later, the outskirts of a bazaar, the gutters clogged with rotting fruit and vegetables. There were a good many khaki-clad soldiers, both white and Indian, and clouds of reddish dust, and everything seemed to be varying shades of copper or brown. Charles explained that this was the edge of the Old City, and I saw elaborate lattice stonework, arches and minarets. I noticed that unpleasant spicy smell again.

'Don't look, darling, there's been an accident,' Charles said, thereby, of course, ensuring that I did. He said something to the driver, who gave a half-hearted shake of the reins.

I scanned the road, and saw a bent bicycle that had been dragged to one side. 'A cyclist?' I said.

'Used to be,' Charles said, grimly, 'I wouldn't look, there's a dead person.' Then I saw the body. He had been flung through the air, and lay crunched, his shoulder pressed into the ground, like a sort of upside down Atlas, trying to bear the weight of the world. There was a brown bloodstain around him, but his face looked so peaceful that he could have been sleeping. I had seen dead bodies before, in the Blitz, and then, as now, I was more shocked by the crowd of onlookers, none of whom moved to cover the corpse.

We drew into Donaldson's Hotel, where Charles was a long-term guest. There was a large main building, and a number of smaller bungalows, all set within an extensive compound. Despite a few half-hearted stabs at imperial grandeur at the entrance – a couple of potted palms, a man in white gloves and uniform, who took my luggage – it was a fairly crummy place, with battered furniture and, I later discovered, lousy food. There were stone paths leading between the bungalows, interspersed with patchy grass and a few geraniums in pots.

We were led to our bungalow, which had a bare, unlived-in look. There was a white-washed bathroom, a bedroom containing a large double bed draped with a greyish mosquito net, and a living room with a low coffee table and a couple of wicker chairs. There were rotating fans on the ceilings, and mesh mosquito netting at the windows and front door, which led onto a small veranda.

Charles, I realised, was still issuing instructions, but I had reached saturation point. I gathered he was going back to work, and I would have time to wash, rest and absorb my new surroundings. 'I'll send Jameel along later to check on you, so don't be alarmed,' he said. 'He's very reliable, and you can ask him for anything you need.'

My suitcase had been left by the bed, and we were alone, husband and wife. 'How did you leave little Charlotte?' Charles asked.

For a moment I misunderstood the question. Comfortable as I was in English, I still sometimes took things a little too literally. 'How indeed?' I thought, remembering my fever, my sore, inflamed breasts, and the large, heavy rock I still felt inside my rib cage, where my heart should be, which I seemed condemned to lug around like a convict. This, however, I quickly realised, was not his meaning. 'She seemed very well, please God,' I answered.

Charles hesitated. 'Does she look at all like me?' he asked. I recognised in his strangely guilty question the sense of fraudulence I'd felt myself, and realised – with a flash of pity – the effort it must be for him to make her real in his mind.

I had often asked myself the same question. 'Sometimes. Not really. It's hard to tell,' I said. She had my darker colouring, but I didn't say this. I also didn't tell him that the person I thought she resembled most was my mother. Although he'd tried to hide it at first, he clearly saw her as a distasteful encumbrance, and an unhealthily strong influence on me, and I took the fact that he hadn't arranged for her ticket to join us as a clear signal that the gloves were off in this respect.

'I'll leave you to rest. I realise it's rather a lot to take in,' he said, and I nodded.

He leant forward and gave me a quick kiss on the cheek. I felt his moustache tickle my skin. I was relieved this was all. I had been afraid that he would expect me to melt into his arms immediately, and I didn't feel at all inclined to do so. I was scared of falling pregnant again. Besides the fact that Charles felt like a stranger, and a rather unappealing one at that, Bobby was so much in my head that I was afraid that my reluctance, and my internal conflict, would surely show.

85

'Things are rather different out here, but you'll soon get used to it,' Charles added, and there was a hopeful note in his voice, as if he were trying to convince himself as much as me.

Vera

I began to feel you move more strongly. The sensation changed from the gentle bubbling, or light fluttering, to definite kicks, and sometimes, great seismic shifts.

I was never-endingly amazed and surprised by it. If Gregor were around, I'd squeal at him to put his hand dutifully on my bump. At first, I don't think he could feel you, although he pretended, to please me. After a while, you grew so strong that, as we struggled to find new ways to accommodate you in bed, you would kick us both at the same time. Sometimes I could see you move in the bath, or as I lay naked on the bed – the bump would become an asymmetrical mound, or begin to wobble of its own accord, or a great ripple would pass across it. Sheila visited again, and felt it too. 'Woah. It's like swimming with dolphins,' she said.

'It's a bit like the feeling of excitement,' I said, trying to explain how the movement ('quickening' was the name the midwives used for it), resembled the feeling of butterflies in the stomach. It wasn't exactly sexual, but felt private, and pleasing, in a slightly similar way. I couldn't get over the fact that there was something in there that wasn't me. I'd be sitting in class, or dozing in front of *Nationwide*, and suddenly start beaming, at the gentle reminder of the secret life inside me.

I began to enjoy being pregnant. Now it was beginning to show, I found myself reaping the concern and attention from other people that actually, I had been more in need of at the beginning, and I liked the idea that I was eating and sleeping for the greater good.

I was a bit happier, and Gregor found me easier to be with. He still spent a lot of time out, though, and we didn't really talk about anything that wasn't in some way related to the baby. I was aware of withdrawing into a kind of baby zone, consumed by uncharacteristic obsessions.

I was in bed, propped up with pillows, eating a banana absentmindedly and turning the pages of a child-care book by Dr Spock. He had to repeat my name twice before I looked up.

86

'What?'

He looked at me helplessly. 'Never mind,' he said.

'No, what?' I repeated, annoyed that he'd distracted me for nothing.

'You used to be so different,' he said, perhaps remembering the earnest girl he'd met on the march, and the slender, barefoot student who'd curled, reading, in his armchair at college. I had become so absolutely self-contained, this relentlessly gestating mama-baby creature that had taken up residence in his life, compulsively feathering its nest and nourishing itself, in such an animal way. It was as if I'd taken up an absorbing and rather gory new hobby, in which he had a limited interest.

'So did you,' I said, crossly, and went back to my book.

My mother sent me a letter. There were details in it that she must have got from Lottie – she knew my due date, and that I'd been feeling sick – and this made me feel furious with my sister. She said she was planning a trip to England later in the year and would I please let her come and visit? She said that she understood I was angry, and that we'd had our difficulties in the past, but she hoped I wouldn't deny her the opportunity to see her grandchild. It made me regret my telephone call – I should have remembered how these things always seemed to result in emotional turmoil. I couldn't quite bring myself, however, to throw the letter away.

The room which we had cleared and painted for the baby became a focal point for my daydreams. I liked its blank emptiness and the smell of the fresh paint – I could stand there for some time, lost in a kind of trance. The few items in there – a borrowed, rectangular plastic carry-cot, a brand-new cellular baby blanket, a pair of tiny bootees – seemed to have a strange power over me. There was something both frightening and compelling about these things that belonged to someone who didn't yet exist.

Sometimes I allowed myself to shop for the baby, wandering timidly through the foreign landscape of strange fastenings and latex and breast pads, the ribbons and bells and gadgets and the minuscule scraps of cloth. 'Can I help you?' said the assistant, pressing a pastel list into my hand, headed 'Baby will need . . .' I didn't mention these expeditions to Gregor. The first few purchases felt alarmingly close to madness, another risky act of faith.

I started to drop food on my bump like an old man, and got a

87

nagging backache, that built throughout the day. My ribs felt sore, as if I'd been beaten up from the inside.

Susie

I built myself into a more combative frame of mind, but it was all smashed again when I next saw her.

Mum was back from the hospital, and very sleepy from all of the pills they'd given her to take, which sat in a large brown-paper bag on top of the fridge. We sat together in the front room. She dozed on the sofa, her head on my arm. Over the fireplace there was an Escher print that had been there for as long as I could remember: one of those optical illusions, of a staircase that goes up as well as down. The faded books were like old friends, looking down from the shelves, and there was a battered stack of board games on the shelf above the telly – Scrabble, Monopoly, Cluedo, Trivial Pursuit. As usual, I found her drowsiness infectious. Touching her for so long felt unusual, and nice.

I wanted to record every aspect of her with my mental video camera. I listened to her breathing, and wanted to absorb her. The weight of her head, her short, wiry hair, her soap and cigarettes smell: if only I could distil it into an equation, keep it in a box of treasures, a necklace of genetic code, like a family heirloom. We still fit together so well, I thought. I was used to the hardness of a male body, and the curves of my mother's frame, despite her new boniness, were so much more accommodating. I looked at the skin of her forearm – warm, soft, becoming a little loose and crêpe-papery – and thought about the life running beneath. How do people actually die, I wondered – what is it actually like? Could she just stop – suddenly, silently? Was she already winding down, like a clock? It's impossible, I thought, and felt guilty for my thoughts.

The two of us went shopping together at Waitrose. The operation was scheduled for Monday, and the weekend stretched before us, bitter and blissful, a pleasure so sharp it felt like pain. Cut loose from everything, all we could do was to live a sort of dreadful parody of before – be brave and go shopping. Mum wore dark glasses, to hide the yellow of her eyes, and her loose-hanging clothes, suddenly several sizes too large, gave her a new elegance. She looked like a fading film star.

The supermarket seemed very posh to me, full of new kinds of food from around the world, fruit and vegetables I didn't even know the names of. I pushed a trolley, and we walked the aisles, the shelves crowded with choices, twenty different types of everything. Mum planned what we were going to eat over the weekend, and bought the ingredients for fresh pesto – basil leaves, pine nuts, pecorino cheese. Discussing this aloud seemed to calm her. 'It's wonderful, the things they have now,' she said. 'Balsamic vinegar is everywhere, and look, dried seaweed, *mon Dieu*. I remember what food was like when I was growing up–,' she blinked, and laughed, '–it could almost make one weep.'

I felt lost, too, trying to suppress a rising sense of panic. Life had become a kind of nightmare, in which something terrible underlay all the old pleasures. I thought I could feel a huge scream building up inside me. I took a ticket at the deli counter. I thought of Mum's friend Cathy, at her husband's funeral – the only funeral I'd ever been to. 'I'm being so bloody British,' she'd said, small and fierce, in her tight black dress, drawing the eyes of the room, like an inverse bride, 'when all I really want to do is to go up to a mountain top and howl and wail and beat my breast.'

A large red number flashed overhead. 'Can I help you?' said the woman behind the softly humming cheese counter, and I realised I was unable to speak, and choked an incoherent apology, and pushed the trolley quickly away.

In the car park outside, I loaded bags into the boot. 'It's surreal, isn't it?' I said, trying to break the self-restraint which threatened to seal us separately, like the cellophaned, shrink-wrapped shopping.

'Yes, it is,' Mum said. 'I sometimes think I should keep a journal, but most of what goes through my head is quite mundane.' I slammed the boot, and we got into the car.

Mum started the engine. 'What makes it all so peculiar is that everything is still the same, still OK on the surface. It's very hard to deal with things before they actually happen. I suppose what I'm saying is that the immediate future is what's important to us – what's for supper, and so forth.'

'Very Zen,' I said.

'Maybe.' We drove back, chasing snatches of sea between the streets. 'I don't mean to sound too ... you know–' she fished for a word, '–other-worldly. I realised the other night that I haven't got much to choose between, style-wise. Along with everything else, this illness is rather limiting from a social point of view. I can be saintly, or I can be scary, and that's it. Sometimes I can be both in the same sentence.'

'You don't have to be saintly for us,' I said.

'Oh, I know. I was a bit worried, because I was getting these great waves of love for the whole of humanity. Then I watched a bit of the VE day anniversary on telly, and it was quite a relief, actually, because I realised it was all still really irritating.' She gave her old, smoker's laugh.

The weather was glorious again, and everything about that weekend seemed excruciatingly beautiful. Mum sat in the garden, in a straw hat, and consoled a steady stream of visitors. 'There are the people who want to cry with you, and the people who offer to do the shopping,' she said, dryly.

Gus seemed to occupy the same space but on a completely different orbit, with the occasional brief sighting at meals. I was still itemising – Mum's voice, from another room; her hairbrush, on the hall table. I made bargains, in my head. Please God, at least five. Please God, make it ten.

We were in the kitchen. The radio was murmuring to itself on a shelf: some typically obscure Radio 4 programme about wading birds. Steve had gone to pick my grandmother up from the station, and Gus was still in bed.

Mum was slicing tomatoes on a big wooden chopping board. She leaned forwards at the table, her heels crossed beneath her chair.

'Do you think we're alike?' I asked. 'Me and you? Toby always says that we are.'

Mum smiled. 'Physically, you mean?'

'Well, obviously I look a bit like you, my eyes and so on. I mean the way I am.'

'Sometimes you really remind me of myself at your age,' she said, using the point of the knife to pierce the tomato's skin.

'Really? I can't see it. I think we're such different people ...'

'I expect I've changed. I was a smug little madam at your age, though, just like you, determined to do it all better.'

This stung a little, but I didn't lash back, or storm off, as I would once have done.

'What changed you?' I said, instead.

90

'Oh,' she gave a sigh, 'the usual things. Divorce, for a start. I'd been with your father for so long, and I had to learn to think for myself, to *be* myself, all over again, without him. I think it started before that, though, so perhaps it was mostly motherhood.' She picked up the chopping board and used the knife to slide the chopped tomatoes into a large bowl, where they pressed against the glass like the result of some violent accident.

'It's only when I had you that being good for its own sake really started losing its appeal. With small kids, there's such a mountain to climb every day, and no one to pat you on the back, and you eventually start to notice that feeling self-satisfied is a bit of a mug's game. Life changed me, and it's probably just as well. Think how unbearable we'd be if we'd never screwed up.' She was on to the cucumber now, but stopped to take a swig of her tea, and reached for her cigarettes.

'There's a little Dictaphone they've lent me from work,' I said, as she lit her cigarette, and leaned back in her chair. 'I was wondering about making a tape recording. If you felt up to it, that is ...' I added hurriedly.

She looked straight at me. I met her eyes, my cheeks burning. 'Of me?' she said.

'Of us. There's lots of things I still don't know about your child-hood ...' I felt wretched. It was like admitting what none of us had so far – that she was going to die.

'OK,' she said, and it was as if she were admitting it as well, and I felt worse, and regretted the whole idea. 'I'd been meaning to talk to you a bit more about all that, in any case.' She smoked deeply, as if it were the only thing that really mattered any more. 'You should ask your grandmother, too. It's her story, as much as mine, and she won't be around forever, either, although I never dreamed she might see me out.'

'Rubbish,' I said, uncomfortably. 'You'll both be around for a good while yet.' We heard the front door, and Mum looked up at me sadly.

Steve came in with my grandmother. She'd retired – after the death of her second husband, with whom she'd lived in California – to a small house in Leamington Spa, stuffed with exotic knick-knacks. I'd always been nervous of her, perhaps picking up on my mother's anxieties ('you indulge those children ridiculously, Vera. You can't let them rule your life'). She was a slight figure, tidily dressed as usual, in a cream blouse, thin chiffon scarf and slacks from Jaeger. She had dark eyes – she'd been a great beauty, I could tell from the photographs, and also something in her bearing – a thin, wiry neck, determined wrinkles around her mouth, and an attitude of scorn towards the world, 'for heaven's sake!' Now I realised I was scared of seeing a crack in her strength. I wasn't sure I could bear it.

'My word, Susanna, don't you look grown up,' she said. Her voice was deep, gravelly, melodious, and upper-class, with just the faintest trace of an Austrian accent (I loved the extra 't's and 'z's with which she seemed to enrich my name).

Then she opened her arms to my mother, and they held on to each other, their faces locked in private struggle.

Helene

I awoke, feeling sticky beneath the sheet. The ceiling fan seemed barely to stir the air. The hotel bungalow was quiet, except for the soft whir above my head and the sound of birds on the corrugated tin roof.

I got up, put on a clean, floral-patterned frock, splashed some water onto my face, and twisted my hair up into a bun, which I fastened with hair-pins. Then I left the bungalow and walked towards the main hotel building, with the vague intention of getting my bearings and perhaps trying to find something to eat. The sun beat down, seeming to intensify the quiet of the afternoon, and heat radiated up from the stones beneath my feet. Where there was no shade, I narrowed my eyes to a squint to protect them against the glare, and thought that perhaps I should have remembered my mother's advice to wear a hat.

The main hotel building seemed very dark until my eyes readjusted. The place was deserted, except for the servants I glimpsed, padding barefoot down the far end of a corridor, sweeping the steps, or sorting laundry through the open door of one of the rooms. I smiled at one of them, and he inclined his head politely, but I didn't know how to speak to him.

Back at our bungalow, a young Indian man in army uniform was folding the clothes I'd changed out of earlier. I was embarrassed and wanted to tell him not to bother, but stopped myself, aware this might sound like a rebuke. He turned as I entered, and salaamed, and I was struck by his large amber eyes, cat-like beneath long lashes.

It was Jameel, Charles's batman and our bearer. Charles had referred to him several times in his letters, but was this his surname or Christian name? ('He's a Mohammedan, darling,' Charles corrected me later, typically managing to be both authoritative and unenlightening). I noticed that he'd brought me a tray of food from the hotel kitchen, unappetising in the heat: some sliced meat and over-boiled vegetables, a glass of orange squash, and a bowl of rice pudding with a dot of jam.

'Thank you,' I said. He didn't speak, but seemed to be waiting for me to say something else, so I introduced myself, unnecessarily, and asked him a few questions: what could I do with my laundry, was there somewhere I could keep the things I'd unpacked?

He spoke good English, but I found him hard to understand. His answer to every question was 'Yes, of course, memsahib,' or sometimes a strange sideways tilting of his head from side to side, which confused me. I moved towards him as he talked, in an attempt to follow him better, but he took a step back, as if he were uncomfortable standing too close to me.

'Will there be anything else?' he said.

'Do you know what time my husband will be returning?' It felt odd to be asking him, perhaps because of the tacit acknowledgement that he knew my husband's routine so much better than I did, but he apparently accepted it as normal. I thanked him again – it felt as if I'd thanked him too many times – and he moved silently from the room.

Later on, Charles arrived, and informed me that we would be having drinks and dinner at 'the Club', which was nearby. While he changed, I applied lipstick and a dab of scent. I watched us both as if from a distance. It was all so normal – a husband and wife going out to dinner together – and yet so new and unfamiliar, so theatrical, that I felt a hysterical giggle building up inside me. I felt as if I were still travelling, still waiting to arrive.

The Club was an old building, with wood-panelled rooms, leather sofas, and an institutional feel. It had a well-stocked bar, and a beautiful garden, shaded with neem trees and japonica. In the golden evening light, the red and scarlet leaves and blossoms –

poinsettia, bougainvillea, and cherry flower – made the borders look as if they were on fire.

Charles fetched me a gin and tonic, and introduced me to hordes of young men, with confusing pet-names and nicknames, and even more confusing job titles – Deputy Assistant Director of Local Purchase, Assistant Deputy District Superintendent – invariably abbreviated to a machine-gun volley of initials. A few of them also had their wives with them. There was a small group of older people seated in one corner, surveying the room with an air of frosty disapproval, bending their heads together from time to time to share some muttered confidence.

'This is Edwina,' Charles said, 'Bunny's wife, you remember.' He guided me towards a big-boned, blonde woman, of about my own age. 'She's terribly good at tennis, so perhaps we should organise a game of doubles? Edwina, this is my wife Helene.'

'At last!' Edwina exclaimed. 'My dear, you don't know how he's been boring us, counting down the days to your arrival. I hope the crossing wasn't too uncomfortable? I hear they pack you in like sardines at the moment.'

I did my best to be charming with the men and reassuring with the women, complaining about the journey and exclaiming about the heat. As on the boat, compared with London, the young people seemed strangely middle-aged, and the middle-aged seemed ancient: tough, tanned and belligerent. I could see a curiosity in their eyes, a slight question mark in their curved eyebrows, and felt a note of entreaty creep into my own patter: don't be nervous, I'm just like you, really I am. From a few feet away, Charles looked over at me, and smiled approvingly.

We ate curried chicken and rice, followed by fruit salad, and rejoined Edwina and Bunny for more drinks. I listened to Edwina rattle off the concerns of her life, under the guise of friendly advice to a newcomer. Her main interest was in the opportunities for sport and organised games, followed by the trials of home-making in the climate, the servants (who were like wilful children, apparently) and the dogs and horses (who were like honorary English).

She asked a cautious question about where I grew up. 'How fascinating,' she said, a sort of distant pity in her voice, and I doubt if she'd ever even heard of Austria. She was from a very pukka army family herself, I gathered, and her father had also served in India for most of his life, 'although I have relatives in

94

Suffolk and an aunt in Bournemouth,' she said.

I tried to make small talk about the Allied victory in Europe, and the general election coming up in England, but was astonished by how uninterested she seemed. The war for her was of course the war in the East, which was still far from over. The news here was all of Mandalay and Rangoon, instead of the Rhine and Berlin. Europe – which was only really England for Edwina – existed as a kind of mythical hinterland, rather than a place in which real events took place. Her England was frozen somewhere between the wars, a place of schooling and one day, retirement, and a symbol of all that was dear and unchanging.

Edwina reminded me of girls I'd known at school, and in some ways this made me warm to her. She was rather overbearing, completely lacking in self-awareness, straightforward in her assumption of complicity, and certain that I would share her preoccupations, because these were the only preoccupations there were. Yet I knew, and she knew too, that we would never be close. I felt apologetic about it, because Charles clearly wanted us to be friends – she was exactly the kind of woman, I suspected in my darker moments, that he ought really to have married – but I could tell that there'd always be a nagging shade of doubt in the back of her mind. She'd never really trust me, although she might not admit this to herself, or analyse why.

Charles and I walked back to our bungalow, arm in arm, beneath a swollen moon. Charles seemed happy, pleased with the way I'd been received, and perhaps also a little tight. I braced myself, expecting him to make some kind of a move, but nothing came. In private, as in public, he was affectionate and protective, and we behaved as courteous, rather formal acquaintances.

'I'm glad you made it out,' he said, as we lay in bed, after taking turns to use the bathroom. 'It's not good for a chap to be out here alone too long. I've seen it in some of the others.'

'I'm glad, too,' I said. Now, surely, I thought, and lay very still, and tense, and thought that perhaps I would almost welcome it, as a release of the awkwardness between us, if it weren't for the risk of conceiving another child. He was Lottie's father, after all, and I belonged to him: through her, he'd colonised me. He didn't reach over to me, however, and after a while I relaxed.

I was still very tired, and my mind started to drift. I thought of my father, who was a great admirer of the British Empire, and wondered what he would say if he knew where I was, and if my mother had had any news. I thought of baby Lottie, too. I couldn't imagine her out there, and so I thought that maybe Charles had been right. Last of all, lying next to my husband, listening to his breathing, I thought of Bobby, and wondered where he was, and if he was alone.

Susie

That evening, Cathy came round again, and we had a barbecue. My grandmother had changed her clothes for dinner, and the smell of her perfume followed her into the garden. She was a bit like royalty – most of the time we more or less ignored her, but her presence added a sense of occasion, and marked the formal start of proceedings.

Mum and Granny did their usual little dance of excessive politeness around each other. I knew that they'd had a difficult relationship in the past, and they seemed rather scared of each other, as if there were an unexploded bomb between them, that they had to pass delicately back and forth. 'Where would you like to sit, Mummy?'

'However you like, my dear.'

'No, really, Mummy, what would *you* like?'

It was like this about every little thing, and then they'd both snap at the same moment, confessing their different preferences, leaving an irreconcilable gulf, and a distinct whiff of resentment. 'Well, if no one objects, I think I'll just sit here,' my grandmother said.

'Yes, you just do that, Helene,' Steve said, with a conspiratorial smile at my mother.

'Isn't this lovely?' my grandmother said. 'Look at all that blossom.' Drifts of it lay over the grass, and you just had to touch a branch for more of the stuff to come floating down, like dandruff.

'The plants are confused by the weather,' I said. 'Apparently everything's happening earlier this year.'

'And isn't it a warm spring?'

'It certainly is a warm spring, Granny.'

We settled down to eat. I felt as if we were trying to duck the worst Sunday evening angst imaginable. 'We're going to have a really good summer,' Steve said, taking a swig of beer. This had become their battle cry.

'What do you want to do?' Cathy asked.

'It might help if I had some burning ambition,' Mum said. 'But I can't think of one, in particular. It would be nice to go back to Roussillon. Maybe watch a bit of the tennis. I wouldn't mind ...' she tailed off. Then she closed her eyes.

'Are you OK?' we all said at once, and Steve took a couple of steps towards her.

'Yes, yes,' she said.

'I'll bet she wouldn't mind getting better,' Gus said, angrily. He put his wine glass down on the grass and went back inside.

I dropped the lamb chop I was eating. It was covered in dirt, and I burst into tears. I couldn't believe how quickly we were all talking, in code or more openly, about her death. Mum put her hand out to me. 'Oh darling, I'm sorry,' she said.

I looked anxiously over at my grandmother, but she seemed oblivious to us, straight-backed on a plastic chair, wiping her fingers on a serviette. Increasingly, she seemed like someone on her best behaviour. She was more relaxed at her home, in her element, with her little rituals – a bowl of salted peanuts with her first gin and tonic, in front of the evening news, telling stories about each of her possessions, the beaten metal bowl from Tunisia, the red plastic lamp from Santa Monica.

'This bulgar salad reminds me of a dish they used to serve in North Africa,' she said. 'What was it called? Do you remember, Vera?'

We stared at her blankly. I felt afraid that I might laugh. She was like a child, absorbing the conversation only when it related to her, or a subject she felt comfortable with, increasingly bewildered if forced onto unfamiliar ground. It made me anxious for her, with an embarrassment that felt closely related to fear.

'Tabbouleh?' my mum supplied.

'What are these yellow bits?' she sounded very concerned.

'Pepper.'

'Tabbouleh, that's right, it was rather like this.'

'Yes, Mummy, that's what it's meant to be,' Mum said.

'You can't see your cunt – do you miss it?' a student said to me at a university drinks party. She was plump, with a reddish face, and like me, she seemed to dare herself to swear, screwing up her face as she did so. I felt sorry for her – she seemed like a nice girl, doing her best to abide by the strange new etiquette, which so easily confused shock-tactics with wit – so I mumbled that I hadn't seen much of it lately, but hoped it would come in useful at the birth.

She laughed. 'We've all been really curious about seeing Gregor's missus,' she said.

The room was very warm, full of polished wood and geometric wall hangings. I was beginning to regret having turned down the offer of a chair. Through the crowd, I could see Gregor, talking to a beautiful woman. I noticed her slender figure, enviously – she wore a close-fitting, ribbed top, and had ash blonde streaks in her long hair. Gregor leaned forward, solicitously, to light her cigarette, and she tilted her head back to draw on it, laughing at something he'd said. Then she started talking animatedly, moving her hands in the air as she spoke.

I was having trouble settling into my new role as a faculty wife. The snootiness of Gregor's colleagues bothered me. I felt they looked straight through me, so involved with the academic hierarchy that they felt this was the only measure of human worth. The students also dismissed me, as a rule, as if my bump were a badge of conformity to some 'straight' or 'establishment' agenda, which meant I couldn't have an opinion worth listening to. I wondered if being pregnant was a bit like being famous: superficially, I drew their eyes, and there was a ready-made starting point for conversation, but there was also this big thing between us that we couldn't seem to get beyond.

The university buildings were new, and striking, like a red-brick spaceship, which had landed in the dazzling green countryside. Most of the people around were quite young, flamboyant and self-consciously eccentric, lolling on the grass banks or floating around the campus in kaftans, capes or crushed velvet, like a cloud of enormous butterflies. It seemed rather unreal to me, like some hippie vision of the future. Perhaps because I had no place in all of it, they seemed incredibly self-important, certain that they were creating a brave new world. At least you walked out of the London colleges into a bustling city, and in Oxford, the ancient buildings kept us in our place, by giving us a sense of context: their isolation allowed them to spiral off, it seemed to me, into increasingly irrelevant orbits of their own.

Slogans were big that year – daubed on to walls, or spray-painted onto bed sheets, and hung out of windows. The humanities students that Gregor taught came up with things like 'Down with the Pedagogic Gerontocracy' and debated whether students were the vanguard of the revolution (much concern was expressed about how to reach out to 'the workers', in the event that one of the muscular, cloth-capped heroes they conjured with such reverence should find themselves on campus). They did things like collecting white bicycles for the Vietnamese ('surely that's the one thing they have enough of?' I said to Gregor, who explained, with exaggerated patience, the symbolism, and the importance of gestures of solidarity). The arts students, in contrast, had slogans like 'Storm the Reality Studio and Retake the Universe' and looser discussions (about really experiencing the existence of the wallpaper, seeing the world in a grain of sand, or why no one had thought of inventing a balloon that, like, went down instead of up). I had no letters after my name, and my inner journey was of a different sort: I felt very out of place.

I had tried to explain all this to Gregor, and he suggested ways I could get involved. He was helping produce a radical campus magazine, called *Reds Under the Bed*, inspired by the underground publications – with such innovative typesetting and design that they were virtually unreadable – which cluttered up our downstairs loo. I did my bit for a while, with the Cow Gum and letraset, while he bashed out belligerent editorials on his typewriter upstairs. I even sold copies in town (people asked why they should pay, since it said 'for a free press' on the masthead, and sometimes got offended by the explicit cartoon on the back). There were still benefits to promote and good causes to support, just as there had been in London, and I still felt deeply about many of the issues. Gregor loved it all, and was very good at it, but suddenly, perhaps after listening to Sheila, just being his little helper seemed a lot less appealing.

'Of course, Gregor's a bit of a heart-throb, as you can imagine,' the red-faced girl was saying. 'I mean, if you go for that smoul-

99

dering Scot thing, and I'd guess you obviously do. He's got all that lecturer shit going on, but he's not hung up on status, you know, he's young, and radical, and kind of cool, and he gets where we're coming from. He puts the sex into Sussex, we like to say.'

I wasn't quite sure how to respond to this. 'Thank you,' I murmured. I wanted to tell her to relax, and to reassure her she didn't have to try so hard with me. It would have seemed rude, however, or patronising, to try. I knew enough of the different masks worn at parties, and the different reactions they provoke, to feel it was all a charade – this wife mask, the latest, it's not me, I wanted to say to her, just as that's not you: don't tie yourself in knots just because of their laziness. Instead, I waved across the room at Gregor, who pretended not to see.

'Some people can be a bit catty round here, but a lot of them are just sexually frustrated, in my view,' the girl was saying. 'They just need a good fuck, probably. But I think he's cool.'

'What do you mean?' I said.

She blushed even redder, and shrugged. 'Oh, you know ...'

'Not really.'

'Only just that I try not to go with the crowd. Listen to the idiots gossiping and shit.'

I waved again at Gregor, and the woman he was with pointed this out to him. He came over. 'Everything OK?' he said. I told him I wanted to leave.

'Who were you talking to, all that time?' I asked, in the car back. I had to raise my voice over the noise of the engine. I was looking for an outlet for the unfocused panic buzzing around my head, like a trapped fly.

'I talked to a lot of people.'

'The blonde. She's very pretty.' I could tell he knew who I meant.

'I suppose you mean Daphne,' he said grumpily. I did feel sorry for him sometimes, in a remote kind of way – there was something about having a pregnant wife that seemed to put him permanently in the wrong. 'She's a PhD student. She's having a bit of trouble with her first chapter,' he said.

'I'll bet she is. Are you her supervisor?' I wondered why she'd never been mentioned. I didn't like the way I sounded: shrill and snide.

'No, Derek is,' Gregor said. There was a pause, as he shifted

100

gear, and the engine hummed in a different key, as the little car tilted down the hill, its soft roof battered by the wind like tent canvas in a storm. 'What's wrong with you, anyway?'

I tried to be honest. 'I don't feel like myself any more. I feel as if you're all making me into someone I don't want to be.'

'What on earth do you mean?'

'I don't know. It's very clever. You people hold all the cards, and then you act so innocent and "what me?" It's all about sins of omission,' I said, darkly.

'The rest of the world?' he said, gently. 'Can't you see how irrational that is?' I was silent. Perhaps he was right, I thought. Perhaps I was being irritable, egotistical, selfish, and impossible to please. Perhaps it was my fault I didn't fit in.

'Look, how about if I drop you home and head back for a bit? You get so tired these days. I won't be much longer, but there are a couple more people I want to talk to.'

'Fine, fine, go,' I said, but I really didn't mean it. Back home, I went to bed, and dreamed I gave birth to an angora rabbit, which I was still expected to breast feed.

Susie

I was cleaning my plate with a piece of bread. 'How do you imagine the cancer?' I asked.

'I don't really hold with all that visualisation stuff,' Mum said. She wasn't eating much, just chain-smoking. 'Darling Lottie, with her voodoo and healing stones. It's rather like these people who keep urging me to fight it. When people say all the time that your attitude is so important, it's as if they're implying that the cancer is some kind of character defect. It's a disease, *mon Dieu*.' For the first time, she sounded as if she might be angry. 'It makes you feel so guilty, as if you got it through personal weakness, or impure thoughts.'

'No one thinks that,' Cathy said. 'No one sensible, anyway.'

'Oh, you'd be surprised. I think that on some level, they really do. People talk such superstitious nonsense. I mean, I'm post-enlightenment, I suppose, in the sense that I know that reason alone is not enough. You need emotion, will-power and what have you as well. But reason has to be the basis. Otherwise we're buggered.'

She drew on her cigarette. 'Like that picture, is it by Goya? "The sleep of reason breeds monsters".'

'But we can still hope for a rational, medical cure,' Steve said. He'd left the barbecue to die down, glowing red and ashy-white in the dusk, and balanced a plate on his ample stomach. 'Can't we? Man, you're a hard woman,' he didn't seem to be joking. 'Can't we at least have that?'

'I don't want to get like one of those AIDS patients you hear about,' Mum said, 'getting excited about every new drug. But yes, reason and optimism. That's the key.'

Lights were beginning to come on in the houses around us. The garden was quite overlooked, and I liked that – there was something magical about the long shadows, and the contrast between our own leafy patch and the irregular rooftops, the balconies of the neighbours, and the fire escapes of the flats behind. I could still remember how the garden had seemed to me as a child. The scale had been all different, and the place had crawled with dramatic possibilities, from the jungly areas by the wall, to the tree in which I'd sat for many hours, legs dangling, or the forsythia bush under which our cat, Leon, had been buried. Cathy's son Will and I had covered each other in paint out here, one sunny afternoon, and the little boy two doors down had been told off for fibbing, when he claimed he'd seen us from the window, leaping around stark naked and bright blue.

'That's not what I meant,' I said, quietly, 'about how it looks. I was just curious. I think of it as black and bubbly, a sort of evil goo.'

'Oh, I see what you mean,' Mum said. 'I suppose I think of it as light brown.' She blew smoke into the evening sky. 'Cigarette coloured, perhaps. Like a nicotine stain.'

It was easy to forget my grandmother, sitting in the half-light. 'Everything OK, there, Helene?' Steve asked. We turned to her, guiltily.

'Are you worrying about me?' She echoed his tone of exaggerated concern so exactly that I suspected for a moment – as I often did – that she was in fact the one patronising us. 'You really needn't. I have everything I need, thank you,' she said.

In the bright kitchen, later, she asked if she couldn't help with something. Steve was upstairs, putting Mum to bed, counting out the pills for her, and Gus was just getting ready to go out. If it hadn't been for my grandmother I might have left the dishes until the morning, but as it was, I started to stack the dishwasher.

'Please, sit down Granny,' I said. I could understand her wanting a job, but I couldn't think of anything suitable. 'You can keep me company if you like. Are you sure you wouldn't like anything else?'

'Do you think you might join me for a little night cap?' she said, in her twinkly, 'forgive an old woman' way. Gus used to joke that she had gin and tonic running through her veins – she'd picked up a taste for it in India – but she was also fond of Schnapps, and I found her a bottle in the kitchen cupboard, untouched since her last visit.

I wondered if I should check she understood about Mum's illness – the possibility I might have to explain it scared me. She got there first, however.

'Do you think they really know what they're talking about, these doctors?'

'I'm afraid so, Granny,' I said.

'And do they have any idea why? It's such a dreadful disease.'

'I don't think so.'

She pursed her lips. 'I suppose one always wants to find a reason.' She probably knew more about death than any of us, I reminded myself, and yet there was this dreadful vulnerability about her.

I explained to her about the tape recording I wanted to make, and asked her if she'd answer some questions. I was worried she might be offended, or horrified, but she actually seemed quite flattered.

'Yes, certainly my dear,' she said.

So after I'd wiped down the sideboard, I poured myself a glass, and sat down with her at the kitchen table, with the Dictaphone between us.

'Now, where shall we start?' she said, and it was extraordinary, just like turning on a tap.

Helene

It was my first real chance to step out from my mother's rather large shadow. Although I had first travelled to England alone, then

I was still only in my teens, and she'd followed me over soon afterwards. For all of my adult life so far we'd lived together, brought closer by our abrupt displacement and our separation from the rest of the family. In India, I might have had the chance to become an authority in my own right, a married woman. It was ironic, therefore, that I'd never felt more powerless, and that circumstances, as well as those around me, seemed to conspire to keep me child-like.

First of all, there was my state of utter ignorance. I had no idea about my new environment, and felt helpless and dependent in every respect. The abrupt narrowing of perspective reminded me of early childhood. At first, I was aware only of my immediate surroundings – the bungalow, the hotel – like a tiny dot of light, surrounded by the dark and frightening unknown outside the compound wall. Gradually my consciousness enlarged to take in the road outside, the Club, the bazaar, the white wooden church we attended on Sundays, and a few other parts of the town, and with each widening, I could laugh at my former fears, and was startled by how limited my horizons had been. It was exhausting, however, this process of discovery, and I sometimes wearied of it all, and longed for a country in which I could imagine what was round the corner, without having to see it for myself. It was hard for me to go out alone, since beggars or curious onlookers would quickly surround me, and besides, Charles was not at all keen to have me wander around without a chaperone.

I had always been good at picking up new languages, but for the first time, I found myself without familiar reference points, and utterly at sea. So many of the words the English dropped casually into their conversation confused me; the way they issued instructions, in a confident appropriation of the local tongues, seemed key to their authority, and something I could never master. They used the most bizarre Anglicised versions of Indian words, as a sort of in-joke (Edwina, for instance, referred to a bath as a 'gussley-wussley', a baby-word from her childhood). Hindi sounded to me like a jangling bag of consonants, 'j's and 'l's and 'b's hitched together in long, unpronounceable hybrids, Urdu a mumbling mulch of vowel sounds and upward inflections, sprinkled with 'ch' like a fit of the sneezes. Even the body language was different, and unreadable. Charles had been studying the local languages for some time, and had a considerable head-start over me in this respect. I found myself as politely perplexed as the Indians I attempted to communicate with. I stumbled and hesitated and mixed up the simplest of words.

I soon discovered that I had almost no responsibilities. At first we had the idea that we would move out of the hotel and find a place of our own, but there was a shortage of suitable accommodation, and we had little experience of housekeeping, so it became clear that by far the most practical option was to stay where we were. Jameel had the domestic arrangements, such as they were, well in hand. Over the first few days, I tried to take an interest, but he answered my questions ('yes, of course, memsahib') with an utter subservience that nonetheless made me feel intrusive, and moved about his work with such quiet efficiency that I was often startled to find him in the room. Charles and Jameel both spoke to me in a similar way, I noticed: polite, smiling, placating, and rather distracted, as you might soothe an awkward child. I quickly decided that it was easier just not to bother.

There was not much to be done, anyway: in England, the complaint of every upper-class woman had been the impossibility of finding domestic help since the start of the war, but here, everything was taken care of. Besides Jameel there was a bathroom wallah and a dhobi who came for the laundry. After the shortages I'd grown used to in London, food and other small luxuries seemed plentiful, if a little repetitive, for those like us, who could afford them. We ate in the hotel dining-room, which served a hybrid Anglo-Indian cuisine ('roast lamb', for instance, was tough-as-boots mutton, if not goat, with a mint sauce) and at the Club, which usually served some sort of curry.

Despite the fact that we spent nearly every evening there, I never really felt part of things at the Club. In India, it gradually dawned on me that my assumption had been wrong – just by marrying Charles, I could not enter into his world, and my relationship with him would never be the sum total of my identity. I often heard people complain that standards were falling, the place was becoming more like an Officers' Mess, and all kinds of strange people were being let in. There was never anything very obvious, and sometimes I thought that Charles was right, and that I shouldn't be so sensitive. Edwina smiled and waved at me, and introduced me to her friends, but afterwards, I sometimes imagined I saw her explaining ('a refugee from Europe', mouthing a word, half swallowing it, with an exaggerated chewing movement, as if it were not quite done to speak it aloud – and I once thought I heard a ginger-haired Colonel exclaim 'a Jewess! How extraordinary!'). Edwina did not invite me to join her tea parties and tennis matches. I mirrored her patronising condescension with a patronising condescension of my own, modelled perhaps on my mother's dignity and immense, unshakable self-belief. I didn't have much to say to them, and they didn't have much to say to me.

I did make one friend: a young Polish woman called Maria who was staying in a neighbouring bungalow. She was as much a fish out of water as I was. She had been interned by the Russians when they occupied Eastern Poland, and then, when Russia recognised the Polish government in exile, she had been released to travel to Tehran to join the Army of General Anders. In Tehran she met and married an Englishman, who had later been posted to India, which is how she wound up in Donaldson's Hotel. We spent many hours together while our husbands were at work. We would share a small quantity of gin, and we'd sit in one of our rooms, beneath the rotating fan, and tipple a bit, and chat. She was getting on very well with her husband. Just seeing them together, and the way they couldn't stop touching each other, made me uneasy.

Charles worked as an honorary magistrate in the Law Courts (or 'Kuchery') in town. Every morning he set off on his bicycle. He had no legal training, and – despite his efforts – wasn't even fluent in the local languages, but he had a clerk, an Indian whom everyone referred to as 'Babu', who prepared all the cases and gave him guidance. I visited a few times, because Charles thought it might be entertaining for me, and I had nothing else to do. One of the cases was quite horrific: a man and his wife had beaten his elderly mother to death because she wouldn't give up a grindstone and a bronze dish which they said belonged to them. Charles sat at a high desk, and heard the case before him, and then the Babu would whisper in his ear, or pass him a slip of paper, and Charles read out his judgement. He had an office, painted reddish brown up to shoulder height, in which every surface was stacked with manila files. He always picked up the telephone to speak to the Babu, even though he was only in the next room.

I waited, with some curiosity, to see if marital relations would resume. For the first two weeks Charles barely touched me, and my initial relief merged with an obscure guilt, a sense that I was falling short in my duties, and failing to be a real wife. Perhaps he

106

could sense my reluctance, or was gallantly holding back because he knew I didn't want another child? Perhaps he didn't want me, or regretted having married me?

When he did make a move, however, it shocked me, and seemed to come completely out of the blue. One night, after an evening of heavy drinking at the Club, he reached over to me in bed, beneath the mosquito net. Finding his way through the confusion of my nightdress, he gave my back and buttocks a silent, fumbling caress, and then lifted himself abruptly onto me, and made a few undirected, quite painful, almost angry jabs, followed by a suppressed groan. There was a moment of silence, while he lay on me, as if we were both a little startled by finding ourselves in this unexpected position, and then he rolled off and turned away.

'Charles?' I said. He lay frozen beside me. I thought I could feel some deep blackness radiate from him: an immense sadness, a huge shame, which seemed to fill the room and leak out into the sticky night.

'What's wrong?' I said.

Again he didn't speak. 'Charles, darling?' I said. A mosquito whined in my ear.

'I'm sorry,' he said, and his voice sounded distorted. We only had intercourse a handful of times in our entire marriage, and each time, he apologised immediately afterwards. 'Let's sleep.'

In the bathroom, I washed myself, standing upright because I had heard that this made conception less likely, with tears sliding silently down my face. I was angry with myself, and my apparent need to be wooed, courted, or seduced. How silly and girlish, I told myself! His behaviour confused me, and frustrated my instinctive need to communicate. It had been so sudden, and dismissive, somehow, like being sneezed on, or spat on. It was as if I were the outlet for some unspeakable urge, which he was unable to acknowledge in words. I felt used, and disappointed. Is this all there is, then, I wondered? It was hardly the great consummation or the sublime act of love which I'd heard described.

I lived for letters. My mother's arrived on thin paper, after a frustrating time lag, and the very sight of the writing on the envelope made my heart leap with fear and anticipation. Despite my eagerness, they were always unsatisfying. She wrote bland, straightforward reports of baby Lottie, and of her unsuccessful attempts to gain news of my father and brother through mutual friends or the Red Cross. I dreaded news from Austria, partly on my mother's behalf, because she had always remained so resolutely optimistic, over the years of silence. Instead, ashamed of my self-ishness, I was hungry for more detail on Lottie – what exactly she ate, how exactly she slept, what she did and how she looked when she did it. Although my mother answered as literally and thoroughly as she could, her descriptions merely served to fuel my appetite.

I didn't write to Bobby, but he was also in my head a good deal. The boat journey seemed so distinct that it was almost as if it had happened to someone else, like a book I'd read, or a film I'd seen. I replayed moments of it, and imagined acting differently, telling him my thoughts and feelings with a fluency I could never have managed in real life. I imagined him taking me into his arms, and kissing me. I indulged in fantasies about alternative realities, substituting him for Charles in our daily life. Perhaps he was my one chance at happiness, gone forever, I sometimes thought: perhaps, because of bad timing, I'd ruined my life.

I missed baby Lottie desperately. I saw babies and young children everywhere. Dark urchins dressed only in a filthy shirt, or scrap of cloth; toddlers with their legs clasping their mothers' strong hips so that their cloven behinds looked as if they had budded from the women's bodies; tiny infants being suckled beneath the folds of the Muslim ladies' 'walking tents' as they journeyed to the bazaar. Children came with their ayahs to play in the hotel garden, which had a swing and see-saw. I watched their games, as they failed to fly a kite in the non-existent wind, or built dung fires to cook little bits of coloured rice in earthen pots. I smiled, and tried to guess their age, and to conceal the mixture of pain and fascination they caused in me. 'Just like mine,' I sometimes said, choked with a bizarre urge to confess something. I wanted the little ones to smile back, to open their hands in benediction, but whether they did, or turned away in fear, either way it was a kind of torture for me.

Chapter Five

Susie

Feeling drained by the heat, I stood up out of the bath, and stepped on to the mat, staining the towelling a shade darker with my wet feet. I wrapped an old bath towel – washed and dried, over the years, to a comforting cardboard roughness – around my pink, shining skin.

The waiting was the worst thing. I'd heard people say that before, but I'd never really understood what they meant. The days felt endless, containing such extremes of topography – huge swings of emotion, great waves of feeling, slow journeys from hope to despair and back again. It stretched you, like an elastic band, until you were about to snap, and then it stretched you some more. Some days felt so long that I couldn't think about time in them, but just lived from one cup of tea to the next.

I dried myself half-heartedly, and then leaned forwards, reaching over the colony of Body Shop bottles and the mug of toothbrushes, to wipe a stripe of steam from the mirror. I peered at my face through the mist, scanning for imperfections, not really seeing a person, caressing with my fingers – tracing my eyebrows, smoothing skin, squeezing a blackhead at the base of my nose. The familiar sight of my own features soothed me, sending me into a vacant, almost mesmerised state.

I stepped back to comb my hair, and tried to see myself as others might. Who did I really look like, I wondered? Mum's eyes and hair, of course, something of Dad in my nose, not much that I could see of any of my grandparents. And what did it really add up to? How much choice did I have in how I stood, how I spoke, the way I laughed, lost my temper, made love, thought, lived? Was there a great-grandmother, or a great-aunt, separated by centuries, who had my face, or who made my mistakes? Was it me, or them, stamped into my genes?

The steam on the mirror was condensing into droplets of moisture, and in the reflection, I caught sight of Mum's stripy cotton dressing gown, hanging on the door behind me. For a moment, it was as if she were standing there. My heart lurched. I made myself turn round, to look at it, and see that it was just an empty piece of cloth.

When I was little, I was afraid of that mirror. I was as superstitious as most young children – I was reminded of that time by the kind of magical thinking I'd found myself drawn to since Mum's diagnosis. A monster had lived in the mirror, and the only way it could get out was if I looked at it (there was another monster that could get out of the toilet if I didn't get to the bottom of the stairs before the end of the flush). Later on, as a teenager, I'd spent many hours staring into it, making minor adjustments to my hair or applying and then removing make-up obsessively, and it had become the focal point for my feelings of helpless self-loathing. By then, the monster it contained was me.

Things had seemed to get more complicated all at once, just after I turned thirteen. I felt too big, bashing into things and tripping over my own limbs. The kids at school thought I was posh, or a wally, or something, and despite the fact that my friend Karen and I had our own thing going, collecting small scented erasers, and decorating our books with shiny stickers from Paperchase, I was beginning to care quite badly what other people thought. The house had felt strange and claustrophobic ever since Steve had moved in – he made fun of me for spending too long in the bathroom, and practising 'Bright Eyes' endlessly on my French horn – and it was particularly crowded that month, because my grandmother had come to stay. Mum was busy, enjoying her job, elated by her new relationship, and very involved in the peace movement, driving to Greenham Common at weekends with Cathy, to 'embrace the base' or 'join hands for freedom'.

One Saturday, she and I went out shopping together. I wore my ra-ra skirt and spangly leg warmers, preoccupied with the possibility of running into one of my classmates from school, and semaphoring unsuspected levels of cool, weekend behaviour. I

110

skipped alongside Mum (who let the side down, rather, I felt, in her knitted cap and cagoule), past the shop windows full of mannequins, ambushed around every corner by our reflections on the glass. I was pestering her about how I wanted to have my ears pierced. It seemed to me that this would open up a whole new category of small shiny things to collect, and besides, I could imagine the gasps of respect, at school, when I casually swung back my hair, and revealed that I'd become someone different, like Olivia Newton-John at the end of *Grease*.

Just after we passed Chelsea Girl, I noticed a man, in a fawn jacket, standing still on the opposite pavement and staring. He looked almost angry – his eyes burned into me – and, although I'd never experienced it before, I instinctively recognised his look of unconcealed lust. I stopped, and looked back at him, then looked away again, feeling grown-up and powerful, but intimidated and embarrassed all at once, and knowing that it was crucial not to show it. I'd wanted attention, but this wasn't quite what I'd had in mind. I looked at Mum, to see if she'd noticed, half expecting her to stomp over and berate him, but she didn't. 'Well, I suppose that's it, now. I might as well be invisible,' was all she said, as if to herself.

Back at home, she came up behind me, as I stood in front of the bathroom mirror, wondering if the ra-ra skirt was actually a bit too short. 'As a young woman, you're subjected to a lot of pressures,' she said. 'The onset of menstruation will change your role in society, and you are being bombarded with images of the feminine ideal as something submissive, emaciated, and often as not chained with jewellery. It's clearly very confusing, but you have to remain strong. Self-mutilation might seem like an appealing idea to you at the moment. Just remember that female genital disfigurement is considered attractive in some cultures.'

It was so typical of her, I thought, to start ranting about something disgusting when all I wanted was to have my ears pierced. She brushed a strand of hair out of my eyes with her hand, and tucked it behind my ear, with a proprietorial caress, and I tried to duck away, too late. 'Your earlobes are perfect,' she insisted, urgently. 'You're beautiful just as you are, remember that. The way you were born.'

'Yes,' I said. 'Like sweaty armpits smell beautiful. Like hairy legs are fine and natural. Like yellow cigarette-stained fangs are lovely. Like having a huge fat bum is great.'

She was silent for a moment, and I felt a sudden qualm, wondering if I'd gone too far. 'Fine,' she said, quietly, but I could tell she was annoyed. 'Do whatever the hell you like.' She closed the bathroom door behind her.

So I went with Karen to a little room over a shop, and came back smelling of surgical spirit, with small silver studs in my ears, feeling sick and wobbly with apprehension, but also elated and giggly, and then surprisingly tearful. With freaky symbolism, on my return home, I noticed a smear of brownish blood in my knickers, my body seeming to conspire with Mum's bizarre theories. She had been going on for years about how I was about to 'become a woman', dropping dark hints at every opportunity (mood swings, headaches, even nose bleeds were solemnly greeted as portents, to the extent where I became scared to complain of almost any ailment). I could hardly bear to tell her: I was scared she'd make a huge, embarrassing fuss. Perhaps I also wanted to punish her, in some way.

So the first person I told was my grandmother. 'I've got my period, Granny,' I said. I suppose I expected – taking my cue from Mum's enthusiasm for the subject – that she'd offer congratulations, or that confiding in her would make us closer. Instead there was an awkward pause, and I wondered if she'd even heard me. 'It's my first one,' I added.

'Oh, really,' she said, and I blushed, as she moved from the room.

So I was left with no choice but to tell Mum. Thankfully, she didn't talk about the moon, and was more matter of fact than I'd expected. She gave me a packet of sanitary towels and told me how to use them. I returned from the toilet feeling grown-up, with my secret – so this is how life goes on, and it's possible to walk around, and do things, and no one even knows.

'My poor lamb,' Mum said, and told me about how the nuns at her school had never referred to it directly, and how she'd used a rag. 'As for the ears,' she said, 'well, I suppose it's a timely come-on for the boys. One way of proclaiming your fertility.'

'You are gross,' I said, my relief fuelling my irritation. There was a sort of inevitability about the argument I'd been rehearsing in my head. 'You think you're so understanding and in touch, but actually, you're selfish and disgusting.'

'Yes, yes,' she said. 'A whited sepulchre.'

It seemed to me to be another way of winning the argument, using words I didn't understand. I could feel the power balance between us shifting, and this both disturbed and excited me. 'Whatever. You're a revolting old witch.'

'Thank you.'

'I can't understand why Dad ever married you. You're a heartless cow who never thinks about anyone but herself. I'm out of here, as soon as I get the chance. And I don't care how I grow up, so long as I don't turn out like you.'

Down the corridor, a decade ago, a door slammed. I splashed cold water on my face, and then blotted it with the towel. Moisturiser, eyeliner, concealer; with clumsy, shaking hands, I composed my features into a mask to meet the world, and it made me feel a little stronger. My arm brushed her dressing gown, and I wondered if after all there might not be something infectious on there, and then felt guilty for even thinking it. Malignant, oncology, carcinoma, terminal – the words whispered in my head, multiplying like abnormal cells.

The things that bothered me most were not the ways in which we were different, but the ways in which we were the same. In the glass, behind my eyes, that look, that steely determination, it's her, multiplying inside me. I turned away, and pulled the light off. That mirror still scared me, I realised.

Vera

At Easter, we took what Gregor kept referring to, with doom-laden emphasis, as our last baby-free holiday. I knew that we had to get away. I wasn't clear about why: if you'd asked, I'd probably have said something vague about having time to 'find each other again'. I think I half knew already – afterwards, it shocked me that I could have suppressed the knowledge so effectively. I was a little mad, around then, whether this was cause or effect of the mental gymnastics I was performing.

We went to visit some old friends, Lucas and Ginny, who had moved to the South of France, with their wild, almost feral toddler, and a shifting constellation of other house guests and hangers-on. The weather was beautiful – hot by day, cool and clear at night –

and to me, it seemed a little like paradise. The miraculous plenty of the markets, the cheese boards and the salad bowls seemed faintly scandalous, in those pre-Waitrose days. Hairy, bare-chested men and head-scarved women sat in the kitchen or round a table outside, drinking wine under the riotously vivid stars. We drove around the rugged countryside, past crumbling huts and peeling posters, the green scrub of the slopes broken, here and there, by the single stroke of a poplar, the poppy-dotted fields unreal to me, like an impressionist painting. In the rear-view mirror, as we rounded the bumpy bends, I saw little villages, with coral-pink and biscuit-coloured houses, clinging to the hillside.

Lucas was one of Gregor's best friends. After several frustrating years in advertising, he had decided to leave England, settling in a village where there were already a few foreign artists, to live very cheaply and paint pictures. Gregor admired him enormously, laughed at all his jokes, and saw everything he did as embodying a courageous disregard of convention. To me, Lucas seemed a bit of a know-it-all, and his unabashed self-confidence made me blush for him. He liked to lecture us on the French names for the birds and trees, as often as not wrong, or horribly pronounced, or his romantic theories about the locals and their customs ('feudal', 'visceral' and 'primitivism' were words he used a lot). There was something undeniably seductive about his personality, however, and the flattering force of his attention. He made charcoal drawings of me lounging in a large wicker chair, emphasising the curves of my belly and breasts, and told me I looked beautiful, and Gregor seemed gratifyingly annoyed, but was unable to object for fear of sounding petit-bourgeois. I didn't particularly like the picture, but found myself participating in the praise just out of a nervousness on his behalf.

In the evenings, I drew my shawl around my shoulders, and watched the insects, dancing with their words: proletariat, intelligentsia, dialectical materialism. Lucas flattered Gregor by treating him as an emissary from the front line of student radicalism, and also spent a lot of time enquiring jokingly about the 'nubiles' in his charge. The loud, English bark of our voices echoed across the hills, undermining our pretensions to peasant life. Because I had studied French, I was the only one of us who could haggle with the stall keepers and joke with the waiters convincingly, and this gave me a new self-confidence, my cheeks tinged pink with the sunshine.

114

Ginny had worked as a photographer's assistant in London in the mid 60s, before ripening into a full-time muse and earth-mother. She took a photograph of me sitting out in the orchard. We spent a lot of time out there together, chopping vegetables or smoking, while her little boy played between the delicate, silvery olive trees, or made toppling towers from the chalky white stones.

I liked Ginny, with her unexpectedly dry sense of humour and cut-glass accent, but she also made me uncomfortable. The idyllic life they led, the unending stream of visitors, seemed like a lot of fun, but there was also, I noticed, an awful lot of washing up to be done, and the chaos, and physical discomforts (a hole in the ground toilet, the ants, the crumbling masonry) would surely get you down after a bit. Ginny's position, so far from home, occasionally seemed a little vulnerable. I suspected that Lucas sometimes slept with his models – he'd been flirtatious enough, even with me ('I confess, dear Vera, I find the sight of a pregnant woman fantastically erotic') – but I was shocked when Ginny herself referred breezily to one of his 'lovers'.

'Don't you mind?' I said.

'He's a very charismatic man,' Ginny said. She was slicing into a silvery onion, and it made her sniff. The vegetables there seemed like an implausible exaggeration of their equivalents at home. 'I always realised he was someone with lots of talent, big passions, and you can't tame a force like that, it would be wrong to try to.' She looked up from the chopping board, straight at me, with streaming eyes, in a way that made me feel suddenly sick. 'Love isn't something that obeys laws or conventions. We have something special, Lucas and I, that goes beyond mere ownership.'

Later, I wondered if Ginny had guessed, because it was on this holiday that Gregor told me, in a moment of weakness, about his own affair. We'd driven to a local beauty spot, a cedar forest, high in the Luberon. We parked in the shade, and walked along dusty chalk tracks, with wild flowers and long grasses in the verges.

I remember feeling pleased to be alone together. For the first time in a long while, we began to talk about our lives in the abstract, almost as if we were another couple; both holidays and views can have a distancing effect. It was a close, rather sticky day, and Gregor was preoccupied with the constipation that always seemed to affect him when we travelled. The trees themselves were a bit of a disappointment – smaller than I'd expected – and Gregor remarked on the pointlessness of the objectives we set ourselves on holiday. 'I always find it a little depressing,' he said. 'We direct all our efforts towards having a good time, chasing the empty dream of personal gratification, and yet pure happiness remains as far out of reach as ever. We kid ourselves that if only we didn't have to work . . . .but I suppose the human condition is such that we're always unsatisfied.'

It irritated me that he used words like 'depressing' and 'unsatisfied', when we were going to have a baby, and everything was about to change forever, but I said nothing. We talked about his career for a while – so long a shared hobby – his frustrations with his colleagues, his doubts about whether he was doing the right thing, his feeling that there was still something missing, aggravated, as usual, by spending time with Lucas. I tried to be encouraging, but I was scared: perhaps I knew we were hovering on some threshold.

I stopped to pee behind a tree, crouching over the scurrying ants and the broken glass and pine cones. Then we carried on. After a while we came to a view, over scrub-covered hills, towards the Mont Saint Victoire.

We sat down on a fallen trunk. 'I'm sorry,' I said, reaching clumsily for the intimacy I knew was lacking, 'If it's been a difficult few months, between us, I mean. I never realised how all-consuming pregnancy would be for me. I suppose it's brought some of my difficulties with my mother back to the surface, as well.' I was surprised to hear myself say this: I hadn't realised, until I did, that it was true.

'It's OK,' Gregor said, 'It's not just you.' First of all, I felt a strange relief – so I wasn't going mad – but then my heart beat faster, as he began to hesitate, and to stumble over his words, like an actor unsure of his part. I was reminded of a conversation I'd had many years before, when I was just fourteen. I half knew already, yet there was still a moment, as he spoke, when the future I'd envisaged swung back like scenery, to reveal dark shadows, behind. The world seemed quite still, waiting for my reaction, and I felt surprisingly calm. The trees spread their bluey green fingers entreatingly, stirring in the breeze with a sound like the sea. Once again, I had the sense of watching myself from a distance, wondering how to respond.

I asked questions: when, who, how, for how long? Gregor tried to answer honestly. I could tell he admired my composure – what a woman – and began to think that it might all be OK after all. He seemed hugely relieved at the chance to articulate the guilt and self-justification that had been echoing inside his head, but his words seemed empty and over-rehearsed. The baby moved inside me, and I remembered the full awfulness of my position, and felt trapped between them. I felt as angry with him for telling me as for anything else, for not allowing me to maintain my charade. I thought of Ginny, and the pity I'd felt for her – other people must feel the same way about me. I felt so humiliated: semblances can be so important.

'I wish it wasn't true,' I said. I felt tired: too weary for the required emotions.

'I couldn't lie to you any more. I've been feeling wretched about this.' He seemed almost to expect me to feel sorry for him, and looking at the misery on his face, the strange thing was that I almost did.

'So you thought you'd make me feel wretched too?'

'I thought you'd want to know. We've always been honest with each other. Sincerity used to be so important to us, do you remember? I used to feel that we could overcome anything, if only we were true to ourselves. Lying to you, I felt as if I was going mad.'

For a moment I struggled for words, unable to comprehend the unfairness of it all. 'Why should I be your Mother Confessor? I've been carrying our child. I've been too sick to move, it's been such an ordeal. And you've been screwing a student. Please. Have you no shame?'

He flinched. 'I know, I know.'

I got up, suddenly, wild eyed. 'What are you doing?' he said.

'I'm going for a walk.'

He followed me along the path, pleading with me, as the light began to fade. 'Look, perhaps we have a choice about how we react to this. Perhaps it doesn't have to be such a terrible big deal, perhaps we can get beyond all the moralistic bollocks we were brought up with. People do, you know.'

'For fuck's sake, Gregor, look at me! Free love is not much of an option for me right now. How can we have an open relationship when I'm like this? And what about your child – have you thought about what all this will mean for him or her? You do pick your moments.'

117

He looked bewildered, waking from a pleasant dream to this scary, grim-faced mad-woman, but unable to retract the fatal words. After a while, I stopped under a tree, my tears coming as the sun finally set, distorting my face with emotion. I felt my features melt into an animal howl of anguish and anger, that seemed to come from somewhere outside of me. There was nothing true, or pure, or beautiful in this life, and any appearance of human closeness was a sham. He wouldn't leave me, though I screamed at him to go. Eventually, I calmed down a little – I couldn't stay there all night – but the act of getting into the car, of letting him drive me, felt unbearable. I seemed to see the whole of our situation already – the banal, frustrating tragedy of it, the dead end we were in.

After that, we had two things that went with us, growing inside of me – the baby, and this new thing, this ugly thing. It was in the thick-walled room in which we slept, finding its way through the shutters every morning with the sunlight; it was in the cool red tiles beneath my bare feet. The landmarks we stopped to look at, in a perfunctory way, the Palais des Papes and the Pont d'Avignon, had been built with it, mixed into the mortar. We tasted it in Ginny's pistou, it smarted on our sun-burned skins. We drove it back in the car with us, in the boot, along with the plastic petrol container of Côtes du Luberon and the cardboard box full of *saucisson* and tinned *cassoulet*.

I was nasty to him, and he took it meekly, his contrition mutating slowly into boredom. 'It won't happen again,' he repeated, on the ferry, before heading off to find the bar.

'We'll see,' I said, turning my back, flinching at the chilly wind, and drawing my coat around my bump.

Susie

We waited for the operation. Every morning, for a week, there was a sign over her bed, NIL BY MOUTH, and we waited for a phone call to say that she had gone into theatre. Every morning, at about eleven, someone rang to say that there were no free beds in intensive care, and they had no alternative but to postpone. It was a strange kind of torture, a bad joke. I felt I no longer knew what was plausible any more.

118

Mum was in torment. One day she was screaming aloud from the itching, and Steve rushed around town, beside himself, trying to buy sheets without starch in them. Mostly she was heavily sedated.

I spent much of my time bobbing around the ward corridor, trying to collar anyone who might have any information, trying not to lose my cool, trying not to be unreasonable. I wondered what Mum would be doing in my place, and telephoned our local MP, and wrote a passionate, carefully worded letter of complaint to the head of the hospital trust. 'Would it help if we had it done privately?' I asked the consultant.

'Do you have insurance?' he asked. The fact that he asked that first filled me with suspicion.

'No, but I expect we could find the money, if it would help.'

'I don't think it would,' he said.

The nurses and the other patients on the ward were full of sympathy. On Friday, they went back to the first plan, and repeated the procedure to drain the bile. This time, it worked. The consultant said that Mum should go home and recover for two weeks before trying again for the big operation. The itching, he said, would gradually subside.

'But won't the cancer grow, in the meantime?' Gus shouted, when I told him. 'Fucking morons. I'd like to torch that place.' He kicked his bike, which was leaning in the hall.

I tried to calm him down. 'They say that it won't make any difference,' I said. 'She can't go on like this.'

'Why are you on their side?' he said. 'You're all over the place, all of you, you keep changing your story.'

'What else can we do?' I said. 'There's nothing else we can do.' I was reminded, suddenly, of Gus as a very little boy, and the tantrums he used to have, flinging himself to the floor in paroxysms of frustration and despair.

'What about a bit of rage?' Gus said. 'She's too young for all this crap.'

'Rage?'

'Rage against the machine. Rage against the dying of the light. Rage against that twat-faced spunk-for-brains *Mr* fucking Thompson.'

'Yes, that would be helpful,' I said, sarcastically.

'At least it would be more honest, more human,' he said. I

recognised the little-boy wobble in his voice. 'At least it would be more fucking alive.'

The glorious weather continued. The beach was crowded with pink-necked people, exposing their white flesh to the sun, and smelled of salt, and tar, and sun cream. Is this hell, I wondered, looking over the ranks of bodies, to the dazzling sea, or is this heaven? And either way, who'd have thought it would be so very beautiful?

Helene

We thought a lot about the prisoners, even if we didn't talk about them. Many of the people we met had relatives or friends being held by the Japanese. They were with us, sometimes as individuals, sometimes as faceless groups, restless and immediate, on an unacknowledged daily basis. They were on our pillows, in our looking-glasses, in our shadows, the way people seep out into everything when they become hypothetical, and no longer pinned-down by their real-live selves.

If my father and brothers were still alive, I imagined they might have been interned somewhere, and were perhaps making their way back through the chaos of central Europe. Dreadful news had been filtering through of the death camps being discovered out there. Before I left England, my mother had already become very preoccupied with looking at the photographs, and trying to spot a familiar face in the crowds of gaunt, hollowed-out survivors. It took some time – years, in fact – for the full horror of what had happened to sink in, and in India this process was further complicated by distance, both geographical and perhaps cultural. The rumours of atrocities, followed by the reports and newsreel footage, were at first merely seen as predictably unsportsmanlike behaviour, further evidence of the enemy's low standards and tactics, and something it was not tasteful to speak about too openly. The people we met drew no parallels between Hitler's doctrines, which had justified such grotesque and bizarre slaughter, and the unchallenged assumption of racial superiority – albeit softened by time and paternalism – which underpinned their own daily lives. I did not think clearly about these contradictions myself, but perhaps it was partly a vague sense of them, as well as my own incongru-

120

ous position, which made me feel so uncomfortable and out of place.

I felt guilty about the relative safety and comfort in which we were sitting out the final phase of the war. However, staying in a hotel for so long sometimes seemed a peculiar kind of internment of its own. The small details of daily life gained a disproportionate importance: we became ridiculously grateful for a well-polished shoe or a change in the menu, and unduly irritated over the many tiny oversights or delays. Powerlessness made us fractious and child-like. There was something of the prisoner's mentality in our insistence on maintaining our little rituals amid a sea of alien strangeness. I occasionally felt that the servants and subordinates who surrounded us might as well be our guards.

The person who made me most awkward was Jameel. I wasn't sure why this was. He was always there, and I couldn't relax when he was around. Perhaps it was the fact that Charles spoke of him so highly, and relied on him so completely, even to help him dress. Any crisis, from a snake in the bathroom to a misunderstanding with the dhobi, required us to call him, like anxious children. More often than not, the solution involved handing over just a little more money – never an unreasonable amount, and always to be paid to someone else. Perhaps I just felt that he played the game too well, mocking us with his complicity. He knew too much about us, while we knew almost nothing about him. I read an insinuation into his polite smile, and an implied reproach into his servile efficiency.

I sometimes tried to put things onto a different footing. 'Do you have a wife, Jameel?' I asked one morning. 'And children?'

I was sitting in the living room, pretending to read. The Club had a small library, and I was making my way through every volume – a few detective stories, and a dusty range of reference works on topics such as pig sticking, or on household management in the tropics.

'Yes, memsahib. I have a wife and three children,' he replied.

I put down my novel, intrigued. 'How old?'

'Only babies. One year, three years and four years.'

'How lovely! But lots of work for your wife.'

'Yes, memsahib,' he said, simply.

There was a silence. I could feel the usual dead end approaching. 'You know we have a baby in London,' I said.

'Yes, memsahib. She is with your mother.'

'That's right.'

He hesitated, unsure of these new conversational rules, but apparently willing to give them a try. 'And your father,' he ventured, 'is he also in London?'

'No,' having gone this far, I felt compelled to elaborate. 'My father stayed in my country. I came to England as a refugee. Escaping from Hitler.'

'You don't look like the English,' he said, and smiled, as if having something confirmed.

I wasn't sure how to respond to this, so I picked up my book again hurriedly, to signal the end of the conversation. I could feel myself flush with embarrassment. He hadn't said anything wrong – and after all, I had drawn it out of him – but it was odd to have him comment on my appearance: he moved among us with such impeccable blankness one almost felt he must be blind. It was not that I was ashamed of who I was. He made me feel, however, that I might be guilty of some attempted deception. Perhaps my insecurity had made me unnecessarily bossy and high-handed? I felt my superiority had been undermined by this revelation, as if there were some element of dishonesty in my position of which I was being reminded.

The contact between different cultures was not at all as I felt it should be. In a way, it was rather like my experience of sex. I had naively expected something mutually beneficial, and life affirming, in this transaction between opposites – reassurance, perhaps, of the things that unite us as people, the exhilaration of communication overcoming all boundaries. Instead, the process was so often tainted by power, and exploitation, and misunderstanding, serving only to emphasise the gulf between us, and our fundamental isolation. Perhaps Charles was right, I thought, and it was best, after all, to keep one's distance.

That evening, I had my first argument with Charles, trivial on the surface, yet loaded with our unspoken disappointments with one another. We were walking the short distance home from the Club. I was thinking about my conversation with Jameel. 'Did you know Jameel has three children?' I said.

'Yes,' said Charles.

'You never mentioned it to me. It makes him seem more – well, more of a person, somehow. To start with, I didn't much like him.'

'What's not to like? He's a decent chap. He's good at his job, unlike so many of them. That dhobi's a lazy old sod, and the Babu needs a good kick up the backside, if you ask me. At least Jameel is reliable.'

'So he should be,' I muttered, 'with all the tips you put his way.'

He stopped walking, and I was surprised by the way he bristled at this – yet maybe I'd said it to wound, subconsciously realising that it would hit some raw nerve. It was dark, and bats flapped in the telegraph wires above our heads.

I could just make out his pale face, and the pink rings around his eyes, where the sun had reddened his cheekbones.

'One needs to keep the wheels oiled. It's only provident. He's very loyal, in fact I don't know how we'd manage without him. Anyway, it's clearly not something you would understand.'

'No, I wouldn't. Because I'm not pukka, am I? I don't know how things are done, I can't deal with the servants. That's it, isn't it?'

'What on earth?' he exclaimed, and looked at me with such unconcealed distaste that I felt like crying. Then he seemed to gather himself, and started walking again. 'I can't believe you're being like this,' he said. He sounded wounded by my betrayal – shocked by the fact that we thought differently, and horrified by the stranger he suddenly saw in me. 'Can't you just see the good in people? Everything gets twisted, when you reduce it all to money like that. It's a grubby, rather low way of looking at things. Frankly, Helene, I find your jumped-up attitude downright ungrateful.'

'I see. And I should be so grateful, shouldn't I?'

The fury and poison crackled between us, and I think we were both frightened by how close we'd come to reaching for the unspeakable insults that seemed to hang in the air. 'I don't think we should pursue this conversation any further,' he said. 'You're clearly not capable of talking rationally tonight.' He was shutting me up, I realised, because we were in danger of being overheard.

We had reached the metal gates of the hotel compound, and the watchman opened up for us. Be sensible, I reminded myself, don't be the hysterical woman he thinks you are. Wire fences, corrugated iron, barking dogs, and hastily constructed sheds set out in grids: the trappings of occupation are not so different, anywhere in the world, I thought to myself, give or take a few searchlights. We walked on, in silence, through the neat rows of dark bungalows.

123

I was scared to phone home. At work, I looked at the telephone every hour, sitting accusingly on my desk. When I summoned the courage to punch out the number, Steve put me on to my mother, who was sniffing. 'I'm afraid I'm feeling very sorry for myself, darling. I don't know why I'm feeling so sorry for myself today,' she said, tremulously.

'I know why,' I said. 'Sweet, darling Mummy. You poor old thing, it's OK. You've been to hell and back.' This probably wasn't the right thing to say; it brought a renewed outburst of sobs. I wondered how I could stay so calm myself.

I had bad dreams. Mum was crying and I couldn't help her, or she was dead and then she came alive.

The next day I rang home again and it was even worse. 'We're having a rough day,' Steve said.

My heart lurched. I was always waiting for bad news. 'What's wrong?'

'Vera's very depressed.' In the background he said, 'Do you want to talk to her?'

I could hear Mum's voice in the distance. 'Tell her ...' she was sobbing, 'tell her how much I love her ...' Then she took the phone. 'I'm OK.' She didn't sound it. 'I'm sorry to, as they say, lay all this on you.'

'Don't be stupid. You're doing so well. I'll ring back later. It's all right. It'll be all right.' I didn't know what to say. There was no reassurance possible – every comfort I could offer seemed dishonest, or patronising.

I telephoned Toby next, because I couldn't get back to work. 'Why is she feeling so bad?' he asked.

'Why do you think? God, you don't have a clue, do you?'

Later that evening, I spoke to her again. 'Why were you feeling so bad?'

'Why do you think?' Mum said, dryly.

'But why specifically, at that moment?'

She paused. 'I've been rather worried about Gus. And about Steve, too, if the truth be told. I'm not sure that they're really dealing with this very well. So last night, I decided not to take my sleeping pills, and I saw the state Gus was in when he got home. I don't mean to sound uptight – I suppose we're not the greatest of role models, after all, Steve in particular – but I've no idea what he'd been up to, he looked really peculiar. As a result I stayed up all night getting myself into a terrible state, and when Steve got up, I let him have it full guns, for setting a bad example, and then went into the mother of all depressions.'

She paused. 'I think maybe I've been trying to be too brave about all this. It's really only just starting to sink in.'

'We're all still in shock,' I said.

'When I was a child, the books and films that were around were very often war stories. It was all about never giving up, escaping against all odds. You know, digging a tunnel out when everyone said it couldn't be done, dodging the guards, and cheating death. No one ever said OK, there's really no way out of here. That makes it harder, because you feel as if you're being encouraged to see things in those terms.'

'Sometimes I think it might be better not to know,' I said.

She was silent, for a moment, on the other end of the line. 'Yes. We're not really equipped to deal rationally with this sort of information,' she said.

Vera

We returned home. The ugly thing, the horrible thing, came with us, growing inside me. For a week, I lay on the bed and wept. The weather grew warmer. Outside the window, seagulls wheeled above chimney pots, in a changing sky. I watched the ripples pass over my belly, the bulge of elbows and shins turning within, like strange sea-creatures breaking the waves, like grotesque shadows on the wall.

I felt an old blackness return: there was no one and nothing I could trust. There were few enough people I'd been close to in my life, and sex had made liars of them all. I cried for the ten years we'd spent together, in which he'd been my best friend; I cried for the people we used to be, and the people we were becoming. Most of all I cried for myself, and felt, once again, like a mistake: the wrong person in the wrong place at the wrong time, someone who should never have happened. I soaked the pillow with tears, crying even in my sleep, imprinting it with the shape of my face, like a shroud.

125

Sometimes the baby also seemed a sinister thing to me now, sucking the life out of me. You seemed like a part of him, an occupying force, part of a wider onslaught, determined to destroy me. At other times, the thought of your innocence devastated me. I had dreamed the perfect world, the perfect marriage for you – I had dreamed them so hard that I had believed my dreams – and yet somehow, I had replicated the mistakes of my parents, and you would be born, as I was, into such a mess. I saw our situation reflected in everything – the news, the house, even the weather. The love and the happiness and the excitement we were supposed to share at this point, when contrasted with the empty parody I felt our relationship to be, filled me with shame and pity. I worried for you, too. Perhaps my sobs shook you, or the bitterness in my fluid would poison you, perhaps the panic and passion coursing through me would speed your heart and sicken your stomach as they did mine. Perhaps my anger and disappointment would twist your features, or your limbs, or your nature, to produce a child born of hate, wide-eyed and strange.

Gregor, for the most part, left me alone, aware that he could only make matters worse. From time to time he appeared, timidly bearing food and drink, enraging me with murmured remarks like 'you must eat'.

'Are you worried about your brat?' I snarled. Or I made dark, elliptical remarks to the wall: 'I will not be your brood mare.'

'Try to calm down. It can't be good for the baby.'

'Fuck you!' I screamed, rising from the bed. 'Fuck your baby!' I smashed crockery, I ripped sheets, enjoying my madness, his fear, my belly swaying before me. 'I want to die,' I shouted.

He scampered a retreat. My chest was heaving, my legs weak beneath me, the healing tears sliding down my cheeks. I heard him moving around the house.

I wanted physical pain, I told myself, to match my state of mind. I would plunge into the fires and emerge anew, I would split in two and leave the weaker part behind, I would shed my skin and become pure. The baby would be my ally – you would love and understand me completely. I would shape you to be strong, to be proud, angry, and unbreakable.

Helene

A month after my arrival in India, we were invited to dinner at Government House with Charles's uncle, who was the Governor of the Province. By then, I had begun to suspect that this branch of the family were less close than had previously been suggested. I looked at the large white building with curiosity whenever we passed. Once I saw a servant trimming the edge of the lawn with a pair of scissors, and a group of men in white, busy with the flag-staff; another time there was a peacock in the driveway. After the embossed cream invitation card arrived, I began to look forward to the event, in spite of myself, as a break from the routine into which we'd so quickly settled. My enthusiasm was increased, I'm ashamed to say, by the thinly-veiled surprise of a number of our acquaintances at the Club. Edwina had also been invited, and seemed startled to hear that we would be there too, and subdued when I reminded her of the family connection.

By then the evenings were oppressively hot. I had nothing suitable to wear, so I had a dress made up from green silk at the bazaar, and was pleased with the result, which seemed to me to be as cleverly made as anything you might see in *Vogue*. I dusted my heat rash with talcum powder, pinned up my hair with greater care than usual, and rolled on scarlet lipstick. Charles looked very fine in his evening dress, like the matinee idol I'd once taken him to be.

There was a doorman dressed in tunic, sash, and puggaree, who helped us down from our tonga as we arrived. Inside the tiled entrance foyer, it was cooler. More servants moved among us with drinks on trays, and there were trophies mounted on the walls. Charles greeted people, while I sipped my drink and looked around. This was more like the India I had imagined. The large ladies made me think of exotic birds, strutting and waddling and eyeing each other, their jewellery glittering on their bosoms. They were attended by men with bent heads, like plainer fowl in the subdued hues of military uniform, or jackdaws, in their dinner jackets. Their squawks and calls rose up to the roof.

Charles's uncle came over to speak to us. He was smaller than I had expected, but had an impressive air of natural authority. 'My dear boy, how are you?' he said, and Charles seemed to swell a little, in the spotlight of his attention. 'And this must be your charming wife.'

'Pleased to meet you, sir,' I said.

'Very nice, yes,' he said, and I got the impression this was a comment on me, rather than the occasion of our meeting. 'So you must be the clever young Viennese girl I keep hearing about?'

'Yes, sir,' I answered, 'I lived there as a child.'

'Then I dare say you're a rather sophisticated sort. A fan of the Opera, perhaps?' he said.

'Oh, I'm not particularly ...'

'I'm afraid you may find this something of a cultural backwater, in that case. Our musical talents are of a more home-grown variety. We have simple tastes, and limited resources. I think you'll find us welcoming, and open-minded, however. Out here, we take as we find.'

'Indeed, your Excellency,' I said, although evidently not enthusiastically enough for Charles, who I could feel flinching beside me.

'Enjoy the evening, in any case,' the Governor said, and moved on, to greet the next of his guests.

A gong was sounded to announce that dinner would be served. Charles and I were seated at the very far end of the table. Men and women were placed alternately, so I was left to try and make conversation with a drunk Captain to one side, and a deaf – and apparently very hungry – Anglican curate on the other.

Between abortive attempts at small-talk, I could hear Edwina's voice, loud and clear as a bell, a few seats away. She was complaining, I gathered, about the meeting of Indian politicians at Simla. 'A ridiculous little man, if you ask me. He's a poseur and a fraud,' she was saying. Bunny, her husband, tried to quieten her, without success. 'But darling,' she went on, 'you've said the same to me a number of times. He thinks he's Christ All Mighty, pronouncing those meaningful-sounding little edicts all the time. All that nonsense about spinning and fasting, as well. It would be funny, if it weren't so irresponsible, but really, with a war on, we can't afford to be too generous with the lot of them. They've shown their true colours and that should be the end of it. It beats me how people can fall for it.'

We ate much the same as we usually did: tinned sardines on toast, mulligatawny soup, then chicken – but it was all very elegantly served, and followed by a beautiful spun toffee basket filled with fruit salad and cream. The room was so hot, despite the frantic fans and the open French windows, that I had little appetite. Faces were flushed, and wet; women dabbed at their necklines, and men tugged at their collars. These are a people as displaced as I am, I thought, suddenly – as precisely and perversely adapted to a vanishing world as the dodo, or the dinosaurs. I'm lucky, though: I'm young enough to change. They're clinging on by their fingernails, shutting their eyes in disbelief.

After dessert, the ladies left the men at the table to drink port, and moved next door. As we went, Edwina took my arm. Despite my distrust of her, I was relieved, since I wasn't sure who else I would talk to, and was afraid of being left conspicuously alone. 'Actually, I've been waiting for a chance to pick your brains,' she said, steering me onto a settee, and lighting a cigarette.

'Really?' I said, flattered, in spite of myself.

She offered me one, and I took it. 'Now do shut me up, darling, if I'm talking out of turn, but I've been dying to clear up a piece of gossip I picked up the other day.'

I felt uneasy, but smiled and nodded.

'You know Captain Hollander was at Cambridge with Charles, a few years before the war? You didn't? Well, anyway, he and Bunny are rather pally these days. The other evening, we were all round at our place after one *chota peg* too many, if you see what I mean, and Captain Hollander mentioned that your husband had been sent down in disgrace, after some scandal in his second year. "*Charles*?" I said, "are you sure?" Because he seems so innocent and you know, butter wouldn't melt. As you can imagine, I was simply wild to know the details, but Bunny, dear old bore that he is, shut him up sharpish, they way he does if anyone even hints at anything to do with sex in mixed company. So I thought I might try and get the details from you.'

She tapped her ash carefully into an ashtray beside us. 'He's frightfully handsome, your husband, and I expect he broke quite a few hearts – before, that is, you charmed him into wedlock. It must have been something quite spectacular, though, for them to pull him up for it. Was she married to the Dean, or something like that?'

I was silent, aware of my thumping heart. 'You don't mind my asking, do you, dear? We're not as innocent as they like to think, are we?'

I felt cornered, and annoyed. The truth was that I didn't know.

Strange as it suddenly seemed, we had never discussed our pasts in that way. Charles had seemed to want to think of me as myself, without a history, and I had been happy to do the same, even though he was older. We had never been through those late-night confessions which seem to raise the ghosts of old lovers, only to slay them, the slow bonding process that I so enjoyed with my later suitors. It hadn't really occurred to me that we might.

I drew on my cigarette, playing for time. The best policy would probably be to mimic her worldly-wise tone, so I concentrated on that. 'Oh Edwina,' I said, 'He's certainly no Casanova. Your English colleges are so easily scandalised. Everyone who's anyone seems to have been expelled at one time or another.'

She laughed, disappointedly. 'So nothing too dramatic, then? I was hoping for a good story.'

I'll bet you were, I thought. 'Nothing worth retelling, no,' I said, and even she was too embarrassed to press me further, until the men rejoined us, loud and liberated by their temporary segregation.

I didn't mention it to Charles. I didn't know how to. It was the first thing in my head, though, the following morning, when I woke in the misty dawn to the distant wail of the muezzin, my temples throbbing from the wine, but my mind racing like a horse out of the starting gate, too fast, too soon. I looked at the bulk of his back, and his arm, flung out in sleep, and he seemed so pungent and animal beneath the sheet, and so remote from me, lost in his secret dreams.

Susie

I knocked on Gus's bedroom door, and then inched it open. There was a slight resistance behind it, which came, I saw, from a crumpled sheet of graph paper on the carpet.

'Hello,' Gus said. He was perched on the bed. He stretched himself, as if waking up – although he was fully dressed, in a sweat shirt and baggy jeans – and raked a hand through his curls.

It was a long time since I'd been into his room, and so I looked around curiously. The walls were covered in posters and felt-tip graffiti. It made me feel old, already confused and irritated by the whimsically named indie bands, Seattle grunge, the deliberately

130

obscure schisms of youth culture, fed, it seemed to me, by marketing – East Coast versus West Coast, Oasis versus Blur. Other aspects, however, had changed remarkably little since I was a teenager – the joss-sticks by his bed, the piece of Indian cotton, which I think might once even have been Mum's, drawing-pinned to the headboard of the bed. The floor was a soup of crumpled essay pages, T-shirts, and Rizla papers. A few shelves were loaded with an incongruously tidy CD collection and an expensive-looking CD player.

'How's it going?' I said.

'Oh, you know.' He gave a charming smile. 'So many petty teen traumas to deal with. Revision, zits, cancer. Life's a breeze ...'

'Mum's worried about you.'

'I'm worried about her.'

It felt like a game of chess, in which I had to corner him. He'd always beaten me at games, in the days when he'd stooped to family interaction of that sort. 'She says you came back in a bit of a state the other night,' I said.

He was quiet for a moment, wondering how to play it. 'I think that's rather hypocritical, considering the booze she's tipped down her neck over the years. Considering the twenty a day habit.'

And look what that's done to her! I wanted to shout. *Do you want to kill yourself, too*? I couldn't bring myself to say it; even thinking it made my feel choked. Instead, I tried a different tack.

'Look, I understand that you've got a lot to be angry about. It's a fucking nightmare, you said it yourself. Something like this brings back a lot of stuff about the past, too.' I tried to talk to him in terms I thought he'd relate to, and not to alienate him with too much psychobabble. I was feeling for the complicity Gus and I used to have when talking about Mum – we didn't seem to have a lot else in common. 'She's always been a bit unhinged. We've had a lot to deal with, over the years,' I said.

'I wouldn't say that. We were fine. Just your average middle-class single-parent fuck-ups. Most people's childhoods are weird. You should hear what some of my mates had to put up with. The people who seem the most ordinary are sometimes the weirdest of all.'

'Maybe,' I said, uneasily. I felt I should be able to help him – to be grown-up yet reachable, a bridge to the adult world – but I always seemed to end up the one sounding peevish and immature.

131

'Don't you remember it as chaotic and frightening?'

'Not really. It was fun. We got to make the decisions, like where to go on holiday, and what to wear to school.'

'And whether to go to school.'

He laughed. 'That too, sometimes. But she made me feel that we were special, and lucky, in spite of everything. She loved us, always,' he said.

'She loved us selfishly, controllingly.'

'So, who doesn't?'

I was surprised by his perceptiveness, and was reminded that although he sometimes seemed so self-contained and male, so like Dad, he'd mainly grown up with female company.

'I suppose so,' I said, grudgingly, unwilling to let it go.

'Why are you always so much harder on her than on anyone else?'

I hesitated. 'I think I apply the same standards to her as I do to myself.'

'Well, chill.' He laughed. 'It's not like I go out and get wasted because of Mum! Not because she screwed me up, not because she's got cancer. I'll live my life, you live yours.' He was triumphant, untouchable. 'You can do the remembering, and I'll do the forgetting. So get off my case. OK?'

'I don't care what you do to yourself,' I said, although I did. 'But Mum's got enough to worry about at the moment ...' At times I felt as if we were all in a juggernaut with no driver, heading towards a cliff.

'You bitches are hard work.'

'Don't call me a bitch! You'll be calling me "ho" next!'

'Ho.'

'You little–' to my annoyance I could think of nothing stronger than '–twerp.'

I wanted to wail for Mum, as in the old days, to appeal to a higher authority, who would wade in and sort us out, as often as not losing her own patience in the face of his quick jibes. The thought calmed me, though, and he smiled again, at how silly we sounded, and just as quickly as my mother would have, I forgave him. 'Just for God's sake try and be a bit sensible, OK?' I said.

'OK,' he replied meekly.

'Hmmm,' I wasn't convinced, but he'd succeeded in making me feel self-conscious, and I turned to go.

132

'I hear that Granny's been talking to you about her "luvaahs"?' he said, with an almost perfect imitation of our grandmother's posh, faintly Teutonic drawl.

'Apparently there's a special word in German for "coming to terms with your own past". It begins with "v" and it takes about ten minutes to say,' I said. 'Anyway, it seems we've all been at it.'

'Isn't it time for the lot of you to declare an amnesty?' Gus said, stretching again. He seemed to exude lethargy, as if he found being a teenager very tiring. 'There should be a special word in German for it as well. Amnesty-against-mother-crimes-gungi-heidi-gung.'

'I always used to think that one day, something really bad was going to happen,' I said, looking out of the window, over the garden. 'I always wondered what it would be like.'

'You should have heard her,' Gus said, following my eyes over the grey slates on the kitchen roof, the trembling leaves, the shed. I was taken off-guard by his sudden seriousness. For a brief moment, I stopped trying to lecture him, and he let his desperate nonchalance drop, and I wanted to put my arms around him, or somehow console him, but I knew that he wouldn't have welcomed it. 'She was howling and moaning as if she was having a fit,' he said. 'I've never heard anything like it. Just sheer, wordless horror.'

Vera

I almost didn't go to the childbirth group. Sheila had suggested it, and even got the details for me, but I expected that I'd be as out of place as I had at the university, and I felt too raw for another failed attempt. 'Perhaps I'm just not the joining type,' I said to her, evasively, down the phone. I felt like a fraud: I was sure my feeble pretence at normality would fool nobody. Our marriage was a sham, and we clearly weren't fit to be parents. Sometimes it felt as if even the pregnancy were just an elaborate disguise.

Gregor was alarmed by the prospect, however, which was enough to make me think again. He mentioned guerrilla fighter-women who gave birth squatting in the jungle, pit workers in the nineteenth century who crouched down in a dark tunnel, and the decadence of a society which alienated us from our true natures, and meant that we required instruction in such things. He was rather scared of Sheila, I think, and the idea of a whole roomful of Sheilas. In the end, it was his reaction, rather than any enthusiasm on my part, which clinched it.

So I drove myself, one wild and rainy night, to a terraced house near the station. The door was opened by an American woman called Alice. I removed my jacket and shoes, to add to the pile in the hallway.

At first it felt faintly ludicrous to be in a room full of other pregnant women, lounging on floor cushions like walruses. Seeing them was a shock. I had been so isolated in the experience, I'd felt as if I were venturing into uncharted waters, and now that I realised I wasn't alone, I was overwhelmingly curious about how it was for them. The living room was something like ours, with crowded bookshelves and spider plants, and a similar selection of LPs stacked in a corner. Rain ran down the bay windows, and a tree thrashed outside. We watched each other curiously, and prompted by Alice, made our awkward introductions. The woman next to me was a petite blonde, with a slim frame that made her large bump look comic, as if she had a cushion stuffed up her jumper: she introduced herself as Cathy. There was a plump librarian, also from the university, called Barbara, and a nervous, dark-haired woman called Linda.

Alice was older than the rest of us, in her thirties, and seemed the more distant for already having children herself. She had a beautiful, lilting voice, with a southern accent. As she spoke, her little girl came padding into the room, and curled sleepily on Alice's lap: Alice stroked her hair, and carried on talking. She explained the three stages of labour, passing a baby doll through a plastic pelvis. I had heard the words she used before – vagina, womb, cervix, ovaries – but usually in a darkly figurative context, as something alarming and obscene – and I had never really thought of them in relation to my own anatomy. We sat, mesmerised, as the little girl fell asleep on her lap, to this peculiar bed-time story. 'I won't pretend it isn't damned painful,' Alice said.

Then there was a break, and Alice carried her daughter upstairs. The room felt quiet and awkward without her, and we all seemed a bit stunned. 'Well, there you go,' Barbara ventured, and we laughed nervously, and agreed how useful it had been. 'I don't

134

know about my cervix, but I'm dying for a ciggie,' Cathy said. Linda mentioned that she'd been getting cramp in her legs, and I said I had too, and then Barbara asked if anyone else could feel a regular bumping, like a heartbeat. Cathy, who turned out to be a nurse, said that it was the baby hiccoughing. Suddenly, we were all talking at once, and I thought, oh yes, this is what I've been missing. There was a warm feeling of being brought together by our physical discomforts, like a war, fought in floral smocking.

Alice came back with a tray of tea and garibaldi biscuits, and joined in. She talked about natural birth, and how she felt it was easier if one could take an active role in it. 'In childbirth, as in the rest of our lives, we risk being objectified by men,' she said. She talked about empowerment, and male chauvinism, and the dangers of an excessive deference to the medical profession. I hung on her every word. It had the force of something I recognised, and already half knew, although I'd never heard it so clearly articulated.

'And how are your menfolk taking it?' Alice asked gently. We all said how lucky we were to have such wonderful husbands, and how understanding they had been, but of course it wasn't the same for them. I had a crazy urge to tell them all about Gregor and his other woman, but I resisted. Just hearing the others venture their first tentative complaints was enough. It was such a relief to hear their worries echoed back, to recognise their fear and their loneliness. Although we'd only just met, I felt a strong surge of fellow feeling, and was embarrassed by the strength of my affection. At the end of the evening, it was odd to see some of the husbands arrive, and to watch the others button up their coats and go back to their real lives, after a moment of such disloyal intimacy. I exchanged telephone numbers with Cathy, who lived not far from me.

I returned home elated, and had another row with Gregor. I wanted to share this new perspective with him: it felt like a vindication, something I'd been trying to say for a long time. I couldn't remember the words, though, my grasp of the language was too tenuous, and it all came out wrong. We pretended to be talking about society at large, but actually, it was far too personal.

'Middle-class women aren't oppressed!' Gregor said. He kept a bottomless store of outrage, it seemed to me, to draw upon at any time. 'A woman with eight kiddies, scrubbing floors and putting clothes through a mangle all day, and then her husband comes back and beats her, that's oppressed, not "oh my God he never remembers to put down the toilet seat." You lot don't know the meaning of the word.'

'Don't tell me how I feel,' I said. I could still feel the ugly thing inside me, whatever it was, and the sense of dread I'd had since our holiday. It was more familiar – I was becoming used to its shape – but I was still too afraid to look at it directly.

I went to bed exhausted, my head swimming with vague, half-remembered scraps of information. That night, I dreamed that he was playing dice with his other woman, on the platform of a tube station. The dice fell onto the track, and we shouted at him not to, but he jumped down to get them, in front of an oncoming train.

Helene

At long last, I received a letter from Bobby.

The sight of his handwriting on the envelope produced a jolt in me, like an electric shock: I recognised the spiky lettering from the poem he'd given me, but he'd never before had to form the 'Mrs' in front of my name. First there was relief – he was alive, at least – followed by a surprising reluctance. He'd become such an important part of my fantasy life, in the involved daydreams I spun over the shimmering, empty days, that I was reluctant to let reality intrude, feeling certain of disappointment.

This will be it, I thought, and realised that I'd actually been waiting for it for some time. This will be the letter in which he lets me know – gently or casually, flippantly or self-importantly – that he's over me. Perhaps there will be someone else – a plucky little ATS or WREN 'doing her bit', even a prostitute in Bombay or Calcutta (he was the sort of man, I suspected, to find an exotic appeal in such an encounter, priding himself on his unconventional daring). Perhaps a few weeks off the boat would simply have put things in perspective. In any case, this would be a fondly apologetic letter, to normalise relations, and tidy up any loose ends.

I could hardly bear to read it. I waited until Jameel had gone out to fetch a few bits and pieces from the bazaar, and tore the envelope with shaking hands. Then I scanned the page, finding myself unable, for a time, to make sense of the phrases. I was so certain of the direction it would take that it took me a while to realise that

136

the gist was quite different. In fact, it was so much what I had wanted to hear that I was almost unable to trust it, suspecting fate of teasing me, and repeatedly reading an irony into his words. Not yet, then, I thought, embarrassed to find tears of gratitude welling up in my eyes – it will surely still happen, but thank God I don't have to face it just yet.

'I have two weeks leave coming up,' he wrote. 'Unfortunately, I find that what I want most to do, rather than while it away getting drunk with a few of the chaps and pretending not to give a damn about anything, is to come and see you (even if I can't manage the elephant or the Kohinoor diamond).

'I have to be honest with you, even though I know you will think me pitifully self-indulgent (I can imagine your face, actually, as you read this). I can't stop thinking, Helene, about our time together on the boat. I remember looks and words that passed between us, and find myself reading far more into them than is sensible. It has helped me get through the last few months out here. I know' (here there was a sentence that was crossed out several times, so that I couldn't read it). 'Let me reassure you that what-ever my feelings, I understand and respect the position that you are in, and would not wish to do or say anything to embarrass you.

'Please write and let me know. I expect I've overstepped the mark, and I'll be surprised to get an answer, let alone a positive one. So if you can't reply, I apologise, and wish you well. If there's one thing I've learned over the past few years, it is that it's pointless to leave opportunities unexplored, or things left unsaid.' He signed himself off as 'ever your loving friend, Robert'.

The letter sent me into a spin, and it was all I thought about for two days. To start with the very idea seemed ludicrous: Charles would never agree, and I could not imagine the two of them meeting. At other moments I thought, well why not? Lighten up, enjoy life a little. After all, nothing had actually happened between us, and the reality of the situation would probably calm us both down – we might even all get on. At other times, giving the lie to my own arguments, I imagined Bobby sweeping up to the bunga-low, pushing Charles aside, embracing me, and whisking me away to some hazy new life.

I finally plucked up courage to broach the subject as Charles was leaving for work. We sat in our bungalow beside the remains of the breakfast tray Jameel had brought in to us: I was still in my

137

nightgown, but Charles was dressed in his customary shirt, long shorts and socks, and bending down to lace up his shoes.

'I think I told you about Robert Miller, one of the friends I made on the boat?' I ventured.

'The one with the RAF?' Charles said.

'Yes, that's him. He's a nice man,' I hesitated, finding new reserves of duplicity. 'I think you'd like him. Anyway, I just got a letter. He's got some leave coming up, and nowhere to spend it. I was wondering . . .'

Charles finished his shoes, and straightened up, slightly flushed from the exertion. He looked at me. I didn't have the nerve to meet his eyes, so I couldn't see his expression, to read any suspicion in his face. 'Invite him here, by all means, if that's what you're think-ing,' he said. 'I know it must be dull for you, with me at work all day.'

'Are you sure?' I said, suddenly afraid of getting what I wanted. 'I don't know him all that well.'

'Why not? I expect the hotel can find a room for him.' He stood, and took a final swig of tea from his cup. 'And I think we could both do with some company, don't you?'

Chapter Six

Susie

In the car, Cathy said, 'You will find the strength to cope. You may not believe it now, but somehow you'll find the strength.'

Gus was shaking as we walked down the corridor. I had never actually seen someone shake from emotion before, and it scared me. We waited outside the theatre as the bed was wheeled out. I was relieved that Mum was conscious, and that she knew already. We walked beside the bed.

Back on the ward, Cathy appeared from behind the curtains. 'Well, we screwed that one up, didn't we?' Mum said. They had found secondary cancers in her liver and they couldn't perform the operation. She was weak and drowsy, and her voice was muffled. 'It's what Mike had, isn't it?'

For a moment, Cathy seemed unable to answer.

'I'm really sorry to bring it all back.' Outside the window it was raining, and from high up, the rain looked like a mist over the trees and houses, blurring with the sea. 'Here it comes,' Mum said, 'the distinguished thing.'

'How do you mean?'

'I'm going to have thousands and thousands of last words.' She was sweetly incoherent, and sleepy, but she said she felt OK. She drifted off in the middle of sentences, but there was usually a kind of buried sense in what she said.

She had a contraption with which to medicate herself, which gave her a shot of pain relief every time she pressed a button. It was meant for after the operation, but they'd decided to give it to her anyway, acting as if it were some kind of a treat. 'We won't

139

tell you what's in it, because it's got a street value of goodness knows,' twinkled the anaesthetist, conspiratorially, when she dropped by to commiserate.

'Diamorphine?' said Gus, sounding a little too interested. 'Cool, my Mum the smack head.' I shot him an angry look.

'Don't worry, it's set so you can't overdo it,' the anaesthetist said.

'I've been planning my own memorial service,' Mum said. Her words made me wince. 'It's like *Desert Island Discs*. There's going to be Bob Marley, Edith Piaf, Jaques Brel. There's a Jaques Brel song I'd like you to hear,' she looked at Steve, and pointed weakly at a CD on the bedside cabinet. *'Ne me quitte pas.'*

Steve looked upset. 'I'm not going anywhere.'

'You'll catch me?' she murmured, with a half smile. 'Because it's as if I'm jumping off, and ...' she seemed almost to have fallen asleep. 'I've heard that one before.'

Gus and I sat on either side of the bed, a head in each of her hands, and she lay, crucified between us. 'My babies. Love each other for me,' she said. 'You two were the best thing I ever did. Steve was the best thing that happened to me, and you two were the best thing I did.'

I could hear mumbled banalities from the other visitors on the ward. The room seemed to me to be full of people in desperate situations saying nothing much very quietly, as if they were afraid of being overheard, 'Did Lesley ring?' or 'Back on the chemo tomorrow'. Cars went up and down the tiny roads below like the bubbles in the drips. People came and went, and at one point my mother and I were alone.

'I don't believe it, Mum. Do I have to believe it?' I said, crying.

'No, it's OK ...' she said. 'It's always strange when people talk about the conscious and then, boumf, the subconscious,' (she used her hand – so skinny now – to make two unsteady slices in the air). 'Because with me at least, I've got so many different levels to my conscious mind ...'

'I've been dreaming about you being ill a lot, and when I tell people they say "how horrible", but I actually prefer it,' I said, 'because then I already know when I wake up. The worst thing is waking up thinking everything is OK, and then remembering.'

'Yes, that's horrible isn't it? Anyway, I was saying ... I believe it on those levels of my conscious mind that are readily accessi-

140

ble.' The rain had stopped by then, and there were gulls, far away like ants, darting in the sky.

'Do you remember when you were very little?' Mum said. 'When we brought you back from the hospital, you were such a sleepy little thing. I used to watch your face ...' she dozed for a while. Just by being with her, I felt almost as if the drugs affected me as well, lubricating the loose, gliding connections that hold a conversation together, like the points on the tracks that determine the route of a train.

'Shall we do some more taping?' she said, the next time she surfaced. 'It's nice to have something else to talk about. Sometimes it seems more real to me than all this ...'

'Why don't you try and rest, a bit, Mum,' I said.

'I'd like to, really,' she insisted.

'OK,' I said, uneasily. 'Let's just see how we go.'

She spoke very slowly, and her voice was weak. Sometimes she seemed to drift off in one of the pauses. I held the Dictaphone up to her mouth, to catch every word, and tried to resist the temptation to finish her sentences.

One of the nurses came and sat with us, to take Mum's blood pressure. I switched the tape recorder off hurriedly, guiltily. 'This is my eldest,' Mum said, volunteering her arm automatically, as the Velcro strips were briskly fastened.

'Lovely,' said the nurse, because Mum seemed to be asking her to.

Then Mum looked at me. 'You'll be all right,' she said.

'Not without you,' I said angrily, tearfully. 'Never.' I buried my head in the bed near her arm. I could hear the hiss of the air, and feel the nurse staring intently at the machine.

'Oh dear, you'll set me off in a minute,' the nurse said.

Vera

Summer came. I ripened, like a fruit, but felt decayed inside, bruised by my fall, corrupted by my own unhappiness. The last days felt unsustainable. I was enormous, and heavy. I waddled around like some joke of nature or improbable feat of engineering – a hippo, or perhaps a zeppelin. The bump swayed proudly before me. I was like a galleon, the sails ballooning.

I hated to be so dependent on Gregor. I could no longer cut my toenails. My belly button had been stretched so wide that it was no longer an indentation, but completely flat. I couldn't pick things up without groaning.

I was haunted by the details of his infidelity, and spent a long time speculating about the girl. He maintained I had never seen her, but she blurred with other people in my head, the women I'd seen on campus. She was thin, inevitably, and supple, and sexually wild. She was modern, and emancipated, and vivacious, her blonde hair falling loose over her shoulders, her life stretching ahead like one long joke. I saw her on the street, on television, and in my dreams. Because I was so large and heavy, and she was so lithe and athletic, I could never get a clear enough view. She was on the cover of magazines, hailed as the spirit of the new age. She was one of the schoolgirls, giggling at the bus stop, as I staggered past.

My ankles swelled up to the size of grapefruit. My feet looked like the feet of an old woman, or a corpse. Gregor helped me, and I snapped at him, and we hated each other. I had become like an elderly relative, bound to him by habit and necessity, by responsibility, rather than desire. I didn't want to be his punishment, it was degrading, but if that was my only option, I thought, then so be it: it began to offer a kind of grim, vindictive satisfaction. I raised my feet on pillows as we slept, in different rooms.

Helene

I counted down the days to Bobby's visit. I tried to give no sign of my preoccupation – aware of how humiliating, and inappropriate it was – but I couldn't help myself. I pictured myself meeting him at the station, perhaps while Charles was at work, and planned every detail of the outfit I would wear, agonising over my choice of scarf. I would be casual but dazzling, beautiful but unobtainable, fresh as a tropical flower, blooming in the dust. I rehearsed the enthusiasm with which I would greet him, concerned that a deliberate nonchalance would give me away. There were moments when I recognised my own foolishness. How ridiculous, I told myself. I'll take one look at him, and he'll become real again, and it will seem laughable, all this pointless agitation, which is, after all,

142

about me and not him. I had never known him well, and might anyway find him changed by the war, or the subcontinent. I told myself I'd know immediately on seeing him how it was going to be – and I did.

Inevitably, it was not at all as I had expected. To start with, Bobby rolled up at our hotel in a curvaceous, shiny black motor car, like a blast from the modern world. In our garrison town of dull army vehicles and worn-out animals, people tended to travel longer distances by train, and so this in itself seemed to give him an unconventional independence. It was the weekend, and Charles was not at work: the new arrival had gathered quite a crowd of curious servants as we hurried out to meet him. I was relieved to see that Bobby looked as boyish as ever, as he stepped out from behind the wheel. He wore mufti – a white aertex shirt and brown slacks, and a cloth hat – and it was hard to imagine that he'd come from the mud and blood of the jungle. There was a new directness about him, however, and he seemed to me to be more purposeful. Ignoring Charles, he took me lightly by the shoulders. 'You look well,' he said.

My cheeks burned: if I'd planned to be a tropical flower, I could feel myself wilt beneath his touch, and every cheery word I'd rehearsed seemed to fly from my head. What would Charles do? It seemed such an intimate greeting that I cringed, half expecting him to fly into a rage and order Bobby away, or even hit him. Instead, they shook hands genially, and as I recovered my composure, I realised they were discussing the car. 'Yes, isn't she a beauty?' Bobby was saying. 'I picked her up in Calcutta. Runs like a dream, given a decent road.'

We had assumed that Bobby would want to wash, and rest, and then slot into our own strangely regimented timetable, like any civilized Englishman. Despite the fact that it was just after midday, however, he announced that what he needed most was a good stiff drink, and insisted we get straight in, so he could take us for a spin. This, again, seemed to tilt the relationship I'd expected, as if we were the ones who had arrived as guests.

The scorched streets were empty at that time. I sat in the back, straining to ease their conversation, shouting over the hot wind and engine noise to supply admiration and enthusiasm at appropriate moments, or the odd point of interest to unite them. The acoustics of the car were against me, however, and although I could hear

143

them reasonably well, they couldn't hear me. ('What's she saying?' Bobby asked. 'Beats me!' Charles replied). I needn't have bothered, anyway. Charles was always more comfortable in male company, and their similar background meant that they spoke the same language, and instantly got on well. I could tell that Bobby's non-conformist streak excited Charles. Perhaps he's actually as bored as I am, I suddenly wondered?

The Club was deserted, but we found someone to serve us, and got drunk rather swiftly, emboldened by our sedate surroundings. Charles and Bobby discovered they had a number of mutual acquaintances back home. Bobby paid me increasingly overt compliments, and rather than being affronted, Charles seemed proud, delighted to have his good taste acknowledged, as if I were the equivalent of Bobby's car. 'Thanks for looking after my wife on the boat,' Charles said, at one point, and coughed.

'Not at all. It was a pleasure,' Bobby replied smoothly, and then laughed, perhaps struck by the preposterousness of the remark. These flashes of honesty, when he seemed almost to be laughing at himself, helped to make him endearing even at his most blatant. 'Really, the chaps were falling over each other for the privilege,' he said. 'I can't claim any very high motive.'

'Well, I'm glad you got there first,' Charles said, and I giggled incredulously.

We drove back to the hotel at dusk, as a distant bugle sounded the last post over at the barracks. The setting sun was large and red. The rest of the town was re-emerging into the evening, which was hazy with the smoke of cooking fires. Bobby drove so fast that I worried we might hit something.

Back at the hotel, we sat out in the dark. Bobby had brought us a bottle of Scotch, which he drank with us. He entertained us with stories of the jungle. There were Brits out there living like natives, he said, burned to leather, and then the US air force, who equipped themselves with air-conditioning, swimming pools, even ice-cream makers. Time passed quickly, and then Charles bullied the staff into providing a late dinner.

I liked listening to the two men talk, and I felt I saw a new side to both of them. Most of the English I'd met so far, Charles included, seemed to regard the war as a temporary disruption to the long-term business of running the Empire, but Bobby, with equal certainty, assumed that British rule in India was as good as over. 'The game's

144

up, old chap, surely you can see that? This war has very nearly ruined us, and I just don't think we can afford to hang on out here. The only question is what kind of a mess we leave behind.'

Charles was intrigued, but unmoved: he said he could understand how it might have looked that way a few years ago, with the Japs on the border and Congress playing silly buggers, but now we had them on the run, the rest would surely fall into place.

'The ordinary Indian just isn't ready,' he said. He had enormous respect for what he called the 'martial races': Sikhs, Marathas, Dogras, Garwhalis and so on. 'I love this country,' he said, with more emotion in his voice than I think I'd ever heard before. 'The men here seem fresh, almost as they were when God first made them in His image. I can understand the people who are seduced by that, but it doesn't do to be starry eyed about the vast scale of superstition and ignorance. There are people here who would rather die of starvation than eat something against their religion. When you deal with them as I do, every day, it's as clear as daylight. Maybe with education, in twenty years, thirty years, but you can't hurry these things . . .'

'You don't think we could win the war but lose the Empire?' Bobby said. He had served with several Indian pilots, he said, and he had gained the greatest respect for their courage. 'They're fighting for their country, don't forget,' he said, 'and in my experience, that's what brings out the real fire in a man. Besides, if we care about the right of nations in Europe to be free, shouldn't the same apply out here?'

I listened to them challenge each other with good humour, increasingly emotional and incoherent. They went back to first principles, stammering out the fundamentals of who they were. I saw their words as maps and murals, rivers of blood, movements of armies, huge shifts of peoples and frontiers, on the walls of the empty dining hall. As we parted, full of plans for the morning, Bobby gave my hand a squeeze.

Charles was uncharacteristically affectionate when we were alone. 'You're right, he seems like a good sort,' he said, as we climbed into bed. 'He's likeable enough, although probably a bit unreliable. I've known men like him before. The war makes them seem cynical, but a lot of it's a pose.' He stroked my hair, so unexpectedly that I had to stop myself from flinching. 'I hope you didn't find it too dull.'

145

'No,' I said. 'I enjoyed listening to you talk about politics.'

'You're a clever old thing, aren't you?' he said.

I couldn't sleep. I knew with certainty that Bobby would ask something of me, and I'd be powerless to refuse. Suddenly, it seemed obscenely clear. Why else was he here? How could Charles not realise? Or did he realise, but not care? It made me feel crazy. Once again, I lay in the darkness, the air from the whirring fan caressing my body, crying out silently for Bobby, but with a new urgency, because he was now so nearby.

Susie

Beforehand, I had been praying for the operation, and felt that I couldn't cope if they didn't do it. Once we found out, though, I felt a surprising calm. A part of me was relieved that at least Mum didn't have to go through that. The small things made me angry, but the big things only seemed to batter me into a docile, rather pathetic gratitude.

A dietician came round to speak to us. Lots of protein, energy, carbohydrates, she said. My new mission became to feed my mother. I was aware that I was being annoying, but couldn't resist coaxing her to take a little more crumble and custard from the blue-green plastic hospital bowl.

The old lady opposite held up one of her high-energy drink cartons. 'Get them on prescription, much cheaper,' she said, and then sucked, dutifully, through a straw. 'I have three a day.'

Mum was desperate to get home. I wasn't – I hoped there was something else, something they weren't telling us, a new drug trial maybe. In a small room, piled with videos and books with names like 'The Clean Colostomy', Mr Thompson, our own particular angel of death, repeated that there really was no treatment he could recommend. He said that we would be put in touch with a hospice, and the very word made me feel sick. Mum wanted to know how long she had – that cliché question, from all the films – but he said that he could only guess, a few months maybe. Mum asked me to leave, so she could ask Mr Thompson questions about dying. I wanted to know – it was worse not to know – but I didn't argue the point. It seemed to be important to Mum to feel there were still small ways in which she could protect us.

146

Outside, Gus had been having an argument with the car park attendant. The attendant had said the parking would cost five pounds and Gus only had a pound and told him to fuck off. We sat on a grass verge with Mum's bags and a potted violet she'd been given, waiting for her.

'We're going to have a really good summer,' Mum repeated, as Gus helped her into the car, but after that, for a few weeks, things got really difficult.

Back home we fragmented and regrouped, moving from room to room, talking and crying, but the normal rules of time and routine and human behaviour seemed to have collapsed. Images stay with me – odd sentences, a hand, a rope, thrown out into the storm. Mum, a shape over the table, crying. 'I'm very depressed,' she explained gently to Toby, who'd just driven down from London. We talked about going to bed. 'So how do we do tomorrow? How do we get up and start again?' Mum said. It wasn't a rhetorical question, she really meant it.

Then we were alone, me and Mum, and I said, with an incredible coolness, the thing that had been frightening me. 'I suppose you must have thought about ... hurting yourself.'

'I stood at the top of the stairs just now and I felt like throwing myself down, smashing my skull. Of course I think about it. I've even planned it, but I'd never do it.'

'Think how it would hurt us.' We avoided each other's eyes. The conversation felt unreal, like a play we were performing.

'I know,' she said, straightforwardly, 'I'd never do it. I couldn't.'

'Are you OK?' we said to each other, all the time.

In the morning, Mum sat at the breakfast table, and sobs came like a burst of gunfire, like a volley of shots. She said something in Latin: '*Deus, deus meus, quare me dereliquisti?*'

'God, where have you ...' Toby, who'd done a few terms of Latin at his school, tried to translate.

'My God, why hast thou forsaken me?' Mum corrected him, teacherly even through her tears, and cried some more. Later on, stumbling around like morons, driving around in convoy, it was the thought of that phrase that set me off.

We had lunch in a pub. 'I do find it difficult,' Mum said, 'when I see old ladies. There seem to be so many old ladies around.'

Some old friends of Mum's had come to see her. Sheila, who

147

was glugging the Chardonnay, was wrinkly but rather glamorous, and had some incredibly important job for Channel 4, and there was a sweet old letch called Lucas, who hugged me hello and goodbye a bit too enthusiastically, with his much younger new wife. There were a lot of people sitting around the table, and some of them were crying, which had become as routine as sneezing. Gus said it was a bit like being at a really awful wedding, that went on for weeks.

'Who was it,' Mum said, 'who used to cry out of boredom? When he was listening to someone boring he used to burst into tears? I can really understand that.'

'Cyril Connolly, I think, used to cry when he didn't like his food,' Sheila said.

'I can really understand that too.'

Back at home, Mum sat down. She had taken to walking with the help of a stick. 'I feel so light, as if I could just float away,' she said. 'I suppose that's getting close to it,' she sounded more interested than anything else. 'It's not unpleasant,' she said, 'but it feels very strange.'

I tried to get her to drink some milk fortified with powder, willing every sip into her mouth, but she seemed more interested in talking. 'People say "let your anger out," and the whole ethos is that it's unhealthy to repress things,' she said, 'but I don't really understand how. How can you separate the red corpuscles from the white, how can you even begin?' She sounded more exasperated than angry, and talked as if it were everyone's problem. 'I just don't understand how they can live, these people who say "let your anger out" all the time.'

'Maybe they've never had anything like this to contend with,' I said.

'Well, *évidemment*. And all this stuff about live one day at a time. Well, fine, *bravo*. But how are you supposed to do that, what does it really mean?'

'They're just platitudes,' I said. 'People don't know what to say.'

'Talking does seem to help a bit, they're right about that much. Those tapes we've been making, and all these old friends who keep coming out of the woodwork. Just comparing notes, comparing stories, keeping a sort of tally. It's odd, how things come round,' she spoke as if she were working something out. 'In literary terms,

148

I suppose, you could say that the anecdotes mesh until they are almost a narrative, and the narrative goes on until it's almost an epic, and there's no big plot or conclusion, but there's repetition and rhythm. Until all together, although there's no meaning as such, the whole thing has a certain . . . *import*.'

'How do you mean?'

'Well, you'll be saying, I wonder what happened to so and so, and there'll be a ring at the doorbell, and it'll be so and so, or someone else who knows them. Or someone will say, I always thought you should do such and such, and you'll say – didn't you know? Nothing mystical. Just a richness of overlapping patterns.'

'Like us oldies do, talking about the past,' Sheila said, flippantly.

'Yes,' Mum said, quite seriously, 'I'm learning how to be old.'

I didn't want to hear these things. The world seemed to me to be a terrible place. Something I'd always known but never quite believed was being confirmed. Any sense of order or justice now seemed to me to be a carefully constructed delusion, and I felt I could see beyond, to the chaos and barbarism outside. I knew, now, how suddenly and completely your reality could be overturned, and this knowledge wasn't easy to live with. I couldn't get into a car without imagining a crash, or answer a telephone without running through, in my mind, the possibilities for bad news. I had a permanently sick, scared, apocalyptic feeling. Back in London, on the tube, marker pen on a white board announced delays due to 'a person on the tracks'. Of course, I thought, death is everywhere. How strange that I never noticed it before.

Mum's condition seemed all-engulfing; it felt as fundamental and far-reaching as the weather. It was as if the mood of all of us, the state of the whole world, was determined by how she felt from one day to the next. Sometimes it felt as if we were all dying together. Everything was suspended, and the world was going to end, and all we could do was after all the most important thing, to sit and make tea, and talk, and talk, and talk about the past.

One morning, I found her sorting through her desk drawers, in the sitting room. She was kneeling on the floor, and the sun shone in blinding squares of light on the sofa, and overlapping piles of old photographs lay around her, like a pool of memories, spilled on the rug. There were photos from her first wedding, and her second wedding. There were photographs of her as a child, or a

149

young mother. There were photographs from holidays, and birth-days, and day trips. She looked happier than I'd seen her in a while, as if she'd received an injection of her old self – more like the plump, annoying Mum of a few months ago. 'Look what I've found . . .' she said, mischievously.

She passed me a pile of my old school photographs. I put my bag down on a chair – I was on my way out, to catch a train back up to London. They were in brown card frames, with a wrinkled texture intended to give the impression of leather. My classmates and I perched in rows on benches, surrounded by wall bars, on a herringbone parquet floor, in the brown and yellow uniform of primary school, then the blue and white of secondary school, inno-cent smiles preceding the obligatory bored pouts.

'And look, there's Will,' Mum said. 'Can you see?'

I tried to feign indifference, but the photographs drew me in, and I sat down beside her, on the rug. 'God, look at me,' I said. Looking at the faces, the clothes, it all came flooding back.

'It's sad, how you're a little less smiley in each one,' Mum said.

'Oh, don't worry, it was just a pose.'

I had been a good girl at school, studious, supercilious and awkward, and had tried to give the impression that fashion was beneath me. At first, I appeared with long socks and a wide smile, standing next to Karen – later, with hair slides and pixie boots, while the other girls in the class had their hair carefully flicked and sprayed into Princess Diana styles. There was Cathy's son, Will, on the back row, in photo after photo, pulling a stupid face. He'd been more at ease, the class clown. There was an unspoken under-standing between us that neither of us would acknowledge our mothers' friendship, or our intimacy as toddlers – we both felt it would be social death to do so. We'd shared a paddling pool recently enough for the fact to seem hideously embarrassing, and most of the time, we were painstakingly neutral towards each other. It was nice, though, this unspoken knowledge between us: he'd stuck up for me once or twice, in the playground, and once or twice I'd let him copy my homework during registration.

Except for that one time on the beach. There was still a very slight spasm in my stomach when I thought about it, something between embarrassment and lust. It was nothing, really, I reminded myself, and so long ago – why is it, I wondered, that these early incidents have such power over us?

150

We were teenagers by then, exams looming, and an end-of-an-era feeling to things. There was a sense – reinforced, perhaps, by the stern reminders we kept getting from teachers and parents – that after all the years of waiting around in playgrounds and bedrooms, now, at last, real life was about to begin.

Karen and I had been to one of the seedy, black-painted night-clubs in town. There were a couple of them, with names like 'Spritzers', and neon cocktail glasses or palm trees over the door, which usually catered for tourists – men with thin ties and mullet haircuts, women with stilettos – but once a week held an 'alterna-tive night', on which we drank Snakebite, and waved our arms around to Soft Cell or the Cure. I wasn't bold enough to be a Goth, although I looked suitably miserable: Karen did a bit better, trow-elling on the eye-liner and crimping her hair.

One night, Will and his two friends were there, too. Unlike most of the boys at school, who were into football and Queen and Bruce Springsteen, Will and his mates were set on their own retro path, as if trying to showcase the youth culture of the past twenty years. Will was a Mod, complete with parka, which he'd tippexed with 'the Who' and a CND sign, and which he tried to keep on in all his classes. He hung around with one punk (a posh kid called Julian), and one Rasta (Asif, who had some difficulty achieving dreadlocks).

We ignored the boys pointedly all evening, but I noticed that Will looked over at us once or twice, especially when Karen got chatted up by a student. Then the last slow dance ended, and the lights went on, leaving us all looking shiny and sheepish, reveal-ing smudged eye-pencil and skin-tinted clearasil, and then we were out on the pavement, in the chilly silence of the sleeping city. Will came over, and said hello. He told us about some party, in a squat near the station, that Julian wanted them to go on to. 'Do you want to come?' he said.

Karen said she didn't think so – she thought boys our own age were decidedly second rate, and those from the same school were even worse – but the student seemed to have vanished, and the evening was in danger of fizzling out, so we ended up walking along the seafront with Will and Jules and Asif, and wandering down on to the shore.

The beach at night gave me the feeling of being on the brink of a vast emptiness, like the edge of a cliff, which was a bit how I felt about my life in general. Jules had a small silver hip flask of Jack Daniel's, and he and Karen and Asif were smoking, using each other as windbreaks in an attempt to light their cigarettes. Will and I went on ahead. I could hear snatches of conversation carried to us on the wind: Jules and Asif trading elaborate insults, partly for Karen's benefit, and reciting musical influences, like mathematical formulae, or magic spells. 'Early Bowie, the Stones, some Talking Heads,' I could hear Julian saying, earnestly.

There were strange, spongy things washed up onto the stones, like giant rice crispies. Will and I sat down beneath the legs of the West Pier, and looked out at the dark waves, smashing the shore, and the moon, which made a silvery path over the water. We had no idea what to say to each other: I was tongue-tied with shyness.

'Is Karen going to crash at yours?' Will said.

I wondered why he was asking, a range of possibilities passing swiftly through my head. 'I expect so,' I said, picking some pebbles up and letting them trickle through my fingers.

'Your mum's quite relaxed about that sort of thing, I expect.'

'Oh yes. It's only in other respects that she's a psycho bitch from hell.'

He laughed. 'I remember she can sometimes be a bit full on. I expect she's a bit embarrassing, as a mum.' He put it so well, I thought, gratefully; he shrunk it back to such a manageable size.

'I've always liked *your* mother a lot,' I confessed. 'When we were little, I was a bit jealous of her. She seemed more like I imagined a proper mum.'

'Yeah, she's a sweetie. Dad can be a bit of a prick, sometimes. They're OK. I'm lucky, I suppose.'

I hugged my knees, and shivered. In the distance, the lights of Palace Pier made starbursts in my streaming eyes. 'Are you warm enough?' he said.

'I'm OK,' I said. I was wearing a flimsy suede jacket, with a ripped lining, and I was freezing. In those days, I was always cold.

'You can borrow my coat, if you want,' he said, almost grudgingly.

'No, no, I'm fine, really,' I protested, but he took off his precious parka – he only had a T-shirt, underneath, and his skinny arms looked ridiculously vulnerable in the moonlight – and draped it over me, and left his arm there, on my shoulder. 'You'll freeze, yourself,' I said. Just expressing concern for each other felt unbe-

152

lievably intimate and risqué. I liked the size of his coat on me, his warmth still inside it, and the glow of pride it gave me, because it seemed like such a trophy. I wondered what the others would say when they saw it. Neither of us referred to his arm: it was as if he'd left it there by accident, or it belonged to someone else.

We talked about what we were going to do after school, which seemed both impossibly distant and scarily close. He said he wanted to go travelling. 'I want to see the world,' he said. 'I expect it's different for you. You lot went off to France every year, and your house is always full of foreign stuff. My parents never get further than Wales.'

He asked me, and I said I wasn't sure. I'd applied to study history, but I was worried, I explained, that it was just the easy option – something I was familiar with, because Dad taught it. I said I wanted to do something useful. 'Not like my parents, who just talk round things endlessly, in circles. Something that really helps people.'

We heard the others crunching up behind us, and Will put his arm down, quickly, and Karen saw his coat on me, and said something cutting about the age of chivalry not being dead, but sounded quite impressed. The lights of a ship twinkled on the horizon, and every detail, every sensation, seemed to me to be loaded with promise.

So, for a short period, something crackled between us. All that week, at school, I scurried down corridors in the dread, and hope, of bumping into Will, or gazed out of windows with a dreamy sense of anticipation, of unfinished business. In my head, he became someone different, something more than any teenaged boy could be. I knew this, and knew I was building myself up for a fall, so I denied my feelings vehemently to Karen, and even to myself, and it was like a kind of schizophrenia. 'What's up with you?' Mum said, when she caught me humming to myself over the bread board one morning. 'Don't tell me you've gone and got yourself a fella at last . . .'

The following weekend, Mum and Steve were going away, and Karen had decided that this would be a good opportunity to have a party at my house. I had a heady new status at school, since everyone wanted to be sure of an invitation, and even the hard kids, who never normally gave me the time of day, started talking to me. Michelle Meatyard, whose sexual prowess was legendary, and who got sent home every morning to change out of her fishnets, said, surreally, that she liked my hair; even Lee Williams offered me one of his chips. We rolled up the rugs, and bought a red light bulb to go in the hall, and six litre bottles of Strongbow, and there was also the rest of Mum's Beaujolais Nouveau in case we ran out of drink. Will made a compilation tape, which he gave Karen in General Studies to pass on to me, and every song contained, I felt, a secret message.

Inevitably, the party was a disappointment. Asif got off with Karen, and Julian kicked our front wall, so that several bricks came off. 'What did you do that for?' I said.

'I'm an anarchist, aren't I?' he mumbled, and then threw up in the front garden.

A thick, party fug – hairspray, smoke, beer and Lynx aftershave – hung in the air. I couldn't imagine the house ever being the same again. Gus kept gerbils at the time, and their cage was full of cigarette butts and bottle tops, and there were empty bottles and squashed plastic cups lying everywhere. After the pubs closed, a lot of bikers I'd never seen before turned up, and by midnight, most of the people I knew had left. Gus – then a curly, precocious twelve-year-old – sat cross-legged on the washing machine in his Superman pyjamas, drinking Newcastle Brown Ale from a bottle, and talking to one of the bikers, a large, hairy man called Shag Nasty, about how he might consider customising his Harley Davidson so it could go underwater. There was wine all over the sofa, someone had broken the kitchen window, and half Steve's LPs had been stolen. Karen and Asif had disappeared.

Will was one of the last people I knew to go. He left arm in arm with Michelle Meatyard. By then, romance was the last thing on my mind: Will shrunk suddenly back to himself, the annoying brat I'd known at primary school with falling-down trousers, remarkable only for his ability to swallow stickle-bricks and bits of Lego. I felt stone cold sober, and was beginning to panic. 'What shall I do?' I asked him, on the doorstep.

'You could wait until they're all asleep, and then burn the house down?' he suggested, with a giggle, as Michelle tugged at his arm.

As it turned out, the bikers weren't as bad as they looked. Shag Nasty offered me a snog, but seemed unsurprised when I turned him down, and even offered, half-heartedly, to help clean up. Mum was fine about the damage: typically, she was more annoyed about the fact that Gus had missed his music lesson, and I hadn't watered the avocado plants.

On Monday, Will came up to me after school, when I was unlocking my bike.

'Were you OK?' he said. 'I felt bad about leaving like that. Actually, I was pretty pissed.'

'I was fine,' I said, fumbling with my lock, haughty and aloof, thinking, don't bother, you've blown it, mate.

And then, before I knew it, we were gone. There were mocks, and A levels, and we were all adrift, like those ninety-nine red balloons floating off into the sky, to gap years, and university places, and jobs in building societies, trading Ikea furniture and cars and flats and relationships for burning ambitions and passionately held beliefs, our parents mutating imperceptibly, over the years, from unpredictable despots to comical nuisances.

'How important it all seemed, at the time,' I said.

I looked over at Mum. She was leafing swiftly through another pile, as if she were looking for something specific, some important element in the jigsaw of her past.

She looked up at me, and smiled. 'I expect it was,' she said.

Helene

Bobby was a hit at the Club. It helped that he was in the RAF, and so young looking, and had been at the front, which was of course rather glamorous. They could sense the fact that he didn't care how he was received, and this gave him an added invulnerability. In the tonga, on the way back, he held my hand, under cover of darkness. I sat, frozen with fear, a mere few feet from Charles, while the two of them chatted amicably. I didn't take my hand away, though.

The next day, Charles went to work. He was very apologetic about leaving us alone. 'What shall we do?' Bobby asked lazily, once he was gone, looking straight at me, with a hint of a smile.

Nervously, I rattled off a few of the limited options available in town, most of which I hadn't seen myself. 'There's a mosque that's supposed to be worth visiting. The bazaar, I suppose, although it's nothing special. Or there's tennis at the Club ...'

'Let's go for a drive,' Bobby said.

155

We struck out for a hill town that I'd heard people talk about. It seemed impossibly distant to me, but I decided to humour him, on the basis that we could always turn back after a few hours.

Leaving the dusty mess of buildings was exhilarating, and the countryside seemed magical. The wind buffed us pleasantly, and the vibrations of the car shuddered through me. Bobby held the wheel in one hand, and reached out to squeeze my knee with his other.

The sky was endless, and turquoise, and unclouded. We saw India gliding by: cowherds with their brown-backed cattle, bundles of hay, and elaborately decorated, jewelled carts. The distinctions between land-use felt unclear: gardens merged with fields, pasture ran into wilderness, nothing seemed hemmed in with the finality of brick or stone. I thought – as I had on the train – of some earlier, fairytale idyll, and said as much to Bobby, who pointed out that the picturesque would be no substitute for the basic comforts of civilisation. We passed mud huts, shacks where bicycles were mended, and an encampment of tents. The roads were poor, but the car was surprisingly robust, and Bobby seemed to keep us going by will-power alone. People ran out to look at us as we passed: they'd never seen such a thing.

After a few hours, we left the plain. The landscape grew hillier, and less parched, and reminded me more, at times, of Europe. We climbed and climbed: in the distance, we could see the dark, rugged mountains. I was afraid of getting stuck on the steep, dirt roads. There were sheep, and strange forests, with towering trees and exotic creepers, and the air felt clearer, and thinner, though still hot.

We stopped the car by the roadside to eat our sandwiches, and children emerged, as if from nowhere, to cluster nervously round the car, and then to chatter at us, in words we couldn't understand. The older ones laughed uproariously at Bobby's slapstick, while the younger ones clambered everywhere, and stroked my scarf admiringly. A young man was summoned who spoke a few words of English. For some reason – the car perhaps – he took us to be Americans. 'Please be so good as to sign your autograph,' he said to us, and produced an exercise book. Bobby drew a cartoon of the two of us standing in front of the car, and wrote 'greetings from England' underneath it.

We reached our destination sooner than I'd expected. It felt miraculous to discover such a quaint little town, perched on the slopes, with a bright red post box, just like the ones in London. It had its own little hotel, an old white building with a wooden veranda, and another immaculate lawn, on which we sat out to drink tea, looking out towards the mountains. A tray of delicate bone china was brought out, with a mirrored tea cosy. 'I'd like to come and stay here with you, one day,' Bobby said, as if it were the most plausible thing in the world.

We explored a while on foot. There was a small bazaar, with chickens in crates, and strange cuts of meat, and a glorious cave of vivid silks and embroidered slippers. The people seemed gentler than in the town we'd left, and less swift to assess our financial potential. We wandered up to a stone church on a hill-top, identical to any you might find in an English village, with stained-glass windows, wooden pews, and brass plaques naming the British, over many generations, who had died young, mostly of fevers, in this apparently tranquil setting.

'What a lot there are,' I said.

'That's nothing,' Bobby said. 'Think of all the Indian children who die; you couldn't start raising plaques to them. The dead are too many to count. I don't ask names any more; I don't know why we bother trying.'

I was shocked. 'But surely it's a duty, the least we can do. "We will remember them," and all that. I mean, that way you can hold something back.'

'Do you suppose it makes much difference to them?' Bobby said. 'I don't know about you, but what matters to me is here, and now.' He slid his arm around my waist.

The vicar came out to speak to us, and Bobby explained about his leave. 'I do hope that you and your wife will enjoy your time with us,' the vicar said, and his misunderstanding – which we enjoyed leaving uncorrected – conjured up a whole alternative life in my mind.

'We should go,' I said. 'We have to get back before dusk.' The roads would be impassable after dark, and Charles would be very worried.

'If you say so,' Bobby said.

He opened the car door for me, and got into the driver's seat. Once the doors were closed, however, he just sat there, in silence, until I began to giggle nervously.

'Was this the face that launched a thousand ships,' he said, in the resonant, 'poetry' voice he sometimes used, that forbade interruption, 'and burnt the topless towers of Ilium? Sweet Helen, make me immortal with a kiss! Dum de dum de dum de dum, And all is dross that is not Helena.'

'Very nice,' I began to say feebly, but he interrupted me with a kiss, full on the lips, and then – just as I registered what was happening, and might have started to panic – drew away and started the engine. My heart was thudding in my chest.

Later on, I rested my head on his shoulder as he drove. 'I've had such a beautiful day,' I said, and at that point, in spite of everything, it felt innocent, and somehow pure between us, with all the comradeship and uncomplicated intensity of a very new love.

Chapter Seven

Susie

Mum had to go into a different hospital, because she had developed diabetes. Arriving at the main entrance, I asked the receptionist where to go. The receptionist looked through pages of handwritten names. She couldn't find Mum's name, so she passed the list over and I had a look myself.

I climbed the stairs to a long, dark, crowded ward, and looked for Mum. There were lots of old ladies. One used a stick to adjust the TV aerial from where she was lying, another lay groaning, another had a plastic mask over her face, and was surrounded by clouds of steam. A very fat lady in a pink dressing gown shuffled around in a pair of fluffy slippers.

I recognised a bag, on a chair. I looked at the old woman in bed beside it, and realised, with a shock, that it was Mum. She'd changed again. She looked so incredibly thin – it seemed surprising that her neck could still support her head, and I could see every bone beneath the skin, with each slow, weak movement. It was as if my mother had been swapped with some shrivelled, flimsy, frightening remnant. Only her hair was the same.

'Do you like the new look?' she said. 'It's AIDS chic, apparently. Finally I get to be as emaciated as Twiggy.'

I helped her into a dressing gown, feeding her arm through the sleeve with the drip still attached, and we pushed it with us along the corridor. We sat on rubber-backed chairs on the landing, near an old-fashioned lift shaft, with a metal grill. 'Look, isn't it funny,' Mum said, pointing at a strange, Gothic door, with a large, handwritten sign taped to it: 'Chapel Unsafe – Do Not Enter.'

159

'How are you feeling?' I asked, after I'd got us both a glass of milk from the ward kitchen. I was shocked at finding her lost in this underworld.

'I've had it up to here with this place,' Mum complained loudly, subversively. 'The old dears, half of them are ga-ga, or incontinent, and as for the completely Monty Pythonesque doctors, they look right through you. They think they're in one of those hospital dramas,' (right on cue, a pair in white coats bustled by). 'I don't really watch them but I know that's what they're thinking. They confuse the drama with the action, you see, rushing around trying to be important. Real hooray Henry types who get a kick out of treating you like an idiot.'

I pressed her to drink more milk. 'And there's a whole underclass of cleaners, who don't speak a word of English. It's like New York,' she said. 'I wouldn't come back here if I was having a heart attack.' This seemed to me a strange thing to say, given the circumstances.

I looked down the ward, at the sad old women, bearing the antiquated chaos with docile equanimity. Maybe they were used to it. Mum said she thought that it might be easier for people who'd been through the war, maybe lost a husband already, and were used to making sacrifices. Or perhaps, weak and dehumanised, passive was the only way to be.

A nurse walked by. 'How are your teeth?' said Mum.

'I just have to stay away from those toffees,' the nurse said.

'She's sweet,' Mum said. 'There are a few. But those doctors! *Incroyable*! They all repeat the same questions – they don't know what drugs I'm on. It's still as bad as when I had you, nothing much seems to have changed. One of them came up yesterday and said, "so who are you? So what seems to be the problem? And how long has this been going on?" I was, well, how far back do you want me to go?'

I was getting a bit nervous in case they heard her and bore a grudge. 'Sssh, Mum. It must be a hellish place to work.' I was thinking, secretly, that the place felt a bit like a mental asylum. 'It must be very hard to keep your compassion.'

'They treat us like loonies. They're the loonies,' she said, as if reading my thoughts. 'Only they don't even know they're in the asylum.'

We took a slow, tottering walk outside, with the drip stand.

160

Mum put her arm over my shoulder to support herself. We sat down, in the dazzling sun, on a low wall, looking at a car park. Mum smoked a cigarette; I rested my hands on the warm bricks.

'Did you hear what happened to that Englishman who was executed in the States?' she said.

'No.'

'They asked him if he had any requests, and he said he'd like some cigarettes. And then they said sorry, he couldn't have any, because it was against prison regulations.'

'God, that's awful.'

'Well, at least they didn't say it was for the sake of his health.'

'I've been feeling a little bit sad,' I said suddenly, forcing the words out, echoing a phrase the twins used.

'Why?'

'Because of you.'

'Because I'm going to die?' she asked. I nodded, and Mum gave an ironic and apologetic smile, acknowledging the strangeness of the situation. 'Well, there's not a lot I can say to that.'

'I just wanted to say how incredibly difficult I'd find it without you,' I said. I was careful to say 'I would' instead of 'I will'. Tenses had become so important to me.

'It's going well, babe. You've got a good life.'

'I know, I know ...'

'Things are in place for you to have a lovely life. I do worry about Gus, about you both, and of course I'd have liked it to be different, but I'm very proud of you as well.'

'I wish you liked Toby more,' I said, peevishly.

She sighed. 'It's not that I don't like him,' she said. 'You have to make your own mistakes, on that front.'

'And there are so many things I'm going to do that I need you to know about. I need to tell you stuff and then get annoyed with your reaction,' I gave a wobbly smile. 'Otherwise, I don't know how to feel about things.' I knew I was being self-indulgent, but once I'd started, there was no way to stop.

'We don't do too badly, do we?' Mum said. 'I know we've had our ups and downs in the past, but I hope you won't feel too angry about any of it. I didn't speak to my mother for years. Do you know about that?'

'Sort of ...' I began.

'I'll tell you. You can record it all, if you like. Secrecy can be

161

very damaging. It's the fact of the dishonesty, almost more than anything else. It's a lot better now that people discuss things more openly.'

I wasn't sure what she was getting at. 'No, I suppose we don't get on too badly, these days,' I conceded. 'I feel much too young for all of this, though.'

'Twenty-five isn't all that young. It never used to be, anyway. I was already pregnant with you when I was twenty-five.'

'I know. But I still feel too young for this.'

'I know, darling.' She dropped her cigarette end on the concrete, and offered me a twisted, tearful smile. 'Believe me, so do I.'

Back on the ward, Mum was overcome by pain. She lay on the bed, her eyes closed, as if turning in on herself. The nurse came over. 'Oral morph,' Mum groaned, and pointed to her mouth. The nurse seemed to me to walk in slow motion – I wanted to stride over and shake her. After what seemed like an age, she brought some over, and Mum sucked eagerly on the plastic measuring syringe, like another cigarette. It took a long time to work.

'They ask about pain as if it should be so simple,' she said, when she could talk again, 'where does it hurt, how much does it hurt, as if it should be black and white. It's actually something that's almost impossible to explain in words. You don't know how bad it is, if you see what I mean.'

I sat by her, and took her hand, lying light as a dried leaf on the sheet, and didn't know if it was better to speak or not to speak. She shut her eyes again.

It was all too much, and I'd had enough of being brave. 'Don't go, Mum,' I said, but I don't know if she could still hear me.

Vera

Leaving work was surprisingly upsetting. I always counted down to the end of term; it was something I longed for, but somehow couldn't see beyond. My colleagues gave me good luck cards and chocolates, and had a drink in my honour, in the local pub. Talking my stuff home in a cardboard box, I felt frighteningly replaceable. I felt I was arranging for my own disappearance, or obliteration. I was launching myself into a limbo-world of waiting – shedding my old self without a new one to step into.

My hospital bag was packed, with carefully folded nightdresses, enormous 'Dr Whites' sanitary towels, shaped breast pads (which made me think of something you might find in a joke shop, or perhaps a Soho sex shop), and a lacy baby blanket. The baby's room was ready, a spooky little shrine of tiny, unworn baby-gros and plastic wrapped equipment.

The antenatal group continued, and reminded me of revision time at school, with some of the women nervously comparing half-remembered facts, and others playing it cool, claiming to be completely unprepared, before letting slip a remark that showed they were as preoccupied with it as anyone else.

Cathy was the first to have her baby, a little boy called William. This information really shocked me. I nearly burst into tears when Alice told us, with a detailed account of the labour, like the analysis you might hear after a football match. It finally brought it home that it was going to happen to me as well. Up until then, on one level, it had felt rather like some kind of theoretical evening class we were all attending.

I got myself measured for maternity bras at a large department store in town. Waiting in the fitting rooms, I felt as if I were in some kind of allegory. In the cubicle on one side, a young woman and her mother were shopping for nylon wedding lingerie and baby-doll negligées in peach ('and don't you want something floaty for the honeymoon, darling?'), while on the other, a sulky teenager was being cajoled into her first bra ('stand up straight, love – now, doesn't that look better?').

I slumped heavily in my chair, waiting for the assistant to bring my new armour (rigid with zips and reinforced elastic), fanning myself with a catalogue full of slender, athletic young models in wholesome white sports bras ('Triumph have the bra for the way you are!') or beaming about their secret girdles and unnoticable support tights. I felt sad about the fact that my own mother was so far removed from all this, although it was hard to imagine her in the role (I had never seen her in her underwear, unless you counted a silk dressing gown, and could only remember one brief and indirect conversation with her about 'the curse'). I felt as if I'd slipped out of something that everyone else was part of – some safety net I didn't have. More and more often, I found myself missing her.

My dreams grew ever stranger. I was taunted by Gregor's young lover, I gave birth to bagpipes from my bottom, the doctor turned into Harold Wilson, and the government gave me a practice baby, which I lost on the London Underground. In my waking hours, though, I felt less scared than I would have expected. The feeling of being engulfed, with a new set of interests and obsessions, made me feel like a different person, and was strangely numbing. The discomforts had reached a point at which I felt something had to change.

Your body betrays you, I realised, with surprise. Perhaps that was why mothers all seemed to have this cynical, world-weary edge to them – this impatience with the uninitiated. Perhaps, I thought, they had realised something that men and the childless only get to know with illness or old age. Your mate, your pal, the one you unthinkingly rely on to scratch your nose, pass the salt, or wipe your bum, will sooner or later just say, OK, enough, no deal. I realised, with the part of me that remained logical, that it was only temporary, but the shock still stung me. I was possessed, a vessel, and it made my ego smart to be so expendable. The race wins out over the individual, and this fact felt unexpectedly cruel when applied to me. I couldn't believe that climbing stairs, or moving fast, or even reaching the glove compartment was suddenly such a problem.

Susie

I returned to London early the following morning. It was a Sunday, and I expected to find Toby still in bed. Watching the back gardens and allotments rattle by, feeling fragile and calm, I looked forward to a retreat into simple sensation. I'd bought a heavy newspaper, but I'd leave it on the floor and climb into bed next to him, in all likelihood, enjoying the relapse into irresponsibility, the day cancelled due to leaves on the line. His sweat would smell of beer and his hair of cigarette smoke; I'd smell of Connex South Central Brunch Muffin and the outside world. I'd know the news headlines – his ears would still be ringing with the music of the night before. I'd nestle into the warm dip between his shoulder blades, and at some point he'd turn over, slide his hands under my clothes, and I'd notice the gentle insistence of his erection.

I let myself in quietly, and picked my way through the junk in the hall, with a half-hearted glance at the pile of post balanced on

164

the radiator. I climbed the stairs, ignoring the flashing answer-phone on the grubby oatmeal carpet. I turned the doorknob quietly, and crept into our room.

As I'd expected, the curtains were still drawn, and the room smelled of sweat and sleep. What I hadn't expected was to find Zoe, curled under my own faded duvet cover.

At first I didn't understand – I thought they must have swapped rooms for some reason, even as Toby returned from the bathroom. Only Zoe's expression – of almost comical horror – told me what was up.

'Susanna . . .' Toby said – a statement, a plea, an aborted explanation.

It was like the jumbled, bizarre, not-quite-reality of a dream, while my brain caught up with this new information, slotting it clumsily into place like a jigsaw puzzle. Zoe was pulling on a disintegrating T-shirt – one of Toby's, to add insult to injury, souvenir of some long-ago rag week. Her tits were rather small, I noticed, with remote interest, but pretty. It was like a bedroom farce: I had an odd impulse to laugh.

Zoe was the first to manage a whole sentence. 'Shit, Susie, I've felt so awful. I didn't want you to find out like this. With every-thing you've been going through . . .'

'I see,' I said, slowly. 'Unbelievable timing.'

'We tried so hard to fight it. We thought about it for the longest time before anything happened . . .'

I could hear her telling the story they'd told each other, in inti-mate moments – how we began. 'Is that supposed to make me feel better?' I said.

'The weird thing is it actually started in our sleep,' Toby stepped in, counsel for the defence, confident, clearly, that he could explain things so much better. 'We stayed up talking, one night, and both fell asleep on the sofa, and when we woke, we were in each other's arms.'

'Oh yes?'

At the note of sarcasm in my voice, Zoe started crying. I felt that they were waiting for some kind of verdict. I knew that anger was called for, but it hadn't yet hit me, and this made me feel strangely powerful. I looked at Zoe's crumpled red face. 'You're acting like someone's died or something,' I said.

They both looked bewildered, and alarmed. They looked at me,

165

then at each other. Whatever else – and they'd dreaded it, rehearsed for it, half longed for it – they were sure, I could see, that it was a big deal. I didn't want to play the scene, make the big speech, be part of their drama. I turned to go.

'Suze,' Toby pleaded, 'you won't do anything . . . you won't do anything, um, *silly*, will you?'

I laughed. 'You love yourselves so much, don't you?' I said.

I walked out of the house, still stunned. On the street, people were purposeful, rushing from place to place, but I had nowhere to go. I sat in a café round the corner, free-falling. My hands were clasped around a styrofoam cup of stewed tea. All the things that had once seemed so important, worthy of endless, probing analysis – my career, Toby, my friendships – seemed like nothing, now. I saw myself spiralling away from the different elements of my life, passing them one by one, tumbling into the giddying emptiness below. I sat there for a long time, staring at the sugar grains on the blue formica table.

Then I walked back to the house, my cheeks burning, focusing on small details – the key in the door, the things I would need. They were surprised to see me; I had obviously interrupted a crisis meeting, a council of war. Zoe scuttled into the kitchen, Toby tried to talk to me again. Ignoring them, I packed as much as I could carry into two suitcases, and called myself another cab. The following morning, I called my work, and arranged for a few weeks compassionate leave.

Helene

It was a very peculiar time. By day, I went sightseeing with Bobby, as we grew gradually bolder in our affair. By night, I tried to muster the semblance of married respectability with Charles, while the two men got on surprisingly well together. I'm ashamed to say that my preoccupation with Lottie lifted, or at any rate merged with the wider anxieties I was trying to ignore, and I left the latest letters from my mother unanswered.

I was drunk on Bobby, utterly intoxicated with him. The smallest indication of favour became loaded with meaning. When we were all together, we would communicate in gesture and implication, and I sometimes thought, am I imagining this? Am I going crazy? I felt his eyes burning into me, and it reminded me of the way I'd felt as I first boarded the *Orion*, under the massed gaze of those hundreds of lonely men.

My relationship with Charles had been a negotiated settlement: the sensible thing to do. With Bobby it was a simple demand: I want you, and the world owes me that much. He had such confidence in the legitimacy of his own desires, and seemed content to wait until I came around. He was returning to active service, and it seemed almost too cruel to deny him whatever consolation I could offer. He was just a boy, really, but I knew that I didn't have the strength or the will to oppose him. He was like a dull ache that wouldn't go away, recurring in pleasant waves throughout the day, interspersed with the sudden, sobering nausea of guilt.

Bobby seemed so different from everyone else in our circle. He wore a battered 'bush hat', instead of the old-style topee, and his speech was full of the Americanisms of the men with whom he'd served. He ate local food from roadside vendors, which most of the English I knew considered tantamount to suicide ('if a dose of the runs were the worst thing I had to worry about, I'd be a happy man') and was happy, if circumstances required, to eat with his fingers, like the Indians did. He took me to places where Charles would never normally have allowed me to go, and opened my eyes to the vivid and extraordinary things around me.

We visited some kind of religious festival he'd heard about, at the shrine of a local holy man. Thousands of people were gathered together; pilgrims had walked for weeks from the surrounding villages. The fields around the shrine had become a vast, transient city, with tents, market stalls, and fires. Great clouds of dust were raised by a multitude of bare feet.

We parked the car and walked. It was impossible to get to the holy spot itself for the jostling crowds, and Bobby and I were swept along by shouting people, holding hands, at times stumbling into a run. There was an atmosphere of excitement, which might easily tilt over into disorder; Charles would have been horrified, but Bobby merely seemed curious, and even infected by the mood. I caught bright details in the shifting mass: garlands of flowers, mountains of sugary sweets, a boy in violet, with an armful of purple flowers, an old man with a monkey peeping from the folds of his cloak. Once again, I thought of the Middle Ages. It could have been a hundred, or a thousand years before – there was not a single motor vehicle, or telegraph pole, or any other trace of the modern world. We were the only white people there: in all likelihood, the people at the Club had no notion this was going on. My mother would probably have been revolted by all these poor, unwashed heathens, but I was inclined to a more romantic view, and was awed and humbled by this huge event I didn't even begin to understand. Perhaps this is how they think of us, I wondered – impressive but inexplicable, with our war, our God, our ships and our cities?

We had so much to explore, and yet nowhere to go that was private. My memories of that time are tinged with lust. Our frustrated desire seemed to over-spill our bodies and escape into the rest of the world, so that every sensation – the hot leather of the car seat, the taste of a mango, the wind in my blouse, the gaze of a passer-by – had a slight erotic charge of its own. Before Bobby arrived, I had been intimidated and strangely shamed by the Muslim men, who stared at my bare arms, or averted their eyes in pious anger from the two or three centimetres of ankle visible beneath my skirt. Now, safe and adored, with an amorous man of my own at my side, I began to accept their fascinated disapproval as my due. They seemed more in tune with – and honest about – these powerful sexual undercurrents, which I now sensed in the most innocent of situations.

Of course I was still trying, in a fairly limited way, to be a good Catholic, and on Sunday, Charles and I went to Mass, while Bobby stayed at the hotel. I made my confession, and tried my best to be honest, although at that stage I hadn't really admitted – even to myself – the situation I was in. I think I said something tentative about finding my eyes, and my imagination, drawn elsewhere. To my irritation, the priest refused to take me seriously! 'My child,' he said, 'I can't give Absolution unless you produce a real sin.' Well, too bad, I thought, at least I tried.

The next day, Charles went back to work, and Bobby and I took a drive. We parked near the Old City, and walked along the narrow streets, which were not wide enough for a car. After a while we found ourselves in a park, which seemed to be deserted but for some loud, bright birds. We sat down together on the dry grass – 'it's OK, just for a minute,' Bobby said, pulling me down, and I thought 'oh God, this is dangerous,' and suddenly Bobby's hands were all over me, and I let out a broken moan, and my skirt was up around my suspenders and I thought 'we can't, surely, not here in the open air.' We were interrupted by a nearby whisper, and a laugh, and sat up abruptly, straightening our clothes in alarm, as a group of young Indian men appeared.

'We have seen you, Sahib,' one of them stated baldly, with a broad, insinuating grin. 'You should take care with such behaviour.' They just stood there, above us, waiting, delighted at this reversal of the normal balance of power, relishing our red faces and disarray.

'What can they want with us?' I thought. It was almost a relief when it came to me: they were after money.

Bobby dealt with it quite firmly, and shouted at them to clear off and mind their own bloody business. After hanging round uncertainly for a while, they gave up and left. They weren't fooled, though, they knew something was up. One wouldn't be so flamingly passionate in public with one's own wife.

In the car, afterwards, I was shaken, and subdued. Desire was one thing, action quite another, and for the first time, I felt really ashamed. All the things in my life which felt secure, and certain, were really very fragile. My marriage to Charles was not much, but it was all I had. Without it I would be penniless, homeless, possibly childless, arguably even stateless. I felt in a flash that I might lose it all.

'I'm sorry, darling. They can't do anything, you know,' Bobby said. 'Just a bunch of no-goods trying their luck. Are you all right?'

I nodded, because to express what I was thinking would be a kind of betrayal.

'That's my girl,' he said, 'it doesn't mean anything.' But to me it felt like a warning.

Susie

The house had a strange, frightening atmosphere. It was like a ship without a captain, tilting into the darkness, the waves crashing above our heads. All the lights were blazing, and people crowded the decks, together but alone, at their private all-night parties.

Gus checked Mum's blood sugar with a little needle contraption, plotting it on a graph on the fridge door, like some kind of twisted science homework, before feeding her temazepam, and going out to get wasted himself. Steve was upstairs, supposedly doing the accounts for the shop, red-eyed and rigid before a screen. When I was in bed, I heard them blundering around, crashing into furniture, trying to get keys into the door. They slept on a sofa or a floor, where I found them, washed up like flotsam, in new formations, in the morning.

I tried to hold things together, sorting her medication, cleaning the kitchen obsessively, emptying the ashtrays and hoovering up the roaches, trying to ignore the roaring in my own ears or the sea water seeping in from below decks. Toby rang several times, but I refused to talk to him. I couldn't think about it too hard, I had no space to absorb it yet. I had the feeling it couldn't end just like that between us, there was too much history. No matter how much I told myself it was over, I felt as if we were merely on hold.

And Mum: she was like the calm at the eye of the storm. Propped up in bed, listening to Mozart on headphones, her head tilted back, her eyes closed, her face ravaged, her body battered, worn away by the elements. She was ugly, terrifying, tortured, but also beautiful in a way, radiating love and intelligence and humanity, or so it seemed to me. I can still see her now, hobbling down a shining corridor with her drip stand, or sitting in the garden, looking at the flowers with a strange intensity.

She was back in the first hospital, on a general ward. She couldn't lift her arm. 'The trouble is, she's a bit ambitious,' the nurse said. 'What was going on when I came in here this morning, Vera?'

Mum smiled weakly, almost guiltily. It surprised me that she didn't seem to mind being talked to like that.

'She'd fallen on to the floor trying to get up, hadn't you, Vera? And Mrs Choudhry in the next bed was trying to pick her up,' the nurse said with affectionate amusement, as you might speak of a child. She said Mum could go back to the hospice. 'You should really wait for an ambulance to take you, but I think it would be all right for you two to take her in a taxi if you'd rather get going right away.'

I dressed Mum and brushed her hair, while Steve went to fetch a wheelchair. I liked doing physical things for her – it made me feel less helpless, and gave me a way to express my affection without being over the top – and increasingly Mum, though

170

fiercely independent, would acquiesce. Her face was now so thin that she looked like a skeleton, with a pinched, scary look. Her eyes were often half closed, and her head sometimes lolled. The phrase that kept coming, unbidden, into my head was 'a living corpse'.

'Can you see there, that vein?' Mum whispered anxiously, pointing to her forehead. I didn't understand what she meant. 'In the mirror it looked really big.'

We tried to do a little more tape recording, but Mum was almost too weak to speak. I could feel a young woman in the next bed watching us, and after a while, she stood up.

'I'm going out for a bit of air,' she said, loudly, to her visitor. 'It's bloody depressing in here.'

I felt a surge of rage, and would have liked to follow her out and scream at her. 'Broken collar bone,' Mum rasped, quietly. 'Apparently her neighbour attacked her.'

'I can see why,' I said.

A half-smile played over Mum's face. 'She's only young,' she paused, to gather the strength to finish her thought. 'I scare her.'

Steve arrived with the wheelchair, and to my surprise, Mum didn't object to sitting in it, as we made one more trip in the large metal lift, with its disembodied voice, and along the buffed corridors, gleaming like ice. Waiting for the car, Mum spoke again about the cards she'd been sent, telling her to 'keep fighting'. 'It's annoying,' she murmured, 'because actually I am fighting hard. Bloody hard. Every single day.' She closed her eyes in the sun.

The drive had a horrific mixture of strangeness and familiarity to it. Seeing my mother in a normal context shocked me afresh. I sat on the back seat, and Mum's hair in front of me was so familiar, so reassuring, and yet her face was so deeply disturbing. I knew I would never sit in a car with her again, and this idea, which I kept suppressing, pushed to become an acknowledged thought. The terrible weirdness of it all hit me again and my eyes kept filling up with tears.

Steve played Van Morrison on the tape deck. He drove, with one hand on the wheel, and Mum's hand in his other. Mum seemed to doze, as they drove, holding hands, through the city in which she had lived. We went past the park, in which she'd walked with a pram, then pushed a bike with stabilisers; past the shops where she'd fished in her purse for pound notes, then pound coins; along

171

the sea front, with the skim and dip of its curlicued lamp posts and railings, its carefree roller-bladers and day-trippers, and the bright, dizzying foreverness of the sea.

We passed near to the house, but we didn't stop. Mum seemed so fragile that we were afraid to have her alone, without medical support. It felt almost as if we were playing truant from the hospital, or out on day release. I watched it all, blurred by my tears, gliding past the windows, an unstoppable stream.

From the first moment, the hospice was an enormous, heartbreaking relief. 'Hello again, Vera,' said the lady on reception. A genteel volunteer offered us all something to drink, and the nurses took Mum into a small single room. 'There, I told you it was nice,' she said. I felt a huge rush of gratitude. I had been so preoccupied with the prognosis, with clinging to the hope of a cure, that I hadn't realised what a difference it would make just to see her treated with dignity and consideration. It hadn't even occurred to me that there might be another way.

The building was a quiet bungalow, with an open box of tissues set on every surface, and a sense of the gentle institutional routines of cooking and cleaning going on behind closed doors. There was a garden in which frail people also stared at flowers and leaves. I sat on a bench and waited, while Mum settled in. I looked at a stained cushion on a reclining garden chair, and, in the way in which these thoughts stubbornly kept presenting themselves, couldn't help thinking of all the people who had sat on it, and were now dead.

When I went back into Mum's room, a lady doctor was there. Mum said that she'd like to spend a week in the hospice and then maybe a few weeks at home. I felt uncomfortable, because I couldn't see how we could manage her at home in that condition. Besides, home was such a mess – it wasn't really home any more.

'And the other thing,' Mum said. 'I'm so very confused ... tired. Is it because of the drugs, or is it because I'm dying?' The directness of the question shocked me, but the doctor answered steadily. She said that it was partly the drugs, and that if her liver wasn't working properly, that could also lead to drowsiness. I wondered what it was about this woman that was so different from the hospital doctors. Perhaps it was that she didn't seem to be afraid of my mother.

After the doctor left, Steve went home to pick up some clean things for Mum, and we were alone for a while. It seemed unimportant – trivial, even, in the circumstances – but I wanted to tell her, anyway. 'Mum, I think I've split up with Toby,' I said.

I could see the effort with which she summoned a response, but she managed it very well. 'Oh sweetie, I'm sorry. Are you all right?'

'I'm OK,' I said. 'You were right, it's probably for the best. At least we weren't married.' I hoped she might smile, or something, at this, but she didn't seem able. 'All I care about at the moment,' my voice started to wobble, 'is you.'

They brought in some dinner, but Mum was too sleepy to eat. I tried to feed her with a fork, but she didn't even have the energy to open her mouth, so I kissed her, and left her to rest.

Vera

The days at home dragged. I lay in bed, feeling too large to even dress. I tried, half-heartedly, to read an improving novel which I'd abandoned at college, many years before – with a doom-laden suspicion that I might never have the time again, and a panicky certainty that there was no way I'd make it to the end. It really felt as if my life was about to stop.

Then, one morning, I woke with a surge of energy. I had a sudden, uncharacteristic urge to clean the house. Imagining soft baby hands crawling on our floor or baby gums sucking on our cushions filled me with horror. The heaps of books everywhere, the tilting shelves made of bricks and planks, seemed to me like potential death-traps. I saw dirt as never before: it was if I'd put on special glasses which revealed the grime on the window frames, and the dust ingrained into the leather chair backs and the upholstery.

I tied Gregor's dressing gown over my huge belly, and began work, sprinkling a white dusting of Vim powder over every surface, working it into a gritty cream, displacing clouds of dust with the inflating bladder of the hoover. I kept going all day, until the house seemed to have shed its old skin and emerged a whole shade lighter.

Gregor arrived home late, smelling of smoke and beer, and I had an urge to scrub him too, or at least to order him straight into the

173

bathroom. 'What's going on?' he said. 'Are you nesting, or some-thing? The house looks as if my mother's been at it.'

'Nonsense,' I said. 'It just really needed doing.' I climbed back into bed, my hands chapped and red, my back aching, but with a kind of grim satisfaction, at having imposed some kind of order on the world.

Helene

The car was like a tin sauna. I could feel my heat rash begin to prickle and my head start to throb. My clothes were damp with sweat, and clung to the backs of my legs and my shoulders.

Bobby started the engine. 'Where do you want to go?' he said.

'Let's go back to the hotel.'

'Would you really rather?' He was apologetic, and a little guilty. I could tell he was also beginning to realise the risks all this entailed for me, but would like to recapture his previous thought-less bravado.

'Yes, I'd rather,' I said.

As usual, he drove faster than was sensible. The objects ahead of us seemed to shimmer in the heat, and an optical illusion made it look as if there were patches of water on the bone-dry road ahead, which evaporated into thin air as we drew near. My instinct was always to talk things through, to try and sort it out, but I knew that there was nothing left to say. We could only restate our posi-tions: his demand, simple and selfish enough, my cowardly prevarication, half-concessions withdrawn in alarm, a dangerous desire to have things both ways. The end of his visit was looming: in a few days he would be gone. There was only so long that we could stay perched on this precipice, enjoying the possibilities of the view. He was too gentlemanly to press me, but I could feel him losing patience with my lack of nerve. We had reached the point at which I had to say yes or no.

We drew into the hotel compound. An old man was sweeping the stone footpaths with a bundle of reeds, and a sprinkler splut-tered fitfully over a shaded part of the lawn. Bobby went back to his bungalow. I wanted to call him back, and somehow make things up. Watching him go, I felt desperate. I didn't think I could bear to lose him.

174

I went back to our bungalow. A little solitude, and perhaps a bath, would have been a great relief. We had been drinking heavily every evening, and sleeping little, and this was contributing to my anxiety. I had become frighteningly good at lying to myself, to Charles, to the world in general, and I felt as if my own grip on reality were slipping away.

As I stepped on to our veranda, I was surprised to hear voices from inside. Charles was sitting in our living room with a young Indian man in a striped tunic. Charles was smiling as I entered, his bare feet up on the coffee table, on which there were also two half-drunk glasses of orange squash. They both rose to their feet when they saw me. The Indian boy – for he was really very young, probably not old enough to have joined up, with just a few wisps of hair on his upper lip – looked nervous.

'Back already?' Charles said. Bobby and I were in the habit of spending the whole day out.

I decided that another half-lie would be the safest approach. 'I wasn't feeling too good.'

'Karim was just leaving,' Charles said. He spoke to the boy in his heavily accented Urdu. The boy mumbled a question, and I caught Jameel's name in Charles's reply. He laid a fatherly hand on the boy's shoulder, and the boy gave a little salaam, and scuttled out backwards through the door.

'Who was that?' I said.

'One of Jameel's cousins,' Charles answered smoothly. 'He's looking for work. I agreed to talk to him, to see if I could help.'

'Why didn't you see him at work?'

'You do look a bit off. What's wrong? Was it something you ate? Poor darling,' he said, 'why don't you lie down and I'll send for some tonic water.'

'Can you help him, then?' I persisted. 'And why didn't you just see him at your office?'

'I'm not sure yet if we need anyone else. I thought it would be easier to see him here,' Charles answered, vaguely. 'Lie down under the fan. You look very flushed – I really don't want you getting sick.'

The bedroom, as usual, was immaculately tidy, and all the windows were open. I lay down on the bed, and noticed that my heart was thumping. Charles brought me a drink, and got ready to go back out.

After he had left, I fell into a light sleep. I had a dream, in which I was supposed to be meeting my brother off a boat, but couldn't recognise him in the crowd. Instead, I noticed one of the nuns who had given me instruction before our marriage. We walked into a warehouse, full of old machinery. 'Really,' I said, 'you needn't have bothered to come all this way. I'm quite all right.'

'I had to,' she said. 'We've all been so concerned.'

Then, as so often in my dreams, I remembered something dreadful. I started to run, realising I had left Lottie alone at the dockside.

Susie

Between hospital visits, I took the twins to the park. The day was very warm, and there was an uncanny silence in the wide streets of Hove, the fat, detached, mock-Tudor houses sitting complacently in the sun. The children dawdled, Billy banging every one of the railings with a stick, as we passed, Megan pulling on my hand as if battling her own, private hurricane. Distances felt greater, with them, and time felt slower.

Billy was in a philosophical mood. 'Um, um, Susie?' he said, seriously.

'Yes, um, um, Billy?'

'What's alive?'

'You mean, what does alive mean?'

'Yes.'

His question made me flinch. They were such uncanny little barometers, I thought, unconsciously registering the pressures in the air around – or was it just chance, my state of mind? I looked at his small, pale face, his big eyes blinking up at me, and he reminded me of Dad.

The easiest thing would have been to talk about death, but I couldn't trust myself to go down that route, so instead I asked him questions. 'Well, let's see, am I alive?'

'Yes.'

'Are you alive?'

'Yes.'

'Is the pavement alive?' We looked down at the sun-baked tarmac. I noticed details when I was with them: the peeling paint

176

on the railings, the weeds at the base of the wall, the kerb stones.

'No,' Billy said.

'There, you see, you do know.'

'Is Elmer alive?' Megan intervened, more, I suspected, in a bid to gain my attention.

'Well, real elephants are alive, but Elmer's not real.'

'What's real?'

'Not pretend.'

'Um, um, Susie?' Billy wanted the conversation back under his control. He seemed to be grappling with ideas which he couldn't quite put into words, and his eyes darted from side to side, as if trying to catch them. 'Are the clouds alive?'

I hesitated. 'Not really,' I said. 'What are you eating, Megan?'

'Just snot.'

At the end of the road, there was a large Victorian church, with a pale green spire. At the gate was one of those wooden notice-boards, which try to tempt you inside with some cardigan-wearing committee's idea of a zany or arresting theological poser. 'Will I see you in heaven?' it shouted at me, in a jaunty red typeface.

Again, I had the sense of stumbling, of accidentally looking down. I blinked hard, and recovered myself a bit, but the question welled up inside me, and as we wandered slowly across the recreation ground, the million blades of grass beneath the huge sky, it overwhelmed me, and the tears streamed down my face.

We sat down on a broken bench. Billy didn't seem to notice that I was crying. He'd found another stick and was using it as a magic wand – pointing it at us, and issuing commands – 'Be a tree! Be a lion! Be a lady!'

'Are you a little bit sad, again?' Megan asked. I nodded, as choking great spasms shook my body.

Crying in front of the children scared me, and made me feel especially unhinged. I felt the risk of losing control, when I was supposed to be the responsible one, or worse, of scaring them. They weren't fluent in the adult responses which restrain and sanitise emotion, forcing it into an acceptable shape, and it felt like a dark and irrational force capable of overwhelming us all. They were matter-of-fact, and surprisingly reassuring, however: more familiar, perhaps, with the ebb and flow of these outbursts, in their own lives. Megan made her hand very flat, as if petting a cat, and stroked my cheek, in a way that was neither gentle nor precise, but still very sweet. Billy discarded his wand, and took my hand in his. 'Are you worried because of your Mummy?' Megan said.

I nodded, relieved not to have to explain.

'Don't worry, the doctors will make her better,' Billy said.

'People don't really die,' Megan informed me, confidently, 'only in stories.'

I was gaining some control over my voice. 'Doctors can't always make people better,' I said.

'Can't they?' I could see their minds working this through, and lost my nerve.

'They can usually, though,' I said, quickly, and gave Billy's hot little hand a pat.

We carried on to the playground, the children sprinting ahead in a ducking, lolloping canter. On the way back, Megan dropped her ice-cream, and it was her turn to cry, and my turn to reassure her. I wondered again how the furious disappointment of a child could be so upsetting – the reminder that things are so often not the way we want, even though we harden ourselves to that, and learn to forget it.

By the time I got them home, Dad was back. He was sitting at the kitchen table, drinking tea and reading the newspaper – manip-ulating the pages with the practiced flourishes I knew so well. When he saw me, he put the paper aside, and opened his arms for a hug.

'It's sweet of you to take them. I hope they behaved,' he said.

'Oh no, I enjoyed it. Nice to do something a bit ... normal.'

'How's it going with your mother?' he said. The familiar ques-tion, now quietly loaded for different reasons.

'It's not good,' I said, 'she's very weak.' Hearing myself talk about it to someone else – particularly him – still shocked me.

He took off his glasses and ran his hands over his long, lined face, as if he were washing it. 'I've been thinking about the past a lot. I suppose it all comes back, at a time like this,' he said.

'She's been talking about the past too,' I said. 'She's been in touch with people she hasn't seen in years.'

He got up to make me a cup of tea. As usual, we were driven back to platitudes by the scale of it all, and the unfairness. There was nothing else to say.

His back was towards me, as he stood over the kettle. 'It's such a fucking awful thing,' he said.

178

It was dusk by the time I got home. There were no lights on in the house, and at first I thought that no one was in. When I went into the living room, however, I was startled to find Steve, sitting on the sofa, smoking in the dark. 'I can't do this,' he said. 'I'm not the right type for it. I can't nurse her and mop her brow and you know, let her die.'

The curtains were still open. Outside, the leaves of the tree blew in the wind, and the lights of other people's televisions flickered through front windows. We seemed to have fallen out of time, and out of society.

I stood in the doorway. I knew what he meant. It felt as if by accepting it, we were allowing it to happen, but by not accepting it, or ignoring it, we were letting her down. The thought his nerve might fail, and that he might just opt out, terrified me. 'You have to,' I said, fiercely.

Early the following morning, I took a taxi back to the hospice. Mum was about to have a bath. I picked out some clothes for her to wear afterwards and went into the other bathroom, with its sinister white plastic handrails and bath-chairs, to rinse out a couple of her things. It felt strange, this new physical intimacy – washing the nightdresses that were so imbued with her, the well-worn Marks and Spencer's underwear, now much too large – but I was grateful for any small labour of love that presented itself.

When Mum was dressed, I supported her under the arm and we hobbled very slowly into the communal sitting room. 'It's funny being given a bath by someone else,' Mum said. I found her a big chair, with wooden arms and an upholstered back. 'I still care how I look,' she said. 'You'd think I wouldn't. I shouldn't, should I?'

She dozed most of the time. I pulled up another chair and sat by her, holding her hand, or studying her face, mentally drawing her, trying to commit to memory the exact shape of her nose, the exact curve of her brow. Her sleepiness made me feel drowsy. Sometimes she would surface, briefly. 'It's funny how ...' she said.

'What?' I said, but she was gone again.

Then another time, 'It's good, really ...'

A smartly dressed woman walked by and said hello. 'Everybody's famous,' Mum said, drowsily, 'I mean, I recognise them ... but I don't ...'

'You don't know their names?'

'Yes.'

179

She woke again a little later. 'I have this sort of dream life,' she said. 'Nothing I can put my finger on ...' Her dry lips stuck to her teeth, and her skull, every sinew, bone or artery perfectly visible beneath the thinnest covering of flesh, lolled against the cushion.

The longest thing she said came a little more fluently, and I wondered if it might have been something that she'd said before, so that the groove was already there, in her brain. 'It's odd,' she said, 'being the first of my lot to do this.'

'The first to do what?' I said.

'To die. I can see the others, when they visit, thinking of themselves as well.'

'And is that all right?' I said.

'That's all right,' she echoed my words back, the way small children do. Several times that day, she reminded me of the twins.

'No, it's not really all right,' I said, with a sudden flash of anger.

'But you know, it might sound arrogant, but if it's all I've got left to do, I'd like to do it well, have a good death. It's something people are so very scared of. Life goes on. I think it helps if you can understand that life really does go on without you. Even if it's hard to believe.'

I tried to wake her for lunch, but she could only manage a couple of sips of milk. Then Cathy showed up. She helped me take Mum back to her room, and showed me how we could lift her back onto the bed by making a sort of chair with our arms. Cathy didn't stay long. Outside the hospice, as she was leaving, we talked. I noticed that Cathy was blinking back tears. 'I remember you were asking whether you should take more time off work now, or wait until later,' Cathy said. 'And I think you're right to take it now. It's just, I had the same worry, when Mike was diagnosed, and someone said to me do it now, don't put it off. And, later, I was grateful they'd said that.'

I said how strange it was, with Mum so sleepy all the time. 'I remember Mike, for the last few weeks, just seemed to be gradually, slowly, drifting further and further away,' Cathy said. Perhaps she was trying to tell me that she thought it wouldn't be long.

Back in the room, Mum said 'I can't do the columns.'

'What columns?' I said.

'Newspaper columns,' she mumbled.

'You mean you can't read them? Would you like me to read them for you?' I said, but she was gone again.

A colleague from the university came to visit, with his wife and their small boy. 'She's very out of it,' I warned them, outside the room. Mum seemed to revive a little, at first, but then she drifted off again, and we sat around the bed in a shocked, stunned silence.

Their little boy was drawing a picture with some crayons, sitting on the floor at the foot of the bed. 'Tiger!' he said.

Mum opened her eyes, and said 'Tiger, tiger, burning bright, in the forests of the night . . .' Quotations seemed to be easier, that day, because she already knew the words.

'She's really a very talented teacher,' the colleague said to me, sounding embarrassed, and also being very careful with his tenses. The only thing to do seemed to be to talk to each other. 'I remember several years back, when she suggested that we change the marking system, you know, she met with a lot of resistance at first . . .'

I nodded, and Mum lay between us, on the bed, her eyes closed. Then he finished the story, a little lamely, and Mum suddenly spoke, apparently from the depths of sleep – 'Brilliant, incisive mind that she was!' she said, loudly. It made us all jump, guiltily, and the man flushed scarlet.

Later on, at teatime, Steve and Gus arrived, and they took Mum outside in a wheelchair. Sitting in the garden all together, it was almost possible to believe this was like all the other early evenings in the garden at home, with me visiting from London, Mum holding court, talking and laughing, and Steve topping up the drinks.

A volunteer from the hospice came and offered us tea. 'Is there anyone else you want to see this weekend?' Steve asked Mum.

'Only Mummy,' she whispered.

'OK,' he said.

A bird hopped across the lawn. There was a sundial, a flowerbed, a couple of trees. I saw and felt it all with such violent clarity. My senses seemed raw, and everything seemed to clamour around me: every blade of grass, every leaf, every twist of the breeze. The world was sharpened – by love, or loss, or fear, I don't know – to the point of pain. It was a strangely exhilarating feeling, in spite of all the misery that went with it.

181

I got up to go. 'Thank you,' Mum said.

'No, thank *you*,' I said, absurdly.

Mum sang 'thank you very, very, very much.' I kissed her again, just in case. 'There is some corner of a foreign field that is forever poo,' she said, with a childlike giggle. Perhaps, I thought, she was wondering the same thing I was: if she'd live through the night, till I saw her again.

Chapter Eight

Vera

I woke in darkness. This was not unusual: I woke several times a night, and nothing particular seemed to have roused me. I squinted at the Baby Ben alarm clock by the bed, and read the fluorescent numbers on the face: it was nearly four in the morning.

I no longer had complete control over my bladder – another unpleasant way in which my body had betrayed me – and my night-dress was slightly damp between my legs. Sighing, I heaved myself out of bed, and waddled along the corridor to the toilet to clean up, trying not to wake myself too thoroughly in the process, the floorboards creaking under my weight. However, as I eased myself back between the sheets, another trickle came out, and then some more.

Gregor lay in the next room, breathing heavily, the cares of the world etched on his sleeping brow. I woke him, and he groaned, then sprang up, eyes wild. Together, we examined the damp patch on my sheet, in the light of the bedside lamp. Perhaps my waters had broken? The phrase had led me to expect something rather more dramatic: a flood of epic, Biblical proportions, or at least a gush, rather than this unseemly seepage.

I telephoned the hospital. An Irish woman told me to come in to be examined. I got dressed, and added a transistor radio and a paperback novel to my bag. We drove through dark, empty streets. The street lamps made tranquil pools of white light on the pave-ment. On the horizon, the roaring sea was black, dragging against the shingle, tilting the lights of the pier on its surface. Gregor helped me out of the car, and put an arm around my shoulder, and for once, I didn't shrug it off. I was in a state of disbelief. I was sure that there'd be lots of false alarms before the baby actually came; I couldn't believe this could really be it.

In the blazing lights of the hospital, we were shown into a shabby little room, and I was given a gown to wear. The Irish midwife appeared; she wore a starched white cap, and had a face rather like a horse. She asked me to lie on a bed, and prodded my belly, and asked me brusque questions.

After a while, a female doctor, wearing bat-wing spectacles and a white coat, arrived to examine me. She referred to me as 'mother', which I found ludicrous and also rather confusing ('would mother please lie down and open her legs'). 'Your husband might want to wait outside for a moment,' she said, but Gregor protested, and was allowed to stay. She used a metal speculum; it was painful and humiliating. 'No, ouch, no,' I protested, turning my face to the side, 'you've got it in wrong.'

'Don't worry, nearly done,' said the doctor.

'Are you feeling all right?' the midwife asked Gregor, who looked a little uncomfortable.

'Not really,' he said. I didn't like him seeing me like that.

The people left. Time passed surprisingly quickly. I soaked through a packet of sanitary towels, as the sky grew light outside the little window. We listened to the news on our transistor radio. We heard chattering and laughing in the corridor as the morning shift came on, and Gregor went outside and bought a newspaper.

Is this really it, I wondered? How extraordinary, the way life just goes on, even if I'm in labour. Can I really be about to have a baby? Then suddenly, I was in pain.

Susie

I took another taxi to the hospice. I felt we were entering a new phase of my mother's illness, with her drifting in and out of consciousness, and I had been wondering how to deal with this. I had resolved to read aloud to her – anything to fill the dreadful, helpless silences of the day before – and had a poetry anthology, *The Everyman Book of Evergreen Verse*, open on my lap. All of the poems I recognised seemed wrong, however, about the emptiness of life or the banality of pain, 'about suffering they were not wrong, the old masters . . .' or the 'patient etherised upon a table'. I was looking through the other end of the telescope, and the poems that had given me a frisson, an insight, in times of happiness and security, were not the ones to offer any kind of consolation. What was I looking for, I wondered? 'How do I love thee, let me count the ways . . .'? I rested my head back against the car seat, realising, with a new exhaustion, that I wouldn't find a poem that said what I wanted.

'Good book, is it, love?' said the taxi driver.

I nodded. I didn't want to talk.

'Romance, is it?'

'You could say that.'

'So d'you work at the hospice then?' the driver persisted.

I felt a rush of anger at the tactlessness of the question. 'No, I'm visiting my mother,' I said. 'She's very ill. Very ill indeed.' Saying it – even reproachfully – made it feel true, and another wave of self-pity washed over me, and I started to cry.

'I'm sorry to hear that, love,' said the driver, and I softened towards him a little.

As I arrived at the hospice, the lady doctor intercepted me in the corridor. The door to Mum's room was open, and I could see her, lying curled on the bed. Immediately, I knew that everything was different.

The doctor explained that Mum's condition had worsened during the night. 'We've been having difficulties controlling her pain,' she said, darkly. 'We've called your father–' I realised she must mean Steve '–and he's coming right over.' I looked straight into her eyes, and I thought I knew what she was trying to tell me. 'We could transfer her back to the hospital, where they'd give her antibiotics intravenously, but I don't think it would make any difference, and I'm reluctant to move her . . .'

I hesitated. 'I don't want her to die in an ambulance, or a lift, or something,' I said, hoping that the doctor would contradict me.

'No,' the doctor repeated. 'I don't think we should move her.'

Inside the little room, Mum lay on her side on the bed, hunched in a foetal position. She looked terrible. With every breath she gave a loud groan, almost a cry of pain. Under the stiff sheets, she wore the white lacey nightdress I had washed for her the day before. The bones on her back, clearly visible beneath the thin straps, made me think of machinery – her shoulder blades stood

185

out, sharp as pistons, beneath the barest film of skin. Her breathing seemed precarious – slow, laboured, and irregular. Something in her pinched, striving expression struck a deep chord with me. I was reminded of a religious image of some sort – the crucifixion, perhaps, or some kind of martyrdom, or one of the statues sometimes carved on tombs. I recognised the face of someone dying, although I'd never seen it before, and realised this could not go on.

'I'm here, Mum,' I blurted, but it seemed hopelessly inadequate, and she gave no sign of recognition, enwrapped in her pain. For the first time, I felt afraid of being left alone in the room with her. I didn't know what else to say or do, and felt utterly helpless and scared.

Helene

I lay awake in bed, and my mind raced. Charles was beside me. We had been pretending to sleep for several hours, it seemed to me, while the fan turned above our heads with no more impact on the temperature than a spoon in a cup of tea, and great waves of unrelenting heat rose up from the parched earth. Now, though, I could tell from his breathing that he really was gone, and I envied him this oblivion. I sighed, shifting position, in the sweaty, crumpled sheets.

We are both pretending almost all the time, I thought. We barely even know we're doing it any more. This act we perform: the happily married couple – we both do it so automatically that we hardly know the difference, but for the unease we feel when we meet a real pair, and sense the blood in their relationship, even when they aren't getting on. What is it that compels us in this charade, I wondered? What a way to live. What a waste of life.

I sat up, and felt under the bed for my shoes, tipping them over before putting them on, in case there was a scorpion inside. I stepped out onto the veranda in search, I told myself, of a breeze.

The hot night was alive with insects. The air seemed to thrum and vibrate with a noise like radio static, made by the agitation of tiny legs and wings. From time to time, something large flung itself against the netting at the windows with a thump.

The stars above looked so near, and so deliriously bright, that I felt I could catch them in my palm like fireflies. My nostrils prick-

186

led with the smells of unfamiliar foliage, after a day in the sun. I was conscious of enormous space, stretching for miles around me, and I felt myself shrink within the teeming thickness of the dark.

Perhaps I was waiting for it, because just then, when my senses were most alert, a thin cry rose up from the low building nearby where the servants had their quarters. It had an unearthly quality, which other people might have read as animal – a cat, maybe – but which my oversensitive radar registered instantly as a baby. I was tuned to it: the frequency corresponded in some way to the silence whistling in my ears, and the shape of the sound-waves bent themselves to some pattern in my brain. I was capable of picking up a whingeing child at the far end of the street, or transmuting the sound of a yelping dog, even a squeaking door. I never stopped listening for it. An exhausting alertness had been awakened within me, which I couldn't now shut off. With or without realising it, I was scanning my environment constantly for this sound.

I took deep breaths, to forestall the clenching anxiety in my stomach. At worst, if I let it escalate, this sense of wrongness and the tightness in my diaphragm could make me pace the room frantically, or run my hands repeatedly over my hair and face.

Hush, shush, I whispered, trying to soothe myself, or the distant culprit, or perhaps, even more hopelessly, my own baby, across the miles of sea. The noise stopped, and I waited for it to resume, straining to hear.

The sounds of the night gained volume to compensate. The cicadas now seemed to me like a million pinpricks of noise, throbbing in time with the stars, and my prickly heat. A dog barked in the distance, and sleeping bodies shifted, under the thin, oddly tilted sliver of the moon. I searched for the outline of Bobby's bungalow. As I had expected (we still joked about his insomnia, but I knew it was a nightly torment to him), the light was still on.

I pulled a thin, pink cardigan over my nightdress, just out of a confused sense of decency, since I certainly had no need of extra warmth. There were square lamps set alongside the paths between bungalows, but the bulbs had been removed, as part of an energy-saving drive a few years before. I found a box of matches, and lit the hurricane lantern that hung on a nail by the door, which I then unhooked and carried by its curved handle. It attracted some of the insects, which circled the flame, apparently bent on self-immolation.

187

Don't think about it too hard, I told myself, or you won't do it. It was too late, though – I'd already contemplated it for too long for my actions to have any natural spontaneity, or for me to be able to consider them objectively. Just let your feet take you. You'll think of some excuse, if necessary. It felt like a dream, leaping jerkily from one impression to another: something, probably a lizard, darting from the light, rustling in the blackness of the leaves, the three steps up to Bobby's door, and then my hand, tapping gently on the wood.

I could see Bobby, through the blur of the mosquito netting, and felt suddenly guilty about disturbing him. He looked up in surprise, and I was flooded with alarm, and the most awful shame. Oh God, this is a mistake, I thought, I should never have come.

He opened the door. His hat and cigarettes lay on the coffee table, which was strewn with papers. 'The lady of the lamp,' he said.

Vera

The pain began in my lower back, but was not localised in one part of my body, or even, I felt, in my body itself, and seemed to fill the whole of the room with a deep, sickening, all-consuming ache. It brought me out in a sweat, and made me feel as if the walls were closing in on me. I tried some of the exercises Alice had suggested, which didn't seem to make the blindest bit of difference. I gasped and groaned and swore at Gregor, and after a few moments, it passed.

The horsey-faced midwife returned to show me to another bed. 'I think I had a contraction,' I said. The midwife did not respond. 'It hurt a lot,' I added, rather lamely. This was all completely routine for the hospital staff, I reminded myself, but even so, the fact that no one explained what was going on, or seemed to take me at all seriously, increased the sense of self-doubt and inadequacy which was nagging at me already. I was in a kind of denial, and couldn't believe that I was really in labour, or really going to have a baby, and it didn't help that no one else gave any outward sign of believing it, either.

It was a very warm day. The pains came irregularly at first. The waiting should perhaps have made things seem slower, but I dreaded the coming of each pain so much that the time in between seemed to race by, and little incidents ran into each other to fill the hours. I slid into that passive, apprehensive state which hospitals induce, seeming to lose any power of self-determination or free will.

Gregor and I went for a walk around the hospital and its grounds. We sat on a bench just outside the doors. Nearby, a group of nurses, like birds in their capes and caps, were talking and laughing, on a break. I gripped the metal railings as another pain overtook me, and studied the paving stones, studded with bottle tops and cigarette ends, intently.

I was shown through the antenatal ward, with its hobbling women and beaming visitors; I could hear babies crying next door. They drew the screen around my bed, and shaved my pubic hair, and gave me an enema; this time, I asked Gregor to leave. It seemed so strange, to be hairless down there, like another layer of nakedness. I felt I was distancing myself from my own body, and thought about being prepared for some kind of human sacrifice. They brought me a pill and a glass of water.

One of the midwives suggested a bath, and this seemed like a surprising idea, but not a bad one, both to prepare myself and to ease the pain. Another blinding contraction hit me as I got in, however, and I was sick into the water. 'I'm sorry,' I said, as the nurse tried to swill the vomit down the plug hole, with a sigh of impatience. As I left the bathroom, I saw another woman in labour being helped along the corridor. I stared with horror at the lumbering and lowing creature, with her distorted body seemingly at war with itself, and still could not relate this to my own condition.

They examined me again, and I expected that they'd say I was about to give birth, but they said I was only 'three fingers' dilated. They took me along the corridor in a wheelchair, to the delivery rooms. Through a blur of agony, I could see two children, giggling at me, as I passed. They took me to a large, empty room, with tiled walls, and a black plastic bed in one corner. There was an operating light, and a bin. It looked stark and sinister as a torture chamber.

'We could have a party in here,' I said, weakly.

'Yes,' said Gregor, 'a labour party.'

By then, pain had begun to take up the whole of my consciousness. I could hear people talking in the background, and our transistor radio, which for some reason was playing some kind of military music, but the pain seemed to dull my other perceptions. They brought me a large canister of gas and air, and told me to suck on the plastic mouthpiece. It didn't help much, but it gave me something to focus on: my deep, rasping breaths and my own moans filled my ears, over the ebb and flow.

Susie

A nurse came in with a trolley of drugs. 'I'm giving her some diamorphine,' she said. 'OK, Vera,' she said loudly, 'I'm going to prick your arm.' She punctured her skin and taped on a small capsule of liquid. She left a large green button with an icon of a nurse on it, just near Mum's hand.

Steve and Gus arrived, shuffling into the room looking nervous and shocked. 'Oh God,' said Steve, when he saw her.

The nurse took us into the next room, which had chairs and a sofa and a television, and a box of tissues on a coffee table. She said we could use the room for as long as we wanted. Gus had a cold, and asked the nurse if there was any danger he could infect Mum. 'Don't worry,' the nurse said, gently, 'you can't make her any worse.'

Then we were alone in the room – a lop-sided, mutant family, a family that barely knew how to talk to each other, stumbling around with its heart cut out. 'You don't get better from something like this, not in an illness like this,' Gus said.

'I was going to read her poems,' I said, 'but none of them seem right.'

Gus said that he would try and write one, and lay down on the sofa with a pencil in his mouth. Steve went next door and sat with Mum, stroking her hair. I made phone calls, from a pay phone in the hallway. I called Cathy, and then Lottie, who was already on her way down to see us with my grandmother, and then, on an impulse, I called my father. I was worried that Lottie might arrive too late. 'My aunt's on her way over,' I told the nurses, as if that might help, as if they could somehow slow things down.

After a while, Gus and I took a turn to sit with Mum. She was still groaning loudly. Gus and I sat in silence. So much had passed between the three of us, words seemed impossible.

190

'Aren't you going to read your poem?' I said, after a while, in desperation.

Gus read his poem. 'Love is the glue, that binds me to you.' It was about floating in candyfloss clouds through a tangerine dream – I could hear the influence of the song lyrics he listened to.

Mum groaned again. 'It's lovely,' I said.

'It's shite,' said Gus, angrily, and his shoulders started to heave. I knew how he felt. Anything we could say or do seemed irrelevant, tactless, insulting even, faced with Mum's condition.

Cathy arrived. She bent over Mum and kissed her cheek. 'You've been the best friend I've ever had,' she said. Mum was so hot, her skin felt as if it were burning up. Cathy wetted a piece of tissue and wiped her face to cool her down. We gave up on the poetry, and put on a tape, some Mozart, on the cassette player by the bed.

Two of the nurses asked if they could come in to give Mum a sponge bath. It seemed like a strange thing to do to a dying woman – I caught a glimpse, through the door, of her arms being wiped with a flannel, her hair gently brushed, 'Eine Kleine Nacht Musik' filling the room – but it also somehow made sense, to prepare her for something important.

Then the nurses were finished. The whites of Mum's eyes were bright yellow, and her teeth seemed very white in contrast. Sometimes her eyes flickered open, often they were closed. Her groans were getting quieter – now they seemed more as if she were trying to speak than trying to scream – or perhaps she was just trying to breathe.

'Her eyes are yellow again,' Gus said. 'Do you think we should tell someone?'

I went to tell a nurse, just to make him feel better. 'Poor love,' said the nurse, giving my shoulder a little squeeze, 'did it frighten you?' I felt annoyed, and wanted to explain that I was older than I looked.

The lady doctor came into the room. Mum groaned and moved and seemed to be trying hard to speak, but couldn't. Afterwards, I wondered what she had been trying to say – 'help me', perhaps, or 'am I dying'?

'She took us by surprise with this,' the doctor said, apologetically. 'If you feel she's in pain, let us know. We're not worried about giving her too much any more ...'

I was worried, because of the groaning. 'Blink if you're in pain, Mum,' I said. Mum just stared.

'Close your eyes if you're in pain, Vera,' said the doctor, but still her eyes stayed open. The doctor looked at her for a while, and seemed to be genuinely moved. Then, rousing herself, she said 'what am I doing, I shouldn't be taking up your time', and left.

Mum gestured weakly at her mouth, to indicate something – that she couldn't speak, perhaps, or that she wanted a kiss, or that she was thirsty. It was the clearest attempt at communication she'd made that day. Cathy moistened her lips with a pink glycerine and lemon stick.

After that, it was changing. Cathy went next door, to call Steve back.

Vera

All of the objects in the room became infused with pain: the iron bed frame, the black plastic mattress, the trolley and the lamps, the bin and the walls. Pain warped the people who drifted in and out, muffled their words, and masked their faces. Hot sickening eddies of it, pulsing layers of it, overwhelming waves of it, carried me off into a more abstract world of pure sensation, something like a dream. I couldn't really see any more, and was deafened by my own screams. Pain was all there was, a thrumming, vibrating force, like God's love, I thought, obscurely, that moves all things.

Between contractions, I pleaded for relief, and begged for drugs like a junkie. They promised me something to help, but it seemed to take forever to arrive, and the midwife moved so slowly that I lost my temper, and cried, 'For fuck's sake just give me some fucking pethedine.'

'There's no need for that kind of language,' said the midwife, sniffily.

I said I wanted a caesarean, that I wanted to die. 'Can't you knock me out, please?' I whimpered. I heard a woman along the corridor give an unearthly yell, and then the sound of a baby, crying.

'Listen,' said Gregor encouragingly, 'a baby.' But it only frightened me; the woman sounded in such agony.

The pethedine didn't really seem to ease the pain, but it confused me, and scrambled the world, so that I was less aware of the agony, less able to process it. I could hear my own words, not making sense – the meaning seemed to evaporate as they left my mouth, as if I were dreaming aloud. 'Where's the ... Did you get the ...' I could hear Gregor and the midwife talking about me, from a distance. No one else can ever feel my pain, I thought, I am alone in this, and it seemed like a revelation. They sounded worried, and I was aware that things weren't going right.

The hours passed like a nightmare, a fragmented mosaic of bright lights, the incongruous military music, and the people coming in and out, recurring like characters in some dreadful situation comedy. I recognised voices from the night before: the Irish midwife, the doctor with bat-wing glasses, a series of anxious conversations by the bed. Someone said the contractions were slowing, another voice talked about failure to progress. I felt relief, each time the pain eased, followed by panic, and despair, each time a new contraction began. There seemed no room left in my perception for sight: I experienced the world through a new geometry of pain, which gave me a sense of being present in the room in a different way, without completely being there.

The midwife finished work, and another came on duty. I couldn't see her face, but her voice was kind, and she seemed to me like an angel, guiding me through the storm, over the rough ridges of agony, holding my hand. 'Keep breathing,' she insisted, 'breathe over the pain, that's it ...' My loud, laboured breaths seemed to impose a kind of rhythm, and made me feel a little less out of control.

In the early hours, I was examined again, and now the discomfort of the examination seemed nothing, a relief, compared to the contractions. 'Go on,' I gasped to the midwife, 'good news, for a change.'

The midwife laughed. 'You're fully dilated, my dear,' she said.

Helene

Bobby looked surprised, and I stood on his veranda, speechless with shame. 'The lady of the lamp,' he said.

He wore pyjama trousers, and no shirt. His torso was slender, but the muscles on his arms and shoulders were well defined, and there were dark curls of hair on his breast and stomach, damp with perspiration, leading my eye down towards the drawstring at his waist. He looked less boyish than when dressed – it was definitely the body of a man, despite the familiar, mocking innocence of his face. Seeing him like that produced a strange stab of feeling. There was embarrassment, most of all, but also a kind of empathy, to do with how vulnerable he looked, both somehow mingled with lust.

I couldn't meet his eyes. I cleared my throat. 'I couldn't sleep,' I said. His bungalow was almost identical to ours in layout, I noticed, but very untidy.

He looked behind me, up the path. 'You'd better come in,' he said.

Inside, he embraced me with a new confidence, as if reclaiming property that was rightfully his. The physical reality of him was a shock, in contrast with the romantic paper figure I had been manipulating in my head. I realised, too late, that by coming, I had lost what control I had over the situation – but perhaps I had known, and that was why I had hesitated so long. Together, we were warm, and wet: I was aware of sweat, saliva on tooth enamel, and his strong, probing tongue.

'Hello,' he said, releasing his grip a little.

'Hello.' I stepped back and smiled ruefully, giddy with kissing and sick with confusion. I covered my burning face with my hands. He took my wrists, and gently pulled them away from my cheeks, and drew me into the bedroom. It was so fast, and so blatant, that I was vaguely insulted, yet I could hardly reproach him for it, having surrendered any claim to modesty. Was this really why I came, I wondered? I suppose it must have been.

He moved a paperback which lay open on the bed. 'Can't we just talk a little?' I said.

'I suppose so. What would you like to talk about?'

'I don't know.'

'I think we've done enough talking,' he said, laughingly, 'don't you?' I still felt dizzy, and he pulled me down easily, the smell of him in the crumpled sheets. He set to verifying things about my body, like a blind man, so intent that it was as if he were trying to memorise my shapes and textures, taking an imprint with his hands. I could feel myself differently through his fingertips – enjoying soft curves and secret crevices, hindered by the obstacle of fabric.

194

'Can we take this off?' he said, and we sat up, and unpeeled my cardigan, clumsily. He resumed his exploration, unbuttoning my nightgown, digging his fingers into flesh, finding the knobbles of my spine, the damp cave of my armpit and the almost skinless vulnerability of my breasts. Then, curious and undaunted, cupping my knees, sculpting the jut of my hip bone, skimming my inner thighs, he found the wet gash between my legs, making me gasp aloud. His simple, unhurried enthusiasm felt like a revelation: so this is how it can be! I hadn't realised how much of a failure Charles had made me feel, with his anxious, guilty attitude. Bobby took such pleasure in me that he made me appreciate myself – for the first time in a long while – and I loved it. 'Stop,' I moaned, in my head, but the word didn't sound, only the moan, and I listened with distant surprise to the animal noises I was making. 'What the hell,' I thought. 'What difference can it really make?'

He slipped off his pyjama trousers, impatiently, so that he was fully naked, and his erect penis might have seemed ludicrous if not for the seriousness on his face. I took off my nightgown, which in any case hung pointlessly open at my sides. A kind of businesslike imperative took over, and our wordless absorption filled the room.

He had a condom – a 'rubber Johnny', he called it – and I had never seen one before. It looked like a dreadfully uncomfortable thing, however, and after a few failed attempts to get it on, he swore, and threw it away. I helped him enter me – a moment of collaboration, of ignored mutual humiliation – crying out involuntarily as he did so. Waves of pleasure, deliciously close to pain, overtook my whole body. I buckled to his thrusts, gasping as he pushed some boundary, making some urgent claim, striving for some unreachable point. We were lost in a strange combination of intimacy and distance – nearer than ever to each other, yet unreachable, within our own sensations. He paused for an instant, as if to prolong the moment, and then resumed with a new urgency. I thought I could not bear it, the sensation was so intense, and cried out louder, and he pushed harder, and again, and then came to a shuddering halt.

One more gasp, and then silence, and the rest of the room, the night outside, re-emerged from the boundaries. There it all still was: the crickets, the sweat, even the faint whine of a mosquito. It seemed we neither of us wanted to be the first to move, out of politeness perhaps, or a reluctance to recognise the situation with

195

words. Gradually reality, and discomfort, intervened. We pulled apart, and he slithered out, with a faint sigh of regret, and we lay side by side on the bed.

We stretched, and rearranged the sheets, and recombined, in a looser embrace, with a tenderness that seemed to mean more, now that a little of the lust was gone. 'OK?' he said.

'Yes.'

'No regrets, then?' he said.

'Not yet. And you?'

'Me neither.' We lay there together for a long while, my head resting on his arm.

I felt several things at once, but all of them were muted. First there was a fond closeness that was almost maternal in nature. I felt overwhelmingly protective – my boy, with his soft, pale skin, his tender under-belly, his pink genitalia curled against his thigh. There was a new, physical revulsion at the idea of his flesh being exposed to the bullets and metal of combat, like someone holding a knife to my own stomach. There was also a faint sadness. Sex was an end to the mystery, and to the bitter-sweet pleasure of self-denial – an end to the romance of the impossible, in exchange for what, after all, was only a physical sensation, however intense. Most surprising, to me, was the renewed appetite it left behind. I had thought that sleeping with him would rid me of something, and simplify things, but actually, I wanted something more than that, and something different. I was scared that I had lost my hold over him, and this already bothered me. I wanted to own him, every thought in his head, every sensation he experienced. Is this love, I wondered?

I felt I should be honest, at least to him. 'I do feel guilty, though,' I added.

'So do I.' I imagined, self-involved as I was, that he also meant towards Charles.

'I don't think he really cares for me,' I said, reluctant to even mention his name. I was justifying myself, and I sounded peevish.

'I've known men like your husband before. Nice enough chaps, most of them, and they don't have it easy. They've no business getting married, though, in my view.'

I let his words hang in the air. By then, even I, in all my naivety, had begun to have an idea of what he meant. His interpretation made me feel better, absolving me of guilt – it was

196

Charles's fault, then, not mine – but I knew it was a little too convenient, given the circumstances, and that things weren't quite that simple. I felt I could consider things with a new distance, and none of it mattered so much any more.

'My poor darling,' Bobby said.

The pauses between thoughts grew longer, and I realised I was drifting, and that I mustn't fall asleep. It would take all my strength to leave him. Just one minute more, I kept saying to myself. We lay together, holding onto each other, in that room that was so like mine, but wasn't.

Susie

Steve, Gus and I were in the room, gathered around the bed. We all touched Mum – a hand or an arm or a leg. Her breathing had slowed, and sometimes seemed about to stop.

I ran for a nurse to come and look. I had a vague idea that they might try and resuscitate her, like on television, with machines and wires and electric shocks. The nurse came to the bed. 'She's very near,' was all she said, but it was enough to reassure me that this was really it, what we had been waiting for, and that they really weren't going to do anything about it.

Steve summoned new depths of strength, and spoke, red-eyed and intense, keeping up a sort of running patter, 'We're here, sweetie, we're all here, my darling, it's OK, my darling, be peaceful, my love . . .'

'Don't go, Mum,' I said. It was the first really spontaneous thing I'd said. The words made a crack in my defences, in the self-control that we were all struggling with, which threatened to undo me, but I was also relieved that I'd spoken what was in my heart.

The tension in the room was almost unbearable. Mum's breathing became slower and slower – with each rasp, we waited, desperately, for the next. Her eyes were open, her muscles were taut, and she looked as if she were reaching out for something. One more rasp, and then it stopped.

The room was completely still, and then our stifled sobs burst into a crescendo. I put my hand on Gus's broad back, between his shoulder blades. The moment of death was very clear, and visible, and awe inspiring.

Peace came creeping in from the corners. The silence was so thick, so tangible, it seemed to solidify around us. A few seconds passed. Mum's eyes were open, her mouth was open, as if she were about to say something, reaching out, to something she could see.

'Can't we close her eyes?' said Gus. I felt it was too soon, and was annoyed that the silence had been broken. I almost felt that, if we all sat perfectly still, things might freeze, and we might prolong the moment forever. I stared closely into her eyes, because I knew I would never see them again, registering the pale blue, the massively dilated pupils, the yellow cornea.

Cathy was back in the room. 'I don't know if they'll stay closed,' she said, anxiously. She wetted a tissue, and pulled the eyelids down, gumming them shut with a little water.

I carried on touching my mother's hands and arms, as if she could still feel me. They were still warm, she still felt alive. She was hunched over, curled on her side. After a while, the nurses offered to move in to 'make her look a bit more comfortable'.

'Can you close her mouth?' said Steve. 'She said she didn't want her mouth left open. She even thought of that.' He gave a contorted laugh.

We stood in the corridor. 'Do you mind if I give you a hug?' Steve said, awkwardly, and embraced Gus and me, one of us in each arm.

Vera

The pushing was very hard. Everything was suddenly the opposite to before, and it was not about fighting the pain but about embracing it. Instead of helping me breathe, the midwife told me to hold my breath while I pushed, and not to scream. I was no longer allowed to use the gas and air. I felt angry that they'd changed all the rules. The effort itself felt rather like doing an excruciating bowel movement, which surprised me. I kept thinking weakly that perhaps I ought to change position, like Alice had said, but nothing seemed to help.

I felt horror and disbelief that this could be happening to me, this frightening metamorphosis, this grotesque division of my body into two. Even at that stage, I didn't really believe there would be

198

a baby. 'Push harder, push longer,' the midwife urged me. 'Nearly there ...' The baby kept going back in again; the midwife explained that it was like the u-bend of the toilet, which added to my confused sense of the weirdly lavatorial. 'Well done,' they kept saying, and I wondered why, because I hadn't done it. I felt a crushing sense of my own inadequacy: it was like on the sports field at school, when all attention had suddenly turned to me, the shouts and cheers urging me on, and I had known with certainty, even before it had happened, that I would stumble, and lose the ball.

The doctor with bat-wing glasses reappeared. Apparently she was called Dr Livingstone. Gregor said 'ah, Dr Livingstone I presume,' and the doctor gave him a chilly look which implied that husbands in the delivery room were one thing, but their lame attempts at humour were quite another, so that I felt ashamed for him, even in my drained and distant state. 'She's not getting a chance,' the midwife explained, supportively, 'the contractions are too weak.'

'I think we shall have to use the forceps,' the doctor said, and, instead of fear, I felt a flood of relief that perhaps there was another way out of this.

They put my feet up in stirrups, and gave me a local anaesthetic. I didn't feel them make the incision, but noticed that they were all wearing plastic aprons, and wellington boots, like butchers. 'You will still need to push very hard, on the count of three,' the doctor said, severely.

'One, two, three.' Perhaps it was fear of the doctor that did it, in the end. I squealed like a pig, or like a newborn baby myself. I felt your head come out, and gave a big push for the shoulders, and then I felt the slither of the rest. I saw you for an instant, being wrapped in a hospital towel, like a very pale alabaster doll, smeared with blood and vernix. The umbilical cord was still looped around you, a strange bluey-grey and pink, candy-striped twine.

I was stunned and horrified, and asked if you were breathing. 'It's a girl!' Gregor said, just like in a film, but I couldn't really make any sense of this information. I could hear him commenting on how quickly the baby's colour was changing. He was in tears – not of joy, but of despair, he later explained – 'you've no idea how bad you looked'. I didn't hear you cry.

I didn't notice the placenta coming out, and they took it away

199

before I saw it. I was aware that they were weighing you while I took more gas and air in order to be stitched up by the doctor. I could see an awful bloody mess, like something from a horror movie, reflected in the lenses of the doctor's glasses, and realised with astonishment that it was me.

Gregor took photos of the baby being weighed, more from a sense of form than by inclination. The midwife looked at the clock. 'Six fifty-seven,' she said.

Helene

While I was with Bobby, something of his air of invulnerability seemed to rub off on me, and it was only when I left him that I realised the risk I had taken. I walked back to my bungalow, taking swift, silent steps, fighting the urge to run, terrified of being seen from the shadows. I tiptoed back inside. To my relief, Charles lay just as I had left him.

I went into the bathroom, to try and calm myself down. The bath was still full of tepid water, from the evening before, and a transparent sliver of Pear's soap lay on the side. I set down the lamp, and got out of my nightdress, and stepped in. Seams of reflected light played over the whitewashed walls, with the tilting of the water. There was a large spider in the corner.

I washed myself, and began to relax. The room was silent, but for a splash every now and then. The water cooled me down, and it felt good to rinse the sweat and semen from my skin. I ran my hands over my body as if they were Bobby's, enjoying my used, slightly bruised feeling, prolonging the echoes of him, a stupid smile breaking out on my face. After a while I stood, sheets of water falling from me, and reached for the crisp, hotel towel.

Back in my nightdress, the water in my hair already mingling with new sweat, I slid carefully back into bed. I was superstitious about even looking at Charles – rightly so, as it turned out – and it was a while before I risked a glance at his face. Although he lay quite still, his eyes were wide open, staring at the ceiling. I shrank away, rigid with alarm.

'Better now?' he said.

I didn't dare answer. I clung to the faint hope that he might have woken while I was in the bathroom, and I didn't want to incriminate myself – although his tone told me I was too late for that. I hadn't decided how to be: apologetic or defensive, honest or evasive.

'You are my wife,' he said, in a low, furious voice. 'I insist that you comport yourself with some dignity. I will not be publicly humiliated, after everything I've done for you. At least have some dignity, you wretched woman.'

'You mean like you do, with your young men?' My voice shook. I knew immediately I spoke that I should not have said that.

He reached over and grabbed my wrist, pinning me to the bed. 'You filthy bloody whore,' he said. 'Do you have any idea how many people warned me against marrying you?' I went completely stiff, and my eyes welled up with tears of shock and self-pity. I could tell he wanted to hit me, and the effort of not doing so made him shake. His contorted face was unrecognisable, and very close to mine.

'Did he fuck you, then? Did he put his hands there, and there?' He felt for my breasts, and then my groin. He was breathing hard, moving his rough, mocking hands over my nightdress, to insult and dominate me, in a crude parody of love. 'Was he better than me? Did he give you what you really wanted?' He wanted to prove something to me and – perhaps more to the point – to prove something to himself: my body was part of an internal argument that I really had no part of. 'Was he stronger than me, more of a man?'

He pinned my other arm down. 'Don't hurt me,' I whispered, shocked at my own cowardice.

'Why not? You're despicable,' he said. He held me still, after that, and went on talking in this vein, about how I'd got my claws into him and was intent on destroying him, about how I'd planned it all from the start. A lot of what he said made no sense. Sometimes he talked about slander and dishonour and our vows before God, sometimes he said I'd 'sensed a weakness' in him which I'd decided to exploit.

I turned my face to one side, into the pillow, waiting for whatever violence he would do to me. After spitting his fury for a while, however, he just began crying. I had never seen him cry before, and this horrified me almost as much as his anger. 'I should throw you out,' he said, and he released his grip on me, just as I thought 'I must leave you, whatever the price'.

He raised himself up in bed, and huge childlike sobs shook his shoulders. For a while we just sat, hunched separately, and I listened to the noise.

I was too shocked to speak, but – immediately, even as the anger of his physical assault subsided – I felt guilt and pity. Shaking, I offered him a cigarette, and we sat and smoked together. 'I'm sorry. I'm sorry,' he said, after a while.

'I'm sorry too,' I said.

'We're a sorry pair, then. We should both pray for forgiveness. God is merciful, and loving. You might not believe this, but I do understand a little of what you're going through, with Bobby,' he said. 'Or at least, I think I do.' I wondered who he'd loved, in the past, without hope of a future. He was trapped, like me, I realised.

'You've every right to be angry,' I said, listening to my voice as if it were someone else's. 'I didn't want to deceive you.' I had no urge to run from him. I knew he wouldn't touch me again.

'What an awful mess,' he said, with a deep sigh. I could only agree, silently. 'You're so very young,' he said, sadly. 'I often forget how young you are.' We sat there, shackled together, by the expectations of others and the bonds of our faith.

The night felt as if it had lasted forever – the bed a ship, crossing vast oceans of dark and obscure emotion. It was a shock to be reminded of the world outside, as dawn broke, slowly, through the shutters, and once again, we heard the warbling call to prayer.

Susie

When we went back in, the nurses had put Mum flat on her back with her arms by her sides, a clean sheet tucked over her torso. She looked more like herself, somehow, more peaceful than she had for weeks, and less like a living corpse. I couldn't believe she was dead. I kept thinking she was going to sit up, like in some horror film, and laugh at the look on our faces.

That face. I'd looked at it so often that I couldn't really see it: it was the one face in the world more familiar than my own. The geometry of it, the relationship of the features, the magic ingredient that made it hers, unchanging through the snaps of a lifetime, echoed back to a dream-time, to the first flickers of my consciousness. That face had once contained, encrypted, the mysteries of the whole world.

Gus went home, but I sat with the body for some time. Mum's neck started to swell, and her arms grew cooler and strangely waxy, with dark spots appearing on her shoulders and hands. Her toes were cold, sticking out from under the sheet. She looked beautiful, to me, and I felt an urge to keep her like that somehow, perhaps to take a photograph. Although only her body was left, I felt how soon that too would be gone, and I could understand why people made masks of the dead. Occasionally, there was a little noise from her nose, a kind of movement of mucus deep inside a passageway, and this scared me. I'd always thought that a corpse would be completely silent. Her chest, beneath the sheet, seemed much too big.

Dad appeared. 'I didn't know whether to come,' he said. 'I hope Steve doesn't mind.' He went in to look at the body. It seemed strange to me, as usual, to see my parents in the same room, my mother and my father. Dad looked pale, and perplexed. 'So much of one's life . . .' he said, again, as he had on the evening I'd told him.

Lottie arrived, with her husband behind her, supporting my grandmother by the arm. I was relieved that they knew already. 'Poor Gus had to tell me. I made him say it twice. It was the car phone, and I couldn't really hear,' Lottie said.

'I tried to call you. I'm so sorry, I'm so sorry you weren't here in time,' I said.

'It was meant to be like this,' Lottie said. 'I feel it was meant.'

When they entered the room, however, Lottie lost her composure. She clutched her sister's hand in a paroxysm of choking tears. 'Oh God, oh God,' she gave a series of explosive sobs. She put her hand over Mum's face. 'She's still warm.' Where her hand had been, the face was smudged out of shape, and the skin didn't relax back into place. I tried to smooth out the wrinkles. My aunt's emotion embarrassed and unnerved me. It made me feel that I should be feeling something stronger: that my aunt had somehow understood what I had not.

She went outside, and we could still hear her crying in the corridor. My grandmother, however, remained uncannily calm. She looked at her daughter's body, lying on the bed. 'She looks quite peaceful, actually,' she said, and then a little trickle of blood came out of her mouth, at the side. My grandmother tried to mop it up, with handfuls of the tissues on the bedside cabinet, but there was more and more.

203

'You don't have to do that,' I said.

'No, I want to,' my grandmother said.

'Is it upsetting you, Granny?' I said. Her composure was even more unnerving than my aunt's emotion. The blood seemed to be endless, and soon we ran out of tissues. I imagined the whole windpipe full of it, dark red and strange. I led my grandmother out, and called a nurse, who came in a plastic apron and plastic gloves to 'clean her up', suddenly very industrial.

Outside, I sat on a bench in the garden. I began to realise that it was really over, that there was nowhere to be, suddenly no more urgency. The hospice vicar hovered nearby, in case we wanted to talk, but Steve and I were resolutely breezy with him, and Dad only wanted to quiz him aggressively on obscure theological points, so after a while he left us to it. Lottie got some sandwiches, and I was surprised to find that I could eat. It seemed strange to me that the other patients in the hospice were still alive.

Steve and Dad were stiff and formal with each other, but very polite, and even rather comradely. My two fathers – how strange, that these clumsy men were now my only parents. A whole new set of rules seemed to apply: death, it appeared, trumps divorce, and the silent female will-power which had held us in our places for so long, like planets circling the sun, was gone, leaving us spinning through the dark, in chaotic new constellations. I wondered how we would live in this unfamiliar universe.

Before leaving, I went back into the little room and saw my mother one last time, only I already knew that it wasn't really her. The blood was all gone. I broke a flower off the bunch by the bed, brought by her colleague from the university, and put it on Mum's chest. The unmistakable smell of that day filled my nostrils: a mixture of disinfectant and sweat, the starch on the sheets and the sweet stench of blood and decay.

We drove back to the house in convoy. Gus met us in the hallway. 'It's much weirder here,' he said.

Vera

Most of the people left the delivery room. The midwife put you to my breast – how peculiar – and you snuffled around a bit and sucked at my nipple, although I couldn't believe that anything

204

would come out. The midwife said I had just missed breakfast, and brought me a cup of tea and some bread and margarine. I felt unspeakably grateful towards her.

'Oh nonsense,' the midwife said. 'It's not much of a meal for someone who's just given birth,' and I had to agree with her there.

It's over, I thought, and for all the rest of my life I must remember to be this grateful for the absence of pain.

You had been dressed, and wore your first nappy. You lay in a clear plastic cot on wheels. There was something ancient about your wrinkly face, a strange mixture of the familiar and the new. You opened your beautiful pale blue eyes, and looked at me, for the very first time.

Chapter Nine

Vera

At first I felt that you were the property of the hospital, and that taking you home would be a kind of theft, something like stealing a library book.

Gregor took our photograph standing at the hospital gates. I clutched a little bundle to my chest. All that can be seen of you is a small, knitted cap which, despite the warm weather, the midwife had insisted you should wear. I wore a plastic name tag on my wrist, and my hands were still puffy – the large, sausage-fingers felt as if they belonged to someone else. My belly was big, but soft and empty, like a slowly deflating beach ball, and my breasts were huge and hard and swollen, beneath a wide-collared nylon shirt. My hair was in bunches, and I wore a defiant smile – the proud new mother – but the thing that strikes me now, when I look at it, is the shock in my eyes. I look as if I'd just survived a car crash.

Gregor drove us home. I sat on the back seat, cradling you in my arms – I was too afraid to put you down in the carry cot. I saw the streets through new eyes, assessing the world as a home for my child. The town looked shabby to me – chip papers blew in the streets, and gulls fought for scraps, like giant, flying rats. Dirt and danger seemed to be everywhere.

The house was full of flowers, in vases, jugs and milk bottles. It smelled like a florists, or a chapel of rest. I felt as if I'd been away for a very long time. The small comforts and the dizzying freedom of home were overwhelming. It was strange not having anyone tell me what to do. Lying in clean sheets, with my baby beside me, was bliss. Gregor had moved back into our bed while

I'd been away, and I didn't have the heart to evict him again. Piles of dirty washing, from my stay in the hospital, lay on the floor.

I couldn't walk, but hobbled tentatively to the sofa, where I lay with you, careful not to put pressure on my stitches, while Gregor brought me food and drink. My breasts – astonishingly – were full of milk, weeping slow white tears all day and night, like some miraculous effigy. It oozed into my bra, it dripped on to the floor when I leaned forwards, and when I lay in the bath, milk billowed from my nipples, like plumes of smoke, underwater. My body felt unfamiliar, ravaged, out of control, incontinent from every orifice. I felt that it belonged to you now.

I was swept along on a strange mixture of elation and fear. Much of the time I was scared: scared of the world, scared for the baby, in a completely new way. I felt as if you might just stop – suddenly, silently, like a clock. The idea that you might revert to non-existence still seemed more plausible than the idea that you were there to stay.

I worried about feeding you – I'd heard other mothers talk confidently of regular and manageable 'feeds', and I fretted over these clues furtively, as if trying to crack a code, reading and rereading the brisk yet confusing advice in my baby-care book. You seemed to want to stay permanently latched on to the nipple, taking a few painful sips at a time, and drifting off to sleep *in situ*; it was not so much an intermittent event as a way of life, and any kind of order or control over this new condition seemed impossibly distant and difficult to achieve. My nipples were covered in red, bleeding sores. I could not actually see the milk go in, and the idea that I alone could sustain this new life seemed highly unlikely, involving a terrifying leap of faith. I was scared for you, but sometimes it felt almost as if I were scared of you, like a question I hadn't revised, like a bomb that could go off at any minute in a public place, revealing me for the charlatan I really was.

I explored your body like a new toy, discovering crevices and moles. Bathing you was another hurdle: I tried to remember how the midwife had shown me in hospital. I snipped through the plastic name tags on your ankle and wrist – like the tags I'd worn myself – with the same sense of the vaguely criminal, of defacing hospital property.

You were crumpled and red, curled in on yourself, ingeniously compact and womb-sized. Your arms and legs stirred slowly,

207

dreamily, perhaps unaccustomed to the lack of constraint, waving in the air as if conducting an invisible orchestra. Your fingers and long toes were so very tiny and thin, the nails like a fleck of dandruff; your nipples were as faint and insubstantial as freckles – I wondered if you would ever, one day, nurse a child yourself, and the idea seemed ludicrous. Your skin was flaky, and did not yet seem to offer adequate protection against the air; your umbilical cord had shrivelled to a dried black scab. I felt as if your body were still my own: having you in another room was almost physically painful, and we seemed scarred in strangely similar ways, still bleeding at the points of separation. You filled your nappies with black meconium, like crude oil. I was nervous about passing a stool myself, because of my stitches, and felt a similarly infantile triumph on behalf of us both.

You were a constant presence, even at night – especially at night. I lived with a permanent sense of crisis. Your little snuffles permeated my sleep long before they became cries, pulling me up through the layers of unconsciousness, from grotesque dreams – accidents and disasters – in which you also featured. As the whimpers broke through into wails, I raised myself from the patch of milk in which I lay, sticky and sore, and lurched, drunken with drowsiness, for the bedside light. I lifted you from the cot, my heart swelling with delight – I slept! And I have you! I arranged pillows, peeling through the layers of soggy night-clothes, the baby writhing and buckling at my breast, your wide mouth rooting blindly, stupidly, sucking furiously at my hand, my bra strap, with increasing desperation. Then, at last, cramming in a mouthful of nipple, the sweetly serious intensity of the sucking started a prickling pain, the tingle of milk flowing through my breast, like electricity through a wire. 'Good girl, good girl,' I murmured.

Gregor lay beside me, squashed into his pillow, flattened like road-kill. I watched the twitch of your neck, swallowing, the curve of your cheek; I felt your softness and weight in my arms. The sucking subsided, and I shifted slightly, rousing you to drink more. I contrived to look at the alarm clock without unlatching you – three something – and prayed that you wouldn't open your eyes. Then you pulled away, and stretched, a little Buddha, and yawned delicately, like a cat. Such a beautiful yawn! Once again it caught me off balance, and my eyes welled up with tears, which rolled down my cheeks, as rivulets of milk dripped on to your tiny feet.

208

I heard the birds outside, the dawn chorus, and my every bone ached with exhaustion.

Managing visits became my new job; it was like being the Queen. Everyone came, and brought presents, and held you, carefully supporting your head, and made much of every burp or hiccough, and took it very personally when you cried or didn't cry, but got a little embarrassed when I cried too. Gregor's parents came timidly, all the way down from Scotland, bringing knitted baby clothes, and a cheque. Lottie rocked you to sleep with an expert air, while her own toddler played with your new toys, and Sheila changed a nappy with a mixture of horror and hilarity.

The notable absence was my own mother, but I thought of her a good deal. She had been through all this with me, and I found myself wondering how it was for her. For the first time, I had an insight into what was involved, and what she might have been feeling. Suddenly, all the rest of it began to feel a little less important, in comparison.

Gregor and I assembled the necessary bits and pieces to walk outside. I hobbled carefully, with small steps, and we both looked intently into the pram, as we pushed it before us, with pride and disbelief. People smiled when they saw us.

'I think I'm beginning to feel a bit more normal,' I said, as if trying to convince myself. I felt as if something – the maternal instinct, perhaps – had ripped through me with the force of a freight train. I looked at the children playing on the swings, and thought about you playing there one day. I amended the thought with a 'please God', in exactly the same way I always had when pregnant, and then wryly remembered the naive idea I'd had – long, long ago, it seemed, though it was less than two weeks – that I'd be able to stop worrying once you were born.

Everything we passed made my eyes well up with tears – the ducks on the pond, the music on a transistor radio. We sat on a bench. 'I don't want her to ever change,' I sobbed, to Gregor.

'You're bound to feel a bit emotional. It's the hormones. Everyone says so,' he ventured.

'It's not hormones!' I insisted. 'That's so dismissive. Maybe something like this actually makes you more aware of the world as it really is – maybe it heightens your senses, and makes you more in touch with life and death.'

'Maybe,' he said, putting a placatory hand over mine.

'I've been on the cusp,' I said, and started crying again. I couldn't really explain what I meant. It felt more like being in shock: sometimes I was sustained by triumphant euphoria, but when this subsided, exhaustion and self-pity came flooding in. I felt as if I'd been transported somewhere outside ordinary life – or as if ordinary life had revealed itself to be something altogether different, altogether more brutal and shocking, than I had previously thought.

We watched you sleep, like a tiny, live doll. Expressions passed over your face like clouds over the landscape, like changes in the light – your eyelids flickered, a little pucker of unhappiness creased your face, then your mouth twitched with what was probably a suck, but could almost have been a smile.

'I wonder what she's dreaming,' Gregor said. 'Don't you?'

Susie

It was a strange, muddled time. The house seemed to have lost its whole logic. Mum's absence felt brutal, ludicrous, and bizarre. I saw everything as if for the first time: things felt brand new, and raw, as if the skin had been peeled. Her bags, back from the hospice, stood in the corner of the living-room. No one knew what to do with them. They were an aberration, and we were almost afraid to touch them, these things that belonged to someone who no longer existed.

Many people arrived – cousins, neighbours, friends, even Cathy's son, Will, back from Slovakia. It was strange to see his face, in the midst of all this, fundamentally the same, but now a grown man. Everyone sat around, talking and crying. The house was full of flowers, half of which hadn't even been unwrapped. Toby sent an Interflora basket, with a note: 'I'm so very sorry. I still can't believe it. Please, can't we at least talk?' People stumbled about in large groups, or drove around in convoy, unable to think for themselves; huge meals and endless rounds of tea were prepared by women who didn't know where things were kept. All this activity helped me a little, by creating a diversion, something to fill the silence, and a sense of occasion to mitigate the strangeness. It was hard to shake the feeling that we were waiting for my mother to arrive.

210

My grandmother remained poised and dignified, which was a huge relief. 'It should have been me,' she said, straightforwardly. She was the only one who really scared me: I couldn't bear her. People took turns to sit with her, and mumble condolences.

Steve sat upstairs alone. People were simultaneously nervous of him and reverential towards him. Cathy and Lottie and I went through Mum's address book and made a list of people to tell. We made the phone calls in shifts. Telling people made me feel cruel – often they would burst into tears, and I would try to comfort them, feeling remote, and calm, and unreal, playing the dutiful daughter. Someone rang to try and sell us double glazing. 'My mother's just died,' I said, feeling a strange mixture of things: triumph, at playing the ultimate telesales trump card; disbelief, on hearing it spoken aloud; and curiosity, about how he'd react. He paused, as if he were also wondering how to respond, and then apologised, and then said goodbye.

I put all of Mum's drugs – the sleeping pills, the laxatives, the half bottle of liquid morphine – back into their large paper bag to get rid of them. 'I'll do it,' Gus offered. I hesitated for a moment, but wanted to trust and involve him; it was the only thing he'd volunteered to do. To question his intentions at such a moment would, I felt, have been unforgivable.

'Thanks,' I said, 'good chap,' and then realised that it was exactly what my mother might have said.

The hospice rang to say that Mum's body was decomposing badly, and could they call an undertaker? Downstairs, people sat around the kitchen table and talked about her, impromptu eulogies about what she was like or what she would have wanted, as if they were comparing impressions, striving for a composite. Sometimes people said things that didn't tally with my view of her at all, or remembered things from long ago, that I hadn't even known about, and this disturbed me. 'She always loved the colour green,' Lottie announced, 'so maybe we should all wear green, in mourning.' I was startled, and sceptical, and wanted to check, only there was no one to check with.

I realised, as they talked, that they all had slightly different Veras in their heads, and that she was someone different to each of them. Without the real Vera to mediate, this was all there was left, these pale, shadowy, personalised half-Veras sitting around her house, quarrelling. There was no official version of history any more, only speculation.

'I keep expecting her to come through the door,' confessed one of my cousins, Lottie's eldest daughter.

I said I was going to take a plate of food up to Steve. Lottie and Cathy both offered to do it, with irritating eagerness, and I said no, it was OK, I would. Upstairs, Steve sat in the bedroom. The wardrobe door was open, and I could see Mum's clothes. I closed it, and gave Steve his food. 'Do you want anything else?' I said.

'No, I'm OK here for a bit.'

'You did brilliantly,' I said. It was a strange thing to say, but I wanted him to know that I was grateful. I didn't know how he could bear to be in there. It was his bedroom too, I reminded myself, and then thought that maybe I actually didn't know how he could bear to be him.

On my way back down, I looked into Gus's room. He was lying at right angles across the bed, with his eyes half-closed in a squint, a look of cretinous rapture on his face, his hands folded between his knees. I shook his shoulder, but could not rouse him, and cursed him, and myself, for trusting him with the morphine. I felt calm, and angry, and strangely bored by the whole situation. I closed the door so no one else would see him, and went back downstairs.

'I'm going outside for a walk,' I announced.

'Are you OK, lovie?' said Cathy. 'Do you want someone to go with you? Will would love to go with you, I'm sure.'

'Sure,' said Will, with a smiling shrug. He was nearly twice his mother's height, and it seemed strange, when I saw them together, that she could have produced such a creature.

We walked down towards the sea. At first I wanted to be alone, but felt constrained by politeness, even under such exceptional circumstances. The sun was setting – a red smudge, at the far end of the beach – and it was the last day on which I'd seen my mother. I felt it might not rise again, or that if it did, it would be the dawn of a whole new world. I saw the same apocalyptic beauty as I'd seen everywhere that summer, in the subtle gradations of blue where the sea met the sky, and the slight curve of the wide horizon, broken by the distant point of a sail.

The sea had always been there, in my life. The idea of a city without water disorientates me – when I arrive somewhere new, I find myself looking, almost subconsciously, for a downwards slope, a stronger breeze, a change in the light. Just as in London

212

the river is the basis of my mental map, so at home, the sea provides a spirit level, an edge, against which everything else can be measured. The sea is space enough for the bigger thoughts, a place like the cathedrals must once have been, where the sudden widening of perspective allows unconstricted feeling, and a sense of the profound.

'I'm sorry,' Will said. 'It must be horrible to lose your mum.' He had the same fair hair as Cathy, and a friendly, good-humoured face, with eloquent eyebrows, which moved as he spoke, adding a counterpoint of sympathy or irony to whatever he was saying. He still had the faint freckles that I remembered from when we were children.

'I suppose so,' I said, thinking what a bizarre turn of phrase it was. 'It just feels really strange that the world still exists without her. That she's really not anywhere – not in London, or in France, or something like that. I can't quite believe that I'm alive if she's dead, you know?'

'I know,' Will said. 'It takes a lot of getting used to. It must be worse if it's your mother. They're so ... so fundamental.'

'It's such a thin line, between existing and not existing. I always knew people died, but I suppose I never quite believed it.' There were joggers, and couples, and parents with pushchairs strolling along the promenade. They had had ordinary days, I thought, with surprise, which would be forgotten by the end of the week.

We climbed down some steps onto the beach. The head of a swimmer broke the water like a seal. There was something awkward about being exposed to one of my contemporaries in this vulnerable state, but Will was gentle and gallant about it, for which I was grateful. The sea dragged on the flint, and our feet slid on the shingle as we walked, making a companionable crunch.

'Your mother was lovely,' Will said.

His use of the past tense seemed wrong. I wasn't ready to let go of her that quickly. 'A lot of the time she irritates me,' I confessed. My use of the present tense made me feel crazy. I watched the patterns on the surface, at the water's edge, the ripples and wrinkles in the foam, like an ever-changing map, with peninsulas and estuaries, islands and lagoons, continents and lunar seas.

'I bet. She was cool, though. She made me want to study literature.'

'You didn't study literature, did you?'

213

'No,' he grinned. 'She made me want to, though. The way she used to talk about things – she made it all seem interesting. She's probably the person who first made me think of teaching.'

It was strangely consoling, I found, to hear that she'd impacted on the world in ways I hadn't known about. I watched a solitary seagull cut a curve into the sky. 'You end up really superstitious,' I said. 'I see that gull, for example, and part of me thinks, maybe that's Mum. Sounds mad, I suppose. It's just so hard to know where she's gone.'

'I remember when my father died. We scattered his ashes a bit further along the coast, somewhere my parents used to go in their biker days, I think. It was a really windy day, and I remember thinking perhaps that wind is Dad.'

We watched the large glassy waves beat their magnificent pulse against the stones, the suck and crash and drag almost as familiar as the heartbeat in my ears. I was soothed by the repetition, and the gradual variation, like music. In the distance, we could see the crazy twinkling of Palace Pier and the dark, flimsy skeleton of the West Pier. I wondered if he remembered that night, so long ago, when he'd lent me his coat. It was as strange, I thought, this motherless state, as the sea suddenly disappearing.

'I was cross and critical for so long,' I said. 'She was just this thing I used to push against, I could barely see her. It seems like such a waste of time, now. There are things I was still finding out, and so many things about her life I never knew.'

'Yes,' he said, kicking at the stones with his foot, 'all those years, there are two sides to the arguments, and then suddenly, it's just an argument you're having with yourself.'

'I think that there's a part of me that saw my parents as a pattern for my own life,' I said. 'Of course I realise that they're not – they're not even a cautionary tale – but it's quite hard to shake. I always think of myself as just at the beginning of everything, but if I died as young as she has, then I'd already be nearly halfway through.'

'It's a sobering thought,' he said. He seemed to hesitate. 'We'd better get on with it. You know, *carpe diem*.'

You can't be hitting on me, I thought, not now. I looked at him. He was smiling, but straightforwardly, without insinuation, and I felt a wave of relief, together with affection. This is how it will always be between us, I thought: on the beach, side by side, he will always offer me his coat. People stay the same more than they change; that's the remarkable thing.

I watched the sun setting, a furious red, blurred by the tears in my eyes. The wind carried faint screams and whoops from the distant funfair. Goodbye, Mum, I thought. Goodbye, goodbye, goodbye.

I slept on the sofa-bed, and one of my cousins had my room. To my surprise, I slept well, and didn't remember my dreams.

Helene

The peculiar thing to me, after a personal crisis, is the way in which people carry on, from day to day, behaving much as before. Bobby's leave ended, and Charles and I each bid him our civil, tight-lipped farewells, crackling with cross-currents of lethal feeling.

Bobby went back to the war, Charles went to work, and in the evenings, we went to the Club, where we ate the same food and talked to the same people. We lived much the same life, communicating little, keeping up appearances, waiting for something – a change in the world, or at least in the weather.

We didn't have to wait long. Our own domestic dramas were, in any case, soon dwarfed by events. News of the Labour Party's landslide victory in the general election in Britain was received as the most sombre calamity in the circles in which we moved. There were a lot of very long faces at the Club that day. I was fairly ignorant about such matters, but most people seemed to be aware that it meant the unthinkable – the end of British rule in India. On the streets outside, young Indian men who had probably never heard of Clement Attlee or the Beveridge Report were cheering and celebrating. Charles muttered darkly about what a mess they'd make of things, these ignorant crooks in London, and how they had no understanding of India and its people. We all agreed with Edwina, that it was terribly ungrateful towards poor Mr Churchill.

Conversely, the Allied bombing of Hiroshima and Nagasaki was widely welcomed at the time. I don't think I heard anyone question it, and none of the newspapers I saw were critical. The mood was one of elation. This awesome secret weapon – about which we had only the haziest of notions – had brought the enemy to their

215

knees, and ended a bloody, drawn-out conflict which none of us could stomach any longer. We listened to the King Emperor broadcast to the Empire, and during the crackly rendition of the national anthem I couldn't stop crying. Thank God, at last the war would finally be over.

I felt ill, and thought that I had eaten something which disagreed with me. Despite this, the news gave me fresh optimism. I found the post-war future impossible to imagine, but I had faith in its potential. We had been waiting for this for so long that just a little extra patience didn't seem too much to ask. Everything would change. I was sure that Bobby would write, soon, with some plan for the future, some way for us to be together. Charles and I would end our fragile truce, and agree to part as friends – we were both sensible people, without malice, and surely it was the only thing to do. Perhaps my father and my brother would even make contact, now that it was really safe to do so. My nausea would pass, and, after a day or so of the usual backache and irritability, I'd 'come on' – my monthly cycle had been irregular, in any case, since I stopped feeding Lottie. Any day now, I thought every morning, under an identical blue sky. Perhaps it will be today.

Then a letter came for me, in a new handwriting. It was from a Flight Lieutenant Godfrey Blatt. Two weeks earlier, and just a week before news of the Japanese surrender, Bobby had been involved in an unfortunate accident, on a routine sortie. No other aircraft were involved. The description in the letter was curiously technical. Bobby's plane had hardly gained an altitude of 300 feet after clearing the runway when there was an explosion. One propeller began wobbling and although Bobby apparently tried to hold the plane steady it crashed at the edge of the airstrip. Fires started at both ends of the plane. Bobby emerged from the plane suffering an injury to the head and covered with flaming gasoline. Men nearby rushed to his aid, and managed to rip off most of his uniform, suffering burns to their own hands in the process. Bobby was conscious for six hours before he died in a field hospital.

Flight Lieutenant Blatt said that he had the highest respect for Bobby both as a pilot and as an individual. He said that Bobby had spoken of me on a number of occasions, and that he had found my letter amongst Bobby's things.

It was particularly hard, he said, to have to report this loss at a time of joy and celebration. He said that although she had been

216

informed through official channels, he would also, of course, be writing to Bobby's wife.

Vera

At times it seemed to me that my whole world had become that house. I stumbled through the same darkened rooms, wielding my breasts like weapons; my ears rang with cries, so I couldn't tell, when I woke, if you had actually being crying, or if I'd just dreamed it; I stood at the windows rocking or jiggling, looking out like an animal from its cage.

Whatever time of day it was, whatever moment I was in, it seemed to me that it was always that time, and that I was trapped in that moment forever. So it seemed to me that it was always the early hours of the morning, as I listened to the whirr of the milk float and the call of the gulls outside; or that I was forever saying goodbye to Gregor on the doorstep in my striped cotton dressing gown, both of us trying to duck the edge of desperation I felt at the thought of another day alone with the baby; or that I was eternally battling along the seafront, with you screaming in your huge, curvaceous, White Cross pram. Yet I would also look at the breakfast dishes and think – my God, was that only this morning? It seemed like a week ago.

You were like a small, snuffling combustion engine, driven by hunger: your mouth a furious, scarlet furnace, waiting to be filled. Sometimes it seemed to me that we were locked in a kind of wrestling match – clothes and nappies on and off, a hand-to-hand struggle – sleeping to gather our strength, between bouts. Often, when I spent the day alone with you, you seemed huge, growing to take up the whole of my consciousness. You became a force of nature, like the weather, and the state of the whole world, my verdict on the day, the way I felt about myself, were all determined by your mood.

I was totally absorbed by you, consumed by you, addicted to you. When you opened your eyes, your face seemed to come alive. You stared, panting with excitement and fascination, or sometimes with what looked like terror, at a flapping curtain or a patch of wall; you'd inch your way up Gregor's chest with a reflex stepping action, or startle, arms splayed, as I put you down. You started to smile – wide, open-mouthed beams and gurgles which filled me

217

with rapture, and made it impossible to drag my eyes away. You began to follow me with your eyes, as I moved across the room. You made little hand gestures whilst feeding – clumsy, flailing caresses, grasping my finger, your fingers finding their way into my mouth, to make a sucky circle, or a raised hand that seemed to say 'not now, please, I'm in the middle of something very important'. It all seemed adorable to me; this little life seemed extraordinary like no other.

The housework became a vast, unwinnable war. The house became like an extension of my state of mind, my prison and my refuge, my labour of love, my cross to bear. I knew its creaks and sighs, its dappled light and smells. How strange, I thought, as the tepid water gurgled from the sink for the thousandth time, that after all, this would be how I would spend my life, wiping this particular formica worktop.

'For heaven's sake, darling, get yourself a char,' Sheila said, on the phone ('but Gregor feels it would be the immoral exploitation of another human being,' I protested weakly, to snorts of derision). I was forever hanging ludicrously small scraps of clothing on the wooden clothes horse, wearily shifting objects upstairs and downstairs, or stirring the plastic bucket, with its foul shit, flannel and Napisan stew festering inside. I was always being interrupted by a choking, bubbling cry, that made my heart sink. I was always going in, to see, with new astonishment, the weird, big-headed human-goblin creature, small limbs thrashing in a tiny white suit, miniature hands scrabbling at its face, struggling to consciousness.

I met up with the other mothers from my group, each self-consciously bearing forth the former contents of their bump. Together, distractedly, in snatched moments between the feeding, changing, winding and jiggling, we examined the details of our new lives, exchanging trivia, comparing neuroses, as if we might thereby arrive at some kind of an answer.

I came to know their living-rooms, and their dilemmas and obsessions, almost as well as my own. Linda's baby was covered in spots, and she'd become very concerned with hygiene; Cathy's baby screamed all evening, and she fretted about what might be in her milk; Barbara's baby wouldn't take the breast, and lost weight alarmingly before she switched to bottle feeding. Their responses to the unrelenting responsibilities of motherhood differed – Linda's bravado self-confidence, Cathy's self-deprecating humour, Barbara's frantic

218

insecurity – and I came to know them as one might know comrades in battle. I was not alone, they reminded me of this – but it was a time when I rarely felt sane.

All this felt harder than anything I'd ever done before, and yet, somehow, the time passed like sand between my fingers. You changed so fast that at each moment I thought yes, this is how it will be, our new lives, now we can begin, and then it would all shift again – I couldn't grasp it before it slid away. I was forever willing the next development, the next milestone, although each, I sometimes felt, took you a tiny bit further from me, a small loss. It was like having a different child every week.

The changes came as if from nowhere. One day you laughed out loud – a gorgeous dirty-great cackle that we took great delight in coaxing from you. Soon after, you started to show fear, and loud noises brought on a look of abject, pitiful terror, followed by a howl. It sometimes felt to me as if your character existed already and was just emerging – it seemed too fast for it to be being formed. It was as if you'd always been there, as if it were all pre-programmed. It made me think back, with new credulity, to my early belief in an immortal soul.

'It's as if she's under water and she's surfacing,' Gregor said. 'She has a very strong presence.'

'What does her presence feel like to you?' I said eagerly, because it was so close to what I'd felt myself.

'Something very fundamental,' he said. 'Pleasure, discomfort, light and shade, all the really deep-down stuff.'

It wasn't that I loved you too little: rather that I loved you too much. You broke down my defences, so that the world seemed too intense, too much. I was paralysed with fear for you, and a devastating lack of confidence in myself.

When we were apart, I felt abnormally light, as if I could just float down the street. I didn't know what to do with my arms. I wanted to tell strangers that I had a baby – that I was needed, and absolutely had to hurry home. I could feel you pulling at me, in my milk – the excess fluid welling up, and the strange, frantic discomfort it produced – drawing me back, as the moon draws the tide. There was only one person who could help me – one hungry little sucker who could siphon off the wretched stuff – and I was the only one, I felt, who could pacify you. It linked us, like an invisible white cord, tugging us together through the air.

219

An undertaker came round, with a clear plastic folder full of coffins, and sat at the kitchen table. He'd just come from The Grand, where a body had been found in one of the rooms.

'How strange, to die on holiday,' I said.

'You'd be surprised,' the undertaker said. 'They often do it deliberately.' Something – perhaps his use of the third person plural – suggested an impatience with the perversities of the dead, the way one might speak of a group of intransigent colleagues with whom one is forced to deal rather too intimately.

'Suicide?' said Gus, with a flicker of interest.

'Not as such. They just get a feeling, I think. Want to be somewhere with happy memories.'

We went through the many options and packages available, like a multiple-choice paper – teak or plywood; flowers in the car or the chapel. Mum had insisted on the cheapest option, which helped, although I could feel myself being drawn into the details, as a potential new focus for my confused anguish, and beginning to worry about what the undertaker might think. He was quick with the reassuring phrases, about many paths to the same God, about how he tried to treat every case as he would want his own relatives to be treated. A bit like an estate agent, I thought; these dark-suited, self-important professionals who appear at the crossroads of life, where once would have stood a rabbi or a priest.

He explained to us, delicately, almost apologetically, that Mum's body was decomposing very badly. 'It's difficult in this weather.' He said that it was our decision, but that it might be advisable, in this case, to have the coffin closed. There was a long pause: no one seemed to know what to say. 'She wouldn't want people to see her looking horrible,' I said, at last.

Steve and I went to register the death. Once again, I had the sense that telling people, especially someone official, made the whole thing a tiny bit truer. The date, the time, the causes 1a and 1b, were all set down on a crisp new certificate. It struck me that your whole life, you have a death-day, objectively speaking just as important as your birthday, only you don't know what it is.

'What a grim job,' Gus said, when I told him about it.

'They get to do the births as well.'

The night before the funeral we slept badly. There was a full moon, and the house was filled with the sound of people moving around, banging doors, flushing toilets, all night long. I felt a desperate sense of apprehension, of moving inexorably away from my mother. Things felt dislocated, and terribly wrong. I looked at the moon and thought that it was the last night that her body would be on the earth. I dreamed, with startling obviousness, about smashing up the kitchen: breaking plates and cups and glasses on the floor, ripping down the curtains, with a violent force.

I got up very early, desperate to bring the night to an end, and dressed in smart clothes. Sitting in the car, in rush hour traffic, we were so worked up that it felt like midday.

There was a sign at the crematorium gate: North Wing, for services at quarter past and quarter to the hour, South Wing, for services at half past and on the hour. I had to stop myself looking for a chimney.

We waited in little knots around the car park, mingling uncomfortably with the tear-streaked mourners from the group before. Dad arrived. He said, once again, that he hadn't known whether to come, which is more or less what he'd said that day at the hospice. The self-centredness of his dilemma annoyed me – while it angered me that he could even have considered not attending, his efforts at chumminess with Steve also irritated me, as if he expected the death to wipe clean the past.

A smart black hearse drew up. We all stood at a distance, afraid of its contents. Four suited men unloaded the coffin and carried it inside. Seeing it felt like a punch in the stomach. My body seemed somehow to have grasped what was going on, even if my mind couldn't. The service passed very fast, in that strange, heightened state which I sometimes felt during exams. Later, I could recall only moments – Lottie reading a poem, Steve bending over double during a song, people passing over tissues and leaning into each other for support. I wondered, with a remote curiosity, if I would cry.

Afterwards, there were drinks at the university where Mum had taught. The Department had gone to a lot of trouble – there were flower arrangements, and nibbles, and trays of wine glasses. I felt like a public figure. People came and cried at me, and I tried to comfort them, feeling embarrassed, removed, and even a little guilty at my own lack of emotion. On an aesthetic level, to my shame, I began to warm to the role I was playing: gracious, dutiful, selfless, and terribly, terribly brave. How tragic, they said, to die so young. They talked about Mum, and her qualities, recasting her in a reverential, 'too good for this world' light, and I thanked them, but resisted – I didn't want her to be so defined by her death. The man who'd visited on the last day was in floods, and seeing me seemed to further overwhelm him. 'It'll be OK,' I said, not knowing what else to say. He looked at me with puzzled concern, through his tears, and I was aware of having hit a wrong note.

It went on and on, blurred by alcohol, like a wedding; a celebration of epic proportions that became like a way of life, the other guests like colleagues one is obliged to endure. People got drunker and more effusive, 'a tireless anti-nuclear campaigner,' they said, 'a pillar of the community', and 'an extraordinary woman in every sense of the word'.

I tired of my part. The knot of sympathetic women around Steve made me angry. I felt sickened, suddenly, by my parents' generation – their self-deluding hippie crap, their disloyalty, somehow, in accepting this so readily, their ill-concealed fascination with the whole drama, feeding off the death like so many vultures. I'd had enough of this nightmareish new state of affairs. Gus had vanished, presumably to get stoned somewhere. I wished I had someone to lean on, and hide behind, someone whose resources I could count on as my own – I missed Toby.

Dad was at my elbow. I turned to him, and noticed a look of twisted concern on his face. 'I'm really sorry, darling, I have to get back. The twins have chicken pox. Carole's going out of her mind. She needs me back there.'

I nodded, coldly. About right, I thought. I wanted to go home, only home didn't exist any more. There was only this peculiar facsimile of home, crammed with the mad strangers who were now my remaining family.

Perhaps I will go mad too, I thought. Perhaps that is what happens if one cannot accept reality, and reality now seemed so completely unacceptable. I will have to become someone else, I thought. I will have to make do with the traces of her left in me.

Vera

There were lovely moments. The baby looked around with such wonder and delight. You stared up at the branches above the pram, or at me, with an eager innocence, an expression of amused attentiveness that seemed to say 'what next, world?' You raised one shoulder in a coy shrug, and kicked your leg, as if curling up with shyness, or smiled at us like a polite, bemused foreigner, who doesn't speak the language, but is anxious not to cause offence. 'It's as if she's trying to memorise your face,' Sheila said, wistfully. I remembered the feeling from my own childhood that the world was a fantastic mystery, full of glorious new sensations, waiting to reveal its pleasures in good time.

Gradually, slowly, painfully, you won control over your own body. At first, you were just a twitching, flailing bundle of reflexes, your eyes rolling wildly, your limbs jerking to strange, involuntary rhythms, like a marionette at the mercy of its strings. In the bath, you seemed happier – I wondered if perhaps the water supported you, and made movement easier. After a while, you managed to edge a hand towards your mouth, to suck desperately on the fingers, to raise, and then turn, your head, to hold your feet, or hold your hands together, and then to do small stomach crunches, in an attempt to sit up.

Before I had you, I always used to envy the physicality of motherhood when I saw it – the easy closeness, the way mother and child seemed to me to move together, so at ease with each other's bodies that they were almost the same organism. And it was lovely, when I remembered to notice it – the way you relaxed when I took you, scooping you up to perch on a hip, or the way you would nuzzle into my shoulder when tired, as if trying to burrow back inside. Like dancing, I sometimes thought, as well as like wrestling, this thing we do together, these moves we practice endlessly, bound by biology, whether we like it or not.

The nights were mad and desperate and interminable, a confused state between sleeping and waking. I became preoccupied with the strange arithmetic of the baby's sleep, and with futile strategies for outwitting the cries that ripped into my rest at such bizarrely regular intervals. At each waking, I squinted at the little alarm clock by the bed and calculated the hours of sleep I'd achieved, the ground we had left to cover. With the dawn came a sense of relief:

we made it; at least that is over. I dreamed of losing you, of accidentally leaving you somewhere, of dropping you or crushing you. I dreamed that the reason I went to the cot repeatedly was actually to give you a cigarette, on which you sucked hungrily, before settling back down.

Gregor was a stranger in this new land – this half-life of dim light and bodily fluids, where the minutiae of living took on crisis proportions and grew to fill, to over-spill, the twenty-four hours of the day. Beyond his role as provider, he seemed superfluous to requirements: too loud, too clumsy, forever at risk of transgressing the mysterious rules which governed our new existence. I wanted his help desperately, yet when he took you from me, I seemed unable to relinquish my role as interpreter of your wants and needs, unable to simply let you be, and would give directions, or worse, hold my tongue with obvious difficulty, until it was a relief to us both when I took you back. Gregor couldn't help at night, since you seemed only to want the breast, and yet he enraged me – whether by sleeping too soundly, or by waking up and moving around. He went back to sleeping in the spare room, and, as the price, shouldering the sarcastic asides, with which I begrudged him his rest.

At best, we were like irritable siblings. I felt I knew him too well, with a new contempt for his sexuality. The myth I'd fostered, over the years – that it was a personalised thing, about me – was destroyed. His appetites now seemed to me a distasteful affliction, rather the way sex was regarded in my childhood, I suppose, before we were all supposed to become so liberated – although I was also increasingly surprised by how little I cared. At worst, the escalation of my fury scared us both. The smallest things could spark it, and I could go in a few seconds from relative calm to the most hysterical, embittered, impassioned hatred – beyond expression in words, or actions – a pure, vindictive desire to hurt.

These new parts came to us like second-hand clothes – well worn, yet unfamiliar, the patches that covered other people's arguments, the thin strings of duty holding it all together – and yet they were such a good fit, so horribly comfortable, that it seemed unthinkable to discard them. Gregor spent even more time at the university, claiming that it was impossible to work in the house. His affair underlay our arguments, an unspoken reproach, a nuclear option, mutually assured destruction. Sometimes I had the terrifying sense that we had no choice, but were compelled to act it out, this time-honoured dynamic, with pointlessly exhausting passion and pain, for the rest of our lives.

I loved the silence that descended on the house when you were finally asleep. A sense of peace and of relief crept out of the corners, and settled over the rooms, over the battle debris, the toys and clothes and soiled nappies strewn across the floor. I opened the kitchen door and walked out into the garden, feeling a little dazed, with cries still echoing in my head, my breasts sucked dry and marked with the scratches of tiny fingernails, my nipples masticated as used chewing-gum, my body sore and mauled.

Under the cherry tree, I sat down, and lit a cigarette. The birth had made me a coward, but it had made me braver, too. At last, I could look directly at the other thing that had been growing inside me for so long. It had seemed so ugly, before, this hideous second foetus, but now that I examined it, I was surprised to see that it was perhaps not as repulsive as I'd thought. Who was it, this small, strange, yet strangely familiar person that I'd been so afraid of? It was me – of course it was – a different version of me, different and disturbing, but growing stronger by the day.

The Old Vera, the Good Girl I'd always been was still there, picking up socks. She was the one who tried so hard to please her mother, her teachers, and Gregor, dutifully parroting their respective catechisms – she was the one who always felt guilty and ashamed about her past. She was weak, though, perhaps she was starving herself away. This new person, whose shape I'd felt for so long – she didn't give a damn about any of them. She was angry, and wild, and unpredictable. She scared and excited me. I didn't know if I could rely on her; I didn't know what she'd do next.

I inhaled deeply, feeling this new self – a part of me that didn't need approval, that could argue, think and flirt – come tingling into my limbs. My thumb played lovingly with the filter; I looked back up towards the house, the curtains drawn on its complacent, inscrutable windows, the boundaries of my known universe.

I thought about leaving, and wondered what would happen if I just walked away from it all, one day. I would tread on the butt, and light up a second, just to prolong the sense of freedom and rebellion, before heading back inside, to tidy up and to sleep.

Susie

At first I thought that time would stop. After Mum stopped breathing, I held my own breath, and didn't want to hear another noise; that evening, when I looked at the sunset, part of me really thought it would be the last. My life seemed to have tilted over a precipice, over the top, on to a blank page. Things would surely just stay still, for a while, as a mark of respect.

Only of course they didn't. The anniversaries – days, weeks, months – were scattered everywhere, like landmines. I would look at my watch, and notice that it was that hour again, or that day of the week, or the month. Growing up, I had always had the sense of moving towards something, taking great strides into a glittering future, but now, suddenly, I was moving away from something as well. Every happiness will now become a sadness, I thought – there'll be a bitter taste to every triumph, a razor blade concealed in every birthday cake. I began to notice changes to my mother's country: new wars to protest about, new multinationals to boycott, new books to read, new packaging on familiar products. Gradually, treacherously, they were building a world that she wouldn't recognise.

I began to see my mother's life as a whole, complete, so that my early childhood felt just as recent as last year. The tapes played on, in my head. Sometimes I felt that she was in me, and that I was living for her. It was like having a kind of double vision; I felt I could see the past and the present at the same time, everything bleeding together. It was like being possessed, I suppose, or haunted.

I went back to work, staying over most nights with a friendly, rather earnest colleague called Sally, who was a little too interested in my problems. People still seemed nervous of me – scared I might break down at any minute, or perhaps that my sorrow might be contagious. I didn't know how much to tell them; it was surprisingly embarrassing. I needed them to know, to make allowances for me, but felt weak for doing so. It would be easier, I sometimes thought, if I could just wear an armband or something.

I collected horror stories. All kinds of cancer, sudden heart attacks, traffic accidents and even peanut allergies – lost for words, people seemed compelled to offer me their own experiences of death. They talked about counselling, about how useful it was for a friend of a friend, and it seemed to me they were distancing themselves from violent emotion, preferring to treat it as an illness. Everything I heard was like an echo of my own pain. The world was full of previously unnoticed horrors. On the train, I looked at the other people in the carriage, and realised, suddenly, that they would all die, imagining the expression on each of their faces. It seemed surprising, really, that one didn't see it more often.

In London, alone in my emotions, things were peculiar, I felt more unhinged, and wanted to rush back to Brighton, where I was the strong one, and more people were involved. At least there, I felt useful. I felt a strange impulse to give up my life, and just try to be my mother, cooking and cleaning for Gus and Steve, my large, clumsy orphans, trying to give the house a heart. I felt gripped by grief, consumed by it, like a disease. I could never tell when it would overwhelm me, filling my ears and eyes, stopping me in my tracks. It was always, always in my head.

Back home, the strangeness of the house was terrifying. After dark was the worst. Pain thundered through the rooms like a rhinoceros – brutal, futile force – crashing against the walls, again and again. The place was filled with echoes of her: her smell on a towel; shoes and gloves, moulded to her shape; even the radio, or a banging door, in another room. It was like an extension of her body. It hadn't caught up with reality. Her things seemed to be waiting for her to return.

Steve never slept, as far as I could tell, but sat very still, with crazy, suspicious eyes. I heard occasional bursts of blundering movement; trips to the kitchen or the bathroom, and then silence. Gus came in late, and I waited until it was quiet, lying in my bed, and then got up, and followed his trail around the house, turning things off or setting them upright. Their male smells, their debris, their foraging rhythms, living off fry-ups and bowls of cereal at strange hours of the day or night, disturbed me. It was as if the children had been left in charge.

Gus started sleepwalking again, which he'd done a few times as a little boy. I met him at 3am, standing on a chair in front of the sink, with the palms of his hands pressed against the mirror.

'What are you doing?' I said.

'I'm looking for a way out.'

I looked at his face, and realised he was dreaming, so I helped him down, and led him back to bed. What if it had been a window,

227

Gussy? I thought. I tucked him in, as Mum would have done, and he nuzzled the pillow and whimpered.

Helene

Bobby was dead. Bobby had been married. The feeling of waking up, and remembering, was horrible. Sometimes the realisation would come upon me gradually, in some grotesque dream-form, on my journey upwards through the layers of my unconscious; at other times I would be fully awake and staring at the ceiling before it hit me, leaving me stunned and winded. I had to mourn my loss without speaking it aloud, at the same time as discovering that he was not at all who I'd taken him for. I was passionately angry, both with him, and myself. Because I could articulate none of this, never mind put it into any kind of order, it felt like a kind of insanity.

The monsoon had arrived, great sheets of water falling from the sky, hammering on the tin rooves, turning the dust to mud, changing the smells of the land, and providing a suitably apocalyptic backdrop to my mood. I suffered for a while from what one would later call depression, or a breakdown, although at the time there was a whole different set of euphemisms for it. It felt a lot like exhaustion. I couldn't get up, dress, or talk to other people. The smallest things would provoke tears or panic, while the larger things brought on a look of puzzlement, or a peculiar blankness. My other longing, for Lottie, returned with a force I'd never experienced, and became a sort of mania. I had bad dreams about her, instead of Bobby, and became convinced that something was wrong. Sometimes it seemed to me as if she were the one who had died, and no one could convince me otherwise. It was my fault, my punishment, for allowing myself to become distracted.

Charles was wonderful. He was gentle, patient and understanding, loyally deflecting the outside world, and nursing me with a tenderness I would never have imagined in him. It was as if he had just been waiting for some vulnerability in me, in order to find a role he could rise to, and a chance to be heroic in his own way. He fed me, brought me drinks, and even bathed me, much to Jameel's surprise and confusion. Selfless sacrifice was one thing he could do, one thing his background and education had prepared

228

him for. I think it was almost a relief to him. I came out of it all thinking – once I began to consider such things again – that things might even work out between us. We began feeling our way towards a new intimacy, and a sexless marriage which, although unorthodox, and far from the romantic ideal, was a comfortable fit, and worked on its own terms.

After a while I told him what I hadn't even admitted to myself – that I believed I was pregnant. I couldn't think about a baby, but spoke in terms of a 'condition'. I was cushioned by my numbness – it would surely be the limits of his tolerance and good faith, which I felt I didn't deserve to start with, but what did any of it matter, anyway? I wanted to be miserable, and despised, and what could he do to hurt me now?

His reaction, once he understood what I meant, astonished me, even in my distanced state. He was delighted, and he never once asked what was – to me at least – the obvious question. After a while I realised that it was very convenient for him, really, as an explanation for my sudden absence from the Club, and long period of bed rest, but he also seemed genuinely excited by the prospect of another child, in addition to the one he'd never met. He kept talking about how wonderful it would be to have a brother or sister for Lottie, and how we'd be a proper family; he seemed to feel that this would be an opportunity to make up for what he'd lost out on the last time. When I did appear back in company, people smiled understandingly, and offered me a seat, and congratulated us, and Edwina and Bunny played at being our best friends again, and said how thrilled they were, and Charles beamed proudly. It all seemed extraordinary to me, but I was quite willing to go along with it. Charles started to make arrangements for my passage back home.

As well as waking up, in the mornings, the other time of day I remember particularly clearly is the dusk. For half an hour before sunset, the colours outside my window took on a purple tinge, and sounds seemed to have an extra resonance. There was the noise of traffic on the road outside, and the shouts of women, or the wails of children from the servants' quarters, as well as the soothing sounds of the hotel: the bangs and shouts from the kitchen, the barking of dogs. The day's passing was marked, as usual, in the different traditions amid which we lived, by the call to prayer and the last post, which I now registered as automatically as one would the sound of church bells in Europe. Later on, I often heard distant music – a military band, playing the popular dance-hall hits of the day with a distinctly Indian wobble.

At times like that, I sometimes felt an almost unbearable nostalgia. It didn't seem to me to be personal, about my own circumstances or grief, but about the whole of humanity. It was hardly specific enough to put into words, but something to do with the agony of change, and the pain of leaving things behind. We can't live our lives at full capacity, I thought, and it's just as well for us, because we surely couldn't take it if we did. It takes a considerable shock to jolt us out of our everyday blindness, and perhaps to see things with their full force, as they really are. Our consciousness is limited by a sort of self-protection, and we take refuge in the blankness of the moment, so that the years slip by unconsidered.

I gazed at the mosquito netting at the window for so long that the sky changed colour behind it, without my even noticing. The fine mesh of threads blurred in and out of focus, so that at some moments they disappeared completely, but at others, they looked as thick and as solid to me as prison bars.

Vera

Before you were born, I did not see my mother for a long time. She lived in America with her second husband, but every couple of years she came back to England for a holiday. She always asked – usually through Lottie – if she could meet me, and I always said no. When you were eight months old or so, however, to my own surprise as well as everyone else's, I agreed that she could come to our house.

'Are you sure?' Gregor said, nervous of unknown alliances, or frightened that this might herald further unpredictable and emotional behaviour.

'She'll be so delighted,' Lottie said approvingly, instantly making me regret my decision.

Cleaning up before her visit, I found myself looking at my home, and my life, from the outside, and wondering what she'd make of it. It all seemed rather humble, rather ordinary – but it's mine, I thought defensively, for better or worse, and the new Vera whispered at me not to tidy too much – why should I? I brushed your hair, however, and rubbed a dab of polish into your tiny patent leather shoes, and changed you again after you got scrambled egg on your cardigan.

The two tones of the doorbell made me jump: her gloved thumb on the white button, set in a black plastic rectangle, a sudden intrusion from the outside world, startling me out of the endless, faintly deranged loop inside my head, 'let's get that nappy off ... now, what else do we need?' I sneaked a quick look in the hall mirror, to calm myself, but was further unnerved by the panic in my own eyes.

And there, astonishingly, she was, on the doorstep, a visitor from another world. Older looking, of course, but not all that much. She looked well: sun-tanned, her hair shorter than she'd worn it before, curled round her face like a helmet. Her brown eyes shone with emotion, her face folding into a smile, not for me, but for you – I'd almost forgotten you, balanced on my hip. Expensive-looking clothes, and handbag – my God, was that a miniskirt she was wearing? It was certainly well above her knee.

'My goodness, this must be little Susanna,' she said.

'Come in,' I said quickly, to curtail the awkwardness over our greetings – I was afraid she might try for a kiss.

We sat together in the front room, and in spite of my resolve not to run around after her, I offered her tea – she'd come a long way, after all – and of course you cried when I tried to put you in the play-pen, so it seemed the natural thing for her to hold you while I made it.

I had been afraid we'd have nothing to talk about, but I'd forgotten that a baby is a great social lubricant, an inexhaustible topic and an almost permanent distraction, to fill any difficult pause. I'd never really considered her grandmother material, but to my surprise, she was really interested. Most people tolerate discussion of children – men as a social nicety, women as a sort of *quid pro quo*, to allow them to discuss their own – but she really cared, in almost the same way as me. 'How does she sleep?' she asked, and 'does she have a good appetite?' and she seemed to approve of my answers – 'just like you', or 'just like your sister', or 'the clever ones often do'. She believed in your potential humanity, projecting personality onto you, in the way that the women in a family love us into being, shaping us into real people as if through faith alone. After ten years of silence between us, it was all still there – like riding a bicycle, which they say you never forget – and after the odd wobble, the memory moved our limbs of their own accord, carrying us along despite our lack of conviction.

We won't discuss it, I realised, with relief and surprise. Perhaps we never will again. It had been a big deal for me. My name, ironically, derives from the Latin for 'truth', but from the age of fourteen, when she confided in me about her affair during the war, I'd felt as if my whole childhood was a lie. My father – and that's how I'll always regard him, because he loved me, and brought me up – was taken from me twice, first by her confession, and then by his death. The secrecy, and guilt, and confusion, and lack of trust, were hard for me to overcome. In her natural affection for you, however, I could forgive her almost anything, and that was why she was there. Besides, I had more of an idea, by now, of how it felt to be trapped in a broken marriage. Life, I had begun to realise, is not the way we plan.

It was strangely ordinary, and on reflection, I decided that ordinary was good. We drank the tea, and went out into the garden. She told me about a weekend trip to Brighton she'd made in the 50s. After an hour or so she looked at her watch, and I found her a train timetable, and we discussed how long she'd need to get to the station. 'Hal's picking me up at Victoria at four fifteen,' she said, and I mumbled something about how she'd have to bring him along too, next time, and was quite ashamed by how thrilled she looked.

She kissed us goodbye, and that was fine, and I could tell she wanted to stay for longer. We watched her back, as she set off along the street.

'That was your granny,' I said to you, just to hear how it sounded, and gave you a jiggle. 'Bye-bye, Granny.' We rarely notice, until the moment is almost gone. Just as you always did, a little too late, you realised what was happening, and started to wave.

Susie

In London, I called Toby, and arranged to go over to the house and collect some more of my things. He sounded pleased to hear my voice, and eager to oblige. I felt nervous about seeing him, and badly wanted to look effortlessly devastating, if at all possible. I wore smarter than usual work clothes, and applied extra eyeliner and lipstick in the toilets before leaving. It felt almost as if we had a date.

I rang the doorbell, even though I still had my key. His ambling shape through the glass, his messy blonde hair, his shy smile, were all so familiar, and I felt as if I had been away on a long voyage. 'You look great,' he said, sounding surprised. I recognised his tone and the look he gave me from the way he'd always been with other people – the way he was when he was actually making an effort.

I sat on the stained sofa, the summer sunshine filtering through the curtains, the dust particles dancing in the air. He fetched me a bottle of Cobra from the fridge. Looking round the house I had so recently considered my own, a territorial resentment crept up on me. My pictures! I thought, childishly. My books! My throw! Where to sit was clearly an issue for him, and he hovered uneasily, before settling on a floor cushion by the telly.

'I'm so sorry about your mum,' he said. 'It must have been horrible. I don't think I ever really believed she would die.'

I didn't reply. I wasn't going to let him anywhere near all that. 'Where's Zoe?' I asked, feeling queasy. I had had neurotic fantasies about them welcoming me together, inviting me into their happy little love-nest.

'She's moved out,' he said. The floor cushion was a bad choice: he could either perch uncomfortably, like a disciple at my feet, or sprawl like a sultan, sipping his beer. 'It was a bit full on, both being here.'

I hesitated, absorbing this information with a surprising relief. 'Are you still, um, seeing her?' I asked, rejecting some of the harsher verbs that suggested themselves.

He was silent, and avoided my eyes, and I could tell that he was. 'I'm not sure it's going to work out,' he said, 'we both feel so guilty. It was a bad way to start.'

It seemed to me that he was repeating something she'd said. 'Do you expect me to feel sorry for you?' I said, trying to suppress the righteous anger that pounded in my chest. 'Or do you want my advice, perhaps?'

'You're good at stuff like that ...' he said, apologetically.

'She's pretty. You always fancied her.' I remembered the elation in the air between them, the heated debates, the bouts of giggling, the breathless wrestling. It all made a sense to me now. They'd suit each other, I thought, bitterly – two blondes, both charmed, in their way – the kind of couple people want to be with. I remembered Zoe's old Year Book, from her High School in the US. She'd written in a Billy Bragg quote, 'help save the youth of America, help save them from themselves'. This – between the hearts and jokes and declarations of undying love – had particularly impressed Toby. 'Your very own Prom Queen to defile,' I said. Increasingly, I reminded myself of Mum.

It felt very strange to sit so close to him without touching. Until recently, it would have been so natural to reach out, and suddenly, this was taboo. It felt a bit like my possessiveness over the furnishings – surely he was still mine? I knew his underwear, his obsessions, the hairs on his back, his sleeping positions. I couldn't believe the swift turns my life had taken, and was bewildered by the sudden negation of the past.

'I'd better get started,' I said, and got up, and went upstairs to get my things.

I filled three cardboard boxes and a bin liner, while he leaned against the door frame. We chatted, surprisingly easily, about old friends, or practical stuff – he still didn't know what day the bins were emptied, and who to ring about the boiler. He was generous with our shared possessions, letting me take anything I wanted, and I found that, faced with his lack of opposition, I didn't actually want that much of it. I think we were both relieved by how well things had gone, and as I finished the last box, he brought me up another beer.

'You're amazing,' he said. 'So calm.' Don't be fooled, I wanted to say, but didn't. 'I do miss you,' he said, looking down. 'It's very weird. It's almost as if you were the one who died. You were always there, and then suddenly, you weren't. I noticed your smell on the pillow, the first week, and it had a very powerful effect on me. I haven't been sleeping at all well, but that helped me sleep better.' He gave a self-conscious shrug, as if to say I know, I shouldn't, but I don't care. He had no reason to behave well with me – no more good opinion to maintain.

I thought of opening Mum's closet, and burying my face in her clothes. 'I didn't die,' I said, starting to cry, 'but it felt a bit like that to me, too.'

He came and sat by me on the bed, and stroked my head, and it was a huge relief just to have a familiar body, on whom I could sob without inhibition. He found me some toilet roll, and I blew my nose and dabbed at my eyeliner, and he gave me a kiss on the cheek, and a squeeze, and then another kiss. 'The people that made me feel like myself were you and her,' I said, incoherently. 'I didn't think I could exist without her. I didn't know who I was without you. It's a bit like being in between personalities ...'

Even when we were kissing properly, it felt somehow platonic, as if we were just old friends who happened to snog from time to time. 'I wonder if I'm really going to sleep with him?' I thought, 'I can't, surely, after everything he's done.' It wasn't that I had any renewed faith in him – I felt I could see right through his words – but I suppose it was just a relief to let go. I could feel him responding – the combination of novelty and habit was hard to resist, and it felt good to have this power over him, and to get some revenge on that bitch Zoe. The familiar choreography of our foreplay had a momentum of its own, a well-travelled road. I let out a deep, wobbly sigh, and wanted to say 'I love you', as I always had, and had to stop myself. 'I've missed you too,' I said, instead.

By the time we had undressed, with the disengagement that involved, it felt worse again. 'Why am I letting him do this?' I thought to myself, as he unhooked my bra, but it felt vindictive to make him stop by then, as if I'd planned the whole thing. The movements and noises I knew so well couldn't deaden my feelings, and my brain raced on regardless. 'Is this OK?' he said, and I nodded, silently. 'How do you want to go?' he asked, later, as if I'd want to discuss the relative merits of different sexual positions, and I said 'I don't care,' and the fact that he should perhaps have stopped then, but didn't, showed how little we had left to lose. It had become like a task we both had to accomplish, by unspoken agreement. It was like ghost sex: we both seemed strangely absent.

Afterwards, I started to cry again. He put his arm around me, but the physical intimacy without trust, without emotional intimacy, felt all wrong. I had always been curious about one-night stands, and in the past I envied Zoe her easy, cheerful promiscuity, but I realised then that I wouldn't have been good at it. The world seemed curdled, and cold, and topsy-turvey, and I didn't know who to trust. I dressed, with belated modesty, and nothing could fill the silence between us.

Waiting on the pavement with my bag and my boxes, I thought, this is it, I can go no lower. Yet I also felt strangely purged, and human again. There was not much comfort in this bleak new landscape, but a spark of self-belief deep inside me kept me going, like a boiler light. It must have been something Mum gave me, right at the beginning. It might flicker, at times, but it would blink back on again, it would never go right out.

Chapter Ten

Susie

I told Gus what I had learned about Mum's father. 'Cool. I always knew Granny was a dark horse,' he said.

It bothered me more than I would have expected. It wasn't the impropriety, or any notion of sin, of course – although I think that side of it upset Mum more than she cared to admit. It was mostly the fact that she'd kept quiet about it for so long. You take it for granted that you know your mother – because if you don't know her, who do you know? She's the person who teaches you trust – if you're lucky, anyway – a model, in some sense, for your future relationships. The fact that there was this fundamental fact of her life that I didn't know about was a shock to me. It was all bound up with the process of losing her. The idea of her that I thought was so secure was shaken, and I found myself unsure of everything. You think you own your past, but you don't own anything, or anyone. Perhaps the truth is that it owns you.

I found it hard to get to sleep, but when I did, I dreamed with a clarity, a luminosity, and a force that I'd never experienced. Often, I was startled by the obviousness of my dreams. It was as if my brain were running a pre-programmed sequence – grief – all by itself, working things out in my absence. I missed her physically, too. I hadn't thought we had a particularly physical relationship, but her smell, her touch, and her embrace, were the things I really sickened for.

I could sense her so completely, it was as if I'd become the air around her. She was curled in a leather armchair, her legs crossed over one of the arms, reading a white book, with red lettering on the cover. She was so engrossed that she couldn't hear me call her, her eyes moving swiftly from left to right, her face blank. I could feel all her textures – her dark brown top, a stretchy ribbed material with small wooden buttons, her rough skirt, with dark red flowers on, her leather sandals buckled over knobbly toes. I could smell the cigarette smoke and Vosene in her hair. She moved suddenly, to turn a page, and it was like watching someone stir in their sleep. She looked so young, and happy, I thought, before we used her up.

When I woke, my face was wet with tears, and I realised that I had been sobbing aloud.

Vera

I stood in the half-light of our bedroom. You seemed to have been uneasy forever, bubbling at first, like a coffee pot coming to the boil, then twitching, puckering your face into a plaintive, kitten-like cry, now buckling and flailing in my arms, wailing. Your discontent seemed immense to me, I could hardly bear it, this all-engulfing anguish, the pain of life distilled into noise, and I was torn between empathy and irritation – 'I know, darling, I know'. I sat down on the edge of the bed and tried to feed you again, but you writhed away, your lip quivering with disappointment, and I felt locked in the moment – eternal, tiresome, desperate – jiggling and crooning, 'ssssh, ssssh, rockabye baby, oh for heaven's sake!'

I heard a car start outside. The curtains billowed in a breeze. Then the cries subsided, and you seemed to grow heavier in my arms, and your wriggling stopped, and I could feel the atmosphere in the room change, as a profound stillness settled around us. I looked down, and could see your eyelids slowly lowering, your head tilted back in surrender, your little hand uncurling. I hardly dared breathe: it was as if a fairy had touched us both with her magic wand, and turned us into statues where we sat.

And as usual, alongside the relief, I was struck with a strange regret. It was nonsense, madness, I told myself. In sleep you no longer needed me, however briefly, and I missed you already. I remembered, suddenly, to breathe in your gorgeousness, the light down on your silky cheek, your exact warmth and weight in my arms, your perfect smallness. Swaying with tiredness, I could

238

hardly bear to put you down, and you stirred, and it seemed to me that you didn't want to be put down either, and I remembered the time when you were part of me, and never put down. I wanted to stop time, and it seemed so sad; it all seemed to be about loss, somehow.

Blinking back tears – such silliness – I laid you gently in the carry cot, carefully, carefully, working my arm loose slowly, peeling us apart. The curtain blew back again, and I heard echoing footsteps, and voices, on the pavement outside. Lighter, freer, but a little lost, as if waking from a dream myself, I tiptoed from the room.

Helene

Gradually, I began to recover my balance, and to repair my mask. Day by day, I grew a little stronger, and the random panic which had paralysed me without warning seemed less of a threat. The prospect of the journey home also revived me. At the last minute, I began to regret leaving India so abruptly, and made a half-hearted attempt to itemise, and remember. I asked the names of birds, and trees, and it occurred to me to describe my surroundings in a letter to my mother; I even found that I understood a little more of the lingo. It seemed that it was too late, though, for all of that: I was already blinded by familiarity, and impatience.

The last days were packed with practical arrangements and goodbyes. I bought a few keepsakes at the bazaar, trying to see the silver teapots and onyx egg cups in a cold-grey London light, as pleasingly exotic, instead of the crudely-made junk I had always taken them to be. The garden at the Club seemed beautiful to me again, and I even managed to muster an affection for Edwina and Bunny, as we swore to keep in touch. There was talk of English dinners and theatre trips, which I felt was probably lip-service, but could all too well imagine – they were the sort of people towards whom one's obligations never seem ended. Jameel – dedicated, inscrutable, as much of a puzzle to me as ever – accepted my parting gifts with a polite nod. You win, I wanted to say, you can keep it all, whatever it is you wanted – only now let me live a life in which I can lie in bed in private, and drop my clothes where I choose, and in which neither of us is forced to efface the other to avoid embarrassment.

239

On the platform, I kissed goodbye to Charles – my husband, my jailor, and my nurse – in some ways still a stranger, in others bound to me like never before. How strange, I thought again, that we are in this together. In spite of the many times we had discussed it, I just couldn't imagine us building a life together in England, and when he described it, I felt he was talking about other people. There was something the same about us, I was beginning to feel, in that we were bred, or compelled, or temperamentally inclined towards exile. I could tell he was worried about me, going so far alone, and this gave me strength.

At every stage in the process, I found myself whispering a secret goodbye to Bobby – to places where I'd known him, or dreamed him. Perhaps it was because I'd made him up, and he'd never really been the man I superimposed on him, that my sense of him was still so extraordinarily pervasive. He was in everything, I found: smells, tastes, the quality of the light.

This time, I enjoyed the long train journey. I had seen such a small corner of the vast continent, and it seemed a shame to me now. The scalding tea, the lives of other people, and the bright cameos we passed were a pleasant diversion. I wanted to lose myself in the rushing of the wind and the singing of the wheels on the rails, the dip of telegraph wires, as we thundered over the sleepers.

My passage back was also a very different affair. The soldiers on the ship – brown, exhausted, demob happy – seemed like children to me now. I fell in with a few slightly older women, travelling back to visit their own children, often for the first time in many years. We compared photographs, and discussed options for schooling, and other such pressing dilemmas, and called each other 'dear', and asked insincerely after each other's comfort. This time, I felt sedate, and matronly. Once I saw a small fish, alive, in the ship's swimming pool, unaware of its journey into colder waters, like my own amphibious passenger. I dozed in a deck chair a lot, letting the occasional nausea wash over me, and looking forward to meals. I played poker, too, for hours on end, or watched the flying fish hurl themselves pointlessly at the sky.

I slept better, at last. Somewhere around Gibraltar, where the skies were already clouded, and the palette of the world more muted, I seemed to wake from India, and Bobby, just as I'd woken, on the outward journey, from the daily concerns of motherhood: as from some vivid, often troubling, and curiously engrossing dream.

Susie

A child's longing for its mother is such a basic, primary emotion, and feeling it with this intensity took me right back to the beginning, almost as far as I could remember.

The house had seemed filled with difference, the moment I awoke. Perhaps it was just the fact that I couldn't hear the radio, downstairs – my mother always switched it on first thing, so she could argue with the news, or hum along to loud classical music, while we were getting up. Instead, the gulls shrieked outside. The cot, on the other side of the room, was empty, and I had that slightly cheated feeling I always got when Gus was up before me.

My parents' bed, where I went first, was empty. Before we got central heating the house was always cold. I wandered downstairs, tentatively, a few steps at a time, like an explorer searching for human life, in my long, lacy nightie and slipper socks – a scratchy, moccasin arrangement kept on with ribbons, so complicated to fasten and undo that I usually slept with them on. I took Pinky Ted (who was already more pale grey than pink) with me.

Dad was in the kitchen, scrambling eggs in an enamel pan. Baby Gus was on the floor. He had an orange stain spreading up the back of his baby-gro, but was perfectly happy, destroying the newspaper which had just been delivered, bouncing on his bottom, scrunching and flapping the pages excitedly.

'Where's Mummy?' I said, suspiciously.

'It's OK,' Dad said, with an unconvincing brightness that only increased my distrust, 'she's gone out. How about some breakfast?'

'No she hasn't' I said. 'She hasn't gone out.' I felt that by insisting, I could make her appear. Perhaps it was to do with my sense of my own importance, or perhaps I got it from Mum, but I had very little faith in anything he said.

'She's not here, treasure,' Dad said. I didn't like the way he looked or smelled (perhaps he'd been up all night), and I could tell I scared him too.

'But where *is* she?' my voice was a high-pitched waver. I could

241

feel a scream coming on – so loud it would make my throat sore, and my fingers tingle from lack of oxygen – and I was calculating whether to let it out, because I also had the feeling that perhaps this wouldn't work on him. He felt in his dressing-gown pocket for his cigarettes, and lit one on the gas ring.

I was used to their fights. I would stand between the two of them, and try to join in, mimicking their tone of voice without being sure what to say, excited but a little disturbed by the game. 'Stop it!' I shouted, or 'you're waking up the owls!' (because owls sleep in the day) or 'you're giving Pinky Ted a headache!' Sometimes they would pause – their faces frozen in mid-flow, contorted with hatred, and anguish, and sudden guilt – but the force of their passion was too strong to resist, and I heard my name in the accusations which resumed above my head. Or I would sit by the banisters, peeling off slivers of paint – thin and stretchy, like the membrane around an egg – not listening at all, until a phrase lodged itself in my head, where it echoed like poetry: 'hysterical fucking banshee'; 'your sodding libido'. Afterwards, I would find one or other of them, stony faced or sobbing, and distract them with my demands or my toys.

'Don't worry. She'll be back,' Dad said, but I could hear the anger in his voice.

He turned off the heat, and rescued the remains of the newspaper from Gus, who started to howl in protest. I glimpsed, for the first time, a bleaker truth, which came back to me again all those years later – that life would just go on without her, except that I would be less safe, and less sure, and so much less important.

Vera

Red, white and blue balloons hung along the house fronts, and strings of flags flapped between the two sides of the street. The town had decked itself out like a sailing ship, flying its colours in full regalia, tilting into the sea.

You were a hopelessly over-excited little girl. You seemed struck by the idea that outdoors could become like indoors, the street turned inside out like a sock, with trestle tables down the middle of the road, and an assortment of chairs from different living-rooms – you couldn't understand why we didn't do it more often. At your primary school, they were holding a special assembly. The children with the best voices had been selected to sing 'I vow to thee my country . . .', and you were very disappointed not to be picked. The headmistress had said that you needn't stand up for the national anthem (she must have said something like 'I'm sure her Majesty won't mind'), and this had started a rumour that the Queen would be attending in person – you burst into tears when I tried, as gently as I could, to set you straight. You loved ritual – it was a source of great disappointment that I wouldn't take you to church – and you were desperate to feel part of all this.

There were plates of sandwiches and sausage rolls, and bowls of crisps, and each paper plate had a paper napkin and a can of Pepsi. The children were stuffing their faces eagerly, the little girls with their identical, pudding-basin haircuts, Gus, a podgy, imperious baby, already with an unruly burst of curls.

I hovered behind them, along with the other mothers, and behind us, the clusters of elderly ladies in mackintoshes. Cathy was there, reprimanding little Will for balancing a paper plate on his head, crisp crumbs all over his face. I'd put you in a red, white and blue tank top, for the occasion, and even I, the staunch anti-monarchist, wore red trousers, although I preferred to see this as an ambiguous statement. I looked perfectly happy, beaming proudly at my offspring. You wouldn't have guessed that my world had ended three months earlier.

This time, Gregor didn't tell me. He didn't need to – this time I knew the signs already, and wouldn't allow myself to ignore them. Things came to a head one evening, when his Head of Department – with whom Gregor had told me he was having dinner – telephoned asking to speak to him. He got back late; you two were already asleep upstairs. I told him I was going out to get some fresh air. He looked confused and panic stricken, especially when I told him there was a bottle for Gus in the fridge, but I left quickly, before he could stop me.

I got the milk train up to London and stayed with Sheila. She was pleased to see me – I think she thought it would be fun, until she realised that I couldn't stop crying. Leaving you two upset me far more than leaving him, but I was in such a state, what scared me most was that I wouldn't be able to take proper care of you. After two weeks, he was so desperate he agreed to leave the house and I moved back in. Perhaps I wouldn't have been so amenable if I'd realised he'd move straight in with his new girlfriend.

For the next few months, I more or less lost it. The New Vera took over, strong in her rage, but she wasn't much of a mother. You were dressed, approximately, and fed, although I often wondered how; I was on automatic pilot, blinded by fury. I followed him back from work, to a tiny pebble-dashed house in Five Ways. There were hysterical scenes in car parks, baby Gus howling in my arms. Words came out of my mouth which I wasn't aware of speaking; I found myself in places with no memory of how I'd got there. Ugly things were said to friends and colleagues, some of his things were damaged, there was even a brick through a front window. I had dreams, every night, in which I was just screaming at him. I composed long, ever-changing letters in my head. 'Are you trying, deliberately trying, to finish me? Because you couldn't have fucked my life up more completely if you'd tried.'

Slowly, however, the grim, grinding routine of my life began to re-establish itself. The days were a chaos of small tragedies – dropped toys and bumped foreheads – and passionate desires, for shiny objects and chocolate biscuits. I ploughed into the wind with the pushchair, shouting tunes from the children's television programmes in my head: 'Well, Jemima, Let's go shopping, Are we walking? No, we're hopping, Hop, hop, hopping mad, Hop, hop hopping'. The inability to suppress one's internal monologue is seen as a sign of insanity: sometimes, I wasn't talking to baby Gus but to myself, and I caught people looking at me strangely. I was desperately lonely. Often, by the time I managed to get the three of us out of the door in the mornings – a localised whirlwind of bribery, threats and pleas – we'd all be in tears.

In the evenings, I resumed work on my PhD. I sat at my desk in the living room – I couldn't bring myself to use Gregor's study. The standard lamp made a calm circle of light, over the disorderly piles of paper and carbon paper, the painted clay ashtray that you had made for me overflowing with cigarette butts. The click of my typewriter filled the silence of the house.

The world closed ranks on me with an icy disapproval. I had forgotten how to speak to adults, and could hear that I was loud, wheedling, bonkers. The moral majority, the women with rain-proof headscarves and string bags, had their suspicions confirmed.

244

'She's from a broken home', the headmistress mouthed to your new teacher, over your head, as you clung to my legs. Even my own kind – the sort of people who made their own yoghurt and candles – seemed uncomfortable with my new status. Couples were afraid of me, our friends felt they had to choose: it was as if I'd become a cautionary tale, a reminder of the fragility of marriage. Even Sheila, without children herself, didn't really seem to understand – she visited, witnessing the bedtime mayhem with bemused horror, or invited me up to London and tried to fix me up with men, but seemed exasperated when I explained that I hadn't lined up a babysitter, or that I was too tired.

Cathy was my lifeline, my one unlikely ally. The other mothers in the group went their own way, one by one, but Cathy and little Will were there, day after day, for trips to the playground or the library, for cups of Nescafé while the children fought over toys, for walks on the beach or emergency consultations over fevers or tantrums. We shaped each other, in those many hours by the wet swings. Cathy was at first embarrassed to hear my ardent, angry feminism take shape, or by my left-wing take on the Cold War, but it pleased me to hear her begin to question some of her received views; I was at first suspicious of, then buoyed up by her pragmatism and easy-going good humour. If a child was crying, I would concoct some elaborate psychological trauma, often to do with Gregor or the state of the world, and Cathy would say 'they've got a tooth coming'; if the housework was getting out of hand, Cathy would blame herself, and I would blame a patriarchal society. Soon, we each internalised the other's voice, as a reassuring note in the blizzard of self-doubt. It was a lifeline, I felt, but it was not much of a life.

We can't be fully aware all the time, I thought, and maybe it's just as well. Doing the washing up, getting the kids to school, getting through the day to watch a little telly in the evening, these are the things that oil the passage of the years. There were moments, though, like cracks, when I seemed to escape from my ordinary, engrossing concerns, and wonder about the fabric of things, or feel for some shape beneath the surface, gone before I could pin it down.

The clouds moved fast in the sky, the red, white and blue dancing in the breeze. 'Smile, everybody,' Cathy said, and took the photograph, freezing us all in time, with the crisps, the Pepsi,

245

the flags in motion. I smiled, because by now I knew that not to was unacceptable, but I'd never felt more of a foreigner.

Helene

After Bobby's death, I really thought that my life was over. I would continue to walk and talk, and maybe even to laugh and cry, but I would never actually *feel* again. I was very young: needless to say, this wasn't the case. The astonishing thing is that there was so much more, both better and worse, to come.

I arrived back to classic English weather – a grey-white sky, with the never-quite-realised threat of rain. This time, the ship took me straight up the Thames estuary to Tilbury, and my mother could meet me with Lottie as soon as I disembarked.

Everyone came out on deck, as we drifted up the river towards the docks. The scale of the ship seemed incongruous, now we were no longer on open water, and we looked a strange bunch, suddenly, in an outdated assortment of warmer clothes: I wore the same woollen suit, with shoulder pads, in which I'd left England. I recognised the fear the women around me were trying to conceal on their faces, as they pointed things out to each other on the bank, because it was something I was very familiar with – the fear of seeming a foreigner, where one claims to belong, and the fear of being left stranded by change. 'Why, I'd forgotten how different English cows are,' one lady exclaimed, as we glided past a herd of Friesians. 'How green it all is,' remarked another, while her friend was startled at the amount of asphalt that had been laid down during the war, even on the country roads.

London was still a dreadful mess. The warehouses and industrial sites on the shore were mostly in ruins, but there were signs of new life: cranes, cockney workers in flat caps and overalls, factories belching their smoke, prefabs going up everywhere, like fresh shoots in the debris – and there was also a lot more real greenery, since all of the bomb sites were now overgrown.

As we chugged slowly, slowly, towards the quay, we looked down onto cheering and waving faces, pink-cheeked in hats, holding flags and home-made banners, and making victory signs. Some of the soldiers threw their caps, and some of the crowd threw flowers, which bobbed in the water. The new force pulling on us was so strong that we made the most hurried of farewells to people who a moment before had seemed like life-long friends, and I felt sorry for those who had no one to meet them.

I spotted my mother fairly quickly, as I made my way unsteadily down the metal steps. She wore her old coat, with a fur collar, and it seemed to me that she looked thinner, and older. I wondered if all the things that had happened to me would show on my face. She had a small child – no longer a baby – in her arms.

When at last we found each other in the embracing, exclaiming crowd, my mother kissed me hard on the cheek, and stroked my hair, and hugged me tightly with her free arm. I was impatient to get loose, to look at Lottie. My little girl was instantly familiar, but also completely changed, with the same eyes on a more grown-up face, under a lovely thick crop of hair. I was mesmerised by her expression, a fantastic collage of resemblances, an endlessly interesting puzzle of the half-known and the miraculously new. I wanted to smother her with kisses, but I had warned myself to go slowly, for fear she would be frightened, and push me away. Besides, I also felt a surprising shyness, so for the moment I made do with stroking her cheek. 'Do you know who I am?' I asked her, gently.

'Who's this?' cajoled my mother.

Her brows were puckered with a look of puzzled concentration. I could see that she didn't recognise me, but was trying to remember something – perhaps what she'd been told. 'Mama?' she said, slowly.

I've missed so much, I thought, and found that I was laughing and crying at the same time.

Susie

Will and I met in a pub in Brighton. 'We should go for a drink some time,' Will had said, and I'd agreed, with a surge of nervous pleasure. It felt strange to be just the two of us, without a family function to endure, without the embarrassing relatives to both excuse and remove us, making us avoid each other's eyes like passengers in a tube carriage. Alone together, of our own volition, people in our own right, I felt both older and younger, and wondered, suddenly, how to be.

247

The pub we were in had been refurbished. We drank bottled Mexican beer with wedges of lime in the neck; the place was full of students in combat trousers, and Oasis blared from a jukebox. I wondered what had happened to all the old men who used to sit round the wooden tables staring into their pints.

'This place has changed a bit,' I said. 'Don't you find it strange to be back?'

'Yes. Thank God it was still pretty much a crumbling backwater in our day,' Will said. 'There's a lot to be said for growing up surrounded by old people's homes – at least it gives you plenty to feel alienated about. We could dream about the big city, and get pissed under the pier. It all seemed so much simpler.'

'I know what you mean,' I said. 'I quite liked the idea that the action was all somewhere else. It felt as if we just had to hang around and wait for our real lives to begin. I look at Gus, and think that all this must be so much harder to deal with.'

'What are your plans, up in London?' Will asked.

'I'm staying with a colleague at the moment. When the money from the house comes through, I think I'm going to put down a deposit on a flat.'

'A mortgage?' he raised his eyebrows.

'I know. But I feel like I've so done shared housing.'

'I was sorry to hear about your boyfriend,' Will said.

'Yes, well,' I looked down at the beer mats, and wondered what exactly Gus had told him. 'Are you really sorry?' I said, suddenly.

'Well, maybe not *that* sorry,' he conceded, with a laugh. We were edging closer to something. 'And he did sound like a bit of a tosser.' I was momentarily a little stung on Toby's behalf, before remembering that this was also my new, considered view. 'But I'm sorry if you're upset about it. It must have come at a very bad time, with all the awful stuff you've been through with your mum ...'

'I'm all right.' I'd resolved to put a positive spin on things, especially with Will. It wasn't always how I felt, but it helped to keep my pride – I didn't want to become a habitual victim. I'd already fallen into the temptation to air my woes a little too often, and the sympathy was nice while it lasted, but it often left me believing my own propaganda, and feeling worse afterwards, as well as slightly sickened, as if I'd eaten too much of something sweet.

'The whole thing with Mum's illness made me braver in some

248

ways. Toby and Zoe were my best friends, but now I realise I didn't even like them that much. You stick with people out of fear sometimes, don't you?' I said.

I went and got us another drink. At least I had a bit of money. That seemed so much more important at a time like this: perhaps I was becoming more of a materialist with adulthood. 'How about you?' I asked, as I sat down again. 'What are you planning on doing?'

'I'm thinking about doing a PGCE,' he said. 'I like teaching, and I think I'd enjoy working with kids. I've applied to the Institute of Education, in London.' He hesitated. 'I think I wouldn't mind being in England for a bit.' He shot me a look that embarrassed me, making me suddenly more aware of the exact geometry of the spaces between us, our hands and arms above the table, our legs and feet beneath.

'Really? I thought you loved it over there.'

'I did. It was a challenge, and it was great fun. But always being a foreigner gets boring in the end. Living somewhere interesting used to seem like enough, but after a while, it wears a bit thin as a justification for your whole life.'

'I know what you mean,' I said. 'Things don't seem very ... three dimensional, do they? I get that coming back, too. In London I only really know people my own age. You have plenty of freedom, but it all seems a bit artificial.'

'Nothing like family to keep you grounded ...' he said, wryly.

'No, but it's true,' I protested. 'Our parents' generation are pretty crap, and Gus and his friends, well, they make me laugh – as if they think they thought of everything – but they do give life more texture, if you like.'

He laughed. 'Here's to texture,' he raised his bottle. 'The rough with the smooth.'

'To roots,' I said, 'I suppose I mean.' We clinked. There was no mistaking his look this time – he hadn't forgotten that evening on the beach, I realised, any more than I had. I could feel myself start to sit a little straighter, touching my neck self-consciously, as my senses prickled awake.

'Roots, then,' he echoed. 'And branching out, as well.'

I stood with Steve, on that first visit to Montreal, in my reindeer patterned jumper, with my big, layered hair, and some dreadful beige coat over my arm, all quasi-military loops and lapels. We were at an observation point on Mont Royal, grinning like bashful teenagers, one of my colleagues between us, still breathless from the climb. 'Smile, folks!' sang out the obliging American tourist, and handed back the camera. Then we turned back to admire the view – the glinting curve of the St Lawrence river, the cars on the bridge like bubbles in a drip, the unfamiliar foliage, the many-windowed towers of the city. It was inspiring, I felt, this brave new world, suddenly so much wider and fuller than I'd realised.

I'd told Gregor about the trip a month in advance, when he'd dropped the children off. I was nervous, as always during those doorstep handovers, with a note of pre-emptive defiance in my voice, the insistence that I had an adult life to lead too, you know – not that I was that sure that I did. Could he have them for a whole week? To my surprise, he was fine about it. Being the guilty party must have become very boring.

'Are you going to get in touch with Steve?' he said.

'Steve?' I was registering the kids, taking stock in my mind – bags, coats, more new toys. As usual, they smelled a little different, and were dressed slightly wrong.

'You remember.' We looked at each other. There was always this surreal mixture of awkwardness and relief when we touched on our shared past – even sometimes just discussing the children. It was as if we were afraid we might accidentally slide into the old ways of relating. Would there always be this feeling, I wondered, of something left unsaid?

'He virtually lived with us in Camden,' Gregor was saying. 'Droopy moustache. Had the hots for you, as I recall. He was from Montreal. I've got an address somewhere, although I expect he's moved on, by now.'

I hadn't intended to follow it up, but I did, on that first dream-like day. I was taken aback, and flattered, by how pleased Steve had been. He rolled straight up at my hotel, and drove me over a high bridge, with the old warehouses and new tower blocks all jumbled together in the misty distance. He still had a silly moustache – but now rather more Freddie Mercury than Frank Zappa –

and that melodious accent, that made his voice seem surprisingly soft, for a man of his size. Attending a conference, with no kids, and the element of surprise on my side, I saw myself anew through his eyes, and felt successful, and attractive.

His antique shop on the Rue Saint Denis was struggling in the recession. We ate pancakes with maple syrup in a shiny chrome diner – thrilling to me, in spite of myself, from the 50s popular culture of my teens. We talked about the past, and I felt shamed by my younger self's lack of interest in his homeland. I liked the way he knew how to deliver baby lambs and drive a tractor; he was amused by the way I said sorry if someone else bumped into me. Things moved fast: it became an early game, seeing how far he could go before I noticed, stepping on my feet or tripping me up, and listening to me apologise.

In the second photo, there are just the two of us, standing in front of some rapids, out of town. There's suppressed laughter on our faces. You can tell that we'd grown closer, by then.

We talked indulgent, sing-songy nonsense. There were swirling clouds, in the big sky, and calling gulls, the water at cross purposes. I felt a dizziness I'd almost forgotten. For some reason – perhaps that I'd known him way back when – I felt none of the weary melancholy that had soured things with the other relationships I'd attempted since Gregor, and none of the resentful guilt about the children.

His moustache felt strange on my mouth. 'Do Englishwomen kiss differently?' I asked.

'Let's see,' he said. 'Mm, sure they do.'

'Anyway, perhaps I'm not the most English of Englishwomen.'

'That's right, I forgot, you're a mongrel too, just like all of us,' he smiled. 'Anyway, you've got yourself a Quebecer, now, baby. We can do English kisses,' he gave me a peck, 'and French kisses ...' Part of me felt silly, self-consciousness interfering with pure happiness, but another part didn't give a damn.

'And sometimes, just for the hell of it, we kiss like the Cubans,' he said, and bent me backwards, giggling and squirming, against his arm.

I missed a lot of the conference. He showed me round, we ate out. He seemed to accept me – both versions, the new me and the old me, and everyone in between. I was surprised to find that he still smoked pot, in the evenings – I'd never had much of a taste

251

for it myself, even when I was younger, and it belonged to a part of my life which I'd left far behind. He had a failed marriage behind him, too ('we got bored, I don't know, she got religion' – 'No risk of that with me, at least. Well and truly inoculated, at an early age') but no children. He seemed sad about that, which encouraged me, but he also said he didn't think he was cut out for fatherhood.

We drove out to see the farm where he'd grown up. There were clapboard houses with porches, and pointy white churches, enormous wooden barns, big Mack trucks, and yellow buses marked 'Ecoliers'. It reminded me of a painting by Edward Hopper, hyper-real in the crisp sunshine.

I watched him drive, enjoying those details of gesture and bearing that seem so absorbing in a new love, and so frustrating in an old. I delighted in the minutiae; it reminded me of watching the children, especially when they were very little. The moustache would have to go, though, I decided. People in England would think he was gay.

'You said it wouldn't suit me in Brighton,' I said.

'Did I? When?'

'Years and years ago, when we first moved down. You helped us take our stuff, when we left London. Do you remember that van you had? It feels like it was last week. We sat in the garden, and you said it wouldn't suit me.'

He seemed surprised. 'Oh, that would've been sour grapes. I mean, Gregor's a great guy, but I was never sure he appreciated you like he should. I was resisting the homemaking vibe myself, in those days,' he smiled at me. 'Anyway, I was wrong. It seems like it suited you very well.'

'But for some reason I really remembered you saying that, and there were many times when I agreed. I thought about it a lot when I was splitting up with Gregor. I thought, I've spent so much of my life being this person, and it doesn't even suit me.'

'You seem OK to me,' he said. Autumn was just beginning, spreading like a bruise over the forest, and into the bluey-green of the hills.

'Oh, yes, I'm all right,' I said vaguely. Then, before I had time to feel nervous, changing the subject it seemed to him, but following my own train of thought, 'I wish you could meet my kids.'

I couldn't bear the house, with everything packed up in crates and a 'for sale' notice outside, so instead, I dropped by at the shop, to see Steve.

The bell tinkled as I stepped in, and he looked up. 'Hello, stranger,' he said.

He was marking down stock for the clearance sale. Shabby old tat, most of it – wooden ducks, dilapidated stuffed animals, obscure agricultural implements and old beer bottles. We used to laugh about how he could clean it up, display it nicely, and sell it on at a healthy profit, to pub landlords or young fogies, looking for a bit of ready-made 'character'. Now, though, it all seemed to be about loss to me, the property of the dead, the contents of other houses cleared abruptly in unfortunate circumstances.

He made me a cup of tea, and I perched on a stool to drink it as he carried on sorting. Our gentle giant. In retrospect, he'd done OK, I thought. I was grateful to him for all of it, over the years: for not trying to be a father to us, for not using cheap tricks to win us over, or cultivating an easy popularity that could so easily curdle into disappointment. There was an honesty about him: we'd been more like co-habitees, and he'd always shown us consideration. His own distrust of authority had meant that he'd never tried to impose his will on us – in retrospect, if anything, he'd been too easy going, particularly with Gus. It was almost as if we'd all been the children together. Most of all, I was grateful to him for giving my mother a happy ending of sorts, for the self-belief and authority she'd grown into with him, which allowed her to avoid the bitter neediness of so many divorcees.

But what did it leave us, now she was gone? Surprisingly little, I realised. Moments of awkward affection. Bafflement that we'd come to share so much history – a middle-aged man and a young woman, with rather little to say to each other – glossed over with an excessive politeness. I'd seen his lowest points, and his loss of nerve, and it wasn't conducive to respect. Our grief was strangely competitive: we were reminders of each other's pain. Loss made us selfish and childlike. In Mum's death, as in her life, there was a sense in which we'd been rivals.

We talked some more, about Gus, and my grandmother, and the weather, but it all felt forced. There were moments when he looked utterly destroyed. I couldn't imagine him without her, and nor, I suspect, could he. He was going back to Canada for a few months: he'd made a good profit on the shop, and could take his time to decide what to do next. I was glad. Watching him rebuild his life, or fail to rebuild his life, either way, it would be painful to me.

When I left, I put my arms around his broad shoulders, and his beard tickled my cheek. 'Be good, Susie,' he said. 'Keep in touch.'

Helene

The astonishing thing is that there was so much more, both better and worse, to come.

Worse was the letter I read aloud to my mother because her hands were shaking too much to open the envelope. The news took some time to reach us: it was several months after my return to England, and I was heavily pregnant with Vera. My mother sat in a little armchair at one end of the gas fire and I sat opposite her at the other end, and it was difficult to read through, but it would have been too cruel to stop or hesitate. German had become the language of the enemy, and it was a surprise to me that I could still understand it. My father was dead. The elder of my brothers, Michael, had survived the war, but the younger, Kaspar, had not. My mother slid forward from her chair and onto her knees, and it was the physical expression of such total despair. She had hoped, right to the end. She just couldn't, couldn't believe it.

Despite – and into the midst of – all this, Vera was born. I had her at the Lambeth Lying-in Hospital, which had been moved out to St Albans. After the birth, they came round with lunch, and it was fish and chips, which was fabulous, with so little food around. As happens, people said the baby looked like all kinds of relatives. Charles's mother turned up again and pronounced her the spitting image of an Aunt Dorothea. 'She doesn't look much like anyone I know,' my mother said. I think that perhaps she suspected, but she didn't really want to be told.

Charles wrote soon after the birth. He had been demobbed, but had spoken to an acquaintance who had offered him a job in Dhaka. He was afraid there wouldn't be much for him to do in England. He wanted me to come back out with the girls as soon as I could. He enclosed a photograph of a white wooden house, where we would live, to help me make up my mind. My surviving brother had plans to emigrate to New Zealand, and my mother intended to go with him.

Many, many years later, I fell in love again. It all came flooding back, then – the sickening, destabilising, disorientating force of it, its power to remake one's self-image and expectations of life, the brighter colours of the world, the excitement and the fear. This was in New York, and not until the 60s, and there was so much of everything – that skyline, and the noise, the enthusiasm, even the food. Sex was better – there was more of that, too, and we had more practice. I was bowled over, well and truly smitten. It was something real, and adult – a conversation between two people – in a way that my early experiences were not. My memories of Bobby, however, have always retained a special poignancy, perhaps just because things never ran their course. That bittersweet intensity seems undiminished by the years, and those months stand out from the rest of my life. They throb with all the things that have escaped me – my youth, my innocence, a whole world, and the many young lives, which were destroyed by the war.

I never spoke about it, for many years. It wouldn't have been fair on Charles, and besides, it was something very private, no one else's business. I did my best to forget, and that was not as hard as I would have expected. There were moments, however, when it took me off balance: hot nights, when the stars seemed close; Vera's pale wrist, dangling from a deck-chair; a fleeting expression in my granddaughter's pale blue eyes. 'Make me immortal with a kiss,' Bobby said to me once, quoting those lines from Marlowe that so appealed to him, and although I thought it pretentious flattery at the time, I see, looking back, that I did the only thing I could to help him last.

Susie

A year after the death, we met to scatter her ashes. Lottie wanted somewhere with water, and there was talk of planting a tree, but in the end, we settled on Devil's Dyke. It was raining on the day, but we decided to go ahead anyway.

Gus brought his pretty new girlfriend. Having a dead mother, he bragged to me, helped him pull – 'they're so sympathetic they can't wait to get their knickers off,' was how he put it – but she seemed sweet, reassuringly strong minded and unaccountably besotted. He seemed calmer, anyway, and I was relieved that someone else seemed so eager for the chance to keep him in check. I was with Will, and it struck me that Mum's death had been bizarrely influential in both our love lives. Steve had flown back for the occasion, looking thinner and older, and Cathy was there, and Lottie, and my grandmother, and Dad came too. Such an incongruous little group, this death club, I thought, brought together by one person's absence – and yet this is my family, now. I was aware that it might be the last time we all met like this, and that felt strange. My position within the generations had shifted, it seemed. The storm has blown our roof off, I thought: we have become the grown-ups.

Lottie clutched a plastic bag with the ashes, which we had asked the undertaker to divide into separate containers. I was scared of the bag, the contents of which I hadn't seen, but I couldn't stop myself from looking at it.

The soft rain settled on our shoulders. I thought of other cars, on sunnier days, crowding the empty car park in my mind's eye – a Triumph Herald, sea blue with biscuit upholstery; a 2CV with the canvas roof rolled back, in which I'd stood as a child, blinded by the wind; a battered red Renault with a 'Refuse Cruise' sticker, full of pieces of Gus's lego and mouldy banana; a big old Volvo, strewn with crumpled newspaper and photocopied handouts.

We set off down the hill in the drizzle. It was rather like looking for the right spot for a picnic. 'There's a nice photo of her sitting about here,' Steve said.

'No, that was further down,' I said, and Dad, who'd actually taken the photograph, wisely kept quiet. We negotiated the slippery, muddy slope in our inappropriate shoes. I held my grandmother's frail arm, as the rain soaked through her thin headscarf. 'Hold tight, or I might go with her,' she said, bizarrely, and I felt a tremor of hysteria, and worried that I might start to laugh.

Then we reached the ridge that marked the edge of the iron age fort, and could no longer see the road above us. Lottie read a poem, as self-appointed master of ceremonies, in an attempt to muster some sense of occasion, but the wind snatched the words from her mouth, and flung them towards the distant farm buildings. She handed us a little pot each. I opened the lid and sneaked an apprehensive look inside. They really were just like the ashes from a fireplace. I'd expected them to have a smoother, less organic consistency. I looked over at Gus, to share an ironically raised eyebrow, or an embarrassed grimace, and saw instead that his face was twisted with emotion. Oddly enough, that was enough to start my tears, mingling on my cheeks with the rain.

My grandmother opened her pot and took a handful of ash. She scattered it wide, and the wind caught it beautifully as it fell, turning it in a twist of air, a pirouette. She took another handful, and another, flinging her arm out with a surprising vigour; there was white dust, on the dense, short grass around her feet. I saw the dust in the creases of her hand and thought that's her daughter, she's saying goodbye to her daughter. In mid-scoop, she dabbed a little ash on her tongue, and I could understand that she wanted to keep something back, within her.

Then the rest of us started to scatter our containers. I took a little pinch from my pot, and another, and considered keeping some myself, and dabbed a little surreptitiously on my neck, like perfume. Unsure of the etiquette, I offered the pot to Will, with a self-conscious smile, as if it were snuff, but he shook his head, embarrassed. Then I shook all the rest out of the little container. The leaves on the bushes rippled as if they were underwater, and a wave of hurt rose up from my heart.

How can I do it all alone? She seemed to be everywhere and nowhere. Goodbye, Mum, I thought again. Don't go.

Vera

On your first birthday, we drove up to Devil's Dyke with a picnic. The warm weather was giving me unpleasant flashbacks to that day – sweaty, sickening, surreal – the year before. Never had a birthday meant so much to me, I thought; how strange that it wasn't even my own.

The bushes were bent out of shape by the wind, growing horizontal to the ground. We ate cheese sandwiches and drank red wine, my pale legs folded awkwardly on a tartan blanket, Gregor smoking distractedly, with that air of performing some distasteful chore that he often seemed to apply, now, to his domestic life. As usual, my head was full of the baby – was she hot, tired, hungry? – so it was almost a relief not to have to make conversation. The

English countryside was spread out at our feet like a rug.

True to your gruelling internal timetable, or as if obeying the week-by-week commands from the mother ship, you were beginning to toddle. You pulled yourself upright, determinedly, obsessively, on Gregor's legs, and when he removed the support, you stood, with bended knees and outstretched arms, like a surfer, as if the undulations of the ground beneath your feet might at any moment send you flying.

'Cou-cou,' I called, a few feet away, and opened my arms to you, and you extended your tiny starfish hands, a proprietorial demand on both sides. Then, as if under the spell of my offered embrace, and sufficiently distracted to suspend your own disbelief, you took a few lurching steps, giggling and snorting with effort and excitement, swaying and jerking like a little Frankenstein, or a paraplegic after months of physiotherapy. I held my breath, my heart thumping, then caught you as you landed hard on your nappy. You buried your head in my blouse, beaming modestly, and I cupped your face in my hands, kissing the soft little cheeks, 'Clever girl, clever girl.' Then I turned you around and set you off to Gregor.

I had caught the feeling several times recently that perhaps its grip on me was easing. The rest of the world was beginning to shade into existence, and this obsession, this strange year of love, so close to madness, this agonising excess of empathy, was receding. Willing every mouthful down, every millimetre grown, every hour asleep – the exhausting, desperate, endless task of urging you into existence might give way, I allowed myself to hope, to simply sharing space. Perhaps, now I'd thrown my pebble into the pond, I could stand back and admire the ripples. Perhaps you would become just a person, like anyone else. Yet every time I thought this, you would do something wonderful, or terrifying, and my heart would lurch, and I'd realise how far we still had to travel.

Watching the little back stagger away, I felt a swell of pride and love. I'd expected to feel something like this on first seeing you, but hadn't. Flesh of my flesh, I thought. Mingled in with the exhilaration was a sharp pain. Regaining my freedom meant losing something of you. It was like giving up breast feeding, which I was resisting, despite the urge to win back some of my own life.

When you were tired, you'd cry for me, then push me away, beat your little arms against me, then bury your head in my shoul-

der. I was something else to you: the world, the status quo, authority, all the things you could rage against but couldn't change. It
was flattering and funny, and sometimes scary, the force of your
will, the irrational intensity. I wasn't sure I wanted to be all that,
or that I could fulfil the brief, and I wasn't sure if you'd ever
forgive me for falling short. You didn't like it when I laughed or
loved or lived in other ways, you wanted to grasp me in your
sweet, sticky, passionate little fist forever. I was aware, sometimes, of the unfairness of my own demands, as well. Your
achievements and disappointments were so immediate to me, and
felt like such a reflection on me, that I could never view you with
rational distance, and so we would each try endlessly, pointlessly,
to control the other.

We may be becoming separate people, but you'll always feel like
a part of me. When you are hurt, I thought, I'll always feel pain,
and when you feel pleasure, I'll always be pleased. I suppose you
have to go, but please don't go too far. You are the dearest thing
that I have ever done.

Susie

I still dream about her sometimes. Now, ten years later – and God,
they go so fast – mourning her feels increasingly like searching for
her. I find traces of her in films or books, or a tone of voice, the
back of a head, the angle of a chin, a radio playing in another
room. I look for her footprints on the earth. It's like an itch I need
to scratch, an old wound that I should know to leave by now.

They say the dead go with you, and her absence grows and
changes as I live. Each corner turned takes us further apart, in a
long goodbye that never ends. She's entwined in every cell of me,
messy, complicated, infuriating, and reassuring. I argue with her
in my head, and it becomes less urgent, but more surreal, wondering what she'd make of it all. Some days I can hear her voice so
clearly, and at others, I fear that I'm forgetting. Most of what she
says I agree with, but I get irritated by her naive idealism, her
superiority, and her unpredictable emotions. Bringing her up to
date, telling her about me and Gus, helps me work out what I think
about it all.

The burden of memory makes me feel older than I should. I've

259

grown comfortable with it, it's become one of the facts of life, so that when, occasionally, people are still awkward or shocked – 'God, I'm so sorry ...' – I'm surprised, and condescending. The greater affinity I have with someone dead than many of the living makes me feel removed, and out of step. There's new contrast to life – darker shadows to emphasise the brightness. Mostly, though, I think I'm happy.

The only one of us who never really recovered, I think, was my grandmother. It surprised me, at the time, how self-contained she'd seemed, but later, I realised that she hadn't even begun her slow-burn grief. The fact of Mum's death never really sank in, and she returned to it, questioningly, again and again. It was something she couldn't accept. In an awful way, dying was easier for her to do, setting things right again. After she had died, three years after Mum, we found an old black and white photograph, amongst her things. It was a slight, young-looking man on a balcony some-where, in RAF uniform, eyes half closed, scored through with a fold. I would have liked to have known more about him, my biological grandfather, from whom, apparently, I got my blue eyes.

Perhaps the rest of us managed to reconstruct the delusion of a safe and just world, in order to carry on. Often, I simply have the sense there's someone that I ought to ring.

Especially now. Still searching, I thought I caught something through the fog: the angle of her chin, or the curve of her face. The sonographer moved the wand on my stomach, nuzzling into my flesh, gliding over the smear of gel, a paper towel tucked over the top of my tights. Will held my hand, and our eyes were glued to the screen.

We were silent, incredulous, and elated. On the monitor, we circled and soared, flesh and fluid parting like mist banks before us. We swooped in again on the tiny, bird-skeleton, the perfect little vertebrae, moving together with clockwork precision. The world changed, in that fuzzy, black and white image. 'It's like the moon landing,' I said.

'Yes,' said Will, misinterpreting my meaning, 'you could just have a tape in there.'

I was expecting a boy – perhaps having a younger brother made it easier to imagine. I was daunted by the messy passion of the mother-daughter thing, the push-pull of intimacy and claustrophobia, the niggling failures and distorted self-images, the idea that one day I too might be judged and despised. I was scared by the thought someone might miss me, and need me, as I did Mum. Still, it was like an itch I needed to scratch, an old wound that I should know to leave by now.

'You want to know, don't you?' the sonographer said.

Will hesitated, and looked at me. 'Go on then,' he said.

I wanted to hear, and I didn't want to listen. It was the kind of information you can't un-know – once it's out there, the cosmos is reordered, and you can never take it back. Under my thigh, my fingers were still crossed, pressed into the plastic cover on the couch.

'I think it's a girl,' the sonographer said.

08779943 26